EX
LIBRIS

Romance Treasury

THE ROMANCE TREASURY ASSOCIATION

NEW YORK · TORONTO · LONDON

These stories were originally published as follows:

THE SILENT MOON
Copyright © 1971 by Jan Andersen
First published in London by Mills & Boon Limited in 1971

THE YEAR AT YATTABILLA
Copyright © 1970 by Amanda Doyle
First published in London by Mills & Boon Limited in 1970

TOWN NURSE — COUNTRY NURSE
Copyright © 1970 by Marjorie Lewty
First published in London by Mills & Boon Limited in 1970

ROMANCE TREASURY is published by:
The Romance Treasury Association, Stratford, Ontario, Canada

Editorial Board: A. W. Boon, Judith Burgess, Ruth Palmour and Janet Humphreys

Dust Jacket Art by David Craig
Story Illustrations by David Craig
Book Design by Charles Kadin
Printed by Kingsport Press Limited, Kingsport, Tennessee

ISBN 0-919860-19-2

Printed in U.S.A.   AO20

CONTENTS

THE SILENT MOON

The Silent Moon
Jan Andersen

The antagonism that throbbed between them was almost tangible, yet seemingly without cause.

"This is not a place for women, Miss Fraser," Ross Andrews snapped, "particularly women who have no experience with this way of living. I've given four years of my life to Nyala and I don't intend to see it ruined by a couple of girls who merely want to be able to say they own a game reserve in Africa!"

Jo was speechless with anger. She had never met a man like the insolent Ross Andrews before and wasn't good at coping with people she didn't understand. But she was a born fighter and determined to stay!

CHAPTER ONE

The letter arrived on a Saturday morning; the only time the three Frasers could be certain of being together. It was addressed to Alan, but Jo saw it first and pounced because of the South African stamp. Sally, the wise one, withdrew it gently from Jo's fingers.

"It's for Alan, not you. And anyway, I thought you said you didn't care one way or the other whether or not you ever heard from him again."

Jo moved uneasily. "I don't. No . . . that's not strictly true; I would like to know what happened to him, if he made his fortune."

"Bruce Farley will never make his fortune. No, I'm sorry Jo, that's not quite fair," Sally added, quickly repentent as her sister's color deepened. "He was rather super, I agree. But not exactly the settling-down type."

"An adventurer, I think was your word for him," Jo said coldly. She was standing at the window as if engrossed in something outside. Only the quick nervous movement of her fingers rolling the blind cord gave her away. "Anyway, who said anything about settling down? Bruce is a prospector, not a bank clerk. He wasn't likely to stay digging for diamonds in Derbyshire, was he?"

"I'm sorry, Jo," Sally caught the edge to her sister's voice and regretted her thoughtlessness. "Of course not. But it just hurts me to see you hurt, that's all."

"Bruce did not hurt me." Jo's voice was so tense Sally knew she had only made it worse. "We liked each other, that's all. And then he went away. The fact that he's no good at writing letters is not—"

"Good God!"

Both sisters swung toward their brother. The first words he had spoken—and strong words for him. He had reached the bulky South African envelope and tipped its contents onto the breakfast table. They stared at the two airline tickets lying there.

"Who are they for?" breathed Jo. "You?"

Alan shook his head. "There are no names. But they can't be for me—and anyway, why two?"

Jo reached over and grabbed. "You must have entered a competition or something." She flipped through the ticket pages, adding ominously. "They're one-way tickets."

From the floor, where the other mail had slipped, un-heeded, Sally retrieved a typed airmail letter. "This might tell you. Read it," she commanded. "I can't bear the suspense any longer."

As Alan read the closely packed page his eyebrows seemed to rise higher and higher. But the only words he spoke were: "Uncle *Harold*! I thought he'd died years ago."

"And now I suppose," Jo put in dramatically, "we're suddenly heirs to a huge fortune."

Alan did not answer until he reached the end of the letter. Then he said slowly, as if his sister had just made the statement, "Well, I don't know about a fortune, but we are his heirs—at least I think we are."

"Tell us," Sally implored. "By the time we've all read the letter lunchtime will be here."

Alan pushed the hair back from his forehead. "Well, I'll try, if I can decode the legal language. It seems that Uncle Harold has just died; he's so out of touch he thinks there's just you and me, Sally. His only asset is a small game park called Nyala on the . . . in one of the countries bordering on South Africa. Get a map, please, some-one."

"And he's left it to us . . . you?" Jo put in.

"I suppose he has, but with strings. As far as I can gather the government wants to take it over, as it's one of the few private reserves left. Finances are precarious, but he wanted to keep it in the family. If we can show we could make the place pay, then in three months the park is ours. If not, the government has it. Hence the tickets. I think that's the gist of it, but you can read the letter if you like, Sally."

Jo said thoughtfully, "I didn't even know we had an Uncle Harold. And what was he doing in South Africa anyway?"

"I'm not really sure," Alan replied. "I know there was some kind of blazing family row and he went there after the war. I must have been a baby and Sally just two. As there's no mention of you, Jo, he couldn't have known you were born. He was Dad's younger brother, but why there should have been this complete break beats me."

"And why should we be his heirs?" Sally asked. "Didn't he marry or anything? People don't usually leave everything to a niece and nephew they haven't seen for 20 years. It strikes me as very fishy."

But Jo's mind had jumped a few paces. "Where did you say this place—this park is? Do we have an atlas, Alan?"

"Yes, on top of the cupboard there, but I don't see—"

Jo had grabbed the atlas and opened it at the right page. "Now, do you remember the South African you brought home for dinner from the hotel last year, Alan? Mr.—"

"Brand. Neil Brand. But what's he have to do with it?"

"Think back, Alan," she said eagerly. "You couldn't understand why he had chosen a small village in the North of England for a stay. And he was terribly anxious to meet Sally and to see our home. Where did he come from?"

"I'm not sure exactly, but it was somewhere in this area."

"All those questions he asked;" Sally put in, "you mean you think Uncle Harold asked him to come and look us over?"

Jo shrugged. "Well, it's possible, isn't it? Although it

doesn't explain why I've been left out. Perhaps he didn't like me. I must say he seemed to take a fancy to you, Sal."

Alan suddenly folded the letter. "Okay, so that's one bit of the mystery solved, but it's not going to do us much good. The game park isn't ours until we've made it pay, and since we can't do that, it is a waste of time to even think about it."

"And the tickets?" Jo put in hopefully.

"Send them back, I suppose. They're only one-way, so we can't go and have a cheap holiday. We'd have to find about 300 pounds to get back. In any case I couldn't get off for three weeks, much less three months." He glanced at his watch. "Heavens, I must fly. I've an appointment at 11."

"Will you be back for lunch?" Usually it was Sally who asked the practical questions, but this time it was Jo, who could barely keep the suppressed excitement from her voice.

"About one-thirty," he called, "but don't wait for me."

After he left, Sally looked at her younger sister. "Come on, out with it. I can tell you've some crazy scheme up your sleeve. We'll do the dishes later."

Jo sat down again. "All right, I have a plan, but I don't think it's crazy, and you must hear me through and think hard before you condemn it."

Some time later, Sally went to get her hair done. It was Jo's turn to stay at home and do the Saturday chores. For once she was glad to be on her own and think things out a little more clearly. The Frasers, she had decided this morning, were getting into a rut.

They had always been a close-knit family. When their parents were killed five years before, the three of them decided to stick together and keep up the house they had lived in almost all their lives. Jo was in her last year at school; though she badly wanted to leave to take her share of the family finances, she was persuaded that a better education would help them all. Sally was already at college and it seemed equally important that she should finish her home economics training.

That first year was very hard, for although there was no mortgage on the house, there was also no more than a few hundred pounds capital. Alan was doing the job he had wanted to ever since he was about 15—working his way up in a hotel business. But he was only 22 and still on a low salary. With his working overtime, Sally doing private cooking in the evenings, and Jo helping in the local supermarket every Saturday, they managed to stay afloat.

On the whole, Jo decided, it was a good life, but now seemed the time for a change. For instance, it was time that Sally, at 24, thought a little about her own future instead of Alan's. She was rarely short of dates and invitations, but she had never felt deeply enough about anyone to give up the even, sunny pattern of her days. She loved the wild, bleak Derbyshire hills and dales that encircled the little town. Nothing gave her greater pleasure than roaming the countryside for hours at a time to add to her considerable collection of wild flowers.

And Jo herself? She could not really have said what she wanted from life. But she had turned 21 just two months ago and felt the same restless feeling overtaking her that arrived with the departure of Bruce Farley. Only to herself would she admit that the ripples of his coming and going had never died.

The sisters had decided that Jo should put her idea to Alan. She knew she had not won Sally over completely, but she was wavering. Since they had always been a family that decided important issues by discussion, she felt that Alan's opinion was vital.

Jo managed to contain herself until Sally had cleared the table and brought in the coffee.

Alan stretched. "Do you two have plans for the rest of

the day? I'd like the car for the evening if that's possible. I'll likely be working late. But first I need some air."

"First," Jo said dramatically, "Sally and I have something to say to you."

He groaned. "I guessed you'd been thinking about those tickets all morning. If you're thinking we can sell them, then you're very much mistaken."

Jo tossed her fine, silky hair over her shoulders. "Don't jump to conclusions, Alan. First answer one question. What is your greatest ambition?"

He frowned. "You know very well what it is."

"You could have changed since last week. Go on, tell me."

As if he were humoring a child he answered: "To buy the Crag Inn."

"I heard that it really might be on the market at the end of the year.'

"You've only heard what the whole town has heard. Are you proposing, my dear little sister, to write me out a check for the 20 thousand pounds I need so badly?"

"Not exactly, but—"

"Then do me a favor and shut up about it. Even talk sets my nerves all on edge."

"All right, Alan, I'll come to the point, but I'll say the same to you as I did to Sally. Don't interrupt until I've finished.

"You said this morning you can't take three months off because you must work. All right, fair enough. Being manager of the Crown is the next best thing to owning the Crag, so you don't want to lose that job."

"Jo, for heaven's sake . . . !"

"No, please, Alan, let me finish. But there's nothing to stop Sally and me taking the time off. I can get a secretarial job anywhere when I return, and I daresay Sally can get a catering position. You could move into the Crown, and we could let the house for three months.

If—and I know this is a huge gamble—Sally and I could keep this park's head above water for three months, then it's ours, or rather yours. You could then sell it and buy the Crag."

As Alan turned to stare at her, she felt a queer little twist of triumph. She could see she had caught his attention.

"But you two haven't the faintest idea how to run a game park. You've never even seen one."

"Of course not. But there must be someone there doing it now. Anyway, it's only small. What do you suppose that means—20 or 30 acres?"

"If it's that small, you wouldn't get 20 thousand pounds for it. I imagine a few hundred acres would be nearer the mark, but don't ask me. My experience of game is the odd elephant and lion at the zoo. Anyway, it's an insane idea. If the finances are as precarious as this letter indicates, how do you think you're going to do any better than Uncle Harold, or his manager?"

"I don't think at all," Jo said calmly. "I just know it's worth a gamble."

"A gamble that could cost you more than 300 pounds," he said with heavy sarcasm.

It was Sally who came to the rescue in her quiet way.

"Look, Alan, I thought it was crazy this morning, too, but I've sat under the hair drier thinking about nothing else, and I don't think we need lose. I agree with you that we may not save the park for ourselves, but it's worth a try. It's the only way you'll ever get that hotel, you know. The bank's never going to lend you the money. And once the Crag has slipped from the old ladies' hands into someone else's, you've lost it for good. And this 300 pounds? Well, I've thought about that too. Personally I don't think the solicitors could leave us stranded there without return tickets, if we are forced to leave. But if things are bad we should recognize it pretty early. One of us will work. I may not be able to earn 300 pounds in three months, but I daresay I could manage half. So we've spent as much as a good holiday for two."

Jo's heart lifted with joy. With Sally on her side, Alan would at least listen. Actually, if it came to that, he could hardly stop them.

He had left the table and was pacing the room. "I don't know; I just don't know; I feel so responsible."

"We are," Sally reminded him gently, "both of age."

"I know, but neither of you has ever been farther than Spain. Heaven knows what the climate's like. I suppose you, Jo, think you might run into Bruce Farley."

Her head shot up in anger. "That's a rotten remark, Alan. I hadn't given him a thought. And in case you hadn't realized it, Africa is a large continent, not a one-horse town like this."

"I'm sorry, Jo, I wasn't thinking. You really are concerned, aren't you?"

Jo smiled. "You're the only one with ambition. Besides, I've thought of living at the Crag too, and if I have to sit three months in the sun to do it, well, who's grumbling?"

"Well, I don't know, it seems pretty crazy. . . ." He turned finally to Sally. "It really rests with you, Sal, since Jo isn't mentioned in the will. I'd have to give you power of attorney or something."

"I'm quite sure, Alan," she said. "I don't think we have much hope, but it's worth a try. Can you imagine Mother and Dad hesitating when so much is at stake?"

He shook his head. "No. No, I couldn't." He reached into his pocket and once more brought out the tickets. "Three weeks today. It's not long, is it? I shall miss you both."

They sat and talked about it until they could talk no longer. Then, as Jo made fresh coffee, Sally suddenly disappeared. She came down ten minutes later, her face dusty, her arms full of books.

"Where on earth did you get those?" Alan asked. He took them from her. All were old, with dust jackets torn or missing.

"How extraordinary!" He opened them one by one. "Two Stuart Cloete novels, four travel books, one about the early diamond days, a biography of Cecil Rhodes, even this, about the Kruger Park. They're all about South Africa." He looked across at his sister questioningly.

"Do you remember when Mother and Dad died and we had to go through all their personal things? Well, there was this trunk belonging to Mother in the attic. It had her wedding dress in it, those old party invitations, all the odd special things she had treasured. And we decided to keep it, didn't we?"

"That's right," Alan said, "only I think I left it all to you."

"Well, these books were at the bottom. I've never thought of them until this moment. Why aren't they on the bookshelves? And why are they all about South Africa? Mother has never been there. Did she have other friends or relatives?"

"I never heard of anyone but Uncle Harold. Put them on the shelves, Sally. You . . . you'll probably both want to dip into them."

Jo gathered the cups. There were the beginnings of another mystery here, but one that made her feel faintly uneasy—and one they might never be able to unravel. Very loudly she said, "Well, I shall start on the one about the Kruger Park. We should be able to pick up some tips from that." And then a few moments later, "For both your benefits, the nyala is a kind of antelope, timid and strikingly beautiful. It lives in bush-covered regions near the water and feeds on leaves, young roots and wild fruits." She grinned mischievously. "I think I'm going to like Nyala."

CHAPTER TWO

Three weeks later, the jet circled the vast Transvaal plateau and descended with a hiss of wheels onto the runway of Jan Smuts Airport.

On the tarmac Jo breathed deeply of the warm, scented air and turned to her sister. "Well, we really are here, aren't we?"

Sally seemed to shake her head. "I think so. I can't be sure of anything this past week, except that I've learned you're a very forceful organizer."

Jo grinned. "For those few kind words, many thanks."

Little more than half an hour later a taxi dropped them outside their hotel in the center of Johannesburg, a noisy throbbing city of straight roads and high, square buildings. But as they had driven through the suburbs, the avenues lined with glorious purple jacaranda made them think they were entering paradise.

The exhaustion that had been building through excitement and worry during the past week hit them almost as soon as they had eaten, and they slept for 12 hours. When they awoke they realized the main part of their journey was about to begin. But before going to the airport again they had to see the solicitor.

They did not learn very much more than the letter had told them. Harold Fraser had made his will several years ago, but it was only in the last few months that he had added the codicil about the game park's ownership.

At one point Jo asked curiously, "Do you think he knew of my existence?"

"Not as far as I know, Miss Fraser. To be honest I knew very little indeed about Mr. Harold Fraser. He was my client, and I dealt with his business affairs, but about his private life I knew almost nothing."

"He never married?"

"No, I believe he was a very solitary person. That's probably why the life out at Nyala suited him. Oh, yes, I did know one thing about him. He had a passionate interest in the Bushmen and, I believe, spent any spare time in the Kalahari studying their ways and their history."

Jo had one more question to ask. "Mr. Scott, we very nearly didn't come because we thought if we failed to make the park pay then we couldn't afford the return tickets. If . . . if the government does buy, who has the money?"

He smiled. "First, Miss Fraser, you need have no worries about returning to England. That will be taken care of. But if you should not succeed in your uncle's wish, then I'm afraid there will be no money. The government will be able to claim Nyala. A strange legacy, you may think, but then your uncle was a strange man. As I say, I knew very little about him except that he was known as a lone wolf. I suspect there was some disappointment in his life, but unlike others in the same position he did not seek revenge, rather atonement. That is why, I imagine, he felt he did not want to make capital out of this game reserve he had been building up with such loving care over 20 years. And the task he set himself could not have been an easy one. It's a forbidding part of the country to live in, and it must have taken a great deal of courage for an Englishman to come to terms with it."

Sally smiled faintly. "Are you warning us, Mr. Scott?"

"No, I don't think so, Miss Fraser. I'm a legal man and I can only go on facts. I think your hopes of success are slender, partly because of the financial difficulties and partly because you know nothing of the climate or terrain. Up there nature can be very cruel. And yet I hope and pray for your success, because I feel strongly that your uncle would like the land to stay in the family—unless of course the government does take it over, compulsorily. Most game parks have been nationalized, you know."

"Did Uncle Harold ever ask for a subsidy from the government?" Sally asked thoughtfully.

"I don't know, but I doubt it, for the very good reason that he would have to seek legal advice before taking a step like that. And he was a very proud and independent man. I feel it would have been a final step for him."

He glanced at his watch. "And now, regretfully, young ladies, I shall have to remind you that your plane leaves in just over an hour. I can only wish you luck and emphasize that I am here to help you whenever you need me. Do you know anyone, or have you any friends in South Africa?"

Both girls shook their heads.

"Then we must really make sure of having a meeting somewhere about halfway through your term."

"Perhaps you could come for a weekend, Mr. Scott?" Sally put in.

"It might be the best, then I could see things for myself. But I believe you have an excellent manager—or warden as he would be known up there. A Mr. Ross Andrews."

"You know him?"

"Alas, no, but he has been with your uncle nearly four years, so he must be satisfactory."

He bade them goodbye. Once more they were on their way to the airport.

In the taxi Jo turned to Sally. "Did you think what I did?"

Sally nodded. "I imagine so. When he mentioned about no money changing hands and Uncle not wanting to make capital out of the Park? If he had only known that all we want to do is to sell. . . ."

"Well," returned Jo firmly, "it's no good feeling guilty or sentimental. It's what we've come out here to do. It's not even as if we knew Uncle Harold. And I imagine neither of us wants to spend our life up on the edge of the desert with no one but lions and snakes for company."

"Oh," said Sally in a small voice. "I'd thought of lions, but not of snakes. Do you think there'll be many?"

"There always are in deserts, aren't there? I've only read about Kruger, so everything is guesswork."

An hour later they were airborne, but this time in a small plane that held only a dozen passengers. Word must have got around as to who they were, for the young pilot insisted they take the two front seats so he could point out some of the interesting features of the landscape.

The plane landed first at the capital, a small dusty town just over the border. Six of the passengers left the plane and two more joined it. When the pilot took off again for the last leg of the flight north, he said over his shoulder, "Now you'll see a bit of the real country. Look out of the port window."

Jo strained her eyes into the endless distance. "It's not like a country at all, more like a great wasteland."

"The original tribes called it the Thirstland. Now there are only the Bushmen left, and they have to struggle even to exist. You can travel for days in the desert without even the scent of water."

"Is . . . is it like that where we're going?" Sally said cautiously.

"It's tough enough, but you're only on the edge. I believe part of the Nyala Reserve is very beautiful. Only the far side of it touches the real desert. But I wouldn't know except from the air. Your uncle—he was your uncle, wasn't he—didn't encourage visitors."

"But—" The question died on Jo's lips. This man was not the one to ask. Undoubtedly his knowledge of Nyala was only based on gossip and rumor.

Once or twice he took the small plane low, to swoop over a river or to show one of the rough tracks across the desert, or the area where the best game gathered.

Just before they finally landed he said in his broad accent, "Well, girls, if you get tired of the wildlife, send me a message and I'll give you both a night on the town. And I mean that. Not many pretty girls in this part of the world. I have to look for my social life down in Jo'burg. And I reckon you won't be seeing much social life. They do say that Andrews has picked up some of the old man's ways." On that faintly uncomfortable note he brought the wheels down onto the runway of an airstrip that seemed no more than a cluster of huts at one end of a baked brown field.

Outside, they walked into a thick wall of heat; even the airport building wasn't much cooler.

Sally clutched Jo's arm. "Do you think we were mad after all?"

Jo shrugged. "Probably. But now that I know we've at least got our air fare back, I'm going to stick it out. I've been alive for 21 years and never had a real adventure."

Sally smiled her gentle smile. "Sometimes I think you should have been the elder sister. We might have made our fortunes by now."

"Silly!" Jo squeezed her arm, "someone's got to keep my feet on the ground, and I'd sooner it was you. Now, do you suppose we're expected, or do we just hail a taxi and drive into the bush?"

As she spoke a tall African in old but beautifully pressed khaki trousers and shirt came from the shadows of the hall, bowed briefly and handed them a letter.

"*Morena* send this, ladies."

Sally opened the letter. It was short and to the point. "Sorry I couldn't meet you. Kari is my right-hand man and will drive you safely to Nyala. Make sure you bring with you the following items, particularly those from the drugstore."

Sally handed the list to Jo. "He must think we're going to get every disease in the book. The rest—well, I suppose he knows what he's talking about."

After they had shopped, Kari escorted them to the hotel for lunch and told them he would collect them in an hour to drive them to Nyala.

"Is it a long drive?" Sally asked.

"Not long, lady."

But Kari's idea of "not long" and their own seemed to be very different. At the end of each hour one of them would ask "Is it far now?" And he would shake his head and repeat cheerfully, "Not far now." And the truck would go rumbling over the hot, dusty road.

The farther north they drove, the more oppressive seemed the heat. To open the window only invited the flying dust. On either side of the road was nothing but endless bush, scrub and thorn. Then they would come to a kind of village, a group of huts with smiling children waving as they passed. Finally Kari had to stop for gas. Jo said firmly, "We must have some water. My sister is not feeling well."

He looked behind dubiously and from a basket in the back produced a thermos. Jo could only hope that the warmish water it contained was fresh, but at that moment she did not particularly care. Sally looked all in. Then Kari returned carrying two oranges and handed them to them in some triumph.

"Good for the ladies."

"Thank you," said Jo, "but please, we have been driving for four hours. You must tell us how far it is now."

"Not far, lady," came the now familiar answer.

"I want to know exactly how far," Jo said inexorably. She pointed to her watch.

"One hour. That is all."

Inevitably it turned out to be two, for shortly after the stop for gas they turned off the "main" road on to one that in England would have been called little more than a farm track.

By now Sally looked thoroughly ill. All the color had

left her cheeks and she was lying back against the window with her eyes closed.

"Would you like to stop for a while, Sal?" Jo asked, when she realized that the continual bumping of the truck was driving her sister beyond endurance.

Sally looked out of the window. There was practically no shade, and even where there was, the temperature was probably not far off 100.

She tried to smile. "I think I'll try to stick it out. I'd forgotten what a rotten traveler I am."

Kari glanced across anxiously. "Soon, lady, soon." And sure enough in less than half an hour he was pointing to a border of tall trees. "That is the river. On the other side of the river is Nyala."

"Thank God!"

Quite abruptly the country became green again, as if rain had recently washed the thorn and the scrubby bushes. They crossed the river on a narrow log bridge and started up another track running parallel to it. But there was no chance to see more because the swift tropical night came down without warning. The only way they knew they had arrived was by the gleam of lights through the darkness.

Jo climbed down stiffly from the truck and reached up a hand to help her sister. "It's all right, Sal, we really are there, and it seems quite civilized."

But Sally was past caring. It was as much as she could do to walk up the few steps of the bungalow, across the veranda and into the large sitting room.

Jo pushed her gently into the low basket chair. "You'll feel a lot better when you've had a cool drink. I'll ask Kari. . . ."

But Kari had already gone ahead and within a surprisingly short time had produced tall glasses of some mysterious fruit drink piled high with ice.

As Sally reached thankfully for her glass a voice behind

her, sharp with command, said, "Don't touch that!" And then, "Kari, take this away. You know what I've told you about visitors." And the two inviting glasses were whisked away.

Jo looked across toward the man who had entered through the open door. A lean man with muscles like whipcord, weathered skin almost the color of copper and cool gray eyes that seemed to hold a faintly unwelcoming look.

Jo met that look with one of anger. "Is your opinion of visitors that low? Hundreds of miles across a stifling desert and we aren't even allowed a drink?"

He looked from Jo to Sally. "To the first part of your question, Miss Fraser, I'm not over-keen on visitors, but once they are an established fact I don't want to act as nursemaid to them. I have enough on my plate."

"So—no drinks!"

"No ice," he corrected, as the drinks were brought in again in fresh glasses. "God knows what damage it could do to your sister in the dehydrated state she's in." He came farther into the room and watched for a moment while they drank, then ordered more. He held out a hand. "I'm Ross Andrews. I won't ask if you had a good journey because it would be an impossible feat without an air-conditioned car."

In the same cool tone Jo replied, "I'm Jo Fraser, and this is my sister Sally."

"I was told a brother and sister were coming."

"No, Alan couldn't get away."

"I see." He eyed them both speculatively. "Have you ever been to Africa before?"

"No." Jo shook her head.

"Well then, you two should be just the people needed to set Nyala on its feet."

Jo stared, appalled, at this taut, sarcastic man. She had not given much thought to the man behind the name of

Ross Andrews, except that he had worked for her uncle for four years, so must have some feeling for Nyala. That she and Sally would be quite so unwelcome had not entered her head. Even now she could not begin to imagine why.

From beside her Sally, always quick to sense the atmosphere, said quietly, in an attempt to change the mood, "Is it always as hot as this, Mr. Andrews?"

"Usually. Did you really expect something like an English summer day?"

Sally flushed at his continued sarcasm, but Jo was already racing in like a young tiger. "Are you always so abominably rude without reason, Mr. Andrews? We didn't ask our uncle to make such a ridiculous will. We didn't ask the solicitor to send the plane tickets. I realize you must have lost almost complete touch with civilization living here, but haven't you enough sense left to see that my sister is not just hot and thirsty, but ill? If there's a bedroom for us, then perhaps we could go to it!"

He seemed about to say something; then, with barely altered expression, he opened the door and called something incomprehensible. A few minutes later an African appeared.

"This is Saku," Ross Andrews said, "he's my house servant and will see that you have everything you want. I usually have dinner about eight-thirty if you feel like joining me." He turned on his heel and walked out into the darkness.

It was about the last thing Jo felt like doing; her anger went on simmering all the time she bathed, changed and helped Sally into bed.

Her sister did look a little better now, but she was too limp and exhausted to do anything more than lie on the spartan-looking bed.

"Can I get anything for you, Sal?" Jo said softly. "Do you think I should try to find a doctor?"

"Out here?" That even brought a smile to Sally's lips.

"No, I think he's probably right. I'm suffering from some kind of heat exhaustion. I just want to sleep until morning. If you could just see that there's a fair supply of that fruit drink. . . ." Her voice tailed off. She was almost asleep already.

Jo went back and examined her own small room, a twin of Sally's. Presumably Ross Andrews really had been expecting brother and sister. It was small and white-washed; the simple furniture was carved and unpainted. The only gesture to comfort was a zebra skin that covered part of the bare stone floor. One thing was fairly certain, whatever visitors came to Nyala, they were not women.

She would have liked to avoid a further meeting with Andrews that night, but there seemed no point in postponement. There was little enough time to establish some kind of working relationship. Besides, now that she felt greatly refreshed, hunger drove her into the living room.

She had barely walked across to the window when Saku was by her side with a drink, saying in his curiously soft, lilting voice, "*Morena* here soon, lady. You sit." He indicated the comfortable basket chair overlooking the garden.

The scent of the flowers was strong, and the sounds of the night were those she had never heard before; the insistent hum of crickets, like soft orchestral background to the real music, the occasional great trumpeting roar that could only come from an elephant, the chorus of some other beast. She was suddenly intensely aware that these were the sounds of Africa; that for mile upon mile, 100 different animals slept or prowled, awaiting the cool of the night to seek their prey.

She did not know what made her turn at that moment—the sixth sense that tells one is not alone, for certainly there had been no sound. For just a second she thought the sinewy brown shape watching her from the corner of the room was a large dog, but almost immediately came the appalling realization that she was face to face with her first lion that was not behind bars.

The animal did not move, but watched her steadily and made strange little sighing noises.

It was only afterward that Jo was able to describe the feeling of complete numbness. She did not even think of running—although there was simply nowhere to run—and the old saying that her limbs had turned to lead was the truest thing she knew. She could only wait for the inevitable, for she could not possibly imagine that a lion would enter a house unless it was very, very hungry. But in a curiously fatalistic way she could only hope he would get on with it soon.

Her numbness was so great, she had not even cried out. The only movement along her entire body was the faint trickle of tears being squeezed from under her eyelids. But she was not even aware of that at the time.

It could have been five minutes or five hours that she sat there, her eyes never leaving the other huge liquid brown ones. So gentle, so friendly, she thought in a moment of fantasy.

Suddenly the spell was broken as the lion started to move. She closed her eyes and her body started to shake uncontrollably. But there was no slashing claw, no ghastly, suffocating death, only a heightening of the soft crooning noise, then a human voice speaking sharply, but quietly. "Goldie, out, out, out!"

When she opened her eyes at last, the lion was no longer there, but Ross Andrews was standing above her chair, a glass of brandy in his hand.

"Here," he said in a surprisingly gentle voice, "drink this."

But the lead was still in her limbs and the tears were racing silently down her cheeks. It was not until he took her head and forced the brandy between her lips that she finally focused on him. Then, as her teeth started to chatter, a rug was thrown round her shoulders.

All she could say was, "Did—did you really hate us as much as all that, Mr. Andrews?"

He turned away from her. "My God, I'm not a monster! I wouldn't have had that happen for all the world. I can't begin to tell you—"

To her surprise she saw that his hands were clenched so tightly that she thought the joints must crack. So he did mind, he really did mind after all.

Somehow, suddenly, he was the one needing reassurance and she said, in a mild understatement, "It's all right, really it is, I haven't come to any harm. I simply did not know what to do, that's all. I've only seen one in a zoo."

"You did what only one person in a thousand would do, sit tight and not scream. I can only offer you an apology. I should have been here ten minutes ago, but I was held up by one of the usual problems that crop up around her. Tell me, Miss Fraser, you're obviously a brave young woman—are you also of the school that believes that the moment you fall off a horse you should remount immediately?"

"Yes . . . yes, I think I am—in theory at least."

"Then sit there, turn around and don't move." He crossed to the open doorway and called gently, "Goldie—come!"

The lion padded back, crossed to Ross Andrews's side and rubbed herself against him, like a large friendly dog. In return he tickled her behind the ears.

"Up, Goldie," he commanded. The great animal stood up on its hind legs and placed both front paws on Andrews's shoulders, who dived into his pocket and produced a banana. Very gently like a delicate cat, the lion took it from him. It was only then that Jo saw it was wearing a heavy leather collar.

"Now, go and lie down over there, Goldie, and not a sound out of you."

Ross poured himself a beer and sat down on the chair near Jo. "I found her as a cub nearly two years ago. She was the only survivor of the litter and had been deserted by the parents, although we found a dead lioness caught in a trap some days later that was probably the mother. Unlike what people think, most lions are easy to tame, and they're the gentlest, most playful creatures in the world; some of their instincts are almost human. Goldie knocked me down one day on the run and I think she really thought she had hurt me badly. She sat in a corner and snarled and spat, sulking like a child who refuses to admit it's done wrong."

Jo found her voice at last. "Is it only you she knows? I mean, will she respond to strangers?"

"Oh, yes, although she won't play with anyone she doesn't know. And you have to make it quite clear who is master. To spoil a lion like a lap-dog is to invite contempt from it. Anyway, it's high time she returned to the bush and learned to fend for herself. I've begun to stake her out on forays to teach her to hunt."

Jo, her fear finally subsiding, decided she must take her lesson to its limits. "Will . . . will she let me touch her?"

"Of course. Goldie, come here."

The lioness padded across the room and stopped exactly between the two chairs. She turned those coppery eyes on Jo again, watching her with that earlier speculative look.

"Behind the ears," Andrews said. "Just tickle her as you would a dog."

As Jo's fingers touched the rough, almost spiky coat, she simply could not believe that two days ago she was sitting in an English suburban house and now she was stroking a wild lion.

Andrews smiled dryly. "Now you're accepted. This is

part of the day's ritual to her. She knows I eat at eight-thirty, and she's always here on the dot."

Like the huge dog she first appeared to be, Goldie padded to the far side of the room, stretched out and, seconds later, was snoring gently.

Ross turned back to Jo. "And your sister, how is she?"

"Asleep. I think she'll be all right tomorrow."

In a formal voice he went on, "I apologize for my apparent discourtesy when you arrived. My only excuse is that I've had rather a lot on my mind lately."

Jo watched him curiously, feeling the apology was only verbal; there was no real depth to it. She had not given very much thought to Ross Andrews, but her mental picture would have been of an older, rugged, even seasoned man. He could not have been much over 30. There was a restlessness about him, as if after a short while, he found a house too confining.

When Saku indicated that the meal was ready, Ross stood politely and waited for her to sit down.

"I'm afraid," he began, "you won't find London standards in our kitchen here. Your uncle only taught what might be loosely described as bachelor cooking. We're big meat eaters and we get whatever fruit is in season."

"We don't come from London," Jo pointed out, "and we certainly didn't fly thousands of miles to find London standards. But there is one thing I would like to know."

"Yes?"

"Why do you find our presence here quite so irksome? You thought highly of our uncle, I assume, or you wouldn't have stayed with him. Surely you must have had some inkling as to what was in his mind over his property?"

"None whatsoever. Your uncle and I worked very closely running the reserve, but he never talked about his private affairs. In fact I didn't even know he had relatives in England until about a year ago. To be perfectly frank, I always assumed he would hand over Nyala to the Parks Board. This is the only private game reserve of any size in the republic."

"But the solicitor said it was small. How many acres does it actually cover?"

"Acres, Miss Fraser?" He raised his eyebrows in faint amusement. "Nyala is about 500 square miles."

"500 square *miles*?" she repeated stupidly. "But . . . but that's as big as a whole county in England!"

"Of course. But out here it's nothing. And as far as big game parks go, the Gemsbok is 4000 square miles and the Kruger over 7000. Directly behind us lies a million square miles of desert. So space, acres, miles—they mean little."

Still stunned by the impact of this knowledge, Jo continued, "Mr. Andrews, does the name Neil Brand mean anything to you?"

"Yes, he's a farmer; one of your uncle's few close friends, as a matter of fact. I suppose you could call him a neighbor, although his property is about 60 miles from here. You know him?"

"We met him when he came to England, although he didn't mention Uncle Harold—in fact we didn't even know there was an Uncle Harold—he must have come to report back on us. That's probably why you never knew of us either." She paused. "You still haven't told me why you resent us here. You do, don't you?"

He shrugged. "This is not a place for women; particularly for women who have no experience of the way of life here. It's tough, unforgiving, often unrewarding. . . ."

Jo shook her head. "That's not your real reason, Mr. Andrews. *You* want this park to go to the government, don't you?"

"Well, don't you think that would be the best solution?" he challenged.

"For whom?"

"The animals, of course. You have simply no idea what it costs to try to keep this place running on a limited budget. In the state we're in at the moment, it only needs one good disaster—like the threatened drought—and we're finished, so is about a third of the game. I've given four years of my life to Nyala. I don't intend to see it ruined for the sake of a couple of girls who merely want to say they own a game reserve in Africa!"

Quivering with anger, Jo stood up and faced him. "How dare you throw these charges at us, Mr. Andrews! You know nothing about us, and before we've been here more than a couple of hours you make accusations, you're rude and you think you can frighten us away with your pet lion. Oh yes, now I really do begin to believe you guilty in leaving me alone with Goldie. I think you would have enjoyed it if I'd lost my head and screamed the place down. Well, you won't get me or my sister out that way. I too can accuse. Perhaps you would like Nyala for yourself. Perhaps you expected my uncle to leave it to you!"

She had touched him on the raw at last. There were white spots of anger under his tanned skin. But, unlike her, he managed to control himself. Unhurriedly he pushed his plate aside and walked over to the open window. There, very deliberately, he lit a pipe before turning back toward her.

"At least, Miss Fraser, we know where we stand—on opposite sides of the fence. Tell me, how do you propose to keep Nyala solvent?"

"You know perfectly well I can't answer that question."

"All right, then let me ask another one. Supposing you do succeed, what are your plans at the end of three months?"

Jo swallowed. She never was very good at lying. But Sally was even worse, so it was just as well she wasn't here.

"I don't know that, either. You'll have to ask again at the end of a month."

"Oh no, Miss Fraser, I won't be doing that—simply

because I won't be here at the end of a month. If you intend to run Nyala, and you seem confident that you can, or you wouldn't have flown out here, then you and your sister must do it on your own. I'm leaving."

CHAPTER THREE

Jo woke to the sound of birds, a morning song of piercing sweetness that made her think she was in England and the thrushes were nesting again. But she opened her eyes to her cell-like room at Nyala, the sun already burning in the sky, the lemon tea on her bedside table.

Pulling her cotton robe around her, she went to the window, but she could see nothing except a dusty courtyard and the truck under its shelter of grass. Somewhere not far away was the sound of human voices babbling away in a strange tongue and, intermittently, the barking of a dog.

She took the tea into Sally's room. Her sister was awake, looking pale, but a great deal more human than she did the night before.

"Hello, Sal, you are better, aren't you? You had me worried."

"Yes, I'm all right, not exactly ready for a bush trek, but I daresay that will come tomorrow. I don't remember much about yesterday except that our host didn't seem too keen on us."

"You can say that again. He even went as far as setting his pet lion on me."

"He did *what*?" Sally's eyes were filled with horror.

"Well, perhaps not deliberately, but he didn't get to dinner on time and left me to make my own acquaintance with the lion. Oh, she's apparently harmless enough, though I didn't know it at the time. Anyway, Sal, we've got problems on our hands and a family conference is called for. I'm going to shower and dress. Shall I come back here?"

Sally shook her head. "No, it's too hot already. The

sitting room looked as if it might be the coolest place."

As Jo entered the sitting room, Saku padded behind her carrying a tray which he set out on a small table on the veranda. There was more tea, fresh mangoes, bread, and a bowl of wild honey.

For the first time Jo looked out toward the front of her new home. The long wooden bungalow was set in a semi-circle of trees overlooking an apron of short stubby grass. A kind of primitive hose snaked from the direction of the river and spurted occasional splatters of water onto the grass. Toward the left there had even been an attempt at developing a shrubbery where poinsettias, purple oleander and sweet-smelling frangipani struggled to grow. There was no boundary to the garden; it just ended. Beyond, to one side, were the trees that bordered the river—she could just see the gleam of the water as it curved away from the house—but everywhere else was the bush, stretching as far as the eye could see.

From behind her Sally said, "It's both beautiful and frightening, isn't it? So vast."

"I know; and do you know one thing Ross Andrews told me last night? By some standards this might be a small game reserve, but not by ours. It's 500 square miles."

"500?" Sally repeated, stupidly, just as Jo had done. "*Miles*?"

"Miles. I'm only just beginning to realize what we've let ourselves in for."

"But surely," Sally went on, "it's only to us it seems enormous. Mr. Andrews has presumably been able to cope. Is there any reason why he shouldn't just because we're here?"

"None. Except he doesn't intend to stay," Jo replied flatly.

Sally stared at her sister. "You mean he's walking out, just because we've arrived?"

"Something like that. It's not so much his disapproval of us personally—although heaven knows he couldn't have expressed that much more strongly—but the fact that Nyala could become ours. He claims we're a couple of novices and Nyala should really go to the state. They would run it properly and presumably subsidize it."

Sally slumped in her chair. "I suppose if we were honest we'd admit that he was right."

"How do we know after one night here?" Jo cried passionately. "How do we know he hasn't got us on a piece of string; that the government isn't bribing him to get rid of us?"

"But—but it's unthinkable!"

"Is it? Sal, if you'd been yourself last night, if you'd sat with him for half the evening, been aware enough to see the way he looked at us, the way he spoke to us! After that nothing seems unthinkable. The point is, are we going to let him push us out?"

"Have we any alternative?" Sally countered.

Jo did not answer. She was a born fighter, but she suspected that this was one fight she might have to surrender before it even began. There were a lot of jobs she would have tackled, even without experience, but she did not think that coping with wild animals was one of them. If Ross Andrews left there was the probability that the rangers might go too. He would have won anyway then, because they would be forced to go to the government for help.

"We could advertise," Jo said.

"And get some other game reserve's throw-out? We wouldn't know the difference."

Jo stood up. "Well, I'm not beaten yet. Somehow, without having to crawl, we're going to make him see reason."

"But I'm not a reasonable man. Surely you've found that out already, Miss Fraser?"

Both girls swung round to the open veranda door. He had approached them as silently as his lion and was leaning against the door, his arms folded, a faintly amused smile on his face.

Jo flushed, but her voice was cold. "Listeners never hear good of themselves, Mr. Andrews."

"*Touché.*" He turned to Sally. "I'm glad you're looking a little better this morning. Did you sleep well?"

"Marvelously, thank you."

"There's one thing about this area—the nights are often cool. In fact they can be extremely cold."

Sally looked from her sister to Ross Andrews. Jo made good friends quickly and easily, but she also made bad enemies. It was time to step in and act as peacemaker.

"Jo tells me you're not going to stay on at Nyala, Mr. Andrews."

"She's quite right."

"Then you must have made the decision before we came. It might have been kinder to stop us making such a long journey."

He shook his head. "My decision was taken only last night."

"Then you mean you made your judgment after meeting us at the end of that long journey. In fact you could hardly say you met me. So after only an hour or so you decided you couldn't work with my sister. It doesn't really seem fair.'

He eyed her thoughtfully. "Probably you've had a one-sided version of what happened last night. I really think your sister believes I set a lion on her. Mind you, I suppose it's as good a way as any to get rid of visitors. I must bear it in mind next time."

Now he was laughing at her. Jo glared at him. She never had been very good at coping with people she did not understand. "So you really are leaving?"

"We can only run Nyala on my terms, Miss Fraser," he answered inexorably.

"And those are?"

"That you hand Nyala over to the state immediately."

Jo was about to leap in when Sally forestalled her with a touch on the arm.

"That's hardly fair, Mr. Andrews," she pointed out gently. "We don't even know yet what is potentially ours. We've seen nothing but this and our two rooms. You tell us there are difficulties, but we haven't the slightest idea what they are. . . ."

Before he could answer Kari ran across the garden, up the steps and started to talk swiftly and with some agitation, pointing to somewhere in the distance beyond the house.

Andrews nodded. "All right, we'll leave in ten minutes. Have the truck ready and my guns." As Kari disappeared he turned to the girls. "I'm sorry, we'll have to continue this some other time. Poachers—by all accounts a fairly large gang. I shall be away most of the day, probably."

"Are you going in the truck?" Jo asked.

He nodded briefly.

"Then I'm coming. What do I need?"

For a second she thought he was going to argue, but he merely shrugged. "As you wish. As long as you know I'm telling you—in front of your sister—that we're not going on a picnic."

"I'm aware of that."

"Then put on some long cotton pants and something with sleeves. You'll need a hat and a pair of comfortable shoes—not sandals. And some of that insect repellent I told you to buy. Oh, yes, and a heavy sweater in case we're back late." He paused, turning. "And you, Miss Sally Fraser?"

Sally smiled. "I would only be a nuisance. No, I'm going to putter about here for the day and find my bush feet, or whatever you call it."

"Fine. Saku will help you with anything you want. Oh, and Miss Fraser. . . ."

"Sally," she corrected.

"Sally, then. If you do see a stray lion wearing a leather collar also puttering about the place, don't be alarmed. I really won't have sent her back to frighten you."

Sally laughed aloud. "I think you're human after all, Mr. Andrews!"

"Ross. But don't run either. Goldie will only think you're playing."

When the ten minutes were up, Jo was waiting in the shade of the Land Rover. When Ross arrived he gave her a cursory inspection. He made no comment except to nod her into the passenger seat. In the back were Kari and two young Africans.

"I like your sister," were the first words he spoke after they had driven away from the perimeter of the house along a narrow dusty track.

"Everybody likes Sally," Jo answered simply. "I don't know what my brother and I would have done without her."

"I was beginning to think you gave the orders."

"Only sometimes, and only because she lets me. But you always know when you've gone too far with Sally."

The track wound its way directly across the bush, through scrub and thorn trees; the white, blowing sand of the desert was everywhere. Here and there were clumps of trees, wild fig mostly, he told her, and a few thorn bushes. A herd of impala came across the track, their graceful leaps bringing the truck to a halt. Before Ross started again he pointed to a clump of trees and an almost imperceptible movement.

"Zebra!" she exclaimed in delight. But today there was no time to stop and wonder at the game; the giraffe munched away at leaves high above their heads, unconcerned at the humans passing so near. There were buck in plenty, and a shy old kudu bull hiding behind some thorn trees.

The day had started well and Jo wanted it to remain one of truce. So she decided no personal questions, no talk of wills or resignations. Instead she said, as they slowed down once more over a particularly bumpy part of the track, "Tell me about the poachers. What are they after? Ivory?"

"Some. Others just want free meat. I suppose any ranger would tell you there are four kinds of poachers. The first we see little of up here. He's the man who merely wants to boast of a kill. He'll go out at night with a light or gun and shoot anythings that moves—mostly harmless cattle. Fortunately there are few enough men here and those know the rules of the game too well.

"The second type is after gain. He wants to sell his meat. He carries a gun which he doesn't always know how to use properly. It's usually through him that wounded—and dangerous—game are left to drag out their last days in the bush.

"Some poachers hunt in packs. They carry spears and usually have half-starved dogs with them. The dogs can follow the game until it gives up and then there's the spear for the last thrust. Today we are after the worst kind of poachers—those who use traps. They've probably come over the border from Rhodesia knowing we have fewer rangers out in the field. But all poachers are a pretty nasty breed. They kill for greed, not hunger. Only the Bushmen kill because they're hungry. And we tend to turn a blind eye to them as long as they only kill in the dry season."

"I heard that my uncle knew the Bushmen well."

"No one knows the Bushmen well. A few have chosen comparative civilization; the villages near the rivers, particularly by the swamp land, but the nomad tribes grow increasingly shy and stay in the desert, driving a few cattle, growing a few meager crops. Your uncle used to spend a week, whenever he had the time, out in the desert. He would take Kari with him and they would use every means to make contact with the Bushmen, just to photograph them." He looked up into the heavy hazy heat of the morning sky. "This will be a bad season for them. The drought has gone on too long already."

From the back Kari spoke excitedly and a few moments later Ross pulled off the main track, across the scrub. Here there was no shelter from the brassy glare of the sun. On the hard, uneven surface it seemed that the truck had lost all its springs. They halted finally in a clearing and without a glance toward her Ross climbed down, followed by the three Africans. After a second's hesitation Jo joined them. She could not keep back the gasp of horror.

The vicious teeth of a trap were still holding the broken end of a once slender foot. The buck, with sad, sad eyes, lay there whimpering in his last agony. Not only was the shattered leg a mass of sharp bone and blood, but one of the haunches had been ripped open. Jo turned quickly away. A moment later she heard the crack of a rifle. When she looked again the eyes were glazed and at rest.

Ross Andrews's face was hard and bleak. "There's your poacher for you. The trouble is he doesn't even check his snares, so the animal is left to die of pain and thirst and at the mercy of other predators. You see," he pointed with his gun as a brown shape slunk round the bush and came out to watch them. "Hyena, bold as brass. He knows now he can have the rest of the kill." Abruptly he turned to Kari. "Well, have you found the tracks?"

"Toward the waterhole, *Morena*."

"Well, we'll try, but I don't hold out much hope. You'd better wait in the truck, Miss Fraser, we'll be about half an hour."

"Can't I come?"

He hesitated only briefly. Already she had discovered he was a man who made up his mind instantly. "If you like. But this isn't the English countryside, you know, and the temperature is around 100."

She lifted her chin. "I'm aware of that. Would you prefer that I spent my three months in a lawn chair in the garden?"

He started across the uneven ground, with one African behind him, then herself with Kari and the other taking up the rear, probably at a pace far slower than his usual one. She thought she should have been nervous, but oddly enough was not, although she remembered distinctly that in her book about the Kruger Park it was strictly forbidden ever to get out of a car.

In front of her Ross held up his hand and the small party was instantly still. Not more than 50 yards away a great herd of blue-black beasts, with tossing horns and shaggy heads, crossed their track as though on the march. There could have been 100 of them, and Jo held her breath in wonder at being so close to her first real game.

When Ross turned back to her she raised her eyebrows in query and his answer came back as a whisper. "Wildebeest." Then the herd was suddenly alerted to their presence and, like a troop of drilled cavalry, they were thundering out of the bush in a tight, almost dancing formation.

They came to within a few yards of the waterhole; the air already smelled sweeter, fresher, and the camel-thorns no longer rasped at their clothes. Under a clump of trees at the far side, two giraffe munched at the high leaves and a few zebra raced away into the distance.

Ross and Kari were on their knees examining the

tracks, but it did not take them long to decide that it was not worth continuing. As she stood and watched them Jo became deeply aware of the sun. There was no shade, no escape from it, but she was determined he should not see her discomfort.

Back in the truck she thought Ross had given up the chase, but she discovered he was merely trying to outflank his enemy. Oh yes, he told her, he knew in which direction the poachers had gone; on foot, about half a day ahead, probably heading for one of the villages on the edge of the great salt-pan. But with the drought setting in, one of their number would be almost certain to check the snares.

Within 15 minutes they found another victim—a buck too, but this time he was dead. Ross cursed aloud and then, at the same time as Jo, he became aware of the faint movement under the thick bush near the dead animal. Cautiously he moved aside the leaves and lifted up a baby fawn, thin and emaciated. The brown, liquid eyes offered a silent plea for help.

Jo looked at Ross. "Will it live?"

"Not in the bush without its mother. It hasn't a hope; it can't be more than a few days old."

"Then what will you do?"

"Either finish it off here while we go on after the poachers, or take it back with us. Even then it has no more than a 50-50 chance."

She met his gaze steadily. "But that's what you're going to do, isn't it?"

"I imagine you're not offering me any choice. Come on, Kari, get going. You'd better drive while I try to get some water down it." He spoke as if he gave in grudgingly, so she was not sure whether his decision would have been different had she not been there.

Suddenly Jo shivered. "Is there always so much death in the bush?"

"Always. But there's life too. That's what the bush is about; the simple matters of life and death. All animals have to kill to live. I told you before, Miss Fraser, it's a cruel country. I'm only here to preserve it from human destruction; to give all the game a better chance, away from the hunters' guns."

The tiny animal in his arms moved slightly and the eyes flickered as Ross put a rag soaked in water into its mouth. Twice it tried to suck the moisture, but the effort was too much as it slumped back again.

Jo touched the tiny, silky head. "It's dead too, isn't it?"

"Not yet. There's still a chance, only a small one."

"I want it to live," Jo said simply, "not just because it's young, and frightened and motherless, but because it seems like a symbol. My first day at Nyala."

"You mean a symbol of hope that you should keep Nyala."

"If you like—yes." She added curiously, "Where will you go, Mr. Andrews?"

"To another job like this. It's all I know, all I care about."

"Have you ever been to England?"

"Oh, yes, I lived there for several years. But I never want to go back permanently. It would squeeze me dry. Once you've known a place of immense freedom, where a man can still be alone and pit his wits against nature, you would never want to go back."

"You don't like humans very much, do you?"

There was the faintest ghost of a smile. "Let's just say I prefer the company of animals. They're more predictable."

They reached the bungalow in time for a late lunch, but Jo knew she would not be able to think of eating until she saw what chance the tiny fawn had. In a small thatched building near the house that seemed to be fitted up as a makeshift surgery, Ross started to feed the animal drip by drip with warm milk from a baby's bottle.

For a while Jo watched, then said quietly, "I think I could manage that if you have other things to do."

"Then hold her comfortably as you would a child; it will be a long job—she's only taking a few drops now and then."

Two hours later Jo was still there, absorbed in her self-appointed task. Ross had looked in on her once, but made no comment. She had volunteered to do this, so presumably she must be left to get on with it. Her arms ached from holding them in the same position, but suddenly the tiny body wriggled, the eyes opened in fear. The fawn was coming to life.

She called and soon one of the servants brought Ross. He took the struggling animal from her and nodded, pleased with what he saw. "I reckon she'll make it after all. We'll put her in one of the cages and let her sleep."

Jo looked down at the tiny creature curled up on clean straw. "She really is straight out of Walt Disney, isn't she?" she said softly.

"Yes, but I warn you, if you keep her here, you'll find you have more than a puppy on your hands. She'll follow you wherever you go."

Laughter bubbled up in Jo. "I really won't mind that. She is my symbol after all, isn't she?"

He shook his head, smiling. "You're a strange one. One minute a fighting cat, the next. . . ."

"Yes?"

"Never mind." His voice changed abruptly. "I would take a rest. You'll be useless to everyone dead on your feet." He turned on his heel and left the room.

In the sitting room Jo found Sally, who confessed she had been sleeping most of the day but really did feel herself again now. "And you, Jo. How did the trip go? I imagine you didn't catch the poachers?"

"No, but we destroyed two of their traps—vicious-looking steel things. If you'd seen, Sally, what they'd done to the animals!" She shuddered.

"You look about all in. Don't forget, you may think you can ride roughshod over this climate, but I say treat it with respect, or it'll get you sooner or later. Did you talk to Ross about leaving?"

Jo shook her head. "No, there was no chance. Besides, if he wants to leave, how are we going to stop him? We're the last people he'll listen to. Why, he even admitted he preferred animals to people. Oh, he knows how to treat them all right."

"Then he won't walk out of Nyala, will he?" Sally said calmly.

"That's just what he *is* going to do, out of spite. He doesn't want us here and he doesn't much care how he gets us out."

Sally leaned forward. "Listen, you idiot, of course he wants to get us out, but from what you've said he doesn't want to leave." She looked swiftly around and lowered her voice. "You've only confirmed what I was thinking this afternoon. Nyala is his life. Do you honestly believe, if he has any feelings at all for the animals, he's going to walk out of here and leave them to be cared for by a couple of green girls? Of course not. He's counting on us believing his threat and going home at the end of the week. But if we stand our ground. . . ."

Jo caught her breath. "You're right, I really believe you're right, Sal. But what are we going to say to him?"

"Nothing. Pretend he never said anything about leaving. And Jo. . . ."

"Yes?"

"Curb your temper. I can see he's a difficult character, but don't bait him or tell him what you think of him."

"That will be difficult," Jo said bluntly. "I guess he's been too used to having his own way around here. And whatever he says I believe he thought Uncle Harold would leave this place to him."

Sally laid a hand on Jo's leg. "Maybe you're right, but don't be too sure. We've been here less than 24 hours. It's no time or place to make snap judgments."

When Jo reached her room she realized she was almost more tired than she had been yesterday. She had had several hours of the most intense heat in her life. She had tried to take in so many unfamiliar sights and sounds. She had just spent two hours almost immobile in a stifling little room with a sick animal. Derbyshire seemed a million miles away.

She flung herself down on top of the sheets, and slept and dreamed. When she woke the room was dark and the air cool at last. At first she thought the thumping on her door was part of a dream, but then the catch snapped and framed in the light was Goldie, sitting on her haunches.

Even now there was a sudden spurt of fear, but she pushed it down quickly.

"Hello, Goldie." Her voice was almost steady.

The lioness padded to her bedside and watched, with that unnerving stare.

Now what? thought Jo. I haven't quite got the courage to get up while she's here, neither do I want to call out and make her think I'm alarmed. So Jo talked in normal tones, then reached out and tickled the alert ears. Her reward was a hug paw placed on the bed. She swallowed, hard.

"Who on earth are you chatting to? Oh . . ." Sally stood in the doorway uncertainly, "I've only seen her from a distance. Are you all right?"

"I think so. I'm not quite sure whether I can calmly get up and walk out."

"I'll get Ross."

"*No*! I'm damned if I'll ask his help. Go on, Goldie, out, out!"

But the lioness took this to mean the exact opposite. With one comfortable leap she was on the end of the bed, her great weight resting comfortably on Jo's bare toes.

"Oh, lord, now I can't even get up if I want to."

"Then I am going to fetch Ross. Pride can be carried too far, even in our family."

But Ross was already there. With his hands on his hips he looked in, his eyes glinting with amusement. "I'm afraid," he said gravely, "you have a fatal fascination for lions and fawns, just as beds have a fascination for Goldie. She simply can't resist one. If you move she won't take the slightest bit of notice of you. She'll simply think she's commandeered your bed for good."

"Then I'd better show her who's boss, hadn't I?" And acting more bravely than she felt she pushed, with feet and hands, until the great body flopped to the floor. Goldie gazed at her with an expression of great sorrow, but with what dignity she could muster, walked out.

When Jo had showered and changed she heard laughter coming from the sitting room. Well, Sally wasn't wasting any time coming to terms with Mr. Ross Andrews. But she bore her sister no resentment because that was Sally's way. She never had liked to be at war. For just a moment Jo hesitated outside her own room. Perhaps she should stay out and let Sally do the negotiating.

Goldie rose in her corner to greet Jo, then thought better of it and slumped lazily back into sleep. But, as Ross stood up, so did an alert brown body. Not another lion, surely, was her first thought. Then she saw that it was a dog, mostly boxer.

"Sherry?" Ross said politely. "Or would you like something longer?"

"Sherry will do fine now that it's cooler."

As he handed her the glass he said, "You'd better come and meet one of the other members of the family." He in-

dicated the dog who had not moved a muscle since she
came into the room. "This is Tau—a foolish name really
since in the local language it means lion. But we didn't
have Goldie when Tau joined us. Even when he was a
puppy they used to say he was as brave as a lion, so the
name stuck." He nudged the dog with his shoe. "But he's
not so much of a house pet as Goldie. He's trained purely
as a hunting dog. Normally I never go into the bush without him, but we thought yesterday he had picked up some
kind of bug."

"How about the fawn?" Jo asked eagerly. "Is she still
all right?"

"So it seems. We're having an hourly watch on her.
She's taken a little more milk and is sleeping again."

Tonight, Jo decided, he appeared more relaxed. Sally's
doing probably, but she felt no resentment toward the
sister who had such a calming influence on her life. If
Sally could somehow make Ross Andrews see reason,
then she, Jo, might avoid losing her temper, or much
worse, having to grovel.

The two sisters could not have been more opposite
either in temperament or in looks. Jo had always been the
outgoing one, rushing headlong into life, meeting new
people, new experiences, with the enthusiasm she inherited from her father. She had also inherited his fiery
temper, his generosity, and his absolute honesty. Much of
her character showed in her face; green eyes flecked with
gold that seemed to catch fire when she was really angry;
the same reddish glints in her silky hair. Usually she wore
it to her shoulders, but had it cut to a more manageable
length before leaving England. Now it hung straight and
even around her almost heart-shaped face. Jo had always
been the first of the family to laugh, the one who loved to
play a practical joke. People either admired Jo, or else
they thought her too outspoken. They never guessed how
uncertain she was underneath, how deeply she needed
someone of her own to love.

She had been quite right when she said that everyone loved Sally. All the right fairy godmothers had been around when her sister was christened, endowing her with beauty, brains and a true gentleness of spirit. It still remained a mystery to Jo why Sally had not married. But if her sister was warm and gentle, she could also be very stubborn.

Her looks came just as directly from her mother who had been dark with intensely blue eyes. Sally also had her slender build with small hands and feet and an air—not completely true—of great delicacy. Jo used to say that beside her sister she sometimes felt like a clumsy giant. She never realized that her tall proud carriage drew many admiring glances.

Jo was day-dreaming. She came to, hearing Sally and Ross talking about the problems of Nyala.

"What do you think," Sally was asking, "Uncle Harold would have done had he lived another few years? Did he talk about the future of Nyala?"

"Yes, sometimes. I think he honestly believed he could keep this place afloat. Because he didn't talk much about his private affairs I assumed he was hoping to put in more capital. I didn't know things had gone as far as they had."

"As far as what?" Jo challenged.

He shrugged. "Well, for example, we badly need a new truck and there simply is no money to buy one. Fortunately I cover a fair part of the reserve on horseback."

Sally looked at him wonderingly, forgetting the immediate question of finance. "But isn't that dangerous?"

"I often have the feeling that Nyala is much less dangerous than Piccadilly Circus. Every car and bus is a lethal weapon, so you regard them with caution. The same with animals. They only attack when provoked, wounded or very hungry; you learn to treat them with healthy respect. The exception to the rule is the rhino. It will charge without any reason at all. It likes to pretend it's an immovable object and wait in ambush for the unwary passer-by. There's only one escape if you're on foot; head for the nearest tree. Even then it's a question of whose patience holds out longest."

"Why?" said Sally curiously.

"An awkward rhino has been known to keep his hostage up that tree for several hours. But if you think I'm trying to frighten you," and here he was looking at Jo, "then I must tell you that there are no rhinos in Nyala."

But while Jo was just as interested in the wildlife of Nyala, she was determined not to be sidetracked from the more important issue of money. Three months suddenly seemed a very short time.

"Mr. Andrews. . . ." she started.

"Ross. Even if we're to be at war it's still simpler."

"Ross, then." Jo shrugged. "I was wondering what you and my uncle did to try to make Nyala pay its way."

"Like what?"

"Like attracting tourists. Taking them out on safari. . . ."

"You've been seeing too many Hollywood movies."

She flushed. What did he think she was—a child?

"Perhaps you haven't seen enough," she threw back, "or rather you haven't learned the lessons of other parks. The Kruger, for instance. They encourage tourists from all over the world. I imagine they couldn't make the place pay without tourists."

He sighed. "We couldn't do it here."

"Why not?"

"Because we haven't the facilities."

Jo was beginning to wonder if she would ever get the better of this man. "I don't understand you," she said at last. "You want Nyala to go to the state, yet surely that's the first thing they would do—encourage visitors." She appealed to her sister. "Don't you think so, Sal?"

"Yes . . . yes, I think you're right." In a quiet, but very determined way she said to Ross, "You could help us if you wanted to, Ross. You must realize that without you there would be no Nyala."

"There are other game rangers."

But Sally went on inexorably, "Did you get along with Uncle Harold? Was he a man to admire?"

"I never met a finer man in my life," was his answer.

Now it was Jo's turn. "Then you can't let him down, can you?"

He stood up and for just a second looked from one sister to another. The expression in his eyes was unreadable, even a little frightening. Then, without another word, he turned and strode out of the room.

CHAPTER FOUR

It was nearly 24 hours before they saw Ross again. When questioned, Saku said that *Morena* was out working.

"Sulking, you mean," Jo muttered.

But after breakfast they were brought a note that he had left. It said briefly that he and Kari were out on trek today on horseback. It would be too tough to consider taking them. But tomorrow he had to go farther afield by truck to inspect some waterholes and he would be glad to give them at least a partial tour of the property. For today would they please stay within the perimeter of the house and adjoining land. They would be perfectly safe as long as they did not do anything foolish.

"Well," snorted Jo, "his opinion of us grows higher by the hour. What does he think we are—a couple of complete dimwits?"

"I think," said Sally more charitably, "he doesn't understand much about women. He honestly doesn't know what to make of us. We're more or less dumped on his doorstep as the possible new owners of the place that's been his home for four years. I think his reaction is probably quite natural."

"I really believe you're on his side," cried Jo.

"Not necessarily. I'm merely trying to see his point of view. If his only thought is for the preservation of the game, then we must seem like intruders."

"If," said Jo darkly.

"Oh Jo, don't think the worst of him just yet. I know he hasn't much in the way of manners, but does that honestly matter? I can think of plenty of people I've worked with quite amicably, while I didn't think much of them personally. After all, it isn't as though we've come out here as brides for Mr. Ross Andrews."

Jo raised her eyes in mock despair. "Heaven preserve us!"

"Well, then. . . ."

Jo suddenly grinned. "You may be right, I don't know, but at least I'll try to reserve judgment for a week. I just have the feeling he's going to rub me the wrong way, although he likes you. I think what worries me most is that we have to take his word on everything. Any decision he makes about which we're doubtful there simply isn't anyone else to turn to—a neighbor, another man who knows the country."

"There's Neil Brand," Sally said tentatively.

"60 miles away, and anyway if he was a friend of Uncle Harold's then he's almost certain to be hand in glove with Ross. I'd like someone around like Bruce."

"Bruce Farley?" Sally's eyes widened. "Now you're confusing infatuation with common sense!"

For the first time since their arrival Jo felt a spurt of anger toward her sister. "Just because you didn't approve of him," she challenged. "You were all wrong about Bruce—simply because he didn't fit into yours and Alan's idea of the kind of man I should marry."

"He was a wanderer."

"Even wanderers settle down," Jo retorted. "Besides, I wasn't really thinking of my own feelings for him. I was thinking that he'd spent years in Africa. He knows something about it which we don't."

"Africa is a big continent," Sally reminded her. "It's possible that a reserve up here has entirely different problems from one, say, in Kenya. Anyway, Bruce—but it won't help much. Let's do something practical today. Let's explore as far as we can and by the time we see Ross again at least we could make some suggestions instead of sitting back and grumbling."

Of course Sally was right. She generally was when it came to finding a way out of difficulties.

Before the full heat of the day was on them they set off to explore the immediate land around the house. From her place in the shade Goldie rose, made a beeline for Jo, then waited expectantly.

Sally said, "Ross was right when he said you'd made a hit with her. I imagine she's going to come with us whether we invite her or not. Do you mind?"

Jo's attachment to Goldie was also beginning to grow. "No, in fact I think I'd be rather glad to have her protection. Who knows what we might meet?" In an excess of bravery she slapped Goldie's rump. "Although I'm not sure that you would be any more use than a cocker spaniel in an emergency!"

They started around the back of the house where most of the outbuildings were. Their first call was to the "surgery" where the fawn's cage had been brought out to the shade and she lay stretched out. Already she was much stronger, for as they approached, she tried to struggle to her feet. Jo reached through the bars and touched her silky coat. "Hello there," she whispered, "you're going to be all right, aren't you?" The tiny animal did not flinch from her touch, but seemed to nuzzle at her finger.

Jo laughed aloud in delight. "What are we going to call her, Sal?"

"I don't know," Sally said, "you must name her. She's going to be yours. It's strange, you really do have a way with animals. I never knew it."

"Nor did I," Jo replied. "There's never really been time at home even to have a dog or cat. And yet I do remember when I was about ten or eleven collecting everything from the woods I could lay my hands on."

Sally pulled a face. "Toads included; mice and moles and that poor old duck with a limp—Jemima Puddle-duck." Both girls giggled.

Jo said suddenly, "I remember reading that the name Holly meant good luck. Well, I think she's going to bring both of us luck. We'll call her Holly. Look, even Goldie seems to accept her."

Goldie was stretched out in the sun watching them lazily, but making no attempt to disturb the fawn.

"One day," Jo said slowly, "I suppose Goldie will learn to kill helpless animals like that. It seems too awful to think of."

"Then don't get too starry-eyed about Nyala," Sally said practically, "I imagine we might see some pretty horrifying things before we leave here. Lions have to eat, the same as buck do."

"I suppose so, but I don't want to think about it. Come on or it will soon be too hot to walk."

Beyond the "surgery" was the big open-sided cookhouse, with an iron range just outside. Sally regarded it professionally. "I believe that could feed a dozen or more—like a huge barbeque."

"And over there," Jo pointed. "They look like the perfect guest huts. I've seen pictures of them in some of the books I've been reading. They're called rondavels."

"My, you have been doing your homework. But you're quite right." The three huts stood away from the house on a patch of scrubby grass. They were round, whitewashed, with a thatched roof rising to a point and a couple of windows each. Inside each was a wooden bed and a couple of plain chairs.

"That's exactly what they are," Sally commented, "sort of guest cottages. With a little paint and some freshening up they could be perfect. I wonder why Ross said there were no facilities. These must have been used in the past. Well, I suppose he has his reasons."

As they walked farther, they kept talking, trying to work out some plan. In a way the whole project fell neatly in two. Jo could concentrate on learning as much about the actual running of the reserve as possible, since that seemed her natural bent. Sally would put all her energies into the domestic side. They both agreed that the obvious way to make Nyala pay was through visitors.

"This afternoon," Sally said, "as soon as I've had a thorough look around I'm going to shut myself away and work out some facts and figures. I'll see what real possibilities the kitchen has and where Saku gets his supplies. The trouble is that by the look of things Ross and Uncle Harold have always lived on local produce; heaven knows what that meat we ate last night was—not any of the things we are used to, that's certain. What we would need is a freezer. We've got our own generator, so electricity won't be any problem. . . ."

"I think," Jo interrupted, "there are two things you're overlooking."

"What are they?"

"One—money."

"And?"

"Ross Andrews."

"You mean in case he objected?" Sally frowned.

"Not exactly. Look, let's walk to the river and I'll tell you when I've got my thoughts sorted out. At least there's some shade over there."

They circled the house and walked down the sloping ground to the edge of the river. It wasn't very much as rivers go and the water was low.

At the point where it touched Nyala's "garden" it was probably no more than 30 feet wide, but surprisingly clear, undoubtedly, Sally pointed out, from the lightness of the desert sand. As they bent to gaze into the glassy calm, a silver shoal of tiny fish raced through the shallows where a mass of feathery papyrus threw a ten-foot shadow across the water. But most beautiful of all were the waterlilies, their white, waxy flowers glistening in the sun. For a moment it seemed as if they were looking down into an English ornamental pool on a hot Sunday afternoon. Small, sharply black and white birds swooped along the bank, in and out of the colonies of nests that seemed to be suspended from the reeds. Then there were others with long red tail feathers and a glossy blue-crested head; tiny birds that darted from one tree to another in search of insects.

"It's like paradise!" Sally breathed.

As she spoke there was a movement among the thicker reeds a little farther downstream. Instinctively both girls walked toward it.

"I thought it was a big fish," Jo said, disappointed.

"No, it's a floating log."

But the log kept moving until it came to the shallows, then the great appalling square-jawed mouth rose slowly from the water and they were both momentarily hyp-notized by the stare of the bulging, ruby-red eyes. Beside them Goldie gave a deep, menacing growl and the spell was broken.

Sally tugged at Jo's hand and pulled her back from the river's edge so sharply that she nearly fell. When they turned back again the great ridged back of the crocodile was again underwater and the river, except for a nar-rowing circle of ripples, was calm once more.

"Paradise!" echoed Jo, horrified.

Sally, recovering from the shock, smiled slightly. "Well, even in the real paradise there was a serpent. And apparently even Goldie disapproves of crocodiles."

But Jo would not be drawn back to the river and moved instead to the shade of a cluster of wild fig trees where she could watch the colorful bird life—darting, flashing colors from a dozen jewels—and forget the menace that lurked beneath the waters.

"I think," she said, "I'm going to feel about crocodiles as you do about snakes."

"Perhaps," Sally said somberly, "but at least you

know a crocodile sticks to the river. I imagine you could trip over a snake anywhere. Anyway," she changed the subject quickly, "you were going to tell me your ideas on safari guests at Nyala."

"Yes." Jo sat down on the hard ground, cupping her chin in her hand, frowning in her effort to sort out her thoughts.

"Well, it's like this," she began at last. "I also think the only way to make this place pay is to have visitors. I'm not worried about the domestic and catering arrangements. We can get around that somehow. But we're not going to persuade people to come to Nyala unless they can go out into the bush and view the game at first hand."

"Yes, that's right."

"Well, I presume most of them will be as green as we are. They can't go unaccompanied, so who on earth is going to act as guide? I can't honestly see Ross devoting his days to organized tours with unwelcome tourists, can you, Sal?"

"Oh, lord, I hadn't thought of that." Then, more hopefully, "But you can drive through the Kruger and other parks in your own car. What's different about Nyala?"

"The roads, I imagine, or the lack of them. You'd have to have a Land Rover or something similar. The springs of an ordinary car simply wouldn't last on even the short journey I did yesterday."

"Perhaps," said Sally in a small voice, "that's what he meant by lack of facilities."

"Perhaps." Jo's green eyes flashed. "But we're not going to give up as easily as that. What do you think the main things we need are—apart from a guide?"

"Money," said Sally bluntly, "the more you look at it, the more obvious that becomes. To get even one small party here we need a new truck, a freezer and a few more home comforts. That's just basic. And from what Ross said, there isn't even enough money to replace the present truck."

"It's all what Ross says, isn't it? How do we know he's speaking the truth?"

"We don't, but I think he is—at least as far as the position at Nyala is concerned. Anyway, we can find out from Mr. Scott the exact amount of money available."

The more they talked the more it became apparent that every turning they took led to Ross Andrews. They could take no decisions without him.

By now the heat beating down upon them was immense. Even Goldie had abandoned them to stretch out and doze. So they made their way back to the house for the cold drinks that Saku always seemed to have waiting.

Sally started to question him about the kitchen. Yes, he had once cooked for many people on the big range, but mostly he used the smaller one inside. Yes, there was a refrigerator—which he called a cold box, but he did not know what a freezer was.

"Where do you get your meat from?" Sally asked curiously.

He looked at her in the faintest of surprise. "Why, *Morena* shoots it. And the fish come from the river, of course. Where else, lady?"

"Of course," said Sally weakly. "Where else indeed?" When he had gone she turned to Jo. "We have a lot to learn about life in the raw, it seems. Do you think safari visitors would want to know what they were eating?"

"Sitting around the table here I think they would, but not if they really went out on safari, camping, etc."

After lunch Saku, obviously bidden by his master, suggested that the ladies should rest during the hottest part of the day. Sally agreed and went to lie down, but Jo was far too restless, her brain turning over and over all the insurmountable problems.

She looked out across the garden, into the bush, where the heat melted into the hazy distance. She suddenly had a great longing to cross the whole of the park and see the desert for herself. There was a great deal here she had to come to terms with; much to learn and a whole new life and climate to which to grow accustomed. But she had the awesome feeling that she would not mind not returning to England for a long, long time. And on the other side of the coin, three months seemed an impossibly short time to achieve anything at all. On top of all that she wanted to learn and had the wrong teacher. She and Ross Andrews could know each other a lifetime and still be crossing swords.

Not wanting to go into the house yet, she wandered over to see Holly. The little fawn was awake and much stronger; when Jo put her hand into the cage, she was even able to stand upright with a little help. Very carefully Jo opened the cage door and lifted Holly out. The warm brown eyes regarded her with complete trust. There was not a single movement of fear. Under the silky brown coat the flesh was beginning to fill out. Any day now, except for feeding, Holly would be able to fend for herself. But would she be safe even in the garden? Jo wondered, remembering the crocodile within a stone's throw of the house. What animals prowled at night when the air was dark and still?

Ross returned in the late afternoon to find her asleep in the basket chair under the trees with Holly curled up in her arms like a kitten.

She woke to see him standing over her. For a few seconds she could not think where she was and she looked at him as a stranger as he stood holding the bridle of his horse. Then one of the servants came and led the tired animal away. Ross looked tired, his thin face drawn and rough with a day-old beard, his shirt clinging to his body.

She focused suddenly. "You look as if you've had a bad day."

"Rough enough, but I don't like the look of things out there. Two of the waterholes are far too low for comfort.

I'm wondering what I shall find nearer the desert. The Bushmen say it's a year of bad omens."

"And do you believe in bad omens?"

He shrugged. "I believe in facts. In these parts omens and facts get confused. You have to learn to listen to the country speaking to you. It can tell you many things. And you have to listen to the natives. What they tell you usually has a grain of truth. Saku will tell you for instance that when the crocs move into the home stretch of the river it's going to be a bad season."

"There was a crocodile over there today," she said quietly.

"Where?"

She crossed the garden to the banks of the river. She pointed down toward the white cluster of lilies just beginning to close. "It swam from the opposite bank," she said, "and stared at us with red eyes. I had no idea that a crocodile could be so truly ugly. I'm afraid we didn't wait to see any more."

"They're nasty brutes all right, but you can make a fascinating study of them. You remember asking about Neil Brand—well, he spends most of his leave crocodile-hunting up in the Okavango swamps. He'll talk to you for hours about their habits. By the way, I talked to him on the radio telephone early this morning and told him you and your sister had arrived, but he already knew by the bush telegraph. He's driving over here on the weekend with his son Sandy to welcome you—bringing a friend too, he said." He nodded toward the river. "We'll ask him to make a couple of good purses out of that fellow . . . don't look so worried, I doubt if there are more than a couple of them about." He paused. "Did you and your sister have a good day?"

She nodded. "We tried to make a few plans. Sally says we can't carry any of them out without your help."

That cold, bleak look was back in his eyes. "I'd like to help, but I won't be here, will I?" He leaned back against the gnarled trunk of a tree and dug into his pocket for a pipe. He seemed a long time in lighting it. Finally he drew on it slowly and said, "Look, I have no objection to you two personally, whatever you may think. Why not call a truce and I'll give you a month's holiday to remember? Perhaps holiday is too strong a word because we're short on time here, but I'll show you what life on a game reserve is really like."

Jo could feel her temper beginning to rise already, but she controlled it. Sally would have approved. "I too would like to call a truce . . . Ross, but not for the ends you want. We haven't come here for a holiday, but to learn. Unfortunately we have to rely on an unwilling teacher. At least you might listen to our plans tonight without walking out on us."

He regarded her thoughtfully. "You're a very determined young woman, aren't you?"

She returned that gaze steadily. "I'm determined to see justice. Is that so great a crime? And it's not just for myself. I don't suppose you know anything about our family, do you?" And when he did not answer she went on; "My parents died five years ago leaving practically nothing. I was still at school, Sally was at college and our brother Alan was just beginning to get a foot in the hotel business. Alan worked day and night to help Sally. Both of them took extra jobs to keep me at school. For five years it's been very tough indeed. Then suddenly the chance of a lifetime is dropped into our laps. An unknown uncle throws out a challenge to make up for those years. We accepted from the beginning that we hadn't much chance of success, but we never guessed that the one person we counted on to give us a chance would set his face against us so strongly. That's what I mean by justice!"

For a long time he did not answer and she had no idea

what effect her words had had on him. She only knew that it was the last time she intended to either bargain or appeal to him. There was simply nothing more she could say that would get through. She was not, as she said so strongly to Sally, going to grovel.

Suddenly he turned and smiled. For just a second she thought he was laughing at her again. This time she knew she would not be able to control her temper. But he held out his hand and she found herself taking it.

"Well, Miss Jo Fraser, I think I must declare you the winner."

"What . . . what do you mean?"

"What do I mean? That will have to wait, until I've washed some of the filth of the bush from myself. Take Holly back to her cage, then go and get your sister. I'll meet you in the sitting room in 15 minutes."

"But what. . . ."

"*But nothing.* 15 minutes."

She didn't have the slightest idea of his intentions, but she meekly obeyed him, first taking Holly back, having a quick wash herself and then rousing Sally.

"We've been called to a council meeting," she said solemnly. "but whether it's for war or peace we won't know for ten minutes."

"You're talking in riddles," Sally protested.

"Just like Ross. He's made some final decision about us and the future of Nyala; but what it is I can only guess."

The dark tropical night had fallen with its imperceptible swiftness by the time he joined them with Tau at his side. First he called for Saku, who immediately appeared with drinks, then he relit his pipe.

Jo was watching him carefully. He had showered away the dirt, but some of the tiredness remained. He must, she decided, drive himself very hard indeed. There was not an

ounce of spare flesh on his bones; he was a man not used
to asking, or giving, quarter.

He looked only toward Sally. "I wish you'd heard the
short lecture your sister gave me. She made me feel—and
sound—the very worst sort of heel. I've thought hard
about what she said, about what you both have said since
you came, and I've decided she's right in one respect—that I haven't given you a fair chance. I haven't
changed my views on what should eventually happen to
Nyala, but I'm willing to try it your way for a couple of
months. I think I can make you see I'm right, but in any
case I can't stand by and watch Nyala run itself into the
ground, so the better success we make now, the better
things will be in the future. But I must say," he warned,
"that unless you two have a few spare thousand tucked
away your chances are very small indeed."

Sally was still cautious. "You do really mean what you
say, Ross? We will all be fighting on the same front?"

He nodded and suddenly he seemed less tired. "I mean
it. I've probably become what you think I am—an un-
civilized brute, like the croc out there." He reached for
his glass and raised it. "From now on it's nothing but
Nyala."

"Nyala," they both echoed, and Jo felt a sudden
soaring sense of happiness. Perhaps Holly had been a
symbol after all. But that would remain her private
thought.

"There is just one thing," he said, "one condition to all
this."

Jo looked at him sharply. He couldn't go back now, not
after all that.

"I gather you both have made plans. Well, I'm willing
to listen to them. I'm aware this portion of Nyala has
many drawbacks. But as far as the actual game and the
reserve is concerned, I expect to be obeyed instantly.
There are no second chances out there. You must abide

by my decisions, which won't, I assure you, be taken
lightly. And I warn you now, I can be tough and bad-tem-
pered, impossible to live with, but as long as you realize
that everything I do is for Nyala, then we should be able
to get along."

He smiled the quick, sudden smile that Jo had glimpsed
outside. "I think that must be the longest speech I've ever
made in my life! It's about time I asked if you two have
anything to say."

"Nothing," said Sally quietly, "except 'thank you.' I
think we both realize it hasn't been easy for you. We'll
just do what we can to help. In the long run it's all for
Nyala, and at least we will have broadened our education."

"Right," he said briskly, "then let's get down to a few
practical details."

So all that evening, with just a break for a meal when
they still went on talking, they tried to work out a campaign plan. Again and again they returned to the same
old problems, lack of men and money.

Ross explained that he only had a staff of 16 game
guards to help him, apart from Kari. And when Sally said
that did not mean very much to her in terms of acres or
square miles, he told her that in the Kruger Park a ranger
was generally in charge of a section of about 80 square
miles—about 500,000 acres—and he had about 20 men to
help him.

"I'm not saying we need that many here," he added
quickly. "The Kruger Park is a highly organized place
which is as much a tourist attraction as anything in
Africa. I imagine they must have a million or more
visitors in the course of a year. But we are understaffed,
especially in experienced men. When your uncle was alive
one of us used to stay here while the other would go off on
trek for two or three weeks at a time. Like that we managed to keep Nyala pretty well covered. Apart from any-

thing else I'm worried about the poaching; the pressure is really on us and I can't always tell if the men at the outposts are completely reliable. I simple cannot get around and see them often enough."

"I suppose," said Sally, "you need another ranger up here."

"I also need another truck," he told her, "and even more important, I need to spend some money on pumping equipment at some of the waterholes. Water, or the lack of it, could be our downfall quicker than anything else."

Some of Jo's high spirits began to evaporate. "What you're saying is that if we're going to try to do any of the things that will put Nyala on the map, then we must have some money first."

He nodded. "That's about it. I suppose that's what I was trying to tell you yesterday when you put up the idea of safaris. It is a good idea, but we can't do it on a large enough scale."

"But we could take about six people," Sally argued, "if we sold it to them the right way. Expensive, exclusive, but with the only home comforts actually at the bungalow. 500 miles of game to themselves. I think I could manage my end of the operation if I could get hold of a freezer. People will take an awful lot of roughing it as long as they can rely on coming back to a shower and some good food."

He was suddenly thoughtful, his teeth clenched on his pipe. "One thing has just occurred to me. Neil Brand has a brother who runs a tourist agency in Jo'burg. I think he has a branch somewhere in the Republic. I have a feeling a fair amount of his business is sending people up to Chobe and the other national reserves. We could ask Neil on Sunday what he thinks the chances are of success here." He turned to Sally. "And I think we should order your freezer anyway. There's enough money in the kitty to cover that. Besides, whatever happens at the end of the three months, we'll be able to sell it. If you tell me what you want I'll put in an order on the radio telephone."

So it seemed a lot depended on Neil Brand. Jo remembered him as a friendly, easy-going man, although her mind's picture of him had become blurred over the year. Now was probably as good a time as any to ask Ross a question that had been mildly worrying her since their arrival.

"Ross. . . ."

"You've got a solution to all our problems." He raised his eyebrows.

"No, I'm afraid not." Was he patronizing her again? "It was your mentioning Neil Brand that put an idea into my head. You said you knew him quite well, and you heard about our existence about a year ago—after he returned from England, I assume. Have you any idea at all why I was never mentioned, not in the will so much, but even as a person? He must surely have told Uncle Harold there were three of us."

"I can't answer that. I only know that your uncle spoke of a nephew and niece in England. You'll have to ask Neil himself."

Jo turned to Sally. "You'll ask him, won't you, Sal? It will sound better from you. I suppose it's not important, but I'm terribly curious."

Sally suddenly stretched and yawned. "I don't think I can take any more discussion about anything," she said. "My brain's spinning as it is. And, Ross, what time did you say you wanted us up?"

"We ought to leave here at five-thirty. I'll get Saku to bring breakfast at five. That will give you half an hour to wake up."

Sally groaned, "I never was any good at getting up," but when Ross glanced at her she added quickly, "Don't worry, I shan't get ill or do anything stupid, it's just part of my temperament. Besides, soon I shall be too busy here to be taking trips out into the bush. That's going to be strictly Jo's line."

Ross was as good as his word. He was already waiting the following morning as the two sisters stumbled out, half-asleep.

But once away from the house the air woke them up. It was crystal clear, sweet and cool, and truly the best time of day. In the east they could see the first fiery glow of the sun as it rose above the distant horizon of the bush. There was even a silvery pattern of dew on the grass. Impossible to believe that in two hours' time that same sun could become an instrument of torture.

"This is Nyala, at its best," Ross told them, "this is the time to see the best of the game. This is the time to bring the safari out and show them the perfection of Nyala. Between now and about seven-thirty you'll see more game than throughout the rest of the day. I wish I had time to stop and show you every animal. But not today. Today. . . ." He stopped abruptly and spoke a few crisp words to Kari. Within seconds he had stopped the truck, then backed it into a screen of thorn trees just off the track.

"What. . . ." Jo began.

"Don't ask questions, just wait."

For a few moments Jo was puzzled. The ground seemed to be shaking under them, as though racked by a series of small explosions. And then, on the very place where the truck had halted seconds before, came the leader of a magnificent herd of elephant.

They marched in stately splendor toward the river; the huge-tusked bulls, smaller cows and a few calves being continually nudged into line by their parents. There must have been 20 or 30 of them, and Jo watched, spellbound, thinking it was worth coming all the way to Africa for this moment. As the last one passed them it raised its trunk and the trumpeting must have been heard back at the house. It was like a great shout of triumph.

Ross waited a few moments before driving off. "You were lucky," he commented. "We don't have too big a herd in Nyala. Sometimes I've spent a week on trek and never caught sight of one. They must be short of water. They drink about 15 gallons a day."

During the first part of that morning Ross pointed out a dozen different varieties of game: giraffe and zebra in plenty, springbok and the huge antelope called eland, several kudu bulls, buffalo and wildebeest and always the graceful springing herds of impala. They saw, briefly, their first wild lion and a pack of wild dogs. The latter, Ross told them briefly, was the only animal of the bush he really hated. Their cruelty was human cruelty, hunting in packs until their prey falters, exhausted, then ripping out pieces of living flesh.

Jo stored away all that day's knowledge, determined to learn as fast as she could and play an active part in the development of Nyala. Sally had her place clearly defined. It was up to Jo to make Ross see that while she might be inexperienced in the bush, she was not afraid.

It was a long day and toward the end they were all tired. Although Sally did not complain, Jo knew she could not take this too often. The combination of heat and rough travel seemed to affect her badly.

They saw a fair amount of Nyala, as far as the scrubby bush broke into desert. Here for mile after mile there was not a single tree, not a patch of shade in which to escape the soaring temperature.

It was the waterholes that worried Ross. One had dried up completely, another was down to muddy silt. It was a poor sign for the game.

They returned at dusk. The two girls were too tired to do more than wash and eat and tumble into bed. But Ross did offer a rare word of praise.

He had not known many people straight from England take to the bush as they had done. "I would like to let you down lightly," he said, "but there simply isn't the time."

The next day Jo stayed at home and helped Sally with the replanning of the house. Sally was making many sorties into the kitchen and eventually confessed to Jo that she was supervising the Sunday meal herself. Although supplies were limited she wanted to show Ross just what kind of a spread could be put on for visitors.

"And this one just happens to be Neil Brand," Jo said slyly.

Sally flushed. "If you make more hints like that I'll thump you! He just happens to be the visitor for tomorrow, and that's all. You're building something up that simply wasn't there. We met him in England for one day, that's all. Not much romance in that!"

"All right, I give in. I really was only teasing."

Ross was working in the early part of Sunday morning, but he was back at the house to receive their visitors. "I wonder," he said, as they watched the dust of the approaching truck, "who his visitor is. It will seem quite strange to see three fresh faces within a week."

A few minutes later the truck pulled up in the small circle outside the bungalow. Neil Brand stepped out and Jo's memory cleared instantly. He came toward her and Sally with a smile. But suddenly her eyes were not on him, but on the man in the passenger seat. She drew in her breath sharply. It couldn't be; it couldn't possibly!

"Hello there, Jo, welcome to Africa," called Bruce Farley.

CHAPTER FIVE

He was even taller and bigger than she remembered. And with his skin bronzed by the sun and hair bleached to the color of flax he was even more exciting than the man who had stormed in and out of her life a year ago. Bruce Farley had been the only man ever to make her feel dainty and completely feminine.

Now, as he strode toward her, his delight obviously matching her own, she felt ridiculously tongue-tied. He gripped both her shoulders and kissed her soundly on both cheeks.

"God, Jo, it's a miracle! I never expected to see you in the middle of nowhere like this." Then his hand was outstretched behind her, although she noticed with secret pleasure that his eyes flicked back to hers. "And Sally. Don't say the Frasers are here in force?"

Sally shook her head. "Not Alan, just us."

There were more greetings from Neil and then the two girls were shaking hands with the small, rather solemn boy who stood beside him, an almost exact replica of his father. He was trying to be polite and patient, but his bright blue eyes were darting all round.

It was Ross who came to his rescue, ruffling his hair and saying cheerfully, "Well, young Sandy, I know who you are waiting for. She's around somewhere. *Goldie*!" he roared.

With a great shout of delight Sandy flung himself at the lion who had appeared round the side of the house, burying his head in her neck as she nudged his back with her head. The only thing his father said, quite casually, was, "Remember what I told you about not running, Sandy. She's too heavy for you if she jumps."

Sally watched open-mouthed, then turned to Neil.

"But there isn't an ounce of fear in him. Aren't you at all afraid?"

"No, only that Goldie doesn't know her own strength. They've been friends ever since Goldie came as a cub. Sandy's pretty good with animals. He probably wouldn't be afraid if he stood in front of a rogue elephant. But Ross has taught him a hell of a lot of sense. I don't think he would do anything foolhardy."

As Ross led the way inside Jo and Bruce were separated. But she was intensely aware of him, impatient for the moment when they could be alone together. Their eyes met and held, as if they were already touching each other.

"Beer, Farley?" That was Ross, sounding more cool and clipped than usual. For some reason she glanced across at him and surprised a look she did not recognize. Was it anger, distaste—Did he really think she was straight out of the classroom?

"Thanks," Bruce replied lazily. "While you're pouring I'll get Jo to show me the garden." He turned his very special smile on her.

"Of course." She was at his side immediately, and she did not attempt to move away when she felt his arm across her shoulders. Rather, she moved toward him. Let Mr. Ross Disapproving Andrews put that in his pipe and smoke it!

She led the way down to the river, but strangely, once they were alone she felt all her old uncertainty return. Was it a coincidence he was here, or. . . .

"How did you know I . . . we were here?" she asked breathlessly.

He held her away from him, teasing, "Bush telegraph."

She sat down on the old tree stump in the shade of the fig trees. That way her legs felt steadier. Perhaps she was wrong after all. Perhaps her delight at seeing him was stronger than his after all. He hadn't even tried to kiss her.

"No, tell me, please. Nyala is a long way from anywhere, even by African standards."

"Perhaps, but not by diamond prospecting standards."

"You mean . . . you heard there were diamonds in this area." Her heart seemed to be squeezed inside her body. So it was diamonds that brought him here. She could hardly bear it.

"In a way." His eyes were bright as he went on, "It started when I was introduced to Neil in a pub just before I finally left Derbyshire—the day before, in fact. Someone thought we would have something in common, both working in Africa. He gave me his card and told me to give him a call if ever I came to this area. That's it really, except I got a tip about an old river bed that could possibly hold diamonds, so I wrote to him. He wrote back and invited me down for a few days, adding how extraordinary that a couple of people from the very town we met in were coming to Nyala. I merely told him to keep it a surprise from you."

Suddenly his voice thickened and the brightness in his eyes was piercingly strong. He held out his arms to her. "Come here, Jo, I can't stand it much longer." And then she was home at last with his mouth hard on hers, her body crushed to his. So it was going to be all right after all!"

When finally, trembling, they drew apart he said, "It's been a long year, Jo. I behaved like a heel, didn't I?"

"There wasn't really anything between us," she lied. "I just wondered what had happened to you."

"Oh well, I told you then I was a rotten letter writer. And I always intended to come up to Derbyshire to say goodbye. But I got a telegram when I was in London, so that was that."

There are telephones, she thought, but wisely kept silent.

"In any case," he went on, "I'm a restless character, I always told you that, too."

"With a girl in every port?" The lightness did not quite come off.

"You don't find many girls in the ports I visit. No, there's only been one girl I really missed, one I wanted to see again at all costs. She came from a small town in Derbyshire. Believe me or not, Jo, it's the truth."

She did not question it, she did not want to question it. It was enough that he was here. Reluctantly, they made their way back to the house.

Just below the steps of the veranda Bruce stopped. "How am I going to see you, Jo? 60 miles in this country is a hell of a way to pop in on your girl. Besides, I can't impose on Neil for too long."

"But you could come over here for a stay, couldn't you?" Jo said slowly.

His face changed. "That's a terrific idea. This is one of the areas I want to cover anyway. And I'm more or less self-sufficient—I've got a Land Rover and a tent. I'm used to living rough. Oh lord, Jo, I can think of nothing better."

"Nor I," she said softly. "But I will have to ask Ross."

"Why? I thought this was yours and Sally's place. He's only the manager, isn't he? He looked a surly devil."

"Oh, he's all right when you get to know him. Just not very sociable. And touchy. At least I'll mention it—not ask—and to Sally, of course." She touched his arm. "Leave it to me, Bruce. There's a little matter of a truck that will decide things."

"O.K., we'll do it your way." He bent swiftly and kissed her again. "It's going to seem a long lunch. After nothing but sweating engineers, you're the most marvelous sight in the world."

Sally glanced at her sister, flushed, eyes glittering, not even trying to conceal her triumphant happiness.

Ross was handing Bruce his tall glass of beer and saying in his least welcoming tone of voice, "Neil was telling me you're prospecting in these parts. Are there any mineral deposits? Surely not."

"I'm only interested in diamonds." Bruce was drinking, sizing the other man up, already aware of that cool, cool current.

"Diamonds around here? Impossible!"

"With diamonds you can never tell," Bruce returned calmly. "A fool's errand or not, it's usually worth investigating. I've been prospecting beyond the salt-pan where they've got a fairly big operation mounted. Now the largest find of industrial diamonds has been made just to the north, in Orapa. So for me it's time to move on. I happened to be with an old Bushman who talked about the minerals he had seen in the north. Oh, no, he hadn't seen diamonds, that would be too much to hope for, but he had studied the anthills and swore there were garnets and ilmenites."

Jo frowned, puzzled. "Anthills? What on earth have they got to do with diamonds?"

"A surprising amount. The ants bore quite deeply into the ground and, if in the deposits they bring up, there are those two minerals, garnets and ilmenites, it's just a chance there could be a diamond pipe. Whether the Bushman knew what he was talking about I don't know, but it's my job to find out."

The lunch Sally had organized was almost as good as any she could produce in England. There was some kind of chilled fish to start with in a spicy sauce, then chicken done as only Sally knew how, baked with lemon juice and with a variety of unknown vegetables. The dessert was a fruit compôte in liqueur.

Quite obviously Ross simply could not believe he was

in his own home. When the second course came up he looked toward Sally. "I know you said you were going to look after the domestic arrangements, but I didn't realize you meant a feast like this. I think I'm worrying," he added wryly, "rather unnecessarily about probable visitors."

Neil Brand looked toward him with raised eyebrows. "Do I guess you're going to open up Nyala after all?"

"I've been bullied into it—at least to thinking about it. But before we go a step further we'll get some advice from you, Neil."

"Me? I'm afraid I can't be much help. I'm just a good old-fashioned farmer who knows how to breed cattle, not entertain tourists."

"But Ross says you have a brother," Jo put in eagerly, "who arranges small safaris. Sally and I have worked out that we could cope with a party of six to eight. . . ."

"Six," Ross put in firmly.

"Well, six, then. But do you think it's too . . . too primitive here for tourists?"

"Not if they get fed like this." Neil Brand's smile was warm with admiration for Sally. He was a weathered, stocky man with bushy brown hair and a quiet, easy personality. He was the sort of man who would not speak often, but when he did people would listen.

He looked thoughtful for a moment. "My brother is always telling me that for every place there is the right tourist. There are many people who think the Kruger has been spoilt now by too much commercialization. They'd prefer to make the trek to Chobe—and that's some trek. But a private reserve might be quite a temptation. I don't think there would be any difficulty at all over parties of that size. As long as you didn't oversell the facilities of Nyala. I'll have a word with my brother anyway. In fact I'll be seeing him next week. I'm off on a short business trip to the Transvaal. Sandy's coming along too."

Sandy looked at his father beseechingly. "Oh Dad, you said you'd think about letting me stay. I could do some of your job, I know I could."

"I know you could, son, but a week is too long to be left to your own devices in this part of the world."

Sandy looked mutinous, but said nothing. His father added, "He loathes trips to town, and I really don't blame him, but our farm's nearly as isolated as this place."

"If . . . if it would help," Sally said tentatively, looking first at Ross, then at Jo, "he could come here and I could keep an eye on him. I shall be around the house most of the time. . . ."

"Oh Dad, please say yes!" The boy's eyes were alight with excitement. "I'd be so good and no trouble to anyone," he added virtuously, holding his breath tightly, waiting for the verdict.

Neil hesitated a moment, but obviously could not resist the utter longing in his son's face. "Well, all right, Sandy, as far as I'm concerned you can stay, as long as it's all right with Ross too." And when Ross nodded faintly, "But you've got to do exactly what Ross tells you when you're outside and what Sally and Jo tell you when you're inside."

With a great whoop Sandy flung himself on Goldie's prostrate form in the corner. "Just think," he cried ecstatically, "a whole week with Goldie! I've never been here for more than a weekend. Do you think we could. . . ."

"Sandy," said Neil sharply, "enough of you for the moment, there are plans to make. To start with I'm not sure how we're going to get you back here. I'm catching the evening plane tomorrow."

"I could bring him," Bruce put in quietly, "the following day, if you like—Tuesday. I should probably be pulling out then anyway." He grinned. "I don't want to outstay my hospitality, Neil." Then he was looking across at Jo, telling her silently that here was her chance to invite him to stay too. But she did not respond. She must choose her moment for that . . . get Sally on her side before she casually dropped the idea to Ross. Peace had been won at Nyala; there was no reason to throw it away unnecessarily.

After a leisurely lunch the party split up, Sally to take Sandy to meet Holly and Ross and Neil to the stables to look over the horses. Jo and Bruce made a pretense of following them, but Bruce pulled her away toward the shade of the river.

"You are going to fix it, aren't you?" he insisted.

"Of course, but after you've gone. There's so much to be done here, so I've got to convince Sally I'm not going to fritter away my time with you. And Ross . . . he's difficult enough anyway; I don't want him to think I'm filling the house with my friends. Everyone who comes here must be seen to have a job. He doesn't like visitors."

"I could see that at a glance. Don't forget what I told you before lunch, Jo, he is just the manager."

"And we can't manage Nyala without him. We're dependent on him and he knows it. Honestly, Bruce, I want you to come and stay here more than anything else, but so much rests on us making a success of Nyala that I daren't risk offending Ross. He threatened to walk out three days ago."

"Well, you don't exactly endear me to him, I must say. Still," he drew her close to him, "I suppose you know what you're doing. I reckon from what Neil said that your uncle was a bit of a character too. Did this legacy come as a real surprise?"

"I didn't even know we had an uncle in Africa, much less that he owned a game reserve. But whether it will ever be ours is another matter. It looks almost impossible."

"Who says that? Andrews?"

"And the lawyer. And our own common sense," she

said ruefully, "but as long as Ross is willing to help us have a go, then I hope we have a slender chance."

"And does he want you to keep Nyala?"

She shook her head slowly. "Not really. He thinks the government would make a much better job of looking after the place. I guess he's right, but at least we've managed to convince him that it simply wouldn't be fair if we didn't try to face the challenge."

They met the others behind the house where Sandy was getting to know Holly. Holly was able to stand without too much wobble and she was now out of her cage, a little nervous, but more curious than anything else about the people around her. She seemed to be examining each one of them in turn. Then as though, suddenly, she had decided exactly where she was going she turned in Jo's direction, tried to run and crashed in a heap at Jo's feet.

Since only her dignity was hurt they all laughed, and as Jo eased her gently to her feet Ross reminded her, "I told you she would regard you as being completely responsible. She's yours, Jo, whether you want her or not."

"I'll help you next week," Sandy offered. "I'd like to look after her too. Goldie and I could take her for walks."

The idea of a lion, a fawn and a small boy taking walks together seemed faintly incongruous to Jo, but she nodded with due seriousness. "Of course I'd be glad of your help, Sandy."

At the river she and Sally were asked to point out where they had seen the crocodile. Neil bent to examine the bank for spoor. "There's one here all right, probably its mate as well. I just hope there aren't any young." He rose and nodded towards Ross. "When I come to collect Sandy in a week or so I'll bring my gear and we'll make a night of it. Want to come?" He smiled at Sally, who shivered slightly.

"What? Hunting crocodiles? I'd be scared out of my wits!"

"It was a big one, then?"

"Enormous!" Sally and Jo spoke in a chorus and did not understand when both men laughed.

Then Neil explained. "They all look enormous the first time, but a real crocodile-hunter will discard anything under ten feet. Up in the Okavango swamps you'll find the killers up to about 18 feet—nasty brutes to attack you on a dark night."

"And you actually like hunting crocodiles?" Sally sounded appalled.

He nodded. "To me it's the greatest sport, just like a good tiger hunt is to another. Crocs are wily creatures, and you can only get them at night. You wait until those red eyes are a few feet away and then aim for the brain—the smallest of targets. You can't just shoot anywhere, because apart from probably not killing the beasts, you'll also ruin the skin. It's only the under-belly skin that is used to make purses and shoes."

Jo listened, interested by what he was saying, then looked down into the calm, clear waters of the river. How impossible it should be harboring one or more crocodiles.

"And to think," she said aloud, "I was going to ask a couple of days ago whether one could swim in the river!"

"You can," said Ross calmly.

"Oh, no! Never!"

"But yes. 300 yards downstream there's a deepish pool, a natural circle formed by the rocks. When Sandy's here next week we'll show you that the crocodiles couldn't squeeze past the entrance. The most that will nudge your legs will be a couple of bream."

But still she shook her head firmly, not to be convinced even by Sandy, who told her seriously: "It's quite all right, Jo, really it is. I've swum there a lot and I've never seen a crocodile. In fact I haven't very often seen one at all, have I, Dad?" And when his father agreed he added, "But he has promised to take me hunting in Okavango when I'm 12."

There was no more time for Bruce and Jo to be alone, but there was Tuesday to look forward to, and perhaps more than that; for she was determined that he should stay at Nyala as long as he wanted to. Suddenly the year he had been away seemed no time at all. There had been no awkwardness, no gap to bridge. And she felt exactly the same about him as she had done at home.

But there was still Sally to face and she hated quarreling with Sally.

After the visitors had left, well before dark, the two sisters walked up the steps together. "Well, Sal," said Jo lightly, "you certainly impressed us all with your cooking. What *was* that meat, anyway?"

Sally's eyes gleamed. "If I told you it was warthog you'd never trust me again, so I'm not going to tell you!"

"It wasn't really warthog, was it?" Jo grimaced.

"No," said Sally with a sweet smile, "but I believe it's excellent grilled."

"Oh," said Jo weakly, "I think I'll stick to lamb chops."

"Which is one thing you won't get around here." At the door to Jo's bedroom Sally blocked the way. "Well," she said quietly, "that was very well maneuvered."

"What was?" Jo said belligerently.

"Oh Jo, you know perfectly well. Bruce Farley's arrival."

Jo swung round on her passionately. "I swear I didn't know he was coming. How could I, Sal?"

"I don't know," Sally sighed, "but I do know you were determined to see him while you were in Africa."

"But I didn't even know where to start looking. Of course I wanted to see him, but I have enough dignity not to go chasing after someone who doesn't want me. Anyway, it was more or less a coincidence. You can ask Neil if you like." She proceeded to tell Sally how Bruce had arrived at Nyala today. At the end she added, with a trace of coldness in her voice, "You still don't believe me, do you?"

"Yes, I believe you, Jo. You have never lied."

"But you don't like Bruce any more than you liked him in England?"

"I don't dislike him. I just don't want you to fall in love with him. You'll end up by being hurt."

"How can you possibly know that?" Jo cried. "You're acting as if you were a disapproving mother or something. I suppose it's because Bruce doesn't fit into any nice neat category. He's a wanderer; he has no settled job. I know all that, and I accept it. Someone has to do the sort of job he's doing."

"Maybe," said Sally inexorably. "I just wish he hadn't come, that's all. I have a feeling in my bones."

"You'll be telling me next you'd rather I fell for the boorish Mr. Andrews!"

"You're hardly likely to do that, but at least I trust him. He does say exactly what he means."

"Thank you very much!" Jo's voice was beginning to quiver. She knew she was at that awful point, halfway between temper and tears. "Well, I'll tell you one thing, Sal, when Bruce returns with Sandy he's coming with all his gear. I've told him he can stay at Nyala."

"You've told him what?" Sally was aghast. "I thought we were here to make Nyala pay, not to entertain your boyfriends."

Jo flushed. "That's very unfair, Sal, and you know it. I want Nyala to be a success as much as you do, if not more. I th'nk Bruce can help. After all Ross keeps saying how short-handed he is. To start with, Bruce has got another Land Rover, and if he wants to prospect here, he's got to do something in return, hasn't he?"

For a moment Sally was silent. "Well, we'll have to talk it over with Ross."

"Ross Andrews is nothing more than the manager here," Jo said cruelly. "Nyala belongs to us—or at least it might do."

Sally looked at her with something like sorrow in her eyes. "I'm sorry to have to say it, Jo, but Nyala was left to Alan and myself. We would be sharing it with you."

"Oh God, Sal, I am a fool. I'm sorry, really I am. I just didn't think, that's all. Nyala isn't mine, is it? It never will be."

"Legally, no, but in every other way, yes." Sally put her arm around her sister's shoulders. "Look, Jo, all this started over Bruce Farley. If you want him to come, then come he must. I can't bear to see you unhappy. After all, I can't spend my life looking over your boyfriends and approving them. Let's wipe out this whole conversation, and I promise to try to put all my reservations about Bruce away and pretend I'm meeting him for the first time next week. But. . . ."

"Yes?" said Jo warily.

"Well, there is one thing—Ross. You're probably saying to yourself that once Bruce is here we can manage without him, but that isn't true. We need him if we're to have a hope in making something of Nyala in such a short time. He's more than just a manager. He's warden here. He runs Nyala. So we must do him the courtesy of asking him if he minds Bruce coming."

"And if he does?" Jo challenged.

"He won't if you ask him the right way. Oh Jo, please, be just a little charitable."

Ross shrugged when Jo said that Bruce would like to come to Nyala for a short stay. "Of course I don't mind. This is your home for the time being, as well as mine. But I don't think he really imagines he'll find diamonds here, does he?"

"He seems to think there's a possibility. Ross, he could

be very useful to us. He knows the country well; he has a truck. When I told him how important Nyala was to us he said he would do anything he could to help."

"Then that's all that matters," Ross said dryly.

In the short time they had been at Nyala Jo tried to work out what made Ross Andrews so unapproachable. One minute he was gentling an animal back to health, the next he was as prickly as a porcupine. Sally seemed able to relax with him. She could not. And yet already she grudgingly admitted he was good at his job, and she had always respected people of ability. If only he didn't regard her with faint contempt all the time. It didn't apply to Sally. Already he treated her as an equal.

On the Tuesday Bruce and Sandy were expected, she watched Ross mount his horse, Brandy, call for Tau and ride off into the bush without looking back. The three of them were like a tight-knit family—a working family. For just a moment she was full of envy at such self-sufficiency. She wished she had asked Ross if she could ride into the bush one day. The day she did that would be the day she made a great stride in earning Ross Andrews's respect. It was strange that while she did not care for him as a person it seemed important that he did not think her a fool. Sally had shown that she could take care of her end of the plans for Nyala. Now she, Jo, had to do the same.

During the morning, she and Sally started to plan in detail for a minimum of six guests. Saku and the other help turned out the three thatched rondavels and scrubbed and hosed the interiors, until they steamed in the sun. Already Sally had investigated the storerooms of the house, found spare mattresses and decided they could furnish without too much difficulty. The main thing missing was color.

"We need," she announced, "some bright cotton for curtains and bedspreads. But where can we possibly find them? I've been all over the house, but it's too spartan to be of much use." Then Sally, ever resourceful, involved Saku in the problem, made him understand what she wanted and returned in triumph.

"He says," she told Jo, "that there's a village about 20 miles from here and they hold a market once a week. We should be able to buy material there that would do. That's when," she added, "we should be able to make use of Bruce Farley. He can drive one of us over at the end of the week."

Sally also put in motion the beginning of a vegetable garden. A patch was chosen not too far from the river and the gardener asked to turn over the earth ready for planting. "When we go to that market," Sally continued, "we're going to pick up every kind of seed we can. There's no reason, as long as we have enough water, why we shouldn't grow most of the things we need. And whatever we can't buy here I should be able to send away for to Johannesburg."

Jo smiled at Sally's enthusiasm. She had no doubts at all that within a very short time, Nyala would have a flourishing vegetable garden. Sally always had the knack of making anything grow.

Suddenly Jo felt rather useless. She could take orders with the best and up to a point she was quite happy helping Sally, but her real job was to learn about the bush: how the game were scattered, what to look for, so that in the end she could share some of the trekking with Ross and Kari. Even more important, she then could take a truckload of visitors on a day's safari.

After lunch, when she had rested for an hour, she wandered to the back of the house. She took a willing Holly for a walk, tickled Goldie's stomach as she passed her dozing under the trees and then found herself at the stable. The gray mare standing there looked gentle enough for anyone to ride. She hesitated only a moment, then called for Saku, indicating that she wanted the mare saddled.

Saku shook his head anxiously. "No, lady, no. *Morena* is not here."

"Is there something wrong with the horse?" Jo asked. "I mean is she dangerous to ride?"

"Oh, no, but *Morena* would not like it."

"To hell with *Morena*," Jo said under her breath. "Please see that she is saddled, Saku," she said calmly. "I am not going far. *Morena* would not mind."

He raised his hands helplessly, but went to find the gardener, who produced a saddle and bridle while she changed into old jeans and a wide-brimmed hat.

The mare was certainly docile and Jo felt at home almost as soon as she was in the saddle. She had no worry about her riding ability, for as a child she had spent many weekends trekking. Her only doubt was being able to cope with the heat and the unknown terrain.

She did the circumference of the garden twice, walking to get the feel of the mare, and as she looked around she saw to her amazement that wherever she went, Saku followed. Eventually she stopped.

"Why are you following me, Saku?" she demanded.

"*Morena* would wish it, lady."

"Well, you can stop it immediately. I'm perfectly all right."

He bowed his head and stood still, but when she started off again he was still plodding along behind.

Annoyed now, she dug in her heels and the mare started to trot. That would show him. She finally turned aroud in triumph and saw to her utter amazement that he was bent low over a bicycle, the dust flying behind him.

Jo pulled the mare around sharply. Two could play at that game! Seconds later she too was crouched in the saddle and the mare was galloping as though the devil himself were behind her. Jo almost laughed aloud. This was marvelous! She gloried in the sense of freedom as the mare galloped on, certain of its destination.

She finally slowed down when both of them were running with sweat, patting the neck and talking easily. What a pity Ross could not see her now. Feeling enormously pleased with herself, she shaded her eyes against the glare of the sun and looked back the way she had come. There was not one track but two. She turned again and saw a third stretching into the opposite direction. Which one had she come along? The first faint twinges of alarm crept up her spine. There was no sign of the house, not even a landmark she could recognize.

Patting the mare's neck again, she said softly, "Home," and obediently the animal trotted off. But where? she wondered a few moments later. She could still be going in entirely the wrong direction.

The track she was on went in a steep curve anyway.

A sound in the bush made her jump and from almost under the horse's hooves an ugly squat animal raced across their path. She yelped in alarm, then strove for calm again. That was a warthog, but what if it had been a lion or a cheetah? Her mouth was suddenly dry as she remembered she was not just slightly lost, but in the middle of an area thick with game—some of it dangerous.

As if to emphasize that she was not alone, several buck fled along the track, followed a few seconds later by a small herd of impala. Jo was suddenly intensely aware of her vulnerability. She did not know whether her mount could outrun anything, or whether she would even care to put it to the test.

She swallowed, her throat dry from fear and the dust of the track. She could not stay here until dusk, so once again she started off, hoping she had guessed right at the sun's direction. Suddenly the bush was no longer friendly but alien, full of unseen enemies.

She must have been riding for 15 minutes before she was certain she was traveling in the wrong direction. By now, surely the house would have been in sight. But she could see nothing on the horizon except two lines of trees. One of those must be the river. She decided on the one to her left and cut away from the track toward it.

As she urged the mare into a trot she heard the thunder of hooves behind her. This time she did not dare look, but dug in her heels. Now they would see how fast she could go.

The voice slowed her finally and when she ventured a swift turn she saw the other horse behind her.

Ross's voice was savage in its command. "Stay where you are, Jo. Don't move another step!" And she felt a tight ball of fear gathering in her stomach.

Seconds later his hand was on her bridle. "Move one inch further and it will be the end of both of us."

CHAPTER SIX

She did not know how long they both waited there, immobile. The brassy sun beat down so fiercely that even the hat she wore seemed an intolerable burden. She could feel the sweat gathering between her shoulder blades, her hands slippery on the reins. She did not dare to turn and look at him, certain that even the slightest movement would bring some fearful disaster.

The wait was interminable, then finally came the merest whisper in her ear. "All right, we're turning, but stay close to me and walk. Don't trot, or canter, or anything, unless I give the order. Is that understood?"

Mutely she nodded.

A few minutes later they came to a small clump of wild fig trees, frightening away two giraffe. There he reined Brandy in gently and she followed suit. By then some of her courage had returned, so had her annoyance at his high-handed treatment of her.

"All right," she rounded on him in a low, fierce voice, "now perhaps you would explain yourself. First your servant chases me on a bicycle, then you go on at me as if I were some kind of halfwit. I can't think what possible kind of harm I was doing a stone's throw from the house."

"All right, Miss Know-all, just point and tell me in which direction the house is."

"Why should I?"

"Because you tell me you're only a stone's throw from it, and because you seem anxious to persuade me you're not a . . . halfwit."

She shut her eyes, prayed, and pointed vaguely over to the left.

"So I was right; you were lost. You hadn't the faintest

idea where you were. Had you gone on in the direction you were going, if you hadn't killed yourself in a particularly nasty way, you would have gone straight out into the desert."

She was silent. Perhaps he was right but he had a particularly unfortunate way of stating his point.

"I know you think I'm treating you like a child," he went on patiently, "but in one short trip you've made just about every mistake in the book. And by the way don't throw the blame on Saku, he had strict instructions from me to take care of you and Sally as if you were his own children. To him that was a sacred trust. Can you imagine what he's feeling like now, knowing that he has broken that trust? He'll be holding himself completely responsible and whatever I say to him in consolation will mean nothing, because his standard is higher than yours or mine."

"All right," she said flatly, "you've succeeded in making me feel like a worm. Could we go back now, even though you haven't told me what the nasty death was that you've apparently saved me from."

He gave a short, dry laugh. "You still don't believe me, do you? You think, because of the winning ways of Goldie and little Holly, that this really is a sort of pets' corner. Out there, only a few yards from where you were, is a wounded buffalo. With the possible exception of a rhino it can be one of the most dangerous and unpredictable beasts in the bush. It has a hatred of the hunter, and while a herd will leave him alone, a single wounded buffalo will turn that hunter into the hunted. It will wait in ambush for him and if necessary double back on its tracks so that he hasn't the faintest idea where it will spring from. Brandy loathes buffalo, but is so well trained that he'll obey me instantly. Your mare, Betsy, would undoubtedly panic unless she felt you were perfectly in command. Now do you understand what I'm trying to say?"

She nodded slowly. "Where . . . where is the buffalo now?"

"Probably where it was ten minutes ago. I've seen no movement from that direction."

"Will you leave it there?"

"Of course not. That's one of the first rules of the bush—never leave a wounded animal. I've been stalking it for the past hour. It was only by chance I saw you. I imagine the poachers have had a go at it. That's the trouble with them, their shooting is simply not accurate enough. Here, you must be able to kill with a single bullet."

He pulled his gun from its pocket in the saddle and checked the barrel. Then he turned to her and his expression softened slightly.

"If I want to get it before dusk, then I haven't time to take you back and come out here again. I want you to wait here, Jo, and please, don't move. You'll be perfectly safe, but if the worst comes to the worst," he added dryly, "you can always hop up the tree. If you hear a single shot you'll know that I've found it. I'll then fire three more in rapid succession and you can come and join me. If you don't hear them, then wait for me."

"I'll wait," she said quietly, "but . . . but isn't it very dangerous for you to go out after it?"

"Only if I'm careless. This is what I'm paid for at Nyala—the protection of the game." Then he was trotting away, directly into the sun.

She watched him go, straining her eyes after him as he slowed to a cautious walk. Only now did she feel ashamed of such foolhardy behavior. She had acted without thought for herself or others—something she did far too often, according to Sally.

In spite of the shade from the trees it was still breathlessly hot. How long, she wondered, would she have to wait here, tensing for that shot?

In the still air it seemed that nothing moved, except a small brightly colored bird that darted in and out of the leaves above her head. She tried to concentrate on Bruce, who would surely have arrived by now with Sandy. Certainly, both he and Sally would have learned of her flight from Saku, so there would be no hope of hiding her foolishness.

It was going to be good to have Bruce here. Her heart warmed at the thought of him. At least he treated her reasonably. Bruce knew both the bush and the desert. From him perhaps she could learn not to make the same mistakes twice. Ross would make an uncompromising teacher. Even now, she could feel the lash of his sarcasm.

As Ross returned to her thoughts she began to wonder why there had been no shot. The hunted turned into the hunter, he had said. Was there any reason why, however careful he was, he should consider himself invincible? She suddenly pictured him lying there kicked and gored . . . and she would not even know.

That earlier, insidious fear crept back into her bones. She did not want to move, nor disobey his instructions, but how long would he expect her to stay there? Darkness could not be too far away and it would come without warning. The thought of being out here at night when all the beasts of prey came out to hunt and prowl was a fearsome thought.

Suddenly a shot echoed on the still, hot air. Drymouthed, she waited for the next three. When they did not come immediately, the gruesome picture returned. So he had missed that one, vital shot. He must have done. . . .

When the signal finally came she could have wept with relief. She urged Betsy into a canter over the thick sandy scrub.

Ross emerged unmounted from the cover of some bushes, waving at her with his rifle. When she reached him he said, "You'd better come and have a look. You won't often see a dead buffalo."

She looked down at the huge rock-like beast, its horns like something from an ancient picture book. Seeing it lying there so peacefully it was hard to imagine death waiting at the end of those vicious horns.

"It seems sad," she said soberly.

"It always is when an animal has to die this way," he answered. "The buffalo is intelligent and cunning. It can be schemingly vindictive, but it's also a proud beast."

He bent suddenly and with a swift movement hacked off the tail which he wrapped up as casually as if it were a belt and stuffed it into his saddle bag.

"A trophy?" she could not resist asking.

"No," he replied calmly, "tomorrow's lunch, probably. Buffalo makes almost as good a stew as oxtail, or even better, probably, if your sister supervises it."

She wrinkled up her nose distastefully. It was one thing not to know what you were eating, quite another to see it freshly killed. She had never before seriously considered how the oxtail she so enjoyed in England started out.

She wheeled her horse around. "I'm sure you're right. Are we going back now?"

He nodded. "Yes. You must be very tired and very hot, I imagine."

"A little," she admitted, "but I think I'm going to get along with the climate far better than I expected. And, Ross . . ." she paused.

"Yes?"

"I want to apologize to Saku. Will he really blame himself as you said?"

"I'm afraid so. He's rather an emotional fellow, unlike Kari, who would regard it as a mark of weakness to show what he was feeling. But he'll understand an apology and accept it. The only thing is . . . and I warn you . . . he'll be even more vigilant in future."

"Oh well, I suppose I deserve it." It was the nearest she could come to apologizing to him.

"And Jo. . . ."

"In the middle of all my criticism there's one compliment I can pay you."

She turned sharply toward him, expecting sarcasm, but finding only an oddly serious expression on his lean face. "You ride like a professional. Did you learn when you were a child?"

"Yes. My father was quite a well-known amateur rider. He entered most of the local races. He taught us all almost as soon as we could walk. Sally was never quite so keen as Alan and myself. Dad used to take us trekking over the Peaks for a day when we were young, then for a weekend when he thought we could manage it. Those were good times," she smiled sadly, remembering her father, "but I haven't ridden very much during the past few years."

"I said I would take you out in the Land Rover for a longish day. I'll do the same on horseback if you think you can take it. It's the finest way to learn bushlore there is. You'll need to know how to find your way by the sun, how to recognize landmarks. But I warn you now, this is only if you really want to reach the heart of Nyala. It will be no picnic and I'm a hard taskmaster. I won't be thinking of you as a girl visiting the reserve, but one of my own trainee rangers."

"I'd like to do that," she said truthfully. "Whatever you may think, I want to learn about Nyala more than anything else. I told you before that the domestic arrangements are definitely Sally's province. This is where I want . . . oh, look Ross, isn't that a truck ahead kicking up all that dust?"

"I imagine," he said dryly, "your friend Bruce Farley is sending out a search party for you."

She flashed an angry look at him. "You sound just like Sally—sarcastic whenever Bruce is mentioned. Has she been trying to influence you?"

"I make my own judgments about people, Jo, and," he

pointed out, "I have only met your Mr. Farley over one lunch. Hardly time to form an opinion."

"Sally formed her opinion in as short a time as that," she responded with some bitterness.

The truck reached them and pulled up with a squeal of brakes. Bruce leaned out anxiously. "Are you all right Jo? Saku is wringing his hands and wailing back there . . . something about a runaway horse. And now Sally is in a real state too."

"I'm fine." Jo tried to keep her voice light. "And I'm sorry to have thrown everyone into a stew. Did you have a good trip, Bruce, and is Sandy with you?"

"Yes, he wanted to come, but Sally said 'no' very firmly." He grinned. "I really believe your sister was imagining the worst. I must say you look a bit tired, Jo, do you want a lift back?"

"No." But Ross already had his hand on her bridle.

"I think it would be a good idea for you to go with Farley. We're farther away than you think."

"No, really, I can't," she protested, but torn between not wanting to give in and wanting to be with Bruce. "What about Betsy?"

"Betsy would follow Brandy into the middle of the Kalahari—and beyond."

Half reluctantly Jo dismounted and climbed into the passenger seat. Bruce reached across her and closed the door. But he did not withdraw his hand. He kissed her gently. "You really did give us all quite a fright, you know."

Unconsciously this time she pulled away. The shadow of Ross Andrews moving off with the two horses had only just left the window. There was no need to go on proving herself to him.

He switched on the engine and started to turn the car. "What's the matter?"

"Nothing . . . I was just thinking I gave myself quite a

fright too. I never realized that this was a country without landmarks."

"Oh, there are landmarks all right, but you have to learn to distinguish them. Look," he pointed, "that tree on the skyline over there. You would be able to pick that out from a range of at least two miles. It has a curious formation in its top two branches. Then here, on your left," he slowed down, "that's not a track, but a trail used pretty often by elephants. Only an elephant pushes over bushes in just that way. Then there are the smaller things like an oddly shaped anthill, an area which a particular animal frequents, even different formations of the land. That's what I look for."

She sighed. "You make it sound so easy."

"No. No, it's not easy; it's just what you have to learn if you're to survive in the bush. This is a harsh and unforgiving country. But it can also be rewarding, so you have to respect it."

Jo found herself relaxing in the truck. She watched the easy, sure way his big hands rested on the steering wheel, the way the sun picked up the golden hairs of his arms.

"You are really going to stay, aren't you?" she said suddenly.

"Oh yes," he turned toward her and his eyes were smiling behind dark glasses, "if you've all agreed to have me. Even Andrews?"

"Oh, Ross is all right, I told you that before. Anyway, he's been crying out for extra help around Nyala. He'll soon find you're not exactly going to be a parasite."

"Oh, I'll work my passage all right," he said lazily. "Only one thing really worries me."

"What's that?" she said alarmed.

"The fact of not seeing you on your own often enough. I'm not sure that I'll fit in with all this communal living. I can't even take you out to dinner."

"No, you'll have to take me out for a day in the bush

instead," she teased him. "Somehow I've got to learn the do's and don'ts of bushlore if we're really going to have safari parties down here."

"I don't really know yet what your position is over Nyala, how important it is to make it pay, and what chance you've got."

"According to Ross, none at all. But Sally and I are determined to go down fighting."

"Then after the meal tonight, we'll go down to my camp and you can tell me the whole story from start to finish. I have only the bare outlines from Neil." As they drove toward the house, he squeezed her hand. "If you want to fight, Jo, then I'm going to help you."

Sandy was waiting for them dancing about on the doorstep with impatience. "Hello," he said politely to Jo, holding out his hand, then—much more eagerly—"Where's Ross, isn't he coming?"

"Yes, in about 15 minutes, I should think," she told him. "He's got both Brandy and Betsy with him."

The boy looked at Bruce with faint accusation. "You could have taken me, you know, Mr. Farley, then I could have ridden Betsy back. She knows me quite well."

"I'm sorry, Sandy," Bruce apologized, "but we didn't even know Ross was out there with Jo. I daresay he'll let you ride later in the week."

Sally came out then, and stood with her hands on her hips watching her younger sister. "Where on earth . . . ?"

With a sigh, Jo interrupted, "If you're going to start telling me off, you can save your breath. Ross did that quite adequately. In fact he told me off soundly enough for two of you. I took the horse out without permission, and yes, I did try to evade Saku, and yes, I'm perfectly all right, and I'm going to apologize to him."

Sally's face softened. "Oh, Jo, you are a fool. I was just worried, that's all. It's years since you've been riding."

"Well, I haven't lost the knack," Jo said defiantly,

"and now if you'll all excuse me I'm going in for a shower.'

From the bathroom she heard the sound of hooves and then Sandy's voice, firing eager questions at Ross. Certainly, with the boy, he had infinite patience. He seemed better at communicating with animals and children than with adults.

When she returned to her bedroom she found she had mistakenly left her door open. Of course, Goldie was curled up snoring gently. Without thought now, Jo pushed her off and was rewarded with a reproachful look and an indignant swish of the tail. She slapped Goldie on the haunch and collapsed on the bed, wishing that Nyala had been able to afford air-conditioning.

Only now, rested, refreshed and alone, did she begin to relive the scene of the past hour. The sight of the massive buffalo carcass returned to her, an almost prehistoric beast in its proportions. She shuddered at the thought of the damage those horns could do. If only Ross was not so insufferably bossy she could probably take his criticism. One tiny corner of her thought could not help admiring his cool facing of a dangerously wounded animal with such complete courage.

The thought of him made her wonder idly how he would run Nyala if he were left completely on his own. A man as unsociable as he was, with no wife, no company but animals and servants, would probably turn cranky. And it would not take too much to turn Ross Andrews cranky.

"Aren't you coming for a drink?" She opened her eyes to find Sally watching her. "I was beginning to think you'd really fallen asleep."

"No . . . no, just a bit tired, but the shower more or less fixed that. I'll be with you in five minutes. Oh . . . and Sally?"

Her sister turned.

"Did Ross produce tomorrow's supper for you?"

She half expected her sister to grimace, but Sally nodded happily. "Yes, buffalo tail; he said it tastes as good as oxtail. And don't look like that, Jo, there isn't a butcher around the corner. We'll have to make use of what we can get here. I've been reading a bit too and I think I'll be able to make paté for visitors. Ross has promised to save the first liver from any wildebeest. And he says that farther up the river are duck and guineafowl. I honestly believe we could produce a very good menu here."

Dinner that evening should have been a celebration, but somehow there was an air of tension around, saved only by Bruce's cheerfulness and the eager questions of young Sandy.

Ross seemed detached; he hardly joined in the conversation, and when the meal was over and they were waiting for Saku to bring the coffee, he walked over to the window and stared toward the river.

Sandy came over and stood beside him. "Are you looking for the croc, Ross?"

Ross ruffled his hair. "No, that's your dad's job. We're going to wait for him to return and finish that fellow off. No, I'm worried about the water supply. We depend on the river and it's going down about an inch a day."

Sally came to join them. "Is it really bad?" she asked.

"It's never bad until the worst has happened, but we're dependent on the river. We should have more pumps at the farthest waterholes, but they're always too expensive."

In the soft light Sally's eyes were glinting. "Should a pump come before a freezer?" she said demurely.

She drew from him the first smile of the evening. "It should, but a freezer is cheaper. Besides, I was beginning to forget what good food is like. Now I'm quickly developing a taste for it."

Jo watched the little scene by the window. She saw the

way their eyes met. Sally certainly had the knack of re-laxing Ross. She could even make him laugh.

Bruce's hand was resting lightly on her shoulder. "Do you want to wait for coffee, or will you have some of my own brew? It tastes good out of doors."

So they slipped away, unnoticed, down to where the river curved sharply around about 200 yards from the back of the house. Here Bruce had organized a small but highly efficient camp site, with the truck facing the water and a small brown tent pitched beside it. Embers still glowed from the midst of a frame of small rocks. Bruce reached up and lit a storm lamp hooked above the tent. It threw the scene into the sharper light, even the folding table and two camp chairs.

Jo gazed with admiration. "You really have made it look like home!"

"Don't forget," he reminded her, "this is my home. I may have to be on the move and travel light, but I do enjoy a few comforts, otherwise this kind of life could grow intolerable."

"But a table . . . and chairs?"

"I need a table because I have paper work to do. And to sit at a table one needs a chair. I also have a camp bed and a sleeping bag. Now, first—coffee."

She had not quite visualized Bruce in these sur-roundings, fending for himself, so utterly self-sufficient. When he had been in England he had fitted in so well there, his tall figure comfortable and casual in its well-cut suit. He was an Englishman home from the tropics, true, but not one from this sort of rough life.

He looked up and caught her gaze, grinning. "I know what you're thinking."

"Well, what am I thinking?"

"That I'm not your idea of a diamond prospector. The ones you've seen are at the movies, old, wizened, grubby, with a few weeks' growth of beard on their faces. Well, things aren't like that any more, although you can still find some of the old-timers just outside Kimberley in South Africa. They look for diamonds in much the same way as they did a century ago. I don't, I look for the pipe that might hide a million pounds' worth of diamonds. Sugar?" She nodded and he handed her the mug.

"And how do you start looking on Nyala?"

She listened, absorbed as he talked of his real love, the search for diamonds. At home he had also talked a little, but it had never seemed quite so real as now, in just the sort of terrain he was describing. He told her how they sank the shafts deeper and deeper until they came to the "blue ground," the rock that was diamond-bearing, when they started to tunnel through the sides, parallel to the surface. He also told her of the year he had spent in South-West Africa, working on the treacherous coast there, where the slow search for sea diamonds was going on.

For a moment she realized he had almost forgotten she was there. "I'm sorry, Jo," he said ruefully, "you started me off on my pet subject. And you really listened. Most women ask questions, but don't really want to know the answers."

I want to know about you, everything.

He said suddenly, "It would solve all your problems if I found diamonds on Nyala, wouldn't it?"

She frowned, puzzled. "But how?"

"Money problems. They simply wouldn't exist. You could even afford to keep the reserve as a private garden. You could certainly afford to get rid of Andrews."

"Do you dislike him that much?" she asked curiously.

"No, of course not. I was just pointing out facts. But I've never liked to be dependent on anyone but myself for bread and butter. You're completely dependent on him. He could so easily let you down."

"He could, but I don't think he will. He has too much

pride." She thought a moment more and added, "I suppose the truth is he doesn't really want to run Nyala commercially. He would like to continue in the same way as my uncle was doing."

Bruce snorted. "Toward ruin, by the sound of it. Look, Jo," he turned to her and gripped her shoulders, "you sound as if you're not entirely happy with Andrews. Even when you praise him, there's a note of doubt in your voice. I'm not suggesting that game rangers or wardens grow on trees, but mostly they're a band of dedicated men, and you could always replace Andrews. Oh, not at a day's notice, true, but I could always get friends of mine to look around."

"No, honestly, Bruce," she said anxiously, "I don't want to run him down at his job. My only criticism is that he has a difficult personality. Just because he and I don't hit it off. . . . In the end it's only the animals that count."

"The humans too, if you're going to make it pay. Anyway, let's forget him and talk about you for a change. I want to know exactly what you've done in the past year."

So she leaned her head against his shoulder and talked. She knew that what she said to him was not particularly interesting, but it was so good to have him here and not to imagine that last year was all a dream. Even the setting was perfect; the soft glow of the fire and the shaded lamps from the house. She was already beginning to recognize the distant sounds of the bush, from the husky shout of the hyena to the barking of baboons with every few moments the faint but distinctive rumble of an elephant.

"England seems a long way away now," he said.

"Another world," she moved deeper into the shelter of his arms. "And you know, it's a funny thing, but I know three months isn't going to be long enough for me here. I feel I could be happy."

He looked down at her. "Why not? You're only trying to express what many people feel about Africa. It's still a very wild and mysterious place. And you know something, Jo?"

"What's that?"

"I had a feeling in my bones that you and I were meant to meet in Africa. That's why I knew I would see you again. There was no need to write. When you're alone as much as I am, there's time to think and there are some things in life one is quite certain of." His arms tightened around her. "This time I'm not going to let you go."

CHAPTER SEVEN

Ross, the following evening, in a surprisingly expansive mood, suggested he should take a busman's holiday and they would all spend the day in the bush. That the trip was mostly for Sandy was obvious, but Ross said he also wanted to make a start on Goldie's training and possibly discuss key points in the reserve that might be suitable for potential visitors.

"It won't be altogether a holiday," he apologized, "because I might have to do some work along the way and make at least one call at a game post, but we should be able to cover a fair amount of ground and see a good selection of game." He turned to Bruce. "I hope you'll come along. It will give you the feel of the place. I might even be able to help you with some of the problems of the terrain."

"And you'd like the use of my truck," Bruce finished lazily. But he was smiling as he spoke.

Ross had glanced sharply at him. "If you're coming, yes," he replied evenly. "I'd like to do the thing properly and take Kari and a couple of others."

Bruce shrugged. "It's all right by me. I want to do a few small engine checks, but I should be able to get that done tonight. What time are you proposing to start?"

"Five o'clock."

Sally spoke up next. "I'm not sure that I'll come, Ross. All-day traveling and I don't seem to go too well together. I don't want to be a drag."

"You won't," he said confidently, "we're not trying to beat any time records. We'll also be making several longish stops; that's one of the reasons why I want the servants along, so that they can give a hand with the food. We'll also take a tent in case we're out of shade at midday. For tomorrow, Sally, we'll go at your pace, not mine."

She looked relieved. "Then I'll come, of course, or I'll find myself back in England without seeing enough game, or the other boundaries of Nyala."

"Fine. And what we will do," he added, "is to assume that you, Sally, and Jo—and Farley—are members of a day safari out from Nyala. We can then see what you would think of the facilities if you were really paying customers."

It all seemed a good idea, Jo thought, until she tumbled out of bed just after four-thirty the next morning. It was still pitch dark and the air cool and fresh, but the effort of rising after not enough sleep and the heavy program of the previous days seemed enormous.

Only two people were quite wide awake, Ross and Sandy—who was dancing around the steps bubbling over with excitement. The two trucks were already out and packed, except for the last few things. Saku was not coming himself, but he was quite determined he should be held responsible for arranging everything efficiently.

At last only the human element was left. Without asking if anyone had preferences, Ross ordered them to their places.

"Sally, I think you'd better travel with Farley, along with Kari and one of the men. You've also got the tent and a fair bit of gear in the back. I'll take Sandy and Jo, with Goldie in the truck with the other men."

When Jo opened her mouth to protest, his only comment was, "I daresay you'd prefer it to be the other way around, but if I'm to teach you anything about Nyala it will have to be like this." His eyes rested coolly on her mutinous expression. "You were intending to set yourself up as a safari leader one day, weren't you?"

Without another word Jo climbed into the truck alongside Sandy. As usual he was right, but oh, the pleasure he took in the smallest of humiliations.

He and Bruce arranged final signals between them for stopping or drawing each other's attention. Then they were moving off slowly, down the main track, heading toward the southwest and the largest game post of Nyala, other than the main house.

At about five-thirty, the first pink tendrils of the dawn crept across the sky. The light seemed to burst all about them—first a cool, soft gray; then as the sun rose, it turned to gold. And with the light came the game, rising silently to make its way toward the river and the waterholes.

They were heading, Ross said, to one of the largest and most important waterholes in the southwest of Nyala, only 20 miles from the border post, almost on the edge of the real desert. Even a few days ago, he added, the water was getting dangerously low.

"Does the water ever dry up completely?" Jo asked curiously.

"It's never done in my time here, but it can do; and then of course all the game moves toward the river. For some it would simply be too far and they would die on the way. Without appearing to lecture you," he added dryly, "this is one of the reasons we need money so badly. If we have money we can buy pumps and if we have pumps we can at least keep some of the holes going."

Just before seven they stopped for breakfast. Within minutes they had put up the tent with its flat canopy and had coaxed the fire into speedy life for the water to boil. The smell of frying eggs in the sharp morning air suddenly made Jo aware that she was really hungry.

They sat around in the shade of the tent, eating and talking about the possibilities of the day ahead. Goldie seemed faintly ill-humored for once, pushing her way into the circle and nudging Ross until he almost fell off his stool. Jo could only assume she did not like traveling. Then she turned away for a second and found herself tipped off her canvas chair and sprawling on the ground.

The others all roared with laughter. Even the Africans grinned at her discomfiture.

"Wretched lion," she grumbled. "Why can't you keep her under control, Ross Andrews? She can jolly well travel in another truck."

He tickled the lioness behind her ear. She merely growled faintly.

"You see," Jo said crossly, dusting off the sand. "She got out of bed on the wrong side this morning."

He shook his head, still smiling. "No, it's not that; she's hungry. At the moment she's contemplating those nice bare arms of yours."

Jo gave a little gasp. She was not used to Ross in a teasing mood. Quickly she rolled her sleeves down. "I thought you always fed her late at night."

"Yes, but not today. Today Goldie is going hunting." He shooed Goldie out of the breakfast circle. With a grunt she lay down under the dappled shade of a camel-thorn.

The family of baboons appeared from nowhere. Their barking could be heard over the still air and though they did not come near the camp at first, their curiosity brought them closer.

"But they're so ugly," Sally said, watching the cluster of hairy gray beasts whose stance from a distance looked so incredibly human. "What do they want?"

"Like Goldie, a good square meal," Ross answered laconically, watching the group. "They must have broken away from the main troop, because this is certainly not their terrain."

"I don't think they're ugly," announced Jo. "They look rather friendly."

"Not baboons," Ross shook his head. "They're mischievous, greedy, predatory animals. They have odd habits too; they move in this tight family group, yet often they won't raise a finger to help one of their number in trouble. They are also extraordinarily destructive. I once mistakenly saved a young baboon from drowning and brought him home. One minute he was almost human, the next he would try to smash the place. And you ought to see the troop elder in action, he behaves just like a despotic dictator."

For a few moments longer they watched the troop, playing like children, tearing up and down the trees, chasing each other, putting on tumbling acts.

There were quite a few young in the group, one in particular who did not appear to have much clue as to the rules of the game. He kept getting left out, wailing and crying, much to the amusement of the girls. Finally he decided to stay close to father. He climbed onto his back and clung there with all his might as the older animal raced up the nearest tree.

But suddenly laughter turned to horror. The whole scene was over in seconds. It seemed that the parent baboon did not want the child just then. He was nothing but nuisance value. He appeared to be trying to shake the infant off its back, who clung with tenacity. Then, in one swift movement, in a terrifying outburst of rage, the parent lifted the encumbrance from its back, bit it hard and tossed it to the ground, 40 feet below.

"Oh, no!" cried Jo, instinctively, and got up to run to where the tiny body lay sprawled beneath the trees.

"Stay where you are," snapped Ross. "They don't like interference; they could just as easily turn on you." He reached in the truck for his gun. As he walked over, the chattering in the trees died to an uneasy murmuring. But when he bent to the ground, the whole troop turned and fled, abandoning the infant.

"It's dead, I suppose," Jo said flatly when he returned.

He nodded.

"I never thought the animal world was deliberately cruel." She was more upset by the little scene than she would have cared to admit.

"It isn't," Ross told her, "but there are animals with a bad streak just as there are humans. But you mustn't condemn them all. If that had been a young elephant calf lying there dead, the herd would have come and carried it away as a sort of ritual. It's their custom. You'll see many sights in the bush that will sicken you, Jo, until you get used to them, but even more they'll fill you with wonder."

"I suppose so." But for the moment she was unconvinced, still seeing that small body hurtling through the air like a football.

Bruce caught her eye. "Here, Jo, some more tea. Drink it." And she took it from him gratefully, glad to have her attention diverted.

Sandy, wanting also to help, stood before her saying seriously, "I don't like those things either, Jo, but you do learn to get used to them. Why, I can remember on the farm when a hyena got one of Dad's cattle before it was dead. All of its guts. . . ."

"Sandy," Ross's voice came sharply across the clearing, "how about collecting Goldie before she falls completely asleep?"

Bruce grinned at Jo and squeezed her hand. "It's all right. I believe all children have strong stomachs and tend to be a bit ghoulish."

It was probably because of the baboons that Jo reacted quite so strongly to what happened later. Goldie had reluctantly awakened and Ross, picking up his gun, said to Sandy, "We're going to give her the first lessons in survival. Do you want to come, or stay here?"

"With me," Sally chimed in. "I'm not moving anywhere until I have to." Already she had stretched out under the awning, lazily watching all the preparations.

"I'd like to come, please, Ross," Sandy said eagerly,

just managing to apologize to Sally. "If you don't mind, that is, Sally."

"Of course I don't mind. What about you, Jo?"

"I'm going too." Jo picked up her hat and sunglasses, looking inquiringly at Bruce, who nodded, taking her by the arm in a comforting sort of way.

So the little party started on foot across the sandy bush toward a larger patch of trees about half a mile away, with Ross in the lead accompanied by the faithful Tau and Goldie, padding on just behind. Kari brought up the rear with Sandy, Bruce and Jo in the middle.

When Jo asked why they had not made their breakfast camp there Ross answered briefly, "Dunes . . . just ahead. We would have had to make a detour of a couple of miles." And as they aproached the shelter of those dunes he asked them to stay as still and silent as possible.

Jo leaned against the hot dry sand. If she closed her eyes she could almost imagine she was in Cornwall, where they used to spend their holidays as children, with the great rolling dunes covered in dry, scrubby grass.

Here there was scrub, uneven and sparse, where it looked as though rain had not fallen for years. Bruce had already described to her the overnight blossoming of the desert when the rains did come. For a short while it became green and cascades of brilliant flowers burst out of the sand as if by magic.

They waited, although Jo was not certain why, until she saw the small herd of impala appear just 200 yards away. They were traveling slowly, stopping every now and then to probe at half-hidden green shoots from the bush. Then, as if at a signal, they all lifted their head and it seemed, in a single graceful movement, they were leaping into the distance.

As the last animal passed their field of vision, Ross raised his rifle and fired. The impala seemed to hesitate for a second in mid-air, then fell, crumpled into a heap.

The sound of the shot seemed to echo in the sudden silence of the bush.

Ross urged Goldie forward. But Goldie still seemed reluctant, hungry as she was.

Jo, bemused, was staring at Ross in utter disbelief. She fond her voice at last.

"Do you mean to say you shot that . . . that beautiful creature just on a whim, just so that you could give Goldie a little afternoon's fun? You're . . . you're almost as bad as that baboon!"

Ross stopped in his tracks. "I think it should have been you to stay at home today, not Sally. If you think and talk that way then there's no place for you in the bush . . . come on, Goldie." His voice sharpened. "We're not having another squeamish one on our hands."

But Jo had not finished. She ran after him, pulling back on his arm. "I'm not joking, Ross . . . this isn't the way I want to run Nyala."

"Nyala isn't yours to run, is it?" he returned in that same cool voice. "And if your stomach won't stand even an ordinary kill, then you'd better go back to your sister. Now."

For just a few more seconds there was silence as they faced each other, anger about to explode into violence. Sandy was already pushing Goldie by the haunches toward the fallen impala.

Suddenly Bruce intervened. "Look," he said roughly, "I agree that that was an ill-timed piece of shooting, especially after the baboon killing. Surely you've got sense enough to see that Jo is upset?"

Ross leaned forward, resting on his gun. "Well, I did think you would have had more sense, Farley. I thought you would help me point out to Miss Fraser that this isn't Kew Gardens."

"I daresay she knows that already. But it takes time to learn the ways of the desert."

"And that's just what we haven't got around here—time! At least not if I follow my instructions correctly and try to make Nyala into a paying proposition."

"And that includes slaughtering buck in front of girls?"

Although his skin was so tanned, Ross whitened in his anger. His eyes were black coals and his mouth tight in his effort to control himself.

He turned deliberately away from Bruce and looked at Jo. "You're not a child, Jo . . . where do you think the meat comes from that you eat every night, that Goldie eats every night, and Tau, every living thing that has to be fed on Nyala? From my gun, of course. I presume you're one of those people who know unpleasant things go on in the world, but as long as you don't actually see them you can pretend they don't exist. What about the beef and lamb you eat at home? Before you start handing out orders about what I should do, what Goldie should eat, you should become a vegetarian. At least you would be trying to stick to your principles. I suppose you'd like me to keep this lion in captivity all her life, so that she would end up in some wretched zoo, simply because no one had the decency to teach her to feed herself. Already I've left it too long, because there's never enough time round here." He looked from Bruce back to Jo, then jerked his head towards Sandy. "Even a nine-year-old boy accepts the simple fact that in the bush if you want to have life there must be death." With that he strode off.

Bruce started after him. "Damned insolence . . . who the devil does he think he is? I'll. . . ."

"No, please, Bruce." Jo restrained him. "It won't do the slightest bit of good."

"You mean to say you don't mind him speaking to you as he might one of the African servants?"

"Of course I mind." Jo did not add that she would have been very surprised if Ross had ever spoken to a servant like that. "But starting another row won't help. I suppose he's right in a way . . . it's his methods I don't like."

"Shock tactics, you'd call them. He's just the cold-blooded type to do something like that deliberately, knowing how you would feel. Come on, Jo, we'll walk back to Sally." He put his arm lightly round her shoulders. "Would you like to pack up for the day and I'll drive you back? You look a little rough."

Ross made no comment when he found her already seated beside Bruce. He merely said, "We'll keep heading southwest to the waterhole, but there's not much of a track, so we'll have to take it slowly. We should then get to the post in time for lunch." He added curtly to Jo, "Watch out for kudu . . . great shy beast, usually found alone, and if you're lucky you might also see roan antelope. This is their part of the country, not to mention lion—wild lion. It will be Goldie's first meeting with her own species, if we see any."

"I expect Bruce will be able to identify them for me," Jo answered stiffly.

When they had been following the leading truck for a few miles—some distance behind because of the dust clouds—Bruce turned to her and said, "Do you really believe Ross intends to try and make the place pay for you?"

She hesitated. "I don't really know; we just have to rely on him. I know you think it's foolish, Bruce, but we have no alternative. Sometimes I think Sally and I are living in a fool's paradise."

"Not if we can get even a whiff of diamonds." He gripped her arm tightly. "No, Jo, it's not as impossible as all that. These Bushmen have an uncanny knack of being right. There's no logic, just instinct. Tomorrow I'm going to start work in earnest. You might not see me for two or three days at a time, but I'll never be more than 20 or 30 miles away. The more self-sufficient I am the better. I'll only need to come to the house for water . . . and to see you."

"I'm glad you came, Bruce," she said. "Somehow you

make everything seem possible." She looked out at the passing countryside, mile after mile of flat, sandy scrub that looked as though it could not sustain a living thing. "I don't want to go back to England," she said suddenly. "Even if Nyala falls about our ears, I don't think I want to go back yet."

"Then stay," his hand was still gripping hers. "There are other parts of Africa, other countries as interesting as this one. But you're not to give up hope yet, Jo. With well over two months to go you and I are going to get this place buzzing."

"Oh, Bruce," she sighed, "I only hope you're right." But even as she spoke she had a curious feeling of disloyalty toward Ross Andrews.

In about an hour they reached the waterhole. Somehow Jo had expected a kind of miniature lake, or even a pan—one of the indents in the ground found all over the country, mostly dried up, some layered with salt, mud or a couple of feet of water—but this was less than a small village pond.

In its own way, Jo saw as she climbed out of the truck, it was quite pretty, like finding a green oasis in the middle of a desert. Round the edges of the hole grew a coarse kind of grass, much trampled by animals trying to reach the diminishing water. There were also small clumps of trees, the first they had seen for the past hour. She heard Ross explaining to Sally that although the water area was small, normally enough filtered through the ground to give life to the game within ten miles. In the hollows where the water collected, seeds were blown. In the short wet season the trees sprang up, giving shelter, shade and a nesting area for the birds.

Ross pushed his hat to the back of his head and knelt to examine the hole, but with his hand he scooped out only moisture along with the desert sand.

He looked up at Kari who was anxiously standing by

and shook his head. "It is bad, *Morena*," Kari replied solemnly. "In two days there will be nothing."

"And there's not a damn thing we can do about it." He looked angrily up into the brazenly blue sky as if seeking some small sign of rain.

Faint depression hung over all of them as they moved back toward the trucks. Then the first of the morning visitors came to drink and they drew back silently to watch. First came the springbok and a small herd of wildebeest. They drank together, yet stayed apart. Quietly Ross explained to Sally and Sandy that there was an unwritten drinking order to some of these scattered holes. The different species came in a regular order.

As the springbok drew back four or five warthog rushed down to the water, scrambling over each other in their haste to reach the moisture.

Then came the zebra, but as they took their place their eyes went up sharply as though the scent of danger was there and they could not understand it.

"It's Goldie," explained Ross. "They can smell lion when it's not really time for the lion. The lion comes last, after the rest of the buck."

And so it turned out to be. Jo watched the pride stroll down to water: a magnificent shaggy-maned lion, the lioness and several younger ones. There must have been about eight in all. And as they came the rest of the game disappeared as if by magic.

Ross pushed Goldie forward, but she took one look at her fellow beasts and yelped in fright, running around to cower at the far side of the truck. She had come across something she simply did not understand.

"Why," breathed Sandy, "she's frightened, Ross, honestly I think she is!"

"I'm afraid you're right," Ross replied gravely. "Just one more lesson for her to learn. She's not proving to be much good as a pupil today." He turned to Sally. "She'd never even seen a fresh kill. She didn't know what to do with it. She's grown indecently tame."

When the last of the animals had gone Kari and Ross returned to the hole, shovelling into the sand all around it, but there was no spread of moisture and Ross finally threw his shovel down in disgust, sweating with the effort he had made.

They all stood in a group watching him, with the same expressions of sympathy on their faces, all wanting to help, but equally knowing that anything said just now would be merely frivolous.

He seemed to see them for the first time and, as if they were all servants, barked out, "Right, into the trucks, there's nothing we can do here."

Bruce backed his truck out after the other one, slamming the gears home. "This is turning out to be a fine safari, isn't it? I don't give your Ross Andrews much chance of pleasing the tourists if he takes his bad temper out on them—or worse still treats them all like a bunch of school kids."

"I suppose he's worried," Jo said helplessly. "The drought must be getting serious."

"I suppose so, but a good warden would have made some provision for an eventuality like this. A drought is always in the cards in this part of the country."

"Oh, Bruce, that isn't fair," she protested. "Heaven knows I'm annoyed enough with him today, but he's only been in charge of Nyala for a month or two. The only thing he could have done was to put in pumping equipment—and that takes money."

He smiled wryly down at her. "Okay, Jo, you have a kind heart and I don't. It's just that the fellow gets under my skin. But you know, if you're going in for the tourist business seriously, you'll have to think whether he's the right man for it. I feel he's going to rub a lot of people the wrong way."

Jo did not answer. He was right about this. The thought depressed her.

She looked out at the unending vista of sand and knew that by now they were right in the heart of the desert. A truly desolate place. She wished they had never come out today.

CHAPTER EIGHT

For the next two days Jo saw nothing of Bruce. He had taken the truck and was prospecting in a desert area some distance from the house. Wistfully she had watched him leave, wishing to go with him but aware that when he was working he wanted no distractions. Besides, there was plenty for her to do here. She divided her time between helping Sally prepare the guest houses and keeping Sandy amused.

This was a way of giving her more instruction. Ross was also working some miles away with one of the rangers, relying on Brandy for transport, so Kari took the truck for two short sorties into the bush.

In his own quiet way he taught Jo as much as both Ross and Bruce had done. Because he was rather shy of her he addressed most of his comments to Sandy, who listened, fascinated; but Jo knew she was also supposed to listen and learn.

He stopped the truck several times when he thought something would be of interest to Sandy. Once he led them to the edge of a shallow pan where, half hidden by the pattern of thin undergrowth, it took sharp eyes to see the lacework of burrows in the hard dry soil. "There will be many, many mongoose there, young *Morena*," he said, "but they will be difficult to see unless we wait and watch. And we have no time. And over here," he moved stealthily forward, "is a place where the honey badger has been. He was seeking the wild honey."

"Can't we stay?" Sandy leaded. "I've never seen a honey badger."

But Kari shook his head. "He is a shy animal, young *Morena*, he will be alone or perhaps with his mate. If he sees or smells you he will not appear, but come, there is an animal I can show you."

Again he walked along, in an easy, almost loping stride. He was rather broad for a Bushman, with rather unusual features. The normally flat features flared into high cheekbones and eyes full of expression. His tight black curls seemed to grow in an oddly triangular shape, giving an air of quiet humor. It was all these unusual characteristics, and his high intelligence, that had made Uncle Harold hire him.

Further around the pan he bent again and tapped at the hard sand. A pair of sharp eyes peered out at him and darted back again; then another pair, and another. Delighted, Sandy knelt down to get a closer look. "What are they, Kari? Not mongoose, I think."

"No, they are ground squirrels, many, many of them, and each generation stays in the same burrows. But this year," he squinted up at the clear sky, "I'm afraid they will be fewer. They are vegetarians, and with no water they will die." In a lower, sadder voice he added, "It will be a bad year for my people too."

As they climbed back into the truck Jo said, "Where are your people, Kari? Tell me about them."

"They come from deep in the Kalahari, lady, and I do not often see them. They are still very wild and do not understand why I have chosen to leave. But they are happy to see me. I do not belong to the Kalahari now, I belong to the Nyala and the *Morena*." He gave a sideways glance at her. "*Morena* will make Nyala grow again . . . no one will take it from him."

"No, Kari," she said, watching the Bushman's face curiously, "no one will take it from him."

"Not the other *Morena*?"

She looked sharply at him. "Mr. Farley? Of course not." But she wondered why even the thought should have come into his mind.

On that day she learned to recognize the heart-shaped spoor of a waterbuck, the pugmark of a leopard; she learned that giraffe had passed by only an hour before and a small herd of buffalo had crossed their trail. A lone elephant had trampled a path through the bush and this seemed to worry Kari, the fact that the beast was alone. Every now and then when the truck was stopped he would bend close to the ground, perhaps run his fingers lightly across the sand and then, his ear cocked, listen. Like so many Bushmen he could hear sounds that no other human could, or perhaps it was not hearing, but a kind of instinct—that a sound was about to be heard.

Jo found she already knew the main animals on Nyala. Some, of course, were easy enough, but the many kinds of buck and larger antelope were easily confused. She now knew the small gray duiker by its quick movements and the two straight, sharp horns rising between its ears. Not too unlike them were the springbok, but they seemed to move in larger herds. Now she could easily recognize the shy kudu with his proud head and white striped flanks, always hiding behind a group of trees, and the tiny steenbuck with its chestnut brown back and lighter chest. She was even beginning to know the kind of terrain in which to look for certain species, which animals needed more water than others and whether they could survive without grazing ground.

She and Sandy arrived back, tired but happy. Sandy, it was plain, could never have too much of the bush. He had an absolutely sure instinct with animals and an insatiable thirst for knowledge about them. Ten to one, Jo guessed, he would end up doing the same kind of job as Ross.

She showered and changed, tickled the waiting Goldie behind both ears, and collapsed in a canvas chair. Within seconds Saku had produced a long, cold fruit drink which she took gratefully, as Sally came in to join her.

"A message came through that the freezer has arrived!" Sally informed her excitedly.

"So you'll be able to stock up with buffalo tails," Jo teased.

"For someone with a large appetite your stomach is very squeamish," her older sister retorted.

"I know. You really ought to learn to shoot, Sal, then you could control the whole thing yourself, from field to table as it were." She pulled a face at her sister.

"What's Bruce doing tomorrow?" Sally said suddenly.

"I don't know. Why?" Jo returned cautiously.

"Well, I could even give you a proper excuse for spending the day with him. We can get delivery of the freezer as far as Nata. From there we're expected to pick it up from the local warehouse. And apparently it's not an awfully wise thing to leave goods lying around for too long."

"I'm sure Bruce would take me if he's back. He said he might be tonight. I'll walk down to his camp later."

"I thought that would make you sit up. You could also go into market there and get some cotton fabric for the guest rondavels. I've done all the measuring today." She paused. "Jo . . . I don't want you to bite my head off, or even accuse me of interfering, but have your feelings changed toward Bruce since you were in England?"

"Yes," replied Jo simply.

"You mean you no longer. . . ."

"I mean nothing of the sort. My feelings are simply much stronger and surer. Bruce is the one person in the world for me."

"But. . . ."

"No buts, Sal, because it won't make any difference to me—except perhaps to turn me against you. Oh, I know he has faults. I can even see that he wouldn't be an easy man to live with, but that doesn't stop me falling in love with him."

"And him?" Sally said quietly.

Jo paused before she spoke. "I think he feels quite a lot for me. The year without news has drawn us together rather than widening the gap, but whether he's a marrying man, that's quite another matter. All I know is that for the moment I'm content to wait and see. The sort of life he lives isn't an easy one."

"He could change it," Sally pointed out.

"And blame me for the rest of his life? No, Sal, even you know that wouldn't be right. But I think I should tell you one thing. . . ."

"Go on."

"If at the end of three months we have to leave Nyala, I'm not going to go back to England."

"You—you mean you're going to stay here, in this country?"

"Not necessarily. I shouldn't think it would be possible to find much of a job here. No, I might go to South Africa or Kenya. I honestly don't know, Sal. I just feel I want to stay somewhere in Africa for a little longer. But," she added wryly, "I still wish we were able to keep Nyala."

Sally crossed the room and came to stand by her sister. "Look, Jo, I'm not going to try to persuade you one way or the other. You're 21 and you have to live your own life. But you're forgetting one important thing. If—and I know it's a very big if—we manage to make Nyala pay for itself there'll be no question of keeping it. We're going to sell it, remember, to help Alan. Not to do that would be a betrayal of all he's done for us, all he's given up for us. You do understand that, don't you, Jo?"

Jo nodded. "Of course I do." But in a way she had conveniently forgotten the real reason why she and Sally came out here. She had merely been indulging in a foolish little dream, thinking that one day Nyala could conceivably be hers.

The two girls started dinner alone. Even Sandy had admitted defeat and gone to bed, hardly able to keep his eyes open. Saku had just finished serving the soup when they heard Brandy clatter into the yard. A few minutes later Ross appeared at the door.

Both of them leapt to their feet, staring at him, shocked. His shirt was torn and streaked with blood. There were deep scratches down his face and he was covered in dust.

"Ross!" Sally cried. "What on earth has happened? Saku," she called behind her, "bring a glass of brandy."

Ross tried to grin. "Not brandy, beer. I think I must have half the Kalahari desert down my throat."

Sally pulled away the shirt from his arm. The blood had dried into thick lines. "You can't leave that for a moment if you don't want to get infected. Where's the antiseptic?"

But Saku was already there with the beer, the anti-septic and a roll of cotton wool. Ross drained the glass at one gulp then pushed the servant gently away. "Not until I've had a shower. I won't look quite such a sight then."

Jo found her voice at last. "What kind of animal did that to you?" she demanded.

"The most dangerous animal in the bush when you're on horseback," he replied, and disappeared into the bath-room.

Sally and Jo looked at each other soberly. "Funny," said Jo, "walking all over the place with Kari and Sandy today, one forgets that some of the animals are dan-gerous."

"Well, he isn't afraid."

"Of course not. You couldn't last a minute in this job if you were afraid. Animals are supposed to scent fear, aren't they?"

They finished the soup, but Sally told Saku to hold the rest until the *Morena* was ready. She then made sure there was a bowl of warm water, some bandages and plaster, which she set on a small table under the light.

Ross emerged still looking tired, but cleaner and fresher, the scratches on his face less raw and frighten-ing. He saw Sally and shook his head.

"Just pass me the antiseptic and a wad of cotton wool and I'll fix this in no time."

Sally merely said, "Sit down here and take off that shirt. Heaven knows what poison the animal infected you with. What was it anyway?" she said as she set to work on him.

His eyes crinkled into a rare smile. "No lions, no tigers, merely a very unpleasant brush with camel-thorn. That's what caused the scratches. I've always said there's more danger in the bush from thorn than pretty well any game."

He winced as Sally dabbed at the cuts on his face. "But why?" she demanded. "Were you simply not looking where you were going?"

"No, not quite that. I was caught napping by another buffalo and had to make a dash for it. I was in thorn country and Brandy simply took to his heels straight through the lot."

"Poachers again?" Jo said.

He turned to look at her. "Probably. I didn't get a chance to do too much investigating." He paused. "I'm sorry if I disappointed you by not getting attacked by a lion. I'm afraid it doesn't happen very often."

Jo flushed. Did he really think she wished that on him? But his humor was so dry she never could tell if he was laughing at her.

By the time Sally was finished with him the cuts looked less angry, but he seemed immensely tired. Perhaps it had been a nearer scrape with the buffalo than he had told them.

He did not demur when Sally hustled him off to bed in just the way she had Sandy as soon as dinner was over. He told them he was worried about the continued decrease in the water supply. The shorter the water became, so the problem of the poachers grew worse; they became more daring, more careless. From tomorrow, he said, he and Kari were going to have an all-out assault on them, getting a rigorous system of patrols that would at least frighten off the worst of them.

Soon after he left them Sally announced that she too was going to bed. The heat had been particularly exhausting that day. Early nights were becoming necessary, for the hotter it became the earlier they all rose, to make the most of the freshest part of the day.

Jo was tired too, but she was determined to wait just a little longer for Bruce's return.

At last, when she was just nodding off, she heard the crunch of wheels outside. She jerked awake and slipped out to meet him. As he climbed tiredly out of the truck it seemed the most natural thing in the world to run into his arms.

He was hot, dusty and sweaty, but the feel of those strong arms around her was immeasurably wonderful. And the kiss that seemed to tell her so much was even better. Then he pushed her away. "Darling, I shouldn't be touching you in the state I'm in."

"I don't mind," she said happily. "I'm just glad to see you back. Go and have a shower and I'll make you some coffee. Anything to eat?"

"No, just coffee—and a can of beer if you can find one."

She made the coffee in the silent kitchen, but thought he would probably prefer to drink it at his own camp, so took the metal coffee pot down there and tried to stir the dead fire into some kind of life. It was surprising how the temperature could drop so quickly at night.

She thought she might have tidied up for him, but the little camp site was immaculate. Here was a man who could pack up at short notice, she thought wryly, as she settled down to wait.

"Well," she said eagerly, as he finally appeared out of the darkness, "how did your first working day on Nyala go?"

"I must have met every tsetse fly in the bush," he answered, slapping himself liberally with lotion, "but otherwise the two days have acted as a preliminary survey. At least I've found the area in which to concentrate and have arranged to hire a couple of men to help with the first slog of prospecting. And it will be another two days before I get to the digging stage—especially as I shall have to go and pick up the men some time tomorrow. Anyway, enough of me—what have you been doing these past two days?" He reached across and let a strand of her hair curl around his finger.

"Brushing up on my bushlore," she answered. "Kari has been giving lessons to Sandy and me. He probably knows almost as much as Ross does. I gather he was with my uncle for nearly ten years."

"And one day, without warning, he'll pack up and leave," Bruce said lazily.

"Not Kari," she answered. "Ross says he has the most incredible loyalty."

"Only while it suits him."

She frowned. "That doesn't sound like you, Bruce."

"Doesn't it? Then I must hide my cynicism more carefully. I've put my faith in others just once too often. That's why I like to work alone as much as possible."

For some reason she felt uneasy at the turn the conversation was taking. She remembered what she wanted him to do tomorrow. Cautiously she brought up the subject of both the market and the freezer. "But please, Bruce, say if you can't spare the time."

"Time? What's time?" he grinned. "If it means spending the day with you, then to market we'll go. But it'll have to be a six o'clock start. Think you can manage it?"

"It's you, not me, that needs rest." She jumped up, letting go of his hand reluctantly. "Till six o'clock, then—and sleep well."

The truck was already waiting when Jo emerged sleepily

into the fresh morning air. Bruce was leaning against the side throwing scraps of wood at Goldie who, surprisingly, was not in the mood for playing.

Bruce turned at the sound of her steps and Goldie relapsed into slumber once more. "Funny," he said, "I don't think she likes me."

"Impossible," Jo laughed. "Goldie loves every one."

"Maybe," he shrugged, "but there must be exceptions to even a lion's love. I should have thought it really was time for her to go back into the bush."

"Well, Ross is trying, isn't he?"

"In a half-hearted sort of way. The only thing is to be ruthless—take her ten miles away, into a good hunting area, and dump her."

"But would she be able to hunt for herself?" Jo watched Goldie uncertainly.

"An animal is like a human. Throw it in the deep end and it will survive. The lion would go hungry for a couple of days and then by sheer force of circumstance have to fend for itself. Still, I'm a diamond man, not a zoologist, so I should learn to keep my mouth shut." He held out his hand to her. "Are you ready to go, Jo?"

"Yes, quite ready." She looked up happily into the sky. "It's going to be a wonderful day."

"Then don't let the others hear you say that. It won't be wonderful at Nyala until it rains."

Bruce drove in an easy relaxed way, talking most of the time, asking her questions, drawing her out about her early life and the background to Uncle Harold's unexpected legacy. She told him so much that she very nearly let slip about the whole purpose of coming to Nyala—a desperate attempt to raise money for Alan. But while she wanted to take him into her confidence, it was after all a family matter, and the fewer people who knew about the Frasers's plans, the better.

The route they took was across sandy, featureless desert, sprinkled only with scrub and thorn trees. There was hardly a movement in the hot, still air and it seemed strange not to be looking for game.

They reached the small town midmorning, after a stop for fruit and tea brewed by the side of the road. It took almost an hour to go through all the formalities of collecting the freezer and arranging for it to be packed into the back of the truck. By then Jo was exhausted by the searing midday heat, so Bruce managed to arrange a cooling shower for her in a small restaurant. When she emerged, feeling fresher again, after a long cold glass of fruit juice, she discovered that there was a market place only 100 yards down the road.

It was a large market, full of noise and color. At every stall where she paused to examine cloth they were immediately surrounded by the fiercest sales technique she had ever come across. Bruce seemed to be able to cope, fending off the unwanted salesmen with dexterity, but whispering that she had better make up her mind soon or the prices would double.

Eventually she sifted through the dozens of rolls of material and chose the least violent colors; a different set for each of the guest-houses, as Sally had suggested. She only hoped Sally would approve of her choice. It was not going to be the Ritz!

After they had taken the parcels back to the truck, she started to work her way through the other shopping list items from seeds to kitchen stores and fresh vegetables.

Of the latter there were plenty, piled up on the ground, tomatoes and avocadoes, potatoes and oranges and strange unrecognizable roots that Bruce told her were yams, the local staple diet.

By the time that was finished Jo needed a shower all over again, but instead it was time, Bruce said, to take her out to the best lunch the town had to offer.

They left in the early afternoon. Happy and replete and very drowsy, Jo dozed on the long journey home, her head nodding from side to side, until it finally came to rest against Bruce's shoulder.

She had no idea how long she had been asleep, but was awakened with a sudden jerk as the truck slowed to a standstill. Bruce was shouting out of the window and a crowd of Africans was gesticulating and shouting back.

Jo felt she had woken in the middle of an unpleasant dream. "What is it, Bruce?" she said urgently. "Why are they shouting at us like that?"

"Because I've run over one of their chickens. You'd think I'd killed their head man or something." He climbed out of the truck and continued the argument in the shade of one of the huts. Eventually he pulled some bills out of his pocket and slammed them on the flat surface of a fallen tree. As far as he was concerned that was the end of the affair and he turned his back on them all and climbed into the driver's seat.

Sheepishly two men slid out of the crowd, each carrying a bundle. Bruce jerked his head at them to get in the back, then without another glance swung the car around and drove off.

"Weren't they satisfied?" Jo said at last, when the worst of his anger had gone down.

"Apparently not. I apologized and offered the money right from the beginning, but all they wanted was another live chicken. As if I could somehow conjure one out of thin air. What a maddening bunch of people!"

Jo was wide awake by now and managed to stay so until the distant line of trees told them that Nyala was not far away. Today she was surprisingly glad to be home. Dusk was just about to fall.

As she climbed stiffly out of the truck Sandy ran to greet her.

"Did you have a good day, Jo? I've missed you today, really I have."

She gave the boy a hug. "I've missed you too, Sandy,

but it's just as well you didn't come. There wasn't any game. And all Bruce and I did when we got there was the shopping."

"Oh well. . . ." he pulled a face. "But before you do anything at all you must come and see Holly. I've been teaching her tricks. I want to see if she's forgotten them."

"Wouldn't after supper do?" Jo said hopefully.

"No, please, only for two minutes. It'll be dark later."

"All right, two minutes." And good humoredly she allowed herself to be led across the grass.

She thought afterward she must have stumbled, but over what she did not know. She was only aware of the slim, dusky shape that reared up from the ground ahead and came at her like an arrow.

She screamed once as a shaft of pain shot through her leg. Sandy turned and his quick eye saw the slim shape shoot off toward the river. Without a second's hesitation he yelled, "*Mamba!*"

"Oh God, no! Bruce," she called faintly. But he was already there, fumbling at her pant-clad leg.

Sandy was still shouting. "You're wasting time. You want a knife, I know you do!" and when Bruce remained with her, rocking her gently in his arms, he raced for the house.

The next few seconds blurred. She was aware only of Ross looming up behind her, pushing Bruce out of the way. There was a short angry exchange between the two men before she felt some rope tighten around her thigh, then the awful pain of a knife shearing without mercy into her leg. Before she could cry out, she fainted.

CHAPTER NINE

She was trying to push her way through a thick, steaming forest to find water. She knew that if she did not find any soon her throat would dry up completely. On and on she seemed to be traveling, no nearer her destination. She would not give in, and yet she knew she must unless she found water. The trees dripped all about her, but when she held out her hand to catch the drips there was only the crackle of dryness.

Suddenly, miraculously, the forest was gone and ahead was a sheet of shining, shimmering water. Or was it a mirage? She started to run, but her feet were leaden and there was a terrible pain in her leg. Only a few yards to go and finally she reached out to the blessed coolness of the water. As she touched it, it disappeared and she cried out at last.

Very close to Jo there was a voice that sounded exactly like her sister's. "I think she's coming to," Sally was saying.

Coming to where? Jo thought foolishly, and as she opened her eyes the nightmare was gone.

"Could I have some water?" she said clearly. At least that part of it was true; her throat felt drier than sand.

She drank long and deeply and looked at Sally properly. "Why are you looking so worried?"

"I . . . we . . . were all worried about you. Snakebite can be a killer around here, apparently."

Snakebit . . . of course, that was the dull throb in her leg. But what actually happened was a bit hazy except that she remembered Bruce holding her tightly in his arms.

"Is . . . is it all right? My leg, I mean."

Sally nodded. "Ross acted like lightning. He was

pumping the serum into your leg almost before I realized what had happened. . . ." She turned as there was a tap at the door. "Oh, Ross, she seems fine, thank goodness."

He hovered in the doorway. Whatever he might have been feeling was masked by a frown. "You had us worried for a moment when young Sandy called out 'mamba.' You've him to thank as much as anyone for swift action—and the fact he knows his snakes."

"A mamba? That's one of the dangerous ones, isn't it?"

"Just about the most deadly in these parts," he told her. "We don't see the black variety, only the green, and to be perfectly honest not many of those. I'm not entirely sure it was a green mamba that bit you, because you've been so lightly affected. Wearing pants helped, of course, so there was only one puncture, but even so the venom is so strong that it would have laid you out for much longer than this." He turned to Sally. "I think that leg will need fresh dressings. Can you manage it, or do you want me to do it?"

"I'll be all right now," Sally told him, "but I'll call if I'm in any doubt."

He turned to leave and Jo pulled herself higher on to the pillows. "Ross. . . ."

He turned in the doorway.

"Thank you."

"All in a day's work. Elephants, lions—humans!" But there was no malice in his voice.

As Sally bandaged her leg, Jo said, "How did he know what to do?"

"I gather coping with snakebite is one of the first things you have to learn round here. He applied a tourniquet, cut open your leg at the puncture and got most of the poison out that way before injecting the serum. When I asked him later he told me that he had taken a first-aid course and he keeps a fair number of basic medicines here. Don't forget the whole of Nyala relies on him. The nearest doctor is about 100 miles away."

A little later Saku brought in a tray of food. Jo was surprised to find it breakfast time. Apparently Ross had also insisted on giving her a sleeping pill to work off the worst of the pain. The African bowed ceremoniously and hoped the lady was feeling better. The *Morena* was a very clever man, was he not?

"Very clever," Jo agreed gravely.

When he had gone and Jo was drinking her coffee she looked toward her sister and said, "Sally, where's Bruce?"

For a moment Sally looked uncomfortable. "He's waiting for Ross to leave the house, then he's coming to see you."

"Waiting for Ross to leave? Why? What on earth are you talking about?"

Sally sighed. "Look, in a moment I've got to go and fetch him. He'll tell you his side of the story and I honestly don't know the rights and wrongs of it, because I was only on the scene as Ross was dealing with your leg. All I know is that the two of them had a dreadful row."

A chill settled on Jo. "You mean over me?"

"Yes, at least over the snakebite. All I ask, Jo, is for you not to take sides. You were unconscious so can't possibly know which of them did the right thing. The only important thing is that you are all right. Personally, I'm glad Ross took no chances. There isn't time to wait and wonder about a snakebite."

Jo pushed her hair back from her face and when she spoke her voice was dangerously quiet. "Well, you haven't told me what the row was about, but you have told me whose side you were on. I think I'd like to see Bruce. Now."

Sally shrugged. She knew when there was no point at all in talking to Jo, so she got up from her chair, staightened out the bed and went in search of Bruce.

Five minutes later his tall figure was blocking the doorway.

"Hello, Bruce," she said softly.

He paused just for a moment, then he was beside her and she was in his arms, so tightly that she thought he would squeeze the breath from her.

"Oh God, Jo, I thought I'd lost you!"

"I'm afraid you don't get rid of me quite as easily as that." She tried to speak lightly, but her voice came out all choky.

He held her away from him. "You are all right, aren't you?"

"Of course. I've got a bit of a headache and my leg aches, but beyond that there's nothing wrong with me. I gather I had a lucky escape. It's Sally, funnily enough, who hates snakes. Ross said—"

The name slipped out without her thinking. She had not wanted to start anything, but it acted like a red rag to a bull.

His fists closed and unclosed. "Andrews? What I'd like to say about that man could not be said in fit company. It's no thanks to him that you had a lucky escape. He'd have had half your leg off if I hadn't been around."

"What . . . what did happen, Bruce?"

He slumped on the end of the bed. "Oh, you were bitten all right, but not by a mamba. At the time Andrews was more eager to take the boy's word than mine. Sandy yelled 'Mamba' and that was the signal for Andrews to go in for amateur surgery. When I tried to tell him, all I got was enough rough handling to knock me off my feet."

"Oh, Bruce, I am sorry. But if it had been a mamba. . . ."

"If. But it wasn't."

"I suppose he could have thought it was not worth taking any chances."

"He could have done anything. What he actually did included accusing me afterward of panicking, of acting like a raw recruit in the bush and finally of trying to kill you instead of saving your life."

"Oh, Bruce, no!" Now she was truly appalled.

"Oh, yes," he answered bitterly. "I could probably have taken it if this hadn't all been flung at me after the great 'Doctor Andrews' had pronounced you out of danger. I can't honestly see us sitting down at the same dinner table after this, Jo."

She was miserably aware that Bruce believed he had come to a point of no return and while she had genuinely tried to do what Sally said—not take sides, her sympathy was now swinging toward him. Anything could have been done and said in the heat of the moment; but to say those things, to accuse another man without justification, simply because he had taken a different point of view, was surely unforgivable.

While she was trying to think of what to say to Bruce, there was a single tap at the door and Sandy's head appeared. But his grin of delight at seeing her sitting up, none the worse for her experience, changed to a scowl as he saw Bruce. In an extra polite voice he said, "I'm glad to see you're all right, Jo. I'll come and visit you properly later. When you're alone." The door closed with a little snap.

"What was all that about?" she asked.

He sighed. "Young Sandy is a faithful follower. Your Mr. Andrews can do no wrong, but I dared to disagree with him, so am cast as the villain."

"But that's ridiculous," Jo protested. "Just wait until I've had a word with him."

"And tried to influence him? I think the whole subject is better left, darling. Even a nine-year-old can say rather smugly, 'But you were unconscious, what do you know about it?' No, forget it, Jo; the main thing is that you're all right. My only comment is to keep an even warier eye on Andrews. A man who can be so brutal could provide all sorts of problems."

Sally forced Jo to stay in bed for the rest of that day, and although Jo grumbled, she found that she must have been tired and so slept on and off most of the day. By the time she got up the ache in her leg had eased considerably. Sally persuaded her to take it easy and produced the first of the guest curtains for her to sew. There was no sign of Bruce, but he had left her a note saying he was going off again for a couple of days, to start some of the more advanced prospecting work.

As she sewed, Sandy came in and sat beside her.

"Did you know Dad's coming back tomorrow? He's going to stay the whole weekend and we're all going croc-hunting."

"You may be going croc-hunting, but not me," she shuddered.

"Oh, Sally says you'll be quite well enough. I asked her, honestly. And Ross says you can come."

"And what if I don't want to?"

"But you must," he said in tones of disbelief. "Everyone wants to hunt their first croc."

She laughed, unable to admit her disgust. Still, if it was part of Nyala life, it might be prudent to say at least she had seen a crocodile hunt.

Bored with sitting around, Sandy announced that he was going to take Holly for a walk. "She'll follow me nearly as well as she'll follow you," he said proudly. "I wish she could come back home with me."

"I know how you feel, Sandy. Just as I wish we could keep her as a pet, but soon she'll have to go back into the bush, just like Goldie, I suppose."

"I know it really," he said. "Ross has explained it all to me. Do you know, Jo, he knows simply everything about animals. Not like—" he stopped himself abruptly, but could not help adding, "It *was* a mamba, you know, that beautiful pale green color. If it had only been *him* there, you'd be dead."

Jo winced at his outspokenness. "Look, Sandy, I'm all right, and that's all that matters. I think we should all forget what happened, and honestly we'll never really be able to say for certain whether it was a mamba or not."

"But you didn't hear what he said to Ross. . . ."

"Sandy!" That was Ross standing in the doorway, looking unbelievably stern.

Mustering his remaining dignity, Sandy jumped up, saying quickly, "I said I was going to take Holly for a walk. I think I'll go now."

Jo watched the small upright figure disappear. "He's very loyal, Ross."

"Too loyal, I'm afraid. If you put that much trust in a person at some time or another you're bound to be disappointed. Still, if Sandy turns out anything like his father, he'll be all right. By the way, Neil will be here tomorrow. I expect you're wondering if he has any news about Nyala safaris."

"Yes. Although. . . ."

He came and sat on the chair opposite her, his eyes narrowed and keen. She wished suddenly she knew more about Ross Andrews, what made him tick. Sometimes he was quite talkative, but never about himself. In a strange way she knew no more about him now than on the first day they arrived at Nyala. It was as though he did not want to get close to anyone, not even a child like Sandy. Was he afraid they would let him down, or that he would let them down? Or had he something to hide?

"Although what?" he was saying. "Have you changed your mind about the safaris here?"

"Oh no," she shook her head vehemently. "It's the only way to make the place pay, I'm convinced of that. But I realize more every day how dependent we are on you."

"And you think I might let you down. Those thoughts don't sound like yours, Jo. Has Bruce Farley been talking to you?"

"No, but now you come to mention it. . . ."

"Look," he stood up abruptly and she saw the closed expression come over his face, "if you're going to bring up your snakebite, then I think it would be better if I left you now."

"That's unfair," she protested, "if you won't even listen."

"You mean I should listen to you telling me Farley's point of view? No, Jo, I did what was right, and if the same thing happened again that's just what I would do. With snakes there's no time to stop and think and discuss."

"That wasn't what I meant," she said tightly. "You know I'm grateful for what you did for me. But that you should attack Bruce simply for holding his point of view. . . ."

"I see, so that's what he told you. It's not important to me, Jo. All I know is that he's your friend, perhaps even something more, if I'm not mistaken; therefore you have a right to have him here. But as far as the running of this reserve goes then what I say goes. Perhaps you'd better let him know that, though you may not think it, I'm a peace-loving man, but I don't like to be told how to do my job."

"Bruce has also spent his life in Africa," she flung at him, stung because he seemed to think he was always right. "Are you so arrogant as to think no one can tell you anything?"

But he had had enough. He glanced at his watch. "I think I've wasted enough time. I just wanted to say that I'm glad to see you up and about. If there's anything you want, just let me know."

"I hope I won't have to."

"I realize that, but the offer still stands. You could tell Farley when he returns that I hope he won't take his anger out on Neil. We'll look forward to him dining with us—and crocodile-hunting if he feels like it." He turned on his heel and left her.

She picked up a magazine, then flung it down angrily. Oh, what was the use with a man like that!

As dusk fell the following evening they heard Neil Brand's truck long before it came into sight. After an earlier show of nonchalance Sandy was suddenly excited to see his father. He tugged at Sally's hand. "Come with me and meet him, I've got so much to tell him."

"Then you won't want me," she laughed, but she allowed herself to be led.

Ross, leaning over the veranda rail smoking his pipe, turned to Jo and said idly, "Has Sally got any strong ties in England?"

"Someone special, you mean?"

He nodded.

"No," Jo answered, "there's no one special." She looked at him shrewdly. "Why do you ask?"

"She would make someone a wonderful wife," he mused.

She turned quickly away, struggling with the small flare of jealousy. Neil, now Ross. Could Sally never do any wrong?

She led the way down into the garden as Sandy and his father, chattering a mile a minute, approached the house. Sally walked alongside them adding her comments when asked for.

"Well, it all sounds great," Neil put his hand on his son's shoulder, "but you mean to tell me that no one has been eaten by a lion?"

He was rewarded by a withering glance that abruptly changed to one of triumph. "No, but Jo was bitten by a snake—a green mamba!"

Neil glanced at the bandage on Jo's leg as he shook hands with her. "Well, you've got scars to prove it, by the look of things. Exaggeration or truth from my son?"

"It was a snake all right," she laughed, "but there seems some doubt about the identification. Anyway, Ross dealt with it very swiftly."

"Yes, he would," Neil said calmly, and turned to his friend. "Oddly enough I was going to ask you last time how you were off for serum."

They all continued companionably into the house, and while Neil showered, Ross poured them all drinks. So Bruce was not coming tonight, Jo thought with a pang of disappointment. She wanted him beside her so much. And yet in another way she was less certain of being able to cope with icy politeness between the two men. Perhaps tomorrow was better after all. Another day to cool down and perhaps she would be able to talk to him first. At least Neil would be a calming influence.

Once again Sally had produced a magnificent dinner, organizing it without fuss, but she pinked with delight at all the compliments.

"We must have guests more often," Ross winked at his friend, as he raised his glass to Sally. "It gets away from the interminable warthog—or buffalo tail!" That last was aimed at Jo, but tonight she was able to laugh with the others.

"Talking of guests," Neil sat back in his chair, happy and replete, "I've had a couple of talks with my brother about your safari idea. He's over-enthusiastic if anything, so I thought I'd better play down Nyala's amenities. He says he could produce six people tomorrow, but can't you take more? I told him no quite firmly—at least until you were organized, but he seems to think this operation could be run something like a private grouse shoot in England. The individuality of the thing being the keynote—living *en famille,* etc. Anyway, I told him I was only the go-between and had no idea how near you were to starting the thing, so he had a proposal to make. As soon as you even think you can cope with, say, four guests, he'll come down himself with three guinea pigs. You will treat them exactly as you would any strangers and at the end of the week he—and they—can tell you where you're going right or wrong, give any suggestions about the future and, of course, about cost. They'll pay their way, naturally, but you did say you had no idea what to charge people. Well, that's his province. Now, what do you say to that?"

Sally looked across at Ross. "I feel a bit overwhelmed. When do you think we would be ready?"

He smiled wryly. "Never, if it were left to me. When do you think you could have two guest-houses ready?"

Sally looked thoughtful. "Well, if Jo and I sew hard, and that now is really all there is, less than a week. But that's only the beginning."

"I know. But say another week to plan supplies of food and make sure the place is in working order, then we could certainly cope with four guinea pigs."

"Two weeks, then," Neil nodded. "I'll radio him first thing on Monday when I get back."

Jo and Sally's eyes met in faint panic. They were now being rushed, when before it had been the other way around. "Do you really think we can manage it?" Jo said faintly.

"You'll have to," Ross pointed out. "Your three months are slipping away. Besides, let's get a test case over. Neil's brother might see all kinds of difficulties that we can't possibly cope with. Then we would have to do a huge rethink."

So the matter seemed to be settled, and once again Jo marveled at the way Ross had coaxed Sally to do what he wanted almost without her realizing. She did not know whether she was pleased or irritated. But she did suddenly think that the prospects of holding on to Nyala were not quite so gloomy after all.

As they sat drinking coffee afterward, Neil looked at them all and, with a glint in his eye, challenged them. "Who's game for crocodile-hunting tonight?"

The girls said nothing. Ross, of course, took up the

challenge. "Well, tonight's good enough for a start, since you've only got tomorrow with us. We could get the feel of the river at least."

Sandy rushed across to his father. "You are going to let me come, aren't you?"

"On two conditions. One, that you go to bed immediately so that you get a couple of hours' sleep, and second, that when we're out you do exactly what you're told, without a single question. If you fail in that, there'll be a three-year wait for the next go."

Sandy nodded and without a word disappeared to his room.

Ross checked the time and said, "Well, I've a couple of things to do first. Look after the girls, Neil, for half an hour; then we'll go out and check the equipment and the boat."

"Aren't you afraid for Sandy?" Jo said curiously. "I know he's marvelously adaptable, but *crocodiles*. . . ."

Neil smiled. "I'm not afraid for him, because I trust him. Even so I wouldn't take him yet to somewhere like Okavango, where it's all done by boats and in the right areas there are more crocs than humans. No, tonight isn't a real hunt. To start with I guarantee there are only two adult beasts and they must be in a fairly limited stretch of the river. I'll be the only one in a boat; the rest of you—if you two are coming—will be on land. I'm afraid you could hardly call this the real thing, but it's a good enough start for amateurs."

Jo was still deciding whether she would join the hunting party and try to rid herself of her fear when she heard Sally say, "Neil, now we both have you on our own for a moment, there's something we wanted to ask you."

"Go ahead, it sounds very mysterious."

"It's about Uncle Harold. You see, we know so little about him. But last year he did ask you to look us up without giving away your connection with him, didn't he?"

He hesitated only a second. "I'm afraid he did. I hope you don't think it was too underhanded. At the time, I did as he asked; there seemed no harm in it."

"No, it doesn't matter at all," Sally said, "but it would be interesting to know why Jo was left out of the will when you must surely have reported that there were three of us. It doesn't matter anyway, because what's Alan's and mine is Jo's too, but we felt there had to be a reason."

"To answer all that properly would be to know and understand your uncle. I knew him and I liked him, but I never really understood him. Deep down he was an unhappy man. He had never talked of his family in England until he heard that I was going, and then he gave me this commission to find out all I could about you. It seemed terribly important to him that I should think a lot of you so that in turn he could have the right image of you all. I think he wanted to feel you could do things for yourselves, just like he did. Hence possibly the odd will concerning Nyala.

"But as far as Jo is concerned, one of the last things he said to me was before I left, 'Find out if there's a third child. After all these years I must know.' Of course I came back and told him that Jo was very much alive and kicking. And that's another funny thing, Jo. I also told him that I would have known you were his niece anywhere. Same coloring, even the same rather forthright nose, if you'll forgive me. I suppose you take after your father."

"No," said Jo flatly, "I was always the odd man out in the family, nothing like either my father or mother."

A sudden silence fell and they must all have been thinking the same thing. Jo was thinking of all those books about Africa in the trunk in the attic.

Neil said gently, "I'm a clumsy great fool, aren't I? Now I've filled both your minds with the kind of doubts that we can never answer. I'm sorry, truly sorry."

"It's all right." Jo got up quickly. "I'll be back in a

minute, just want to get my croc-hunting gear together," she finished with an attempt at lightness.

She went to her room and leaned out the window into the cool of the night. So the mystery was solved—or was it? She thought of her parents and how happy they had been together before they died, and even the special place, as youngest of the family, she had had in her father's heart. Those facts she was quite, quite sure of. So whatever had happened in the past had no influence on her present life, only the fact that she was here, at Nyala now.

It was foolish to be so suddenly moved near to tears. More than anything now she wished she had met her uncle—just once. But wishing was only for children, so she dashed her face in cold water and dried it thoroughly, then turned to go back.

No, she didn't feel sociable now.

She sat in the darkness feeling suddenly lonely, wishing that Bruce was here. Was she really the outsider she felt herself to be at the moment?

In a pool of light from the house she saw Ross walk across the yard. He hesitated a moment as though he sensed he were being watched. He was alone and did not seem to mind. But his life was dependent on none. In some strange way that provoked her. One day she would show Ross Andrews she was not the willful child he thought she was. One day she would be able to take him down a peg or two.

CHAPTER TEN

From ten to ten-thirty the household seemed to be in a whirl of activity. Both girls wisely kept out of the way, except when asked to do a specific job. When everything was ready they woke Sandy.

All were wearing long pants and boots when they met outside for final instructions. Kari and two others were also there to lend a hand.

Neil examined the sky. Fortunately it was a dark, moonless night, the only real possibility for successful hunting. Ross had marked the crocodiles down to a particular stretch of the river and that had been sectioned off with weighted netting into two halves. They would do one tonight and the other tomorrow.

In the boat was Neil, gun at the ready, with Kari acting as both steersman and oarsman. They would start to move silently down river, in complete darkness, to give as little warning as possible, hoping to pick up the gimlet glare of those ruby red eyes. Ross and the others would move down the bank, always ahead of the boat, hoping for a chance shot. Otherwise they had ropes at the ready to haul their captive ashore, and also an ax for the final blow across the spine.

Jo was not exactly looking forward to the event, but she could not be left out now and, besides, tense excitement was being generated through them all. Even the Africans, used to a surfeit of game, were aware that a crocodile kill was unusual at Nyala.

For the first hour nothing much happened, as Kari rowed steadily downstream, slowly, going from bank to bank whenever the river broadened.

Suddenly there was a subtle tightening of the atmosphere, and although nothing had actually changed, they were all still, waiting. Even the quiet dip of the oars had ceased.

Jo strained her eyes, staring at the dim outline of the boat, and the space just ahead of it. As the lamp at the prow was switched on, where Neil was sitting with gun poised, she caught a glimpse of the two jutting red eyes, glowing, just a few inches apart. As the monster became aware of the boat, it rose slightly, ready to submerge, and at that moment Neil fired.

He hit it all right, Jo saw that, but it was not to be the end of this particular crocodile. She had heard stories of the horror of thrashing tails and the great horny bodies maneuvering to tip the marauding boat, but somehow, seeing this great beast in action was much more horrifying than mere imagination. The spray from its lashing tail drenched everyone, but all the men stayed exactly at their posts, waiting for the moment to kill.

Sally clutched at Jo. "It looks terribly dangerous. Nothing would ever get me in one of those boats!"

Jo felt too afraid for Neil and Kari even to answer. The light from the prow of the boat picked out the scene like something from a science fiction movie.

Suddenly the monstrous head reared high above the water; there was a single shot and as it started to sink, the men on the bank threw the rope and hooks. A few minutes later it lay on the bank. Cautiously both Sally and Jo approached and looked down. Most animals, however wild, looked peaceful, almost harmless, in death; but not the crocodile. The rows of vicious teeth were still locked in a snarl.

Neil landed the boat and came to examine his catch. "Not a large one, I'm afraid, but female. The point is, has she any young around here?"

"Or a mate," put in Ross.

"If he's around, then we'll find him tomorrow, but if by

any chance we don't—well, he won't stay around here for long, a single lone croc."

Sandy was bending down, fingering the horny skin with interest. "What's it worth, Dad?"

"A lady's small purse, I daresay, you mercenary young scamp. Now, off to bed with you, pronto!"

Sandy's face fell and as he backed away added, "You're not going to skin it tonight, are you?"

"No, we're not. It's much too late. Don't worry, I won't let you miss anything."

Sally was still looking taken aback when Neil said to her with a smile, "I'm afraid he's still going through the ghoulish stage."

Sally shuddered. "I envy him. I wish I had such a strong stomach."

"It's something you'll get if you stay out here long enough."

He gave orders for the crocodile to be left immersed in water until the morning, then he would supervise the skinning operation. Both Jo and Sally turned thankfully away.

Ross was relieved that at least one crocodile had been found. "You've earned a celebration drink, Neil, doing my dirty work for me."

Neil shook his head. "You should know by now it's not work to me, but pleasure. It's good to get my eye in shape before going up to Okavango."

As they walked back to the house Jo said curiously, "What's it like up there, and how many crocs do you get in a night?"

"On a good night maybe six or seven. It depends how lucky I am, or how energetic, and how many men I take with me. As to the country, it's difficult to describe. On the edge of the swampland is a broad river, crystal clear and wonderful to drink. You can see pike and bream and incredible shoals of sardines. And on its banks are some of the most beautiful butterflies in the world, painted in every brilliant color you can think of. And of course there are the birds, blue rollers, bee-eaters, and sacred ibis, again in every imaginable color."

"It sounds like paradise."

"It is but even paradise has its serpents, mosquitoes and tsetse flies, and the dangers of malaria and sleeping sickness. And," he added dryly, "you have to watch out for rabies!"

They had moved into the sitting room and Saku produced nightcaps for them all. Jo discovered she was very wide awake and persuaded Neil to go on talking.

"Well," he continued, "you have to get used to the smell of croc—you had a slight whiff of it tonight—then you go inland, into the real swamps. Sometimes the river is only a few feet wide, sometimes there are broad lagoons. Everywhere the vegetation is thick—tall reeds stretching endlessly along the banks, with papyrus and all kinds of trees. The land is dangerous; you're never quite sure whether you are stepping onto terra firma, or merely an island, looking safe enough, but in reality composed of all the entangled roots of the reeds.

"The swamplands have a kind of beauty all their own. You either love it or long to escape from it. It is certainly another world. And the game . . . well, apart from the crocodiles, you'll find plenty of hippo . . . and very tetchy they can be . . . as well as leopard and elephant. You've also got to get used to even more mosquitoes, tsetse flies and particularly nasty leeches." He looked across at the two girls, listening enthralled. "Well, have I put you off for life, or do you want to come on my next trip?"

Both laughed and Jo said stoutly, "Well, give me another few months, until I've overcome all the problems of Nyala, then I'd be willing. But I don't think I could ever really get used to the crocodiles. One is bad enough, but seeing them in quantity. . . ." She shivered.

As they finally stood up, stretching, agreeing that it had been a wonderful evening, the headlights of a truck pierced the darkness outside. Jo's heart leaped. Bruce was home!

Neil, knowing nothing of the tensions between Bruce and Ross, said, "What a pity. Bruce looks as if he's arrived just an hour too late. Still, let's hope we have the same luck tomorrow night."

Jo doubted whether Bruce would come up to the house that evening, but he had apparently run short of water and arrived only a few minutes later, carrying an empty drum.

Neil hailed him. "I was just saying you'd missed all the excitement. Crocodiles. How have you been doing out in the prospecting field?"

"Too early to say. There are both good signs and bad signs. I'm a poor speculator. Anyway, good to see you again, Neil." He smiled at Sally and came directly across to Jo and kissed her.

She felt rather than saw Ross's disapproval. That made her response more eager. There was something very final about a public kiss, almost like an announcement. She put aside the thought that with all the difficulties that still lay ahead, it might have been better for their relationship to remain private.

He let his arms rest possessively across her shoulders. "How's the leg, darling?"

"Much better. I only notice it if I'm standing for some time. There was so much going on this evening down by the river I didn't even give it a thought. Neil caught a vicious-looking crocodile. You'll have to come and look at it in the morning." She found herself speaking quickly, as if to cover up his intimacy toward her.

Ross said abruptly, "For me, it's time for bed. Thanks again, Neil. I'll see you in the morning."

"Did you remember to lock up Holly?" Jo asked him. She had made herself responsible for this before the snakebite, but had forgotten for a couple of days.

"Of course. She's as safe as houses. But you do realize it will soon be time to let her join her own kind?" He was watching her with that cool, unnerving gaze.

"Naturally," she retorted, "but not just yet. She's still only a baby."

"Even babies have to grow up," was his parting shot.

Once again Jo went to bed angry with Ross. He still took pleasure in rubbing her the wrong way. She would have liked to go out with Bruce when he took the water back, but as she made the move, Sally's hand was like steel on her arm.

Outside their bedrooms, Jo shook her off. "You're not my guardian, you know, only a sister."

"Even a sister can tell you two not to make such a public display—I know, I know," she added tiredly, when Jo started to protest, "it's not my business to stop you falling in love or making a fool of yourself. But you know perfectly well how difficult things are here and with a potentially explosive situation between Ross and Bruce, heaven knows what could happen. Just at this very moment we need a happy working team if we're going to put on a show for this first safari, not friction and bad temper."

"You've made yourself perfectly clear," Jo said coldly. "Now, do you mind if I go to bed?" she closed the door behind her with a snap.

Jo was awakened by an odd noise outside her window. At first she thought it was a bird, until she realized it was some kind of tapping. She glanced at her watch. It was not even six o'clock.

She threw on a housecoat and crossed to the window.

Bruce was outside clad only in a pair of shorts. He put a finger to his lips and beckoned to her to come down to his camp. She nodded and did not stop to do more than comb her hair and slip on shorts and a shirt.

The coffee pot was already heating on his small fire. He looked up at the sound of her steps. "I couldn't sleep, so I decided to wake you up to share my wakefulness with me. Did you mind?"

"Did I mind? Don't be silly." She took the hand held out to her and sat down beside him. "I . . . I would have come down last night, but I didn't think it was a very politic move."

"Don't tell me Jo, that you care what people think."

"Of course not." Her denial was immediate. "At this moment I care about you very much, but I also care about Nyala. You want it to be a success as much as I do."

"Naturally. Come here, I can't have you looking as worried as that."

When he let her go, she was breathless, wondering why she was even faintly worried at him kissing her last night. Let them all see. Let them all know. She was proud of their feelings for each other. But somehow she must try to keep the peace.

"Bruce," she began, "I've got a favor to ask you."

His eyes half closed and he smiled lazily. "I know, be friends with your Mr. Andrews."

"He's not my Mr. Andrews, and I don't want you to be friends with him, just to get along with him until things are settled one way or another."

"Why not ask him?"

"I will if you want me to, but I hardly know him, at least not in such a personal way."

"Aren't you being a little naïve, Jo?"

"Naïve?" She was puzzled. "I don't know what you mean."

"No, I don't believe you do. You may not know him in

what you call a personal way, but he would certainly like to know you a little better."

She stared at him. "You must be mad! He thinks I'm some kind of nincompoop he's got to put up with for three months. He hardly ever tries to make the best of it, except when he's being patronizing."

"Then you haven't seen the way he looks at you. Why do you think I marched in and kissed you like that last night? Not just to embarrass you, Jo, I promise you. No, to show them what I felt about you. To stake my claim, if you like. Even your sister has been influenced by Andrews. The next thing we'll hear is that Neil Brand is joining in the general disapproval."

"Oh, Bruce, I don't know what to say. You're wrong about Ross, I know you are. It all stems from my wretched snakebite."

"No. No, not really, although it didn't help. I'm afraid my opinion of him isn't as high as yours. I think he probably knows a fair amount about game, but I don't think he runs this place half as competently as you think he does. I suppose you've thought what he would gain if he could persuade you onto his side."

"His side? But I'm not on anyone's side," she cried. "Only Nyala's. I love it here; I really do. To me Ross is just part of the place like Kari, or Saku . . . or even Goldie," she said helplessly. "You can't really be jealous, Bruce."

"I am. I'm jealous of any man who looks at you like he does. Covetous is the word. Ross Andrews is out to feather his nest, nothing more. And that's the reason I don't trust him with you, or Nyala."

Jo did not know what to say. She always knew that loving Bruce was not going to be easy, but that he should feel so strongly about Ross was ridiculous. Somehow she had to convince him that Ross was merely doing his job. With absolute certainty she knew his opinion of her was not very high. And it really didn't matter except—except there was something disconcerting about that cool, calculating gaze he sometimes turned on her.

Suddenly there was a noise from the house. It sounded like Sandy shouting. And then the calling became shrill. "Ross, Ross . . . Dad! Please come quickly!"

Jo jumped up, startled. "Something's wrong, Bruce, we must go." She let go of his hand and started to run across the patch of land from the river.

The commotion came from the back of the house. There she found Sandy, sobbing wildly, clinging to his father. Beside them Ross stood, watching the swinging door of Holly's empty cage, his eyes empty of emotion.

Jo looked from one man to another. "Where is she?"

"The door was open like this," Ross said bluntly. "Someone must have come after I did last night."

Jo's heart sank. She knew what little chance a trusting young animal like Holly would have in Nyala. "Have you looked for her?" she demanded.

"Not yet."

"Well, let's start." And when Ross hesitated she added savagely, jerking her head toward Sandy, "Well, it's worth doing something, isn't it?"

It was Ross who found Holly's remains, not 300 yards from the house. When he told Sandy, quite directly, yet with great gentleness, the boy did not flinch. The bush was a hard school in which to learn. And after all, his crying had already been done.

But Jo was near to tears, remembering the gentle brown eyes, the delicate movements, the gradual building up of absolute trust. One of the worst things in the world, she decided, was to have one's faith shattered.

Sandy went off with his father and Saku told them that breakfast was ready. Jo turned to Ross. "No one would have deliberately opened the door, it's just not possible. I suppose checking to see that it was closed was too lowly a job for you after all. If you'd only asked me last night, or Sally. . . ."

"You judge people harshly, don't you? Your standards for others are not very high. But, of course, I forget, I'm the sort of man who sets lions on visitors, so it would be quite in keeping to throw a mere fawn to the predators."

"Now you're being sarcastic," she returned, perilously near to tears. "Why can't you ever face the truth?"

"Because I happen to be a man who feels very strongly about the truth." Now his face was black and thunderous. Only five minutes ago it had been full of gentleness when he talked to Sandy. "I may have many, many faults, but telling lies is not one of them. Before you accuse so wildly just look into the purity of your own motives. You've got to grow up, Jo. I don't think we shall get Nyala successfully on its feet as long as your friend Farley is here."

"That's exactly what he said about you!" she hurled back at him.

She hadn't meant to say that, because she was now doing exactly what she had begged Bruce not to—raise the already sizzling temperature at Nyala.

They were still standing facing each other, perhaps both wishing they could retract the hurtful words, when Sally came out. She quickly took in the strained atmosphere, but it was to Ross she turned.

"I think," she said, "there's a message coming through to you on the radio telephone."

"Thank you, Sally," he said politely, and as he turned to go he paused. "Oh, by the way, your sister really does think that Bruce Farley can do my job better than I can. Perhaps you would talk things over with her and decide once and for all whether you want me to stay or not. It's your decision, Sally. There's only room for one warden at Nyala."

Sally watched him go, then looked at her younger sister up and down. "Well, you really are determined to muck things up, aren't you? Why," she sighed, "do you have to lose your temper every time you get upset?"

For once Jo did not hit back at Sally. "It was Holly," she said helplessly. "I kept thinking of her. If I hadn't been bitten by that wretched snake then it would still have been my responsibility to see she was locked up. Instead, it was left to Ross, and he failed."

"Are you so sure about that?"

Jo raised her shoulders and let them fall again. "What else could it be?"

"I doubt if we'll ever know," Sally said, "so it would be better not to toss the blame around without being sure of facts. Holly is dead and it's horrible; but even Sandy is man enough to admit that he realized that soon Holly had to go back where she came from, and the same thing could have happened there. Only he added, very wisely, 'In that case we would never have known, would we?' "

When Jo was silent, Sally went on inexorably. "Tell me, Jo—if you don't think much of Ross and I don't think much of Bruce, what do we both think of Neil? Would you trust his judgment, instinctively?"

"Oh, yes," said Jo, walking straight into the neat trap prepared for her.

"He told me earlier on that he thought that Ross was one of the finest game wardens in Africa. If he failed anywhere it would be because his sense of responsibility was too strong for his own good. He said a lot of other things too, but I won't bore you with them. You might not listen to me. Anyway, that's the man whom you and Bruce Farley are doing your damnedest to denigate. What he needs is a bit of help with the job he's trying desperately to do, not criticism."

Jo swallowed. Perhaps Sally was right, she was too confused and upset to think straight.

Sally touched her arm. "Come on, Jo, let's go in and have some breakfast. I personally can't do anything constructive on an empty stomach." And as they both turned to go, she added softly, "I had a good evening yesterday. I shall always remember it. You enjoyed yourself too, didn't you?"

Jo nodded. She still did not trust herself to speak. In spite of her dislike of crocodiles the evening had been rather special.

"And I'm not going to say it was because Bruce wasn't there," Sally said dryly.

Jo found her voice at last. It came out small and tight. "There's something you ought to know, Sal. Even if I ever admit to being mistaken about Ross, that still doesn't alter the way I feel about Bruce."

"I didn't expect it to," Sally replied. "I just wanted to know where we stood, that's all."

Jo tore her mind away from her own problems and said impulsively, "You like Neil, don't you?"

"Yes," answered Sally, and her cheeks were faintly pink, "I've never met anyone quite like him before."

They came in to find both Ross and Neil in the sitting room, gulping down a cup of coffee and snatching a bite of breakfast.

"What is it?" said Sally. "Has something else gone wrong?"

"You could say that the day hasn't started well." Ross yelled for a servant and told Saku to find Tau, and be sure there was plenty of gas in the truck.

Sally waited. She had learned that Ross would tell them in his own good time.

"I've just had a message from the ranger over on the eastern border to say that he thinks that the only water-hole in operation there has been poisoned. It seems," he added, glancing from Sally to Jo, "that I'm not looking after your interests very well after all."

CHAPTER ELEVEN

"Poisoned waterhole?" Jo repeated foolishly, not quite understanding. "What does that mean?"

"By my reading," he said in a tired voice, drained of emotion, "someone has chucked something unpleasant into the last few inches of water over there. The water will be death to drink, so we'll probably lose all the game in that area that can't move fast enough to either the river or fresh water, unless it rains. Unfortunately the eastern border is most vulnerable, because it's about the most widely spaced hole on the reserve.

"Ah, Neil," he turned in relief as his friend returned, "I'm glad you're around. We're in trouble." And he explained with the minimum of words what had happened. "I'm going over there immediately. Do you feel like coming?"

"Of course. I'm ready now, except for collecting my gun. Would it help to use my truck? I've only just had it serviced, so it may be in better shape than yours."

"Anything is in better shape than ours," Ross said wryly, "but it might be a good idea. It will leave ours free for Kari if he needs it. Unfortunately he's off on a regular 24-hour check-up; probably won't be back until later this morning." He turned to the girls and spoke brusquely.

"Tell him exactly what's happened when he comes. It's the Koanaka hole. It seems fairly certain that if this is serious, then the same band of poachers who've been troubling us recently are responsible for this. There's even a remote chance he's seen something of them, because he's been traveling in an easterly direction. If he's got any idea at all of tracking them, tell him to take anyone he can and go off in the truck. But no rough stuff," he warned. "They'll be armed, probably four or five of them.

I just want to get them off the reserve before they can do any more damage. Understood?"

Sally and Jo nodded.

"Is there anything at all we can do?" Sally asked.

"No, thanks, just keep an eye on Sandy and on the radio telephone. There's an unusual amount of static on it. Oh, and you could ask Saku to pack up some food."

But Saku needed no telling for a job like that. Food was all ready by the time Neil had filled his own truck with gas.

They went outside to watch the men leave. Tau was in the back of the truck and Goldie stood beside Jo. The lion seemed uneasy and made little whimpering noises as she watched Ross leave, almost as if she knew her beloved master was driving into trouble.

Neil started up the engine. "Take care!" Sally called. Both men turned and smiled and waved at her.

Jo said nothing to Ross, but after he had gone she half-wished she had. His face was a tight mask of anxiety.

"It's times like these," Sally said slowly after they had gone, "that you realize how helpless we are and the absolute value of men like Neil and Ross."

"Neil, yes," Jo said sharply, "but I'm not so sure about Ross. It was he who said he had let us down, not us. Perhaps he was right."

"Oh, Jo, now you're being ridiculous; you saw how he looked. What on earth do you think he could have done to prevent something like this? The only thing we can hope for is that there's been some genuine mistake and the waterhole isn't poisoned after all. How on earth would anyone poison it, anyway?"

"With all the odd things growing in the bush," Jo pointed out. "How do you think the Bushmen poison the tips of their arrows? There must be dozens of concoctions in a vast country like this."

"Well, apart from that, let's get one thing clear Jo—if,

when they return there is real trouble, just you even hint that the blame may lie with Ross and I swear I'll see that you never get a cent of Nyala!"

Jo stared at her gentle, easy-going sister. "You really must be joking."

"I've never been more serious in my life."

Without thinking, Jo snapped, "Isn't it time you made up your mind which of those two you're hanging your shirt on?" She stalked off to find Bruce before she could see the whiteness of her sister's face.

Bruce was cleaning the points of his truck. He looked up as she came down the slope to the river.

"Well, darling, I'm sorry to desert you like that, but I thought there were enough people crying over the loss of one pet fawn."

For a second she didn't know what he was talking about. What had happened since had pushed the tragedy of Holly out of her mind.

"I suppose," he added, "your friend Ross had left the cage door open."

"Perhaps, but I doubt if we'll ever really know. Anyway, there's been more trouble to take our minds off Holly." And she told him about the waterhole.

Bruce stood up and stretched his big frame, then wiped his oily hands on a rag. "That sounds like one more nail in the coffin of your frien ' Andrews."

"What . . . what do you mean?" she said quickly.

"On an efficiently run reserve that kind of thing simply doesn't happen. That's why you have a staff of rangers, to prevent troubles like that. Something must be wrong somewhere in this set-up, and while Andrews obviously didn't do it himself he has to be held responsible, just like in any business. You know, Jo,' he added, seeing her worried face, "with just a few more "accidents" like this what little stake you have in Nyala will slip right away."

She was silent for a moment, then, as if trying to prove

a point to herself, she said, "Neil said he was a very good game warden."

"Jo, my love, Neil Brand is a very good man and like all good men he believes the best of everyone. Andrews is his friend, isn't he? Look, I'm not saying he doesn't know anything about animals, game in general, but that's a far cry from being wholly responsible for an area the size of your own county at home."

Again Jo was silent. She suddenly felt very low in spirit; the need to get away from Nyala, away from Sally and all her disapproval, was stronger than anything.

She said at last, "Will you be staying here today, Bruce?"

"No, I'm going to the site, leaving shortly. I'm just getting to an interesting point there. Today may even prove whether it's worth my mounting a decent-sized operation." Her face fell so much that he added casually, "I suppose it's no good asking whether you'd like to come along too? I'll be back around dark tonight."

Her face lit up with joy. He bent down and kissed her. "You're a marvelous girl, Jo. You don't try and hide your feelings. I like that." He glanced down at his watch. "If you could be ready in 20 minutes, we'll make a start then."

Sally was angry when she told her. Sandy also looked disappointed, but she noticed he did not ask to come. He was still influenced in this general feeling against Bruce.

He followed her down the veranda steps where, a few minutes later, she was putting on stronger shoes. He watched her for a long time before saying suddenly, "I asked my dad if you might marry Mr. Farley. He said you could if you wanted to. You're not going to, Jo, are you?"

"I don't know, Sandy," she replied honestly. "I like Mr. Farley very much; but we haven't talked about getting married yet."

"Well, I jolly well hope you don't," he said fiercely.

Jo was puzzled by his attitude. "You mustn't say things like that, Sandy. Mr. Farley is a very nice man. Besides, you didn't feel like this about him when you first came over, or when he drove you over here from home."

"That was before your snakebite," he pointed out.

"Look, Sandy," she said gently, "you think he acted wrongly about my bite—well, I honestly don't know, but you can't go through your life disliking people because they do one thing you disapprove of. Everyone makes mistakes."

"It's not just that," he retorted. "He doesn't like Ross, and anyone who doesn't like Ross is my enemy. And I don't like the way he talks to Kari and Saku and his own men. Dad and Ross wouldn't say the things he does."

Jo had no answer to that because she did not know what he meant. It was time, she decided, to end this conversation. She went inside and told Sally what she was doing, reminding her unnecessarily to pass all the messages on to Kari.

"That's something I'm not likely to forget," Sally said in a chilly, un-Sally-like voice.

"I suppose you think I should stay here."

Sally sighed. "Probably, but today it's better that you're out of my sight. One of us will say something more we'll regret."

Jo's spirits began to lift from the moment the house disappeared behind the morning haze. It seemed hotter than ever and Bruce had warned her that his site did not have much shade, but it was not too far from a tiny branch of a river.

They reached the area after about an hour and a half, driving through a part of the reserve Jo had not seen before. There seemed little game, apart from small groups of buck, in this part, but more than likely what there was was taking refuge from the heat.

He had chosen an open area, with just a small group of

trees under which his two workers had built a rough shelter and a small cooking fire.

She watched, fascinated, during the next hour while they dug a deep square pit from which Bruce extracted the sand and gravel, washed it in one of the open drums of water that had been brought from the river, sieved it, then finally turned the sieve upside down on the makeshift sorting table.

He explained to her, "If there were diamond here it would come to the top in this way, because it's heavier than the rest of the gravel."

"I suppose you haven't found anything yet?" she asked, picking over the fine material with her fingers, enjoying the cool wet feeling of the gravel, wishing she could be the one to make the first strike.

"No, I'm a long way from that, but I have found some interesting minerals, which are just the kind that would have been washed down the river with diamonds thousands of years ago."

"But there's no river where you're digging?" she remarked.

"I know, but this is where the expertise comes in. I'm gambling on the fact of this area once—oh, hundreds of years ago—having been the course of the river. I spent the first two days here surveying, after hours over at Neil's place studying the map. Geologically it's possible. These rivers generally changed their course over the thousands of years."

As the day wore on Jo found it too hot to remain near where Bruce was working with the minimum of shade. He seemed impervious to the heat, but she went over to the shelter of the trees. Even here, she reckoned the temperature must be well over 100. She sat back and wondered idly how far away Ross and Neil were, whether their worst fears had been founded.

As usual she had spoken too impulsively to Sally this

morning. She loathed quarreling with her sister. Perhaps both she and Bruce were judging Ross too harshly. Certainly she never found herself looking for the best in him, only the worst.

Very stongly an unbidden picture of him came into her mind. That taut, worried expression masking all his other feelings. Perhaps he did care deeply about Nyala, after all. Perhaps he missed Uncle Harold more than they realized. Perhaps . . . but she closed her eyes, not wanting to think about Ross Andrews. He was too disturbing a man.

From above her Bruce spoke. "Time for a break, darling. And you look desperately worried. What's wrong?"

She shook her head, not wanting to confide in him. Instead she reached out her hand and let it rest in his. "I wish," he said softly, pushing a damp strand of hair away from her forehead, "I could always look up from my digging or washing and see you sitting there."

He sat down beside her and poured her a glass of lemon from the flask that already seemed too hot to hold. "You know, Jo, you and I could do wonderful things together, even with this place. When you and Sally own it, which by God, I'm going to make sure you do, there's nothing you won't be able to do with it. Let's drink to that day, Jo darling, even in tepid lemonade."

But she paused, guilty suddenly that she had not after all taken him completely into her confidence.

"Bruce. . . ."

"Yes, darling?" He bent and kissed her and she clung to him, as though afraid he might vanish once again.

"There's something I haven't told you."

"A secret?"

"No . . . or rather it's something that Sally and I decided to keep to ourselves. Our plans for the future. You see, Nyala can never really be ours."

He drew away from her, frowning. "You mean you don't think it's possible to make it pay? Well, I. . . ."

"No, not that, although I do think we have only a small chance. No, if we do prove we can manage, then as soon as Nyala becomes ours, or rather Sally and Alan's, then we're committed to selling it. That's the only reason we came out here. I never dreamed I would fall in love with Nyala," she said sadly.

He gripped her with both arms and for a moment his anger was quite frightening. "Sell it? Sell Nyala? Jo, you must be out of your mind! Who's been getting at you—Sally?"

"No, no, of course not. Please, Bruce, you're hurting me. I'll tell you why, only you must try to understand."

"Go on," he said ominously.

"Well, it's Alan, really. He sacrificed so much for Sally and myself. He's had his heart set on one dream for years now. He wants to buy a small hotel right on the edge of the moor called the Crag Inns. Oh, it's a marvelous place; in an English way, very wild and beautiful. Now it's for sale for the first time, and he thinks he could get first option, because the old ladies who own it have a soft spot for him. Unfortunately, he hasn't a hope of raising the money, even half of it. But with Nyala, this is one way Sally and I can help him."

Bruce raised his hands and let them fall helplessly. "So you would let all this go for a . . . a whim of your brother's?"

"It's not a whim, Bruce, and I told you I have no choice. Alan is my brother; I suppose a very special kind of brother. And while it will break my heart to part with Nyala, unless I won the lottery or a premium bond or something, nothing would make me change my mind. In any case the final decision would rest with Sally. I couldn't fight against that."

His eyes were closed as if in pain. She had seen Bruce angry briefly, but usually his big square face was full of laughter. She had never seen him like this. And why? In some ways his concern was curiously misplaced.

"And to think," he said despairingly, "to think what I wanted to do for you, what I did for you. . . ."

"What do you mean?" She stared at him.

But she was not going to find out that day. There was a sudden flurry of movement from the center of the site. The two men working there suddenly put down their spades. They seemed to be jabbering excitedly and as Bruce strained his eyes and muttered, "What the hell's wrong now?" they both started to run over to the distant thorn trees.

With one accord Bruce and Jo stood up.

"There's someone over there," Jo said sharply. "It's not an animal, it's a man."

"One of their pals, no doubt. If they don't get back to work in ten minutes, I'll dock them an hour's pay."

But Jo was not listening, only staring. "It may be an African, Bruce, but there's something wrong with him—see the way they're pulling him along. Please, we must take the truck along and see if we can do anything."

"As you wish." He got up grudgingly and walked across to the truck.

A few minutes later he drew up in a cloud of dust, where his two workers were supporting the other man. His leg was bleeding and almost useless, while his dark face was a mask of sweat and pain.

"Oh, Bruce," she cried, "it's the one we call Kwane, Kari's assistant. Please find out what happened. He can hardly speak any English."

For the next few moments Bruce and Kwane jabbered away, each only half understanding the other. The man could not stand, so Jo persuaded him into the passenger seat of the truck. He leaned back against the seat, physically near the end of his endurance.

"Bruce, what is it, please tell me," she pleaded.

"As far as I can understand some poachers had a pot shot at him, and Kari's gone off after them."

The man's hunted eyes looked from one to the other. "No, no, Kari sick. Very hurt. Find Kari."

"There, you see," she flung at him, "there is something seriously wrong. Kari's hurt!"

"The fellow's dramatizing things. Good grief, Kari's a Bushman; he can find his way out of anything."

"Not if he's shot like this man," she snapped. "We've got to get him back to the house and then send out some help."

"Look, Jo, you're a babe in arms as far as this country is concerned. These men are used to far tougher hazards than this. I can't afford to go dashing back when all he needs is some clean water and disinfectant, both of which I have. Come on, we'll get the truck back in the shade."

"And Kari?" she said tightly.

"I've told you, he's an African. He's well able to take care of himself."

They reached the trees, and he handed her the first-aid box and some spare drinking water. She did not trust herself to speak.

He smiled down at her. "Take that martyred expression off your face, Jo, it doesn't suit you. You can't put the wrongs of all the natives to rights, there are other more important things."

"Like diamonds?"

He shrugged. "For the moment, yes. I'll go down and finish up as quickly as I can. A couple of hours and then we'll be on our way."

But as she started to clean up the man's wound, something she had never done before, she realized immediately that a couple of hours would be much too long. The bullet was probably still in there. She soaked a dressing in antiseptic and bandaged it on rather clumsily. She then gave the man a tot of brandy. It was probably the wrong thing to do, but he looked simply terrible.

Then she hesitated, staring across at where Bruce was engrossed again. But of course there was no real choice. If she was going to be able to live with herself there was only one thing to do.

She placed half the supply of drinking water in the shade and most of the carefully wrapped food. She then climbed back into the truck, switched on the engine and, without a backward glance, drove off in the direction in which they had come.

She thought she heard Bruce call out, but still she did not look. Her only fear was that she could not find the way. She thought the man beside her had lost consciousness.

At first there was only one track, but after a few miles it divided and she had to slow down, faced with her first decision. Kwane opened his eyes and pointed a feeble hand to the right. She breathed again. In that way they reached the house in under two hours.

Within five minutes Saku and the only other man in the house had lifted Kwane from the truck and onto the cool of the veranda. Sally came out and took the dressing off the wound. The only question she asked was, "Where's Bruce?"

"He . . . he wouldn't come." While Sally went indoors to investigate the main first-aid kit, Jo turned anxiously to Saku.

"Please, Saku, before he loses consciousness again, you must ask him about Kari. I think Kari is in some kind of trouble, but I can't understand what."

The two men conversed in undertones. Finally Saku stood up slowly, his face torn with emotion. "Lady," he said, "some poachers ambushed the Land Rover. They dragged Kari off with them. When he," he nodded toward the sick man, "tried to help they shot him. They do not like Kari, because they say he is Bushman gone white.

This man fears they will do something bad to him. He also said Kari knew how the waterhole was poisoned. He was off to tell the *Morena*."

"The same poachers, of course."

Saku shook his wise old head slowly. "No, he said it was a white man. A man who cares more for the white glass than the animals."

"White glass?" she repeated. "What can he mean?"

"Diamonds, lady. Diamonds."

Her heart seemed to kick with a sickening thud. Kwane was delirious. Even he had been turned against Bruce. She stood up quickly. "The only important thing is to help Kari, and for that we need Ross and Neil."

From behind her Sally said, "I'm afraid we're in more trouble. The radio telephone is so thick with static I can't raise anyone."

"Not Ross?"

"No, nor the doctor."

"There will be a storm," Saku said flatly.

Jo looked up at the brassy sky and thought he was dreaming. But Bushmen were supposed to know these things, weren't they? They would smell rain hundreds of miles away.

Jo turned to Sally. "Can you cope with Kwane?"

"I don't know. I'll have to try. My first-aid knowledge is rather limited."

"Well, it's better than mine. There's only one thing I can do, Sal—drive over to the eastern post and find Ross."

Sally nodded. "Yes, you'll have to. I'll keep trying the radio telephone."

Within minutes Saku had produced a map of the reserve. She prayed fervently she would be able to follow it. With that, and Saku's excellent directions, she reckoned she had a good chance.

She went out to the truck. The engine caught, then

coughed and died. Ten minutes later there was still not even a spark of life.

"Can you—" she started toward Saku.

He shook his head mutely.

She swallowed. There was only one way open to her now. Briskly she gave her next orders. "Saddle Brandy for me, Saku, and you'd better put everything in the saddlebags you would put for the *Morena*, including a gun."

Sally caught at her arm. "You're mad, Jo, you can't go all that way on a horse. If you don't get lost you'll have no protection from . . . from anything."

"So you're suggesting I leave Kari to die, because I'm a bit scared? Look, Ross has told me that the most dangerous thing on horseback is camel-thorn. It's still the hot part of the day, so there won't be much game around."

"And the gun? You've only tried it a few times."

"It's to fire when I get near to the post."

"Please, Jo . . . if you got lost."

"I won't. Besides, Saku says it's one of the easiest trails to follow in the park. Even he thinks I can manage it."

When Saku came to tell her that Brandy was ready and saddled, she kissed Sally quickly and said, "Don't worry about me, it's . . . it's just another adventure. And, Sal, I'm sorry about saying those things to you. Perhaps you're right about Bruce. I don't know. At the moment I can hardly bear to think about him."

Saku shook her hand gravely. "You are a very brave lady. *Morena* will be very proud of you."

"That's something, I suppose," said Jo dryly. She kicked her heels into Brandy's flank and rode off toward the lonely desert.

CHAPTER TWELVE

Jo had been riding for just over two hours. She had stopped only once for a drink of the now warm water she carried in a large metal flask. At first she had been very hot, but at last she found her second wind and the heat was no more than mere discomfort. She felt she had temporarily come to terms with it.

She had also been frightened when she turned around and could no longer see the familiar landmarks. Now even those fears had been overcome, or perhaps merely suppressed, although not her watchfulness. It was one of the things both Ross and Kari had drummed into her; once you were no longer frightened of the bush then it was easy to get careless. Just like that first time she rode out.

Actually she had seen little except the friendlier kind of game: a herd of zebra, plenty of impala and other buck. Once when she stopped, a hyena stared at her from the undergrowth. In the distance she had seen a pack of wild dogs. She had also heard the trumpeting of elephants, and only then did she feel the need to urge Brandy forward, but when she realized the sound came from the west, probably a mile or more away, her heartbeat steadied again.

She had consulted the map several times, but once they were well on the trail she realized Brandy knew by instinct where they were going. With luck she should be within firing distance in another hour. She fervently hoped so, glancing up at the sky. Of one thing she would be very, very frightened indeed—spending a night in the bush alone. Strange, the sound of thunder had never been very far away, although rain appeared an impossibility.

Until now she had concentrated on her journey. It had seemed very important to do that for her own safety. But there was another reason, of course. She did not want to think about Bruce.

She would not allow herself to think of the implications of what Kwane had said. She simply did not believe it. But deep down lingered the faintest suspicion of doubt. Bruce had callously abandoned a man because he was black—no, two men, if you counted Kari. It had not occurred to him that these two men were more important than his own work—just for a single day. The discovery of this side of his character had numbed Jo until now. Could she really love a man who had no room in his heart at all for his fellow men? She thought about the others' reactions to Bruce. Both Sally and Ross had instinctively been against him. Had they seen a darker side of his character much earlier? Then there was young Sandy. They say a child instinctively judges another human being. Well, certainly Sandy knew his own mind. *Oh, Bruce, Bruce, can I really love you one minute and doubt you so dreadfully the next?*

There was something else that only now came to the surface of her mind—his anger that she and Sally intended to sell Nyala, if it became theirs. He obviously had not understood that however much you hated the result, you could not go back on your word. But why had he been so angry? Nyala was nothing to him. Even if he found diamonds he would still reap the rewards. Or was she the way to a personal stake in Nyala?

Her sickness at even the thought of such a ruthless betrayal had made her jerk Brandy to a halt. No, not that, never, never, never.

"Get out of my mind, Bruce," she said aloud. She would talk to him later. For the moment she must put all her energies into finding Kari. She dug her heels into Brandy's flanks and he responded instinctively.

Just under an hour later she saw in the distance a clump of trees, the first she had seen for a long time. It must be the post. She drew the gun from its saddle holster and fired three times into the air. Five minutes later she saw the cloud of dust that could only mean the truck was on its way.

She patted Brandy's smooth neck, now wet with sweat. "Thanks," she whispered. "One thing, Ross was quite right about you. You're a truly faithful friend."

With a squeal of tires the truck stopped and Ross jumped out.

"My God, Jo, you must be mad! No . . . no, something must be wrong. Here, let me help you down."

"For once," she said shakily, "I think I need help. I'm practically glued in the same position."

He almost lifted her from the saddle, then gently led her to the truck. "You can talk in a moment, when we get back." He patted Brandy's rump, pointed in the direction of the post and said, "There, off you go." The horse trotted off and was soon a small cloud of dust.

The post was little more than a wooden hut set amongst the trees, but there was a chair, some blessed shade and reasonably cool water. The two Africans there seemed amazed that a woman had ridden so far. Neil thoughtfully produced a bowl of water and a sponge to cool her face and hands.

"Now," said Ross, "if you feel up to it, tell me."

So she started from the moment Kwane had appeared at the edge of the prospecting site to the point where the truck wouldn't start.

Neil was immediately puzzled. "But couldn't Bruce fix the truck? It was surely something minor since the thing had been well looked after."

"I . . . I drove from the site alone, with Kwane."

"You mean he wouldn't come?" Neil was incredulous.

She could not bring herself to answer.

"Right," said Ross, carrying on quickly, "you say Kwane told you this story about Kari. But have you any idea where they were when the poachers appeared?"

She nodded, pulling the map from her pocket. "I marked the place where the Land Rover was last left. Saku explained to me what Kwane told him."

"Good girl!"

"A girl in a million, I'd say," Neil said, and Ross looked down at her with an odd expression. For just a brief second his hand rested on her shoulder.

"Right." He went on, "They say troubles never come singly. We must take the truck and find Kari just as soon as we can. I don't like the sound of this at all. The trouble is I daren't take either of the men with me, Neil. It would leave this place wide open."

"I daresay you and I can cope," Neil said quietly, "but it might be a longish job."

It was Jo's turn to make an observation. "I don't think we can leave Nyala just like that with no one there and the radio telephone out of order. To start with I'm sure that Kwane needs real medical help, much more than Sally can give. Then—then there's Bruce. He's stuck out in the bush with no means of transport, no means of communication. But Kwane comes first," she added quickly.

The two men looked at each other. "I suppose," said Neil, "I could ride back, once Brandy is rested. Taking the short cuts the truck can't manage, I should be there in less than three hours."

"There are only two hours to darkness," Ross pointed out.

"At that point Brandy can get me home blindfold. I think probably Jo is right. If I can get the truck going I can come out and help. You'll also need more gas. The only thing is—Jo."

"She could stay here."

Jo looked about her. She never was very good at merely waiting. "I'm going with Ross," she said clearly. "Another pair of eyes and hands might be useful."

"But you've been riding for four hours," Ross protested. "You must be exhausted."

"I must admit to a sore behind, but as long as you don't put me on a horse again. . . . And if there's any chance of a real wash and something to eat I'll be as good as new." It was almost the truth at that moment. Or was she trying to prove herself to Ross?

While the men made all the other preparations, she was shown to a primitive outhouse where a bucket was rigged up as a kind of shower. She even managed to wash her dusty, thin cotton blouse, reckoning it would be dry by the time it came to leave.

With her hair wet and shining, her body blissfully cool, wrapped in a rough sheet, she came back to the hut and tucked into the tin of corned beef, the can of beer and bowl of fresh fruit. By the time that was over she truly felt a different person, apart from the general soreness of body.

About an hour after she first arrived Ross was leading the way out to the truck. Neil had already left, having made sure Brandy had had some food and water, a good rub down and as long a rest as possible.

Jo had watched them leave. "Will Brandy be able to make it?" she asked anxiously.

Ross nodded. "Brandy's a very tough horse, used to intense heat and rough terrain. Also he hasn't been galloped to a standstill. He'll be tired, but Neil won't drive him hard."

About an hour after they left the post they found the abandoned truck tilted at an angle off the track. Although the windshield was smashed it seemed otherwise undamaged.

Ross peered in. "I should think Kari managed to get rid of the ignition key. That would be his first thought—to immobilize the truck."

He stood, a taut, lonely figure in the gathering darkness of the bush, examining the ground for any kind of track. Jo tried to make herself useful by starting a search for the key, but it was a hopeless job.

After a while he said, "They're heading northwest. Why, I wonder? There's hardly a thing over there. I don't like the look of it at all. But I'm going to find Kari. I've got to," he added fiercely. "Kari is a man who would give his life for a friend."

Jo came to stand beside him. "Can you do anything tonight?"

"No, we would only lose them. I'm afraid it's a question of resting until first light. Do you think you can take it?"

"Of course."

"Yes, that was a foolish question to ask. You've already shown that. You've made your own sacrifice for Kari. That was the kind of decision back at the prospecting site no girl should be asked to take."

"Was it?" she said in a muffled voice, turning away from him. "I imagine anyone would have done the same thing."

"Perhaps. Perhaps not. Not when it could change the course of your life."

Suddenly, with the depth of his understanding, all her resolve broke. She was tired, drained of feeling, and she had been dry-eyed for too long. She sank down onto the sand and wept.

For a few moments he let her cry. He knew she needed to cry. Then he put a glass into her hand and ordered her to drink.

She gulped down the brandy and stared at him, tortured, hardly knowing who he was. "He didn't care," she sobbed, "he didn't care that they were both human beings, and there was no one else to help. Kwane could have died. Kari might be dead already. You can't love someone like that, can you?"

"Love can withstand many tests, I imagine," he said quietly, "but once it's shaken to its very roots, then there's no going back. I learned that a long time ago. But did you really love him, Jo?"

She shook her head from side to side. "Now, I don't know. I only know I thought I did. And there's something else you don't know. Kwane told us that Kari knew who had poisoned your waterhole. A white man; a man seeking diamonds. I kept telling myself that he must be wrong. Why should Bruce want to do a thing like that?"

"I can't answer that, Jo. I hope, I really hope it isn't true."

"If it were true," she said dully, "he wouldn't want Kari found, would he?"

He took hold of both her shoulders and raised her to her feet.

"I don't know that either. I only know that we both have a job to do, and we're both determined to do it. First we're going to make a fire. I want you to find me as much dry thorn and brush as you can—small and big stuff. It's something we have to keep going all night. Then you're going to make some coffee, and we'll have a snack before we sleep. I want to check over the truck so that we'll be ready to leave by dawn."

She was glad of things to do, and though she was tired, it was better than sitting doing nothing. By the time the fire was going and the coffee prepared, he had run the engine sweetly and pulled out the seats of one truck to make her a bed in the back of the other. For himself there was a rug and pillow on the ground near the fire.

She looked uncertain. "Will . . . will you be all right?"

"Fine." He grinned for the first time that evening, the firelight etching the sharp bones of his face. "I'm used to it, and anyway there's not enough flesh on me to make a good eating proposition."

Afterward they cleared up, and then he helped her up

to the back. "Sleep well, Jo," he said softly. "Remember your first night under the stars. The great thing about unhappiness is that it never lasts."

"I've tried to make you unhappy, though, haven't I?"

"No, because you never really meant it."

"But I did," she cried passionately. "I've been abominable to you right from the beginning. I should have trusted you, but I always act before I think. And I listened to Bruce, too."

"Look, Jo." He reached in and covered her hand resting on the side. "Look, Jo, if there's any blame, then it must lie equally with me. I never wanted you or Sally, or anyone, to come and disturb my particular paradise. I'm intolerant, I know I am. That's probably why the girl I was going to marry walked out on me. I could never imagine that anyone could feel about Nyala the way I do. I saw it all changing and I didn't want change. I merely deceived myself."

"No, we deceived you as well, Sally and I. Since I want there to be no misunderstanding from now on I have to tell the other thing that will turn you right against us all over again."

He laughed very quietly. "You mean that if Nyala is yours you intended to sell it!"

She gaped at him. "But how did you know?"

"I didn't know, I guessed; it seemed so obvious. Then I asked Sally. I knew she couldn't lie. I understand why you are trying to do it. At least it's an honorable reason."

"Bruce didn't. But then Bruce wanted Nyala for himself, didn't he?" She asked the question quite calmly. His lack of response was answer enough. After all, she was the only one who had not seen through him.

"I'm glad you told me now, about the selling. I kept telling myself that you would, in your own good time. Sally said you were too honest a person for your own good. Now go to sleep, Jo; we have a lot to face tomorrow."

"All right. And Ross—"

"Yes?"

"Thanks." She bent forward and kissed him impulsively.

Jo woke to the rumble of thunder and lay for a moment trying to get her bearings. She had slept soundly from the moment she put her head on the makeshift pillow.

Now there were other sounds in the darkness—the crackle of a fire newly stirred into life and the clink of metal cups. She peered out to find Ross outlined in the flames, bending over the coffee pot. She combed her hair and pulled on her blouse, then jumped down to join him.

"Sleep well?" he asked.

"Yes, marvelously. I'm still a bit stiff, but otherwise ready for anything." She glanced down at the fire. "Good heavens, ham and eggs? It seems almost too civilized, but it smells out of this world."

"With the sort of day ahead of us that I envisage, we shall need something inside us. Dawn will be breaking in less than half an hour. We must be ready to leave at just that moment."

She thought of Kari; it was no longer just an adventure. "What hope do you really think we have, Ross?"

"I don't like to estimate things like that." He cocked his ear at another rumble of thunder. "That's the thing that worries me. We want rain more than anything else, yet if it does rain every track will be wiped out, and we won't have a hope of finding him. But thunder can roll around the skies for days here before a sign of rain."

"Saku said it was going to rain," she said, suddenly remembering.

"Then you may be sure it is. That's Bushman lore."

They ate their breakfast in companionable silence;

then, as Jo started to clear up, he said, "I want to tell you something, Jo. From now on my whole effort is being concentrated on finding Kari. If I appear to be unsympathetic to your tiredness, or drive you on when you want to stop, that's the only reason."

"I know," she nodded. "I only hope I'm as tough as I think I am!"

As the first pale streaks of dawn crossed the sky, Ross started the truck and drove into the desert. He had left a note for Neil on their general direction, but that was all they could do.

For an hour he drove on steadily, stopping every now and then to examine the tracks. At the end of that time she said, "I know I can manage this for a time. It would be better if I drove and you gave all your attention to the track.

Without a word he nodded, and changed places with her.

It was nearly four hours before he called a 15-minute halt, to cool the engine and have a drink. She was already aching with tiredness, and she could feel the beginnings of blisters on her hands from having to grip the heavy steering wheel against the force of the rough terrain. But nothing would have drawn a complaint from her.

They had a fresh orange each, and he made her take a glucose tablet. The heat was like a dull interminable ache all about her. She wanted to ask him about their progress, but knew he would tell her when he thought it necessary. She turned and found his eyes resting thoughtfully on her.

"I have a problem," he said. "It concerns you."

"Yes?" She waited.

"If we drive on for more than another few miles we shan't have enough gas to get us back. Now do we carry on until we run out and hope that Neil will have followed the trail I've laid, or do we drive to the only clump of trees I know for about five miles, leave the truck hidden and walk?"

"I imagine you would prefer to walk, wouldn't you?" she said with more calmness than she felt.

He smiled, and for a moment he looked happy. "You're learning, Jo Fraser, you're learning fast. We'll make a good bushwoman out of you yet. I could leave you in the truck, of course."

She did not even bother to answer that one, but climbed back into the driving seat, waiting for him to close the passenger door.

They reached Ross's hiding place and camouflaged the truck as best they could. At least now it could only be seen about 20 yards away. In a canvas bag slung over his shoulder he packed some food, as much water as they could carry and a few essential medical supplies. The only other thing he needed was his gun.

Jo had not given the matter of actually walking in the bush—or rather desert now—any serious thought. It was just as well, she considered some time later, or she probably never would have left the security of the truck.

There was practically no shade and the sand made walking both difficult and tiring. Worst of all was the heat—dry, gritty and utterly unrelenting. Jo walked behind Ross because it was easier following his footsteps than finding her own. She was like an automaton incapable of any thought except covering the ground. She did wonder how far they would walk, for with every step forward there was one to retrace. All the time the thunder rumbled overhead, and while she longed for the blessed release of rain, she knew that was one thing she must not pray for—yet.

Ross turned and smiled encouragement at her, but he never spoke. He never changed his step except once, when he stopped abruptly and put his arm out so that she stumbled against it. She saw the tiny black snake slither away into the sand.

They had not seen any game since they started walking. It was just as well, Jo thought. She could not move any faster than she was going now.

Then Ross stopped again. This time he knelt to examine marks on the ground. Even she could see that it looked like a disturbance in the sand. For the first time she asked him a direct question. "It is human, isn't it?"

He nodded. "If I'm wrong, then we can't go much further. There's nothing but desolation ahead, and no human could survive out there. We shall have to turn back and wait for Neil." He cupped his hands around his mouth and called a strange high-pitched sound that was like one animal calling another.

At first there was nothing. The silence and desolation were complete. Then Ross called again.

Jo lifted her head sharply, awakened at last out of her stupor. The sound was so small that it could have been nothing. But Ross had heard it, and he jerked his head at her to follow him. From somewhere she found the energy to keep up with his increased stride.

It was another 15 minutes before they found Kari. Jo barely smothered the gasp of horror. He was bound hand and feet to a thorn tree and sagged against his bonds. His back was a mass of scratches from the terrible thorns with his face almost drained of life.

While Jo hacked him loose Ross got the first few drops of water down his throat. He opened his eyes and in a queer cracked voice said, "I knew you would come, *Morena*."

Together they eased him to the ground. Ross cradled him in his arms, taking the pressure off that dreadful back, tipping more water drop by drop into the dry, swollen throat.

Ross asked him only one question. "How long, Kari?"

"Yesterday afternoon," came the whispered answer.

"Will he be all right?" Jo asked.

"I think so. I hope so. Bushmen have a strong sense of survival. What I don't understand is why Neil isn't here. He should have caught up by the time we started walking. That's why I didn't want to take the truck farther. I suppose it could be something seriously wrong with the truck."

"I don't think so," she said slowly. "It was running perfectly well until I actually arrived back at the house. And I know Bruce was very fussy about its servicing."

"Then we must just walk and hope."

"And Kari?" She looked down at the sick, exhausted man.

"Thank God Bushmen are small."

"You mean you're going to *carry* him?" She was aghast.

"If you can manage bag and gun. I have no choice."

That walk back to the hidden truck was a nightmare. Some of the time Jo felt she was actually sleepwalking. But if she found the conditions unbearable, what of Ross, who would walk for perhaps a quarter of a mile, let down his burden, rest for a few minutes, then start again.

Most of the time Kari was unconscious, but once he woke and begged, "Leave me, *Morena*, please leave me . . . you cannot carry me." But Ross merely put him over his shoulder more firmly and trudged on.

When they reached the truck, there was enough water for a long drink and to sponge their faces and, more important, Kari's back. She watched Ross do it, as gently as if he were handling a child. She felt extraordinarily moved by the sight. She handed him the bottle of anti-septic, feeling tears of relief gather in her throat that they had come through this far together. She knew one thing with complete certainty. There was no other man who could have done what Ross did; no other man who could make her feel so proud or so humble.

There was no questioning who should drive. Ross would not have had the strength, although he would have died rather than admit it. She did not even wait to be asked, but climbed back into the driving seat.

It was better than walking, but not a great deal, because with passing time the fiery pain in her hands seemed to cloud her thoughts. But they were able to go just a little faster. And by the time they reached the other, abandoned truck, they were on some kind of track.

Again Ross was puzzled, for there was still no sign of Neil. It could only be that he had had to rush Kwane to medical help.

Nearly 24 hours after Jo had set out yesterday she saw the landmark of trees in the distance. Could it really be Nyala, or was it just a mirage? She knew at this point that she was just about at the end of her endurance. Ross was still supporting Kari, keeping his back away from pressure, holding him against the continual bumping of the truck.

They were all out in front to greet them, having seen the familiar cloud of dust. Kari was lifted by willing hands of his own friends, and Jo was helped down by Neil and Sally.

Neil said abruptly. "How bad is he?"

"We got him in time. Look at his back, then a sedative and a long sleep. He'll be all right by morning." Ross looked around. "I suppose you had to use Farley's truck for Kwane?"

"You suppose wrong," Neil replied grimly. "I got it going almost immediately. Since Kwane was holding his own and we'd managed to get a message to the hospital the only time the radio telephone functioned, I decided I ought to pick up Farley first. He was only an hour or so away. If necessary we could then both drive Kwane toward town." He paused.

"Go on." It was Jo who said that, knowing that the grimness of Neil's expression concerned Bruce in some way.

"On the way back here we had a few . . . words, then I came in to check on Kwane. By the time I came out again he'd driven off and left us all flat."

Jo felt sick. But calmly she said, "Then it must have been true about what Kari had seen him do?"

"I'm afraid so, Jo," Neil said gently. "When I accused him he didn't really know that Kari had seen him. It was enough to scare him off. I should have had the sense to keep my mouth shut. At least we might still have had the truck."

But it was no time for explanations. All Jo wanted was the blissful cool of a shower, clean clothes and something to relieve the burning pain from her hands.

When she came out of the bathroom Goldie was curled up on her bed as if to welcome her back safely, and Sally was waiting with a pot of salve. "Here," she said severely, "give me those hands."

Jo winced, but some of the pain was soothed away almost immediately. She watched her sister for a moment before taking a deep breath.

"I'm sorry, Sal."

"What on earth for?"

"I was wrong about Bruce, and you were right, after all."

"I may not have cared for him much," Sally said soberly, "but I never expected anything like this. Why do you think he put poison in the waterhole? What did he hope to gain?"

"I keep thinking about it," Jo answered, "and I still don't really know, except that he wanted Ross to get the blame for anything that went wrong. He badly wanted us to get rid of Ross. And I was tempted, wasn't I?"

Sally laid a hand on her sister's arm. "Well, the past is past, and if you can try to forget Bruce I think you'll be happier."

Jo shook her head, saying wryly, "I can't forget him, **but** I promise you every single feeling I had for him was smashed to smithereens. He could have been responsible for the deaths of two men. Kari couldn't have lasted very much longer. And Kwane?"

"He'll be all right. It seems he was mainly suffering from loss of blood, but again he couldn't have survived in the bush with a wound like that. By the way, Jo, I must rub salt in a little more deeply. Neil says he's fairly certain there isn't a hope of diamonds on Nyala. He always thought that Bruce just wanted an excuse to be near you. I think Neil is probably right."

"Of course he is." Jo caught her sister's eye.

Sally gave one of her rare blushes. "Well, I'm not ashamed. It looks possible that I shall be the one to stay out here, not you."

"Oh, Sal, how marvelous!" Jo hugged her sister. "I like him too. I like him very much. And then of course there's Sandy. We'll both be related to Sandy!"

"Hey, hold on a minute! We haven't really got as far as that. But we both seem to feel exactly the same. I think we knew that first day at lunch. I can't really believe it yet." She glanced down at her watch. "Here, it's time to eat, and then you must go to bed. You must be exhausted after a day like that."

"I think I probably am," Jo said, "but I'm also hungry and I want to see how Kari and Ross are."

Ross was in the living room pouring drinks and answering eager questions from Sandy. He put a glass down beside Jo, then took hold of both her wrists and turned her hands over.

"You drove all that way and never said a thing." His voice was low.

"I couldn't," she answered with a brave attempt at flippancy. "The chauffeur had gone off duty." She changed the subject swiftly. "Is Kari all right?"

"Yes, he's sleeping. Thanks to you, we got him well in time."

After they had eaten Ross went to check on Brandy, to see how well he had survived the grueling journey. Jo felt the sudden onset of tiredness, but before she went to bed she decided on a last walk, down to the river, to where Bruce had had his camp.

She looked about her. Apart from the remains of the fire, and the signs that someone had left hurriedly, it was difficult to think that this had been a man's temporary home. She felt no nostalgia, no regrets, nothing at all. It was as though Bruce's actions had cut off her emotional need for him at the roots.

She stood for a moment watching the gentle movements of the river, the way it swirled as it came to a group of rushes and then moved into a pool of calm. The night was warm, but not too hot; impossible to imagine the oven-like temperatures of today's trek.

As she stood up to make her way back to the house and to the welcome thought of a long, long sleep, she became aware of the figure standing against the trees.

"How's Brandy?" she asked softly.

"Like Kari, he's tough." He paused. "I came to tell you how sorry I am about Farley. You must feel very . . . cast adrift."

"Because I came down here?" She looked about her. "No, it's strange, as I told Sally. After what's happened I can feel nothing, nothing at all. I only came down here to prove it to myself. I'm even beginning to wonder about Holly's death. Perhaps he was even capable of that. I don't know. I don't think, deep down, I could ever have been truly in love with him. I was probably in love with a sort of dream. Anyway, I've woken up, so don't let's talk about it."

"Shall I tell you something, Jo?" And when he saw her quizzical expression, "I think, like me, you belong to Africa. You have a feeling for it."

She sighed. "I only know I don't want to leave. But tell me something truthfully, Ross, and this time I'll believe you. Do you think we can make Nyala pay on its own?"

"No," he said bluntly. "Oh, with the help of a few small safaris, we can manage for a little longer, but without real capital I'm afraid it's a lost cause. I mean it when I say I wish from the bottom of my heart it wasn't true, but in two months' time we shall have to face facts. But there is one thing, and now it's my turn to make a confession to you—and Sally—but I'll do that later."

She waited, aware of the tiny grip of fear in her stomach. He was going to leave them after all.

"As you know," he went on, "at the end of three months Nyala—if our attempt fails—has to be handed over to the state. What I have learned and kept to myself is that although they make no payment for the actual property, they would have to make an offer for what are loosely called fixtures and fittings—everything that's not the actual game park which your uncle owned. It would work out at something in the region of 10,000 pounds."

"10,000 pounds?" she repeated stupidly. "But that's a lot of money! And if," she said with growing excitement, "Alan were to sell the house and add that money—why, he would probably be only about 5,000 pounds short. He could cope with that himself with mortgages and things. Oh, do you really think that's so, Ross?"

"Yes, I'm as certain as can be. But what about your house? You and Sally?"

"I don't think Sally will be going home for long, do

you? And me—well, the hotel would be my home whenever I wanted it."

"But you're not going home yet, are you?"

"I . . . I don't want to. But I think Sally will agree that if all this is so, it's foolish to fight for something you can't win. We must hand Nyala over before it's too late. You would remain warden, wouldn't you?"

"There's a good chance of that. And I'll need help, you know, Jo."

"Not my sort of help?" she said unsteadily.

"Just your sort of help." He took hold of her wrists and looked down at her hands again. "I keep wanting to hold your hands and to thank you for bringing me to my senses."

"Isn't the shoe on the other foot?"

"No. I've learned more about myself in the last three weeks than in the past four years. I really believed I wanted to shut myself off from the world. And then you—and Sally—arrived, and I saw that there were still girls in the world who wanted to give, not take everything, who really believed in something and were not afraid to speak their minds."

"Sally, yes," she smiled, shaking her head. "Everyone knows that about Sally, but not me."

"True, it was easy to see in Sally. Look at Neil—one day and he was lost. But you—you were a challenge, Jo, and all my life I've loved a challenge. And I knew you must be all right," he teased, "when Goldie took to you. She's friendly, but fussy."

Suddenly the thunder, hovering all evening, rumbled so loudly that it could only have come from overhead. He looked upward and shouted with joy.

"Jo, look, look, it's a miracle at last! It's going to rain!" And with that the first spots fell. Before they had turned and run for the house, the whole sky had opened.

They stood on the veranda, watching, laughing in their delight. And then suddenly he pulled her head toward his shoulder. "It's going to be a good day tomorrow, Jo. It's going to be a good day for both of us."

"Yes," she answered softly, "I rather think it is." Together they turned and went inside.

THE YEAR AT YATTABILLA

CRAIG

THE YEAR
AT YATTABILLA

Amanda Doyle

The promise of a new life had brought Maddie and her young brother, Skeet, from London to Australia. Now she wondered at the wisdom of the move.

It wasn't just being alone in a strange country, struggling to make the derelict station of Yattabilla into a home. When you came right down to it, the problem was Stephen Darley.

"Why can't you be sensible about the whole thing, Madeleine?" he asked harshly. "Give up. You're city-reared, even if you are Gerald Masterton's daughter. You're just a foolish, misguided, stubborn child—"

"And not your type," she finished for him. "You've already made that clear." How could she possibly be in love with a man like that?

CHAPTER ONE

Maddie Masterton looked at the face of the man sitting in the chair adjacent to hers in the family solicitors' gloomy office and pondered on its strength of jaw and impenetrable cast.

The gray eyes, thoughtfully narrowed at this moment, were pale and glittery against the deep tan of lean, grooved cheeks. They exactly matched the paleness of the man's tropic-weight gray suit, Maddie noted, subconsciously approving its perfect cut and the way it fitted those awesomely broad shoulders. As he flicked ash impatiently into a large, wooden ashtray on Mr. James Opal's desk, she noticed that his fingers were long and brown, the nails well cared for. He was a long, brown, impatient sort of man altogether, she decided judicially, wishing now that the cold gray eyes weren't fastened upon her in quite such an unfriendly fashion.

Beneath the window, with its nondescript cream lace frill that did no more than blur the skyscraper opposite the traffic rumbled and roared along George Street. The Sydney rush was at its morning peak right now, and Maddie, who had had to hurry to this early appointment, clenched her teeth on an impending yawn, and hoped she gave an impression of businesslike alertness and vigor, qualities that positively exuded from the occupant of the other chair. Those qualities came at her in overwhelming waves as the gray eyes clashed with hers again in a way that made Maddie quite breathless and caused a steely cymbal of warning to clang the last sleepy cobwebs from her brain.

Mr. James Opal, of Opal, Rose and Heming, adjusted his spectacles and plunged tactfully into the breach, as if aware that the build-up of tension had become almost explosive.

He cleared his throat and picked up the typewritten sheets in front of him.

"Shall I—er—just refresh you both on the—er—salient points, then Miss Masterton?" he queried, and without waiting for her further assent, proceeded to do so in a flat, legal voice.

". . . being of sound mind, do hereby bequeath to my only daughter Madeleine Janet Masterton the property of Yattabilla and the residue of my estate, apart from the aforementioned individual bequests, providing that the said Madeleine Janet Masterton, at present believed to be domiciled in England, fulfills a term of one year's residence on Yattabilla, as earnest of her intention to inherit, and to cherish the property in the manner in which I myself have endeavored to do, without the physical assistance or moral support of either herself or her mother during this past number of years. In the event that either my executors are unable to contact my daughter within six months of my decease, or, having been contacted, my daughter for any reason defaults in thereafter fulfilling a period of one year's continuous residence on Yattabilla, I bequeath the property in its entirety to my neighbor Stephen Gainsborough Darley in appreciation of his invaluable friendship and concern during my illness."

Mr. Opal stopped speaking, and surveyed his listeners.

"Well, Miss Masterton? Mr. Darley?"

Maddie opened her mouth and closed it again. She felt a curious tide of unreality swamping over her.

"Something to your advantage," they had said when they contacted her in London, adding that her passage would be paid from her late father's estate.

"Something to your advantage."

Maddie could still remember the morning that that phrase dropped into her life as vividly as if it were yesterday, instead of two whole months, several oceans, a whole hemisphere, away. After all, it had been bound to make an impact, hadn't it? Especially when you happened to be a struggling stenographer, with minimum shorthand speeds and a little brother to care for as well.

Maddie hadn't mentioned the little brother yet—not to anyone.

Even Mr. James Opal, of Opal, Rose and Heming, did not know about Skeet, and neither did Mr. Stephen Gainsborough Darley.

It almost seemed as if her very own father hadn't known about Skeet either, and that was something that puzzled Maddie very much right now. It not only puzzled her but added to her sense of unreality, because Skeet was so alive, so full of mischief and fun, so demanding, so *expensive*, that to Maddie he was the only reality in this whole impossible situation. It was her father, Mr. Opal, Stephen Darley, Yattabilla itself that were the dream!

Skeet had been Maddie's reason for making the long sea voyage from the familiar comfort of the dingy London scene to this sprawling, turbulent, heat-hazed city, with its ink-blue harbor and gracefully arched bridge; its still-new skyscrapers and teeming inhabitants, the women gaily clad, with a slim, brown-legged gaudiness against the blazing gold of the Australian sun, the men bronzed and casual compared to the formality she was accustomed to. Lots of them wore shorts, even in the city. Here everything was new when measured against the drab ancientness of the British capital. The buildings, the jetties, the pavements, the gardens, the statues—all had a quality of newness that belied a mere 170 years or so. There was an all-pervading feeling of excitement, adventure and experiment in the air, as of a great city emerging from urban adolescence into cosmopolitan adulthood.

Maddie had sensed that excitement immediately and was aware of its momentous nature. She felt caught up in it already, as though her own life was somehow bound up in its pulsing promise of great things to come. She wished she could communicate her new awareness to Skeet, too, but of course he was too young to understand.

He just looked about him, at the bridge and the sea and the ferryboats and the yachts, with wonder in his wistful blue eyes, and trust on his pale, freckled face. Trust for *her*, for Maddie. Trust that she had done the right thing for them both in bringing him across the world to this frighteningly strange, hot city.

Now Maddie was wondering if Skeet's trust had been misplaced.

Had she done the right thing, after all? She had never envisaged that "something to your advantage" might not be a cash legacy at all, but a derelict station away in the middle of nowhere where she and Skeet would have to endure a year of what sounded incredibly like a prison sentence.

And after that year—what?

It had taken all of her savings to pay for Skeet's passage, beyond a little she had retained for what she called "safety money."

She wondered now about Yattabilla—about all the implications.

There seemed little doubt that the property itself was derelict—the house, at any rate—because Stephen Darley had ground out his cigarette—and was saying tersely, finally, "It's preposterous! I've said that all along! Miss Masterton could never live there! It's absolutely out of the question, even for a year."

His voice, in the last sentence, had reverted to its deep, pleasant, drawling sound, but even when it drawled, it had an edge to it. The edge matched the coolness in the narrowed gray eyes.

"Why is it preposterous?" asked Maddie, suddenly, perversely in disagreement, although a moment ago she had been inwardly shuddering at the mere idea.

Something about this man disturbed her and put her on

the defensive. Perhaps it was his decisiveness, his self-assurance, as though he was accustomed to having his orders obeyed and his every utterance unchallenged.

Maddie was challenging him now, and he did not appear to like that.

An impatient frown gathered on his teak-brown forehead, bringing his thick black brows together in a disapproving scowl.

"Because, Miss Masterton, your father never did a thing to that homestead, that's why. Not one solitary repair did he do after your mother ran out on him."

"She did *not* run out on him!" Maddie was indignant.

Stephen Darley leaned back in his chair and raised one brow, very expressively—horribly expressively, it seemed to Maddie—then he fished in his pocket for the makings to roll himself another cigarette.

"We won't argue about that, if you don't mind," he retorted imperturbably, as one might brush aside the remark of an ignorant child.

"But I do mind! I—I won't have you sitting there, suggesting that my mother—that she—"

"Leave it, child." That was a command—quietly and courteously spoken, but a command, nevertheless.

Effectively silenced, Maddie watched helplessly, but with a reluctant interest, as tobacco was rubbed between calm brown palms and tilted deftly onto a wafer-thin sliver of paper. Wretchedly, she noted the absence of even the tiniest tremor in the lean fingers that were fashioning the neat cylinder so capably.

She herself was shivering with reaction—a combination of shock and anticlimax and the knowledge that she had let Skeet down after all.

"You're overwrought," Stephen Darley observed when he had drawn on his cigarette to his satisfaction. "Furthermore, I suspect you have only the haziest knowledge of the subject in question—and indeed, it's quite irrelevant to the present discussion. The fact remains, that, for *whatever* reasons, Yattabilla homestead is in an unthinkable state for a sheltered young English girl, unused to either the conditions or the climate."

Maddie's oval chin tilted ominously. "I'm not English," she corrected coldly. "I was born on Yattabilla, so that makes me as Australian as you are."

"Can you remember anything about it?" He shot the question at her abruptly.

"N-no, not really. But I—I remember my mother telling me that I was born out in the country."

"The country! You make it sound like an afternoon jaunt down to Sussex!" He shifted his weight impatiently in the small leather chair. "You can't remember, Miss Masterton, because you happened to be a mere child when your mother ran out on Gerald Masterton. From what I can gather, she took you straight to England, which makes you English by habit and upbringing, and totally unsuited to roughing it out in the *country* here."

Maddie hated the way he stressed that word. She hated his whole, disparaging attitude.

He was obviously trying to rattle her, to shake her already dwindling confidence. He didn't want her to come to Yattabilla, that much was certain. Of course, he wouldn't, though, would he in the circumstances? If she did not come, if he could somehow frighten her off, the property would come to him in due course. Maddie glanced at his set, stern features, wishing that she could read the unreadable. If she could, she was pretty sure that her guess would be right. That was why he was being so obstructive just now.

"The property itself, the—er—station? Is it in good order, or is it, too, in a *derelict* condition?" Maddie couldn't keep the sarcasm from her voice.

Stephen Darley regarded her gravely. His eyes did not waver. "No. The property itself is anything but derelict—quite the reverse, in fact. Your father's loneliness drove him on and on, but his energies were all directed to affairs outside the homestead, Miss Masterton. I expect his memories inside it were too painful to dwell upon, but anyway, his efforts to improve the place paid off. Yattabilla is a station in extremely good working order. Your father laid on plenty of bores that are in excellent condition. Water means everything once you get out into those parts, and your father secured his position in that respect to the best of his ability. Yattabilla is well watered and well stocked. Yattabilla steers have a well-deserved name at the sale yards. After a spell on a fattening property, they do well at the abattoirs, too. As regards the sheep stock, it's in a strong-wool area, with an unavoidable dust and burr problem, but your father was improving that aspect steadily. His wool-clip was nothing to be sneezed at and increasing every year."

"I see." Maddie hadn't the faintest idea about steers and abattoirs, burrs and wool-clips, but not for the world would she have shown her ignorance to the hatefully well-informed Stephen Darley!

A faint smile relieved the sternness of his weathered features. "I doubt if you do, actually," he retorted mildly, but with a disconcertingly cynical accuracy.

Maddie flushed. "I see that it could be a desirable property, anyway," she returned pointedly, stung by his perception. She wanted to hurt him just then, wanted to wipe away that confidence, erase that—that—smugness.

His firm lips tightened. "It *is* a desirable property, Miss Masterton," he agreed coolly, "especially, as you are no doubt thinking, to the owner of the neighboring station. Together they could be quite an outfit, couldn't they, and moreover very convenient to run as a single holding? I realize that that's what you're hinting. That, however, has little bearing on your own particular problem, hasn't it—the derelict homestead?"

The gray eyes were crinkling a little bit at the corners,

almost as if they were thinking of smiling. If they smiled now, it would be a triumphant smile, Maddie knew that for sure.

Oh, Skeet, Skeet, what have I landed us in? she was thinking desperately. Where, now, was the pulsing promise, the glowing sense of adventure?

"I have no problem, Mr. Darley," she informed him coldly, rashly, "although I do appreciate your apparent concern." She turned back to the waiting Mr. Opal. "I intend to fulfill the conditions of my father's will and claim my inheritance," she continued proudly. "Perhaps you will be good enough to furnish me with all the necessary details, if I call back at a convenient time?"

"Of course, of course, Miss Masterton. The decision rests with you alone, although you may find it advisable, even necessary, to alter your mind during the course of the period of residence. Most unwise. Most unwise. I shall do nothing to dissuade you, but I cannot help feeling—" here a reproving shake of the head "—that you would do well to heed Mr. Darley's views. He was, after all, one of your father's closest acquaintances and is a trustee of the estate in addition."

Stephen Darley had risen from his chair.

Standing, his height and breadth were formidable. The office suddenly seemed smaller, suffocating, claustrophobic.

"I—I shall return tomorrow to discuss the journey," Maddie said rather breathlessly, and with a formal nod, managed a fairly dignified exit that cloaked a curious weakness in her limbs.

As she clattered down the dark stairs and out into the glare of the street, her mind was beating a tattoo in her brain.

What have I done? What have I done?

Oh, Skeet! It's too late to turn back now!

Maddie plunged into the crowd, felt a firm hand taking

her arm, and looked up to find the Darley man at her side.

"I want to talk to you," he said as he piloted her across the busy street. "Perhaps you would care for a cup of coffee?"

"No thank you," she returned formally, grateful that she had a genuine excuse. "I have to meet someone. I've already been much longer than I'd thought."

Skeet would be waiting for her at the dairy bar where she had left him.

"May I call on you, then, at your apartment? Where are you staying?"

"It's a good way out from the city center, I'm afraid," she hedged. "And there's nothing, really, that we have to say to each other in any case—not for a year, anyway!" added Maddie wickedly, because she resented his domineering manner and still longed to assert herself.

The hand on her arm tightened viciously. The lean fingers bit into her flesh so savagely that she almost winced aloud. She knew that she had struck home with that last remark.

She was halted then and there, and pulled around abruptly, face to face with Stephen Darley, while the people jostled past. His expression was carefully inscrutable. Only those biting fingers had revealed his annoyance.

"You will meet me for dinner tonight, Miss Masterton. I have only a couple more days left. We'll go somewhere quiet, but as your father's friend and trustee, there are certain points to be cleared up. That's just what I mean to do, so don't put me off with more excuses. We know virtually nothing about you, remember. At what time, and where, shall I call for you?"

Maddie looked up and met an imperious gaze. It was quite useless to argue, she could see that.

"You don't need to call for me," she replied evasively,

thinking of the dingy boarding-house—of Skeet, too.
"I shall be waiting for you wherever you say."

"The Blue Balcony, then, at eight."

Before she had time to more than nod, he left her.

Maddie could see his tall, tanned figure, making its
way through the crowd toward the next pedestrian
crossing. Only the bruise that was beginning to throb on
her soft upper arm reminded her of her promised dinner
date later. The Blue Balcony, at eight. Maddie had a
feeling that she was not going to enjoy her evening out.

When she reached the dairy bar, Skeet was sitting at
one of the little tables, disconsolately fingering the bent
straw in his empty glass. His freckled face brightened at
her approach.

"You were an awfully long time, Maddie. I spent my
last ten cents ages ago. Can I have another milk shake? A
pineapple one this time?"

She ordered one, and an ice-cream soda for herself, and
carried the two drinks back to the table.

"Did it go all right, Maddie? Is everything going to be
all right?" The child's pale face was taut and anxious. Although, at ten years of age, he couldn't possibly understand all the implications, he had sensed his sister's own
tension; had realized that they were both on the brink of
some new decision and that Maddie had been strangely
apprehensive and worked up when she had left him earlier
this morning.

"Yes, darling, it's going to be all right," Maddie told
him reassuringly.

Then she smiled at him, and Skeet felt better, because
Maddie had a very lovely smile indeed. It curled her wide,
sensitive mouth at the corners and showed two rows of
pretty, even, white teeth. It made tawny lights dance in
her sherry-colored eyes, too, and brought a tinge of color
to the flawless, creamy skin of her cheeks and throat.
Sitting there in her simple green shift, with her blonde

hair hanging straight and silky to her shoulders, even Skeet could see that she was very pretty, really. He bet everyone else thought so, too. He had seen people looking at her when she came in just now, the way they always did. You had to admit that her hair was eye-catching, with that lovely natural honey color.

He smiled back at his sister and pulled again at the straw, drawing in his cheeks as he did so. He watched with satisfaction as the yellow liquid ran up the straw, and then back again, as he blew instead of sucking. There was a noisy gurgle and a pleasing froth, but Maddie frowned at him, and her smile disappeared.

She seemed preoccupied, because she didn't openly rebuke him—just sat there staring at her own soda drink without speaking.

"Did you see the man?" prodded Skeet curiously.

"Mm? Yes. Yes, I saw him. I saw two of them, in fact. I have to see one of them again tonight, Skeet. You'll be all right with Mrs. Prowse till I get back, won't you? I'm sure you could watch her television if you asked her nicely."

"Yes, I could, couldn't I!" Skeet was obviously pleased at the prospect. "Mrs. Prowse is nice, I think. But I don't like Barney. I hope he's not there."

Barney was their landlady's son, a gangling youth of 13, who enjoyed annoying Skeet by calling him "pommy" all the time.

"He'll probably be doing his homework," comforted Maddie. "Anyway, Skeet, you'll have to be a bit tougher and learn not to mind what people say. You won't have to put up with him much longer, because we're going away soon. We're going away on a great big adventure."

"Gee, Maddie! D'you mean—leaving Sydney? We've only just got here!"

"Yes, I know, but we're going to return to the place where I was born, Skeet. Remember, I told you? It's called Yattabilla. We're going to have a home of our very own, not lodgings in a stuffy, old boarding-house with no garden or view."

"Gee!" Skeet was impressed. He sucked the last of the pineapple mixture up the straw noisily and then asked off handedly, "What will Robert say, Maddie? Will he be coming too?"

Maddie felt her color rising. She, too, had been thinking about Robert Manners. It was going to be difficult, leaving Robert, because she had come to depend on him for moral support in her moments of uncertainty.

They had met on the ship to Australia. Robert had sailed from Durban, and had immediately drawn close to the two lost-looking young people on his own deck. He had just completed a surveying mission for a project in Cape Province. He was ready to relax and allow himself to be caught up in the revelries and superficial acquaintances that typify a brief sea-voyage.

He was a clean-cut, fair, young man of 26, and this had been his first trip abroad. It had been a successful mission in every way. There was already a hint of possible promotion for him when he reported back to his firm in Sydney. He hadn't intended any deep involvement when he struck up a friendship with Maddie and Skeet, but he soon found that her wistful uncertain air was oddly appealing. It aroused feelings in Robert that he hadn't know he possessed—manly, protective feelings that made him want to shelter Maddie. He had a horrid suspicion, from what she had told him, that she was on a wild goose chase, and would have been far better advised to remain in London, bashing a typewriter with her firm of importers.

It wasn't very long before Robert realized that he had fallen in love with this slender, fine-boned girl, with the sherry-colored eyes that danced in those fleeting moments when her expression of anxiety gave way to gaiety, and that curtain of silky hair that was the envy of every other woman on board. The nicest thing about Maddie—the thing that had really won Robert—was her complete ignorance of her own charms, or the effect they had on him. Several times he had been on the verge of confessing to his emotional state, and on each occasion he had stifled the impulse. Keep it light for now, he told himself, with the native caution that was a part of his character. Perhaps, when he returned to Sydney, heard just how far his promotion might take him, had his hoped-for increase in salary, he could think more seriously about offering Maddie something more lasting and worthwhile than the present set-up. In the meantime, it was better to maintain a more brotherly angle. Not for anything would he have caused that anxious, wistful air of Maddie's to deepen into even greater apprehension.

Robert had been 100 percent successful in cloaking his feelings. Thinking about him now, Maddie was aware only of a sinking regret that she would have to part from him before they had really known each other.

Life was like that, she supposed. Just when you met someone rather special, who seemed to be on your own wavelength, you were whisked away on some new adventure, so that you never knew about the "might-have-been."

It was debatable, too, if a year at Yattabilla could be termed an adventure—not an agreeable one, anyway, although for Skeet's sake she must try to pretend that it was. If she didn't manage to regard it in that light, her courage might fail her altogether.

"Robert?" she said now, abstractedly, in answer to Skeet. "No, he won't be coming, Skeet, not to Yattabilla. He has things of his own to do right here in Sydney. Remember, he's been away for quite a long time, too. He'll have a lot to catch up on."

"Oh." Skeet sounded depressed. "Will it be just you and me, then, Maddie?"

"Yes, Skeet, just you and me. It will be fun. An adventure!"

Maddie tried to sound bright and convincing, even though little butterflies of dread were fluttering around inside her.

"Does he know we're going?"

"Robert? I'll have to tell him. I'm going to see him tomorrow night, so I shall tell him then."

"Will you be out two nights in a row, Maddie?"

"I'm afraid so, darling. I didn't know about tonight, you see, when I said I'd meet Robert. But after that we'll be together all the time at Yattabilla. You can watch Mrs. Prowse's television, Skeet. I know she'll let you."

Her brother followed her dolefully from the dairy bar.

"I hope Barney has lots of homework—both nights," he evinced miserably.

Maddie ignored that. There were times when she just had to ignore the things Skeet said, because she was helpless to do anything about them.

This was one of those times. She had to meet that frightening Mr. Darley tonight. He had been insistent; there was no point in avoiding the issue. In a way, he did have a certain moral claim to information, she supposed, since he appeared to have known her father better than anyone else and moreover, was an appointed trustee. And she had to see Robert before she left Sydney. One couldn't just disappear without saying goodbye to someone who had been as good to her as he had. It might be difficult to make him understand, though. He had thought her quest from London to Sydney to be too frivolously uncertain to warrant giving up the small measure of security she had won for herself and Skeet. What he would think when she told him about Yattabilla was all too predictable.

Once they were on the bus, Skeet cheered up. They went right to the top, near the front, where he could look down on the beetling, bright roofs of the cars streaking

along beneath them, and ahead right up the crawling
length of William Street to the Cross at the end of the
straight. There they hopped off and went into one of the
numerous delicatessens. Maddie bought some sandwiches and cold, sliced sausage. She had tomatoes and
some cucumber in their room at the boarding-house.
Mrs. Prowse had given her the use of an electric kettle
since she didn't "do" meals, she explained, except breakfast.

Maddie had discovered that eating meals out could be
a very expensive business. That was why she now made
herself and Skeet as cheerful a picnic as she could in their
room. Then she took him walking down to Rushcutter's
Bay.

The little boy would have liked to stay there longer.
There were yachts bobbing on the sparkly green
water, people playing tennis, and swings in the playground. Maddie had to use all her powers of persuasion
to urge him back with her to the rented room, so that she
could wash her hair and prepare for her evening appointment.

She dressed with meticulous care that evening. She
wasn't quite sure why, except that it was necessary to im-
press Mr. Stephen Darley, somehow, and to bolster her
own shaky confidence.

She opened the cheap, veneered closet and regarded her
few dresses.

The Blue Balcony. Maddie had passed it, although she
hadn't been inside, of course. It ran the full length of the
second floor of a building overlooking some beautiful
gardens, with the harbor in the background. Its long
French windows opened onto a wide wrought-iron balcony, where people could be seen sitting under a milky
glitter of stars in the warm, night air. The entire façade of
the balcony was edged in blue and gilt, the windows were
framed by heavy chintz curtains with gold-fringed edges.
Within floated the muted sounds of music, and from time

to time one caught a glimpse of white-jacketed waiters hovering attentively over the tables inside, or balancing trays of drinks for those on the terrace.

Maddie lifted her best dress from its hanger. It was a simply swathed affair of navy chiffon, with long transparent sleeves. It had cost Maddie two weeks' salary. It had been her sole extravagance, and amid the cotton-clad gaiety of the tourist throng on board ship, it had seemed an unwarrented one—one of those stupidly impulsive buys one later regrets.

Now, she was grateful for its morale-boosting perfection. She clipped earrings in her lobes and set about contriving a sophisticated hairstyle by sweeping her hair up from her nape and securing it with the aid of a small switch. That way it made her appear older, more assured, she thought with satisfaction. Maddie couldn't be expected to know that the nape of her neck, now gracefully exposed, looked extraordinarily young and vulnerable. Her quick glance in the mirror did not reveal that fact. It only reflected her creamy skin against the dark, complimenting navy, and the golden sheen of her hair beneath the pallid light bulb.

Maddie made up her eyes with care and subtlety, touched gentle color to her lips, and went to say goodnight to Skeet. "You'll promise to go to bed at half-past nine, Skeet?"

"Ten, Maddie? Couldn't it be ten? After all, you're going out and having fun, aren't you?" He eyed her reproachfully, hopefully.

"Ten, then, Skeet," agreed Maddie weakly. She sometimes thought she was too lenient with Skeet. It had something to do with trying to make up for his having no parents.

Fun! If only he knew.

Closing the door quietly behind her, Maddie went to catch a bus back into the city.

CHAPTER TWO

It was a rebuff to discover that Stephen Darley had not even bothered to change into something more formal. Even so, she was aware, as she followed the waiter over a sea of soft carpet to a small table in an alcove, that her escort possessed an air of distinction and ease of bearing that drew the eyes of other diners to him. He saw her seated and then took possession of the plush, padded leather bench opposite.

If he was at all aware of a social lapse in not being as formally attired as others about him, he gave no sign. There was certainly nothing apologetic about the imperious way in which he signaled to the head waiter, who came hurrying over, volubly attentive.

"Good evening, Meestair Darley. And what is your wish tonight?"

Stephen Darley ran a practised eye down a long menu whose list of tempting dishes appeared endless to Maddie, and in a gourmet class she was totally unaccustomed to.

"Oysters, Luigi?"

"Yes indeed, Meestair Darley. The best. The sweetest."

"You care for them, Miss Masterton?"

Maddie blushed faintly. "I've never tasted them," she felt bound to admit.

'No?" His eyes traveled over the elegant, upswept hair, the sophisticated swathe of navy chiffon, and came to rest at that girlishly vulnerable throat in a way that made Maddie feel overdressed and foolish. He turned back to the waiter then, saying easily, "In that case, we'll have them cooked, Luigi. Oysters Kilpatrick, the consommé, and chicken Leonora."

Maddie was relieved that the decision had been made

for her, even though she struggled with annoyance. She would have liked to look longer at that amazing menu. It would have been something to tell Skeet, only Stephen Darley was so obviously accustomed to taking command that he had whisked it away. Apparently he saw no reason to consult others over their personal preferences.

Grudgingly, she had to admit that his choice was perfect.

The oysters were succulent, delicious in their crispy cloak of bacon. The soup was steaming hot and appetizing; the chicken pure delight.

There was a pleasant interval between each course. Maddie sipped cautiously at her tall-stemmed glass of dry white wine and watched the couples who came and went, passing their table on their way to the small area of dancing space. Mr. Darley, of course, did not ask her to dance—she hadn't expected him to. As she watched him eating, she was conscious that an air of remote politeness existed between them. It was only slightly more comfortable than that edge of concealed antagonism.

He ate as if he were genuinely hungry, without self-consciousness. When he looked up and caught her watching him, he must have read her thoughts.

His grin was sudden, boyish, and for the first time there was a hint of an apology in his tone.

"I'm sorry to be making such a glutton of myself. I've been in a hurry all day—a series of appointments. I hadn't time for much in the way of food."

Maddie met his eyes and saw the gray glint of humor there, a call for a temporary truce. She saw, too, for the first time, the tired shadows around them, and that the little lines that fanned out from the corners were more deeply etched than she had supposed them in the morning. His mouth, when unrelaxed, was taut with fatigue.

He must be a very important man to have appointments right through the day and responsibilities that didn't allow him time off even to eat. One of those responsibilities had been the entrustment of her own father's estate—one of the appointments, too.

Maddie felt a brief wave of compunction and uncontrolled sympathy. She felt she had been allowed a tiny glimpse behind the man's barrier of reserve and inscrutability. What she had sensed there had been almost human.

Maddie, in fact, was so pleased that she had had that tiny peep into the nature of the man, even fleetingly, that she smiled. It was the wide, complete, beautiful, curling smile that Skeet secretly admired. She had no idea, of course, that it warmed her little brother through and through like a spreading rush of golden sun. She didn't know that her sherry-brown eyes softened and laughed, too, with the curling of her expressively mobile mouth, or that her teeth glinted pearly-white against the pale coral of her lips.

For a split second, Stephen Darley's hand was arrested in its function of conveying food neatly to his mouth. It was a moment of utter stillness, when even the carved granite planes of his face, the severe outline of his head and shoulders, were as still, quiet, and thoughtful as the Sphinx itself.

Or maybe Maddie had imagined that pause?

"Don't apologize, Mr. Darley. I do understand—and one would have to be blasé indeed not to enjoy such a delicious meal."

He inclined his head politely. The reserve returned. "You'd better call me Steve," he told her, then, formally, "since we will of necessity be seeing a certain amount of each other in the future—and I shall call you Madeleine. No need to ask your name. We had the devil of a search for Madeleine Janet Masterton, I can assure you. It's a name I'm not likely to forget in a hurry."

No truce after all! thought Maddie. He resented her. He would always be annoyed with her for turning up at all.

"And are you still intending to pursue this madness?" he asked abruptly, when Luigi had set their pineapple before them with a flourish.

"I don't see that it's madness," she argued stubbornly, her eyes on her plate, hardly noticing or appreciating the delicious tang of the cold fresh fruit against her palate. "That is, unless you're suggesting that my father was mad in making this stipulation?"

He looked at her, then, very gravely indeed. "I'm not implying any such thing, Madeleine. Gerald, your father, was my friend. A valued friend." He hesitated, searching for words, still holding her eyes with his. "The thing you have to remember is that he was also a very lonely man, particularly toward the end, when he was too ill to go on employing sheer physical effort and preoccupation as a means of escape from his personal loneliness. His domestic life was inevitably an unbalanced one, and possibly his judgment became a trifle unbalanced, too. Otherwise—" he offered her a tailor-made cigarette from a slim silver case, took one himself when she declined "—otherwise he would have been more awake to the complete unsuitability of his suggestion. He had little idea of the type of girl his only daughter might turn out to be. It was quite unrealistic to expect a young thing, city-reared at that, to take on the occupancy of a crumbling station-homestead, even for a year."

He cupped his hand to his lighter, pulled on his cigarette, and exhaled. With his head thrown back, he gave her a level, extraordinarily persuasive glance.

"Will you see reason, or do I have to make you?"

"Black coffee, madam?" That was Luigi. If he hadn't interrupted at that particular moment, Maddie might have been really rude.

When Luigi had departed, she replied with deceptive mildness, "You can't make me, can you, Mr.—er—Steve? I think you may have very good reasons for not wanting me to come to Yattabilla, but the final choice is mine, isn't it? That's what Mr. Opal told me, at any rate, and my intention remains firm. I hope you didn't invite me out for dinner tonight for the sole purpose of altering my mind, because if so, I'm afraid you've been unsuccessful."

Steve did not answer immediately. Instead he smoked in thoughtful silence.

Maddie found his poise unnerving. He was a difficult adversary to cope with, no matter how hard one tried, and she was hopelessly aware that he knew far more about what she intended taking on than she did herself. It was both annoying and humiliating not to be able to ask all the questions she was curious to have answered. What was the Yattabilla place really like for instance? Where was it? How remote?

Lilting music wafted around them as Maddie sat primly, all her questions unasked.

Watching with a secret pang of envy the diners about her, she noted that they were couples or foursomes who were obviously enjoying each other's company far more than she and her own companion. Some young things were dancing close, with every appearance of being deeply in love. Others were more circumspect, probably on the brink of a more tender attachment, the way she and Robert might have been—but for that year at Yattabilla, which was soon to take her away.

She leaned back against the soft upholstery, letting the music wash over her and ease away some of her tension.

Steve Darley appeared to be still occupied. Maddie studied the stern angles of his profile covertly, looked at the hand lying carelessly along the table where he had half-turned in his seat to stretch out his legs more comfortably. It was a squarish hand, broad over the back, with long, square-tipped fingers that for all their strength had a certain sensitivity. Remembering that biting grip of his this morning, she wondered idly what it would be like to be held in those arms—properly held, like those young lovers over there, for instance. Would it be capable of tenderness, sympathy? Maddie doubted it. His love would have to be one of mastery and subjection.

"A liqueur, Madeleine?" Steve's voice broke into her thoughts.

Luigi was back again, hovering.

"P—pardon?"

"Cointreau for the lady, and my usual brandy, Luigi, please."

"I—didn't really want one," she murmured a trifle ungraciously, as Luigi darted off. He might have at least waited for her to say, she thought resentfully.

"Nonsense. It will do you good," he contradicted brusquely, surveying her with narrowed eyes. "The wine helped a little, but you're not at ease with me, are you, Madeleine?"

Maddie felt embarrassed color assail her cheeks.

"You aren't a very easy person," she mumbled incoherently. "You d-don't make things very easy."

"I could," he retorted more gently, "if you would allow me. But you won't, will you? You've put a mental barricade up between us, and that cancels out whatever I say—isn't that so? In fact, you're scared stiff of me! You've been as terrified as a rabbit since the moment we came in, and I'm wondering why?" He smiled faintly. "The female sex doesn't find me quite so overwhelmingly unapproachable as a rule."

Maddie's cheeks were on fire. The wine had given her a heady glow, a feeling of unfamiliar recklessness.

"I—think you're being beastly!" she flashed, with a show of spirit. "You've been amusing yourself at my expense the whole evening, haven't you? And as for the reputation with the female sex upon which you no doubt pride yourself, as far as I'm concerned, I'm perfectly satisfied that you remain unapproachable, if you want my candid opinion."

"*Touché!*" A reluctant grin spread over his tanned features. His teeth were white, and their crookedness was oddly attractive, she had to admit, even if his self-conceit was deplorable.

Steve lit another cigarette, sipped his brandy. Then "Let's forget the personal angle now then, shall we?" he drawled with deceptive pleasantness. "That, I'm afraid, brings us right back to where we came in. Madeleine, I'm going to make a suggestion that I want you to consider seriously. That is that you pass up this whole crazy scheme. Contest your father's will, if you like. As his daughter, you have certain legal rights. You could be successful if you go about things in the right way."

Maddie saw that he was utterly sincere or that he seemed so, at any rate. Leaning toward her to stress his point, eyes fixed gravely upon her face, it was difficult to believe that he was being anything but genuine.

"Do you think, then, that my father was —that he wasn't of sound mind when he made that will?" she asked. "Could I contest it on the grounds of well, insanity?"

It was hard to bring out that word in connection with her very own father, even though she couldn't remember him. She felt vaguely disloyal, unfair to the shadowy picture of an ill, frustrated, disappointed and lonely man.

"No, I don't think that at all. I've told you already. He was simply misguided. Clearly it was an error of judgment."

She was silent, considering.

Error of judgment or not, she couldn't do things Steve's way. It cost money to take legal proceedings, and it might be months and months before anything was settled. There was also the very real possibility that she might lose the action, too, and she would already have forfeited the chance of a year's residence. She'd have lost everything. Mr. Opal had said that she must be at Yattabilla within six months of her father's death, as "earnest of her intention to inherit." Yes, those had been his words, and four of those months had gone already. It had taken the Sydney people nearly two to track her down in London, and then a further eight weeks to get ready for the journey and sail.

No, it was impossible. She couldn't do things Steve's way, because she couldn't run the risk of possible failure. For herself, yes, but not for Skeet. How could she possibly support Skeet and at the same time fight a legal action? And why was Stephen Darley so keen for her to do things this way? How did she know that, whatever he said right now, he might not seek to have the will upheld? He had everything to gain by doing just that. He would be a formidable opponent; a wealthy one, too. Maddie shuddered at the mere idea.

"Come on, Madeleine, you can see it's sense. You can't possibly go out and live alone on Yattabilla. You haven't the foggiest notion of what's involved, have you? Just admit it, and we'll get down to the alternatives, there's a good girl."

Steve's voice was cajoling, almost kind.

Maddie swallowed. She wished she could trust him, but she knew she couldn't. He was a hard-boiled businessman, wasn't he—the sort who had appointments all day when he came to the city, important appointments that allowed him no time even to eat. He wasn't the kind to hand over a property like Yattabilla on a plate. The house might be derelict (she found herself even doubting him on that score, too), but hadn't he admitted that the cattle were a satisfactory source of income, and the wool-clip increasing? He must have some ulterior motive in urging her to take this latest, unorthodox step. Maybe he even knew that she would lose her case, and that it would be the quickest way to dispose of her and claim the place for himself.

Fresh doubts assailed Maddie. She found herself meeting those concerned, level gray eyes and simply longing to trust him, but she fought against the feeling, although she would certainly have welcomed a shoulder to lean on just then. She had never felt more alone—except for Skeet, of course.

Maddie braced herself. She had been subconsciously nerving herself, all evening, to tell Stephen Darley about Skeet. This seemed like as good a time as any to do it.

"I won't be alone on Yattabilla, actually," she stated, trying now to sound very casual.

"No?" The black brows opposite rose sceptically. "Who'll be with you, Madeleine? Don't tell me the lady has a husband stowed away somewhere? With that untouched look about you, I simply won't believe it."

"There's Skeet." She couldn't even joke, her voice felt too stifled.

"Skeet?" He had stopped smiling.

"Yes—Skeet," croaked Maddie. She was making a bad job of this.

"And who exactly is Skeet?" Steve was asking carefully. Funny how such a big, athletic man could sit so very still. His words dropped like pebbles into the stillness that he himself had created.

"Skeet's my brother."

"Your—brother!" His exclamation was startled, incredulous. It was evident that, whatever he had been expecting her to say, it certainly had not been that. "Impossible!"

"Don't say that," pleaded Maddie, agonized.

Her face was dead white, her eyes huge, naked with misery and doubt. The doubt had been there ever since this morning, ever since the moment when Stephen Darley had said, "You were a mere child when your mother ran out on Gerald Masterton." It had haunted her right through the day, through the picnic in the room, and the walk to the Bay, and swinging on the swings, and everything. It had been with her all the time she was getting ready for this rendezvous, and it had caused her to give Skeet a clinging, despairing hug when she had left him.

Skeet hated being hugged, she knew that, but the dreadful doubt had made her do it.

"I'm sorry, Madeleine. I shouldn't have said that." Steve's deep voice was contrite. "You surprised me, that's all. I had no idea that your mother had ever married again."

"She—didn't," Maddie stated baldly. She knew he was looking at her, but she couldn't bring herself to meet his eyes. Instead, she let her fingers play with the tiny, fragile liqueur-glass, because she had to be doing something. "She was a good mother, Steve," she added in a strangled, defiant tone. "She was good to Skeet and me."

"I'm sure she was," came the soothing, tactful murmur.

Then silence.

"She wasn't like you're thinking, Steve. She was kind and pretty and—oh, lots of fun. Maybe we didn't have much security. We never stayed in one place for long, but we did have fun. She was always impetuous, I suppose, but gay and generous too. We always did everything together. It was as though she was trying to make up to us for the things we didn't have—you know, a proper home, a father, and so forth."

"What about—er—Skeet's father? Didn't he accompany you, even for a while?" he asked quietly.

Her eyes were wounded. The doubt had curled itself up into a ball at the base of her throat. She shook her head.

"There was no one—nobody like that, I mean. Just Mom and Skeet and me. Skeet was terribly bereft when—when we lost her. That's why I'm taking him to Yattabilla." A pause. "I can't remember Yattabilla, Steve—not anything about it. You said this morning that I was only a child when Mum ra— when we left, so it's understandable, I suppose."

Silence.

"Skeet's only ten. He's a whole ten years younger than

I am." She was speaking almost to herself, as if she had forgotten the presence of the big, quiet man on the other side of the table. "If I'd been ten when we left Yattabilla, I'd remember it, wouldn't I? Wouldn't I?"

"Where were you when you were ten, Madeleine?"

"I can't remember. Melbourne, I think. I went to school there for a while. I was a boarder, because Mom had some sort of a job. Then we flew to England."

"From there?"

"Yes."

"And Skeet was born in England?"

"In London, I think. Yes, I'm sure. Mom used to say he was a true cockney—because of the Bow Bells, you know," she added with a wan smile.

Surprisingly, Steve Darley smiled back. It was a slow, thorough, deliberate sort of smile—kind, sympathetic, very gentle. You'd almost have thought his eyes were tender. Almost—if you hadn't known he was a tough business type, playing poker-faced stakes for a valuable property.

"It figures, Madeleine," he said reasonably. "You'd be too young to know what was going on—at ten your mother would have kept it from you—but she returned to Yattabilla, although you didn't. She came to try for a reconciliation with Gerald, I remember that now. I was in my first year at the University at the time. She'd doubtless have left you with some friend in Melbourne."

"What happened?" Maddie could only whisper.

Steve shrugged. "It didn't work out. She was there maybe a month, six weeks. Then she left—for good. She had to get your father's consent to take you to England, I remember. She hadn't the same problem with Skeet, it seems," he added dryly.

"You mean—?"

"I mean that Gerald Masterton never knew he had that

son, Maddie. Your mother left the country without telling him."

"Oh-h!"

Maddie expelled her breath.

For some reason, she felt giddy, and her limbs had turned to jelly. She sat slumped against the seat, fighting back the tears which threatened. She mustn't cry in front of Stephen Darley. He was the sort who'd have very little patience with sobbing women, she was sure. She blew her nose, wiped her eyes surreptitiously, and then glared at him, wet-lashed.

"I'd have loved him just as much if he hadn't been," she stated huskily, and surprisingly, Steve seemed to understand exactly what this oblique pronouncement meant.

"You're the loyal type, I can see," he agreed, but there was a hint of the old irony back in his voice. "Don't let loyalty blind your common sense, though, Madeleine. Yattabilla isn't the place for you, with, or without, Skeet. Why not pack in the idea?"

Maddie felt tired, relieved, and emotionally confused. Maybe that's why she became so annoyed just then. Afterward—many times afterward—she was to wish that she had not, because it seemed to her in retrospect that that was the moment when she and Steve Darley drew wide apart, finally and irrevocably. Even the former, wary footing receded in the face of Maddie's hot words, leaving only a tenuous bridge of distrust between them.

"Don't bother to go on. Because nothing and nobody is going to stop me from going! I'd be simple if I couldn't see that it would be to your advantage if I didn't go at all, wouldn't I? It's enough that you should hint the most uncomplimentary things about my very own mother, and have me almost out of my mind all day, but you go altogether too far when you suggest that I forfeit my inheritance as well."

After a minute of astonished silence, during which

Steve Darley was obviously wrestling with his own temper, he spoke again. His words were as chill and unfriendly as the coldness in his eyes.

"I'm sorry that that's how you feel, Madeleine. In future, I shall say nothing to imperil your youthful illusions, of that you may be sure. Even so, I doubt if you'll cherish them for very much longer."

Stony-faced, he summoned Luigi, paid the bill, and escorted her down to the street below.

"I'll put you in a taxi," he said coldly.

And that was just what he did. He summoned the nearest one, repeated the address she gave, paid the driver, and bowed an ironic farewell.

Maddie felt uncomfortable all the way back to the boarding house—chastened and ashamed.

She found it difficult to get to sleep, and when she woke up in the morning, she was unrefreshed. She took Skeet into the city again and left him in the sunny Botanical Gardens while she saw Mr. Opal once more, and found out the best way to get to Yattabilla. It seemed that an 11-hour train journey was involved, in order to reach the nearest township.

"I am not very certain of the exact distance of the property itself from the town of Noonday, but you will be in a better position to arrange transport for the final leg of the journey once you are actually there." Mr. Opal regarded her with troubled eyes. "Most of the graziers thereabouts would seem to possess their own private air-transport, Miss Masterton. Of course that simplifies the whole procedure, and cancels out the remoteness of their position to some extent. Mr. Darley, in fact, will be flying back himself shortly. If you would like me to mention that you intend making the journey yourself by a less pleasant means, I am sure he could be prevailed upon to offer you a lift?"

"Definitely not!" Maddie was horrified at the mere idea. She hoped that she would not see Stephen Darley again, ever. "We—I'll take the train, Mr. Opal. I prefer to be independant."

"The night train is preferable, in that case. There's an overnight sleeper service that obviates the tedium a little. I should advise you to reserve."

"I'll do that," promised Maddie.

She returned to the Gardens for Skeet, and together they made their way to the office at Central Station. Her spirits sank when she learned that the sleeping berths for the next four nights were reserved already.

"I can put you on the waiting-list, Miss—Masterton, did you say the name was?"

"No, don't worry. We'll go by the day train instead." She was possessed of an urge to get away from Sydney now, away from the drab boarding house, and the embarrassing memories of her evening with Steve Darley, away from Messrs. Opal, Rose and Heming, to the promise of her new life—hers and Skeet's. "Is it possible to reserve seats—one and a child's, Sydney to Noonday?"

"No problem, miss. The day trip is never booked up the same."

"I'd rather be sure, though. The day after tomorrow, then, please."

The booking clerk wrote neatly on the reservations, deftly punched the date on, handed her the change.

When Maddie ran up the steps and into the sun once more, she found that she was clutching Skeet's hand rather tightly. She felt, now, that the step had been irrevocably taken. There was something very final about those two little cardboard tickets in her handbag, something frighteningly final.

Maddie quelled her pangs of apprehension and took Skeet into the nearest dairy bar again. He was going to miss those milk shakes. Or maybe he wasn't. One doubtless had milk at Yattabilla; some fruit-flavored syrup and an icecube could do the rest.

She was in a happier frame of mind when Robert called for her that evening. She felt comfortable in Robert's company. He was not so very much older than she was herself, and his views on life were youthfully uncomplicated and enthusiastic. She pushed the intrusive image of Steve Darley's cynical mouth and jaded eyes from her mind and concentrated instead upon Robert's boyish charm as she was dressing for her engagement.

Tonight there was no need for special effects and impressions. This evening she could just be herself. Therefore the navy chiffon stayed where it was. Maddie chose a full-length cotton skirt which she had made herself especially for the voyage. In the tropics its gay riot of strong colors had been appropriate and gave a cool, fresh effect. With it she wore a plain white shirt and left her hair falling in its usual straight, shining curtain to her shoulders.

She had phoned Robert and broken the news of her impending departure, because she did not want their last evening to be spoiled by lectures and recriminations. After his initial disapproval had been voiced, Robert had finally agreed to say no more about it and had invited her, instead, to come dancing with him to a nice little place he knew of.

When they arrived at the "nice little place," she could see that it was a very grand place indeed. It must be stretching Robert's pocket to the limit to take her there. Dear Robert! He was doing her proud on what was to be their last outing together for some time to come, and she was secretly very touched.

On the dance floor he drew her into his arms and held her tenderly. "Sweet Maddie," he murmured into her ear. "I'm going to miss you, you know that?"

"Me too, Robert. But I'll write sometimes, and I hope you will too,"

"Of course. And a year will soon pass. I might even be able to come out and see you, but I don't know yet where

I'll be based. They may send me off on another contract, for all I know."

"Would you like that?"

He pulled a wry face. "I suppose I would, except that it would prevent me seeing you as I hope to. A lot can happen in a year, though, Maddie. By the time it's gone, my own future may be secure enough to—well, to say things to you that I can't say just now."

Maddie's eyes had been roving casually over Robert's shoulder as they danced. Suddenly she felt herself stiffen uncontrollably in his arms.

Across the room, a head taller than most of those about him, she could see Stephen Darley. Yes, it was Steve. There was no mistaking that erect carriage and the way he held his well-shaped dark head. It was tipped a little to one side just now, because he was listening to something his partner was saying and smiling urbanely. In his dinner jacket and tucked white shirt, he looked as saturninely handsome as the Devil himself, and as far as Maddie was concerned, every bit as dangerous.

Now he was laughing with outright amusement, and the girl in his arms made a satisfied little *moue*. It was a coquettish gesture, and Steve's answer was to jerk her closer, right against him, so that his face was in her hair and her head was pressed against his shoulder.

Maddie dragged her eyes away. "Let's sit down, Robert," she begged rather breathlessly. "It—it's hot for dancing."

"Aren't you feeling well, Maddie?" He was immediately concerned.

"Yes, I'm all right. It's just—maybe I'm tired."

"It's been too much for you, this whole business. I wish you didn't have to go through with it. Surely there's some other way?"

And let that plausible villain over there get Yattabilla? Never!

"No, Rob, this is the best and only way. Truly."

The other couple were leaving the floor now. Fortunately they were sitting on the opposite side of the long, narrow room. The girl was dark and striking rather than pretty. Her figure, in a classic gown of heavy, white crepe was as near to perfection as any Maddie had ever seen; her skin was deeply tanned, smooth as honey. She looked like a bronze Grecian statue.

Maddie drew a sharp breath. Steve Darley was looking directly at her, across the crowded room. She knew he had seen her. There seemed to be a thread of electricity connecting them just now, and Maddie could feel its current running right through her. It wasn't a pleasant feeling. She looked away.

After that, her evening was ruined. She spent the remaining time taking pains to avoid that other couple. It was a relief when Robert said that they must be going. At last!

To do so, they had to walk right past Steve's table, and as they did that, Maddie found her eyes drawn compulsively to him, in spite of herself. There was no answering flicker of recognition—just a bleak, blank stare. She knew, then, that he was aware that she had purposely avoided him throughout the evening.

A couple just ahead of them blocked the way for a few moments, so that she and Robert had to continue standing quite close to the others' table, waiting to pass. As they stood, the girl's voice reached her. It was smooth and resonant, with perfect pitch and diction, as one might expect of a bronze Grecian goddess.

"What unusual hair, Steve. Do look, darling. Isn't it wonderful what can come out of a bottle these days? So foolish to meddle with nature, don't you think—and the color's quite fatal with that skirt, the poor child."

Maddie's face was aflame as she followed Robert past them to the exit. She gritted her teeth and wooden-faced, allowed him to hand her into a cab.

Hateful goddess! Hateful creature! They both were!

Maddie sank back thankfully into the comforting, concealing darkness of the taxi, glad that Robert, at least, was unaware of her humiliation.

Those cruel words, that beautiful dark head, that proud and perfect figure would be etched on Maddie's mind forever.

The most humbling thing of all, though, was the knowledge that Steve Darley had witnessed the whole thing. Maybe he had even been an accomplice, in thought, at least.

Maddie tried to forget the way he had been looking at the goddess before she spoke those words that had made Maddie glance away and stumble hastily forward, out of their sight. It had been a look of pride, of possesion, of knowledge that his companion's flamboyant beauty was the envy of every other man in the nightclub. Steve Darley had doubtless thought it worthwhile to get out his dinner jacket for her, no matter how many business appointments he had had that day. And Maddie betted that she wouldn't be sent home, alone, in a taxi, at the end of the evening, either.

Recalling his austerely handsome face, and the way his brown hands had drawn the statuesque, white-clad girl close against him, Maddie found to her dismay that she was trembling.

CHAPTER THREE

Skeet licked the tips of his sticky fingers and wiped his hands on the cuffs of his khaki shorts, blatantly ignoring his sister's frown.

The carriage was full of flies and heat. It was difficult to decide which was the worse, thought Skeet morosely. Certainly the heat was there all the time, whereas the flies came and went.

He wondered idly where they went, in between their intermittent invasions. Maybe to the next-door compartment, where there was a baby howling, and a pungent smell of orange juice that mingled with the cloying sweetness of talcum powder whenever you walked past. Or maybe they went right outside, away from the train altogether, in search of cooler air. That's where Skeet would have gone, if he had been a fly on this train. Not that the air did look much cooler out there, but at least it would not be as boring as in here.

All day they had been trundling monotonously through the country. At first, the deep blue gorges and startling orange escarpments of the mountain ranges had provided some excitement. Skeet had felt fresh and alert, and there had been Maddie's picnic to look forward to. After the mountains, they had descended to undulating gentle slopes with shiny creeks, swaying poplars, and pretty green plots of clover and lucerne.

By the time the picnic was eaten, the train was pushing its way steadily through a wheat-belt of rich red soil dotted over with bright, oily-leafed carrajong trees, but that was hours and hours ago now. The picnic was finished, and so was the pretty scenery.

Both were behind them. All that was left was a paper bag with a few bulls'-eyes in it, and a single stick of licorice. The endless expanse of flat, parched country was broken only by the occasional relief of an odd, small railway siding no more than a shed—a signal-box. Sometimes a general store squatted in the shade of a few dejected eucalypts.

Skeet reached for the remaining licorice stick and bit a small piece. He planned to make it last, since there was nothing else but bulls'-eyes left, and he was sick of them. In fact he was sick. The first faint queasiness had assailed his stomach a few moments ago, but Skeet resolutely ignored its warning. You had to do something, cooped up here all day. What was there to do but read and eat? The comics were finished, so that left eating.

When the licorice, too, was finished, he lay back and dozed. He must have actually gone to sleep, because when Maddie pulled at his shoulder to wake him up, it was completely dark. The train had slowed and was grinding noisily over a series of points at the approach to a proper railway station.

Skeet sat up and rubbed a round peep-hole in the dust on the window-pane, peering out. You couldn't see much at all, except for lights shining out of the darkness, and a lot of people scattered along the platform, waiting for the train to come to a stop.

"Here, Skeet. Take these. Quickly!" Maddie handed him the comics, a canvas tote, and the bulls'-eyes. "Put them in your pocket and hurry, Skeet. We're here!"

"Here" must mean Noonday, Skeet supposed sleepily. A silly name, Noonday, especially when it was pitch dark outside. It was night in Noonday. Skeet would have giggled at that thought—would have repeated it to Maddie, but she was busy cramming the waste papers from the picnic into the small bin provided. Anyway, he was still feeling sick.

It was worse when he stood up.

Skeet pushed two of the bulls'-eyes a little desperately into his mouth, stuffed the bag into his pocket as Maddie had suggested, and followed her along the corridor.

People ahead of her had already opened the door and were stepping down onto the platform.

Maddie stepped down, too, and pulled the cases after her.

"Come on, Skeet."

It was quite a jump, when your legs were short with the shortness of a mere ten years.

Skeet jumped down after Maddie, and when he did so, his stomach seemed to be left hanging up there somewhere in the sky. He stood for a moment, waiting for it to subside, but it didn't. Not really. It settled somewhere in the upper part of his chest, even though he stood quite still.

"Come on, Skeet!"

Maddie sounded impatient. She was, in fact, hot, tired and irritable, and very uncertain, but she didn't let Skeet see that. Only her impatience showed through, because she had to get her little brother to move, to stop him just standing there holding up all the traffic.

He chewed the sweet remaining in his mouth, swallowed it, and uttered thinly, "Maddie, I feel sick."

"Well, you can't be sick here," she told him with some asperity. "We've a long way to go yet, Skeet. We have to get out to Yattabilla somehow. Sit on that bench while I make some inquiries, and don't—oh!" Her words faded into a gasp of pure dismay.

"Good evening, Madeleine. A comfortable journey, I trust?" Steve Darley inquired urbanely.

He had suddenly materialized out of the dispersing crowd and stood before her, calm and debonair in a pair of pale drill slacks and open-necked shirt with rolled-up sleeves.

Maddie, hot, sticky and dishevelled, felt at a distinct and immediate disadvantage.

"You!" she exclaimed. "I hadn't expected to see you, Mr. Darley."

"No, I can see you hadn't," he agreed smoothly. "And

I thought we had settled for christian names. Mine's Steve, if you remember. This is all your baggage?"

He tucked a large case under one arm, took up the others and the canvas tote abandoned by Skeet.

"Yes, that's it. But I—I have to make some inquiries first," she hedged breathlessly. It was humiliating not to know exactly where you were going next, or how precisely you were going to get there, especially when it happened to be the place where you'd actually been born.

Steve's face creased with amusement. As he smiled, his white teeth glinted in the yellow dimness of the platform lights. "If you mean you want to ask where Yattabilla is, and how to get there, why not say so? And you needn't bother right now. That's why I came in to meet you. In any case, we're going no farther than this tonight."

"We?" Maddie asked coldly.

"We." The grin was quite devilish this time. "We'll stay at the hotel overnight and get an early start. It's a good 60 miles, and you look whacked." He seemed about to add something to that, changed his mind and said instead, "Is this your brother?" nodding to where Skeet sat slumped on the platform seat a short distance off.

"Yes, that's Skeet."

Steve walked over, looked down at the disconsolate small form. "Hello, sonny. What's your name?"

"Skeet Masterton."

"No, your real name?"

The little boy hesitated. "Anthony Edward Masterton." He had to put his head right back, the man in front of him was so tall. "I feel sick, mister."

Steve, like Maddie, ignored that.

"Come on, Anthony Edward, on your feet," he said briskly. "The hotel's just across the street. You and your sister will feel better when you've had a wash and eaten some dinner."

Dinner! Skeet's tummy turned right over, like a porpoise in an ocean swell. His palms were clammy. He had to almost run to keep up with Maddie and the big man who strode silently through the railway building and into the street beyond.

It was a wide, tree-flanked street, almost completely deserted. They crossed it and walked along the other sidewalk for a bit.

Steve Darley slowed, aware of the dragging steps behind him. When the child caught up, he asked conversationally, "What's Skeet short for? It's an odd sort of name."

"I dunno." The owner of the odd name was not inclined to be helpful.

"Say I dunno—I mean, I don't know, Mr. Darley—please, Skeet," Maddie prompted automatically.

"I dunno what it's short for, Mr. Darley," he obliged.

"Steve will do," said that long-legged individual, turning once more to Maddie. "Skeet?"

"It's short for mosquito. It was a joke of Mom's, at least, that's how it started. When he was little she used to say he was as pestiferous as a mosquito. We started calling him Skeet for short, and it sort of stuck," Maddie informed him.

"I see. In here, then, Skeet." He guided them into a shabby but comfortable reception hall, put down the cases. "Wait here for a moment."

Skeet blinked up at his sister. "Maddie, I feel sick," he whispered urgently.

"Not here, Skeet," she pleaded, glancing uneasily at the man's broad back, across at the reception desk now. "Not here. Just hang on, Skeet."

"I can't hang on!" The little boy's voice rose ominously, caught the ear of the big brown long-legged man.

Steve swung around and acted immediately and without ceremony. Skeet found himself scooped up under one arm just like the suitcases had been, and borne with complete lack of dignity, but with creditable speed, through a door at the end of the hall. Maddie, beyond humiliation, could only wait helplessly for their reappearance.

When they returned, Steve's face was unrevealing, Skeet's pea-green. The man sat the child down on a leather seat against the wall and asked kindly, "Okay now, sonny?"

"Okay, mister—um—Steve." Skeet's freckled face smiled up drowsily. He rested his head back and closed his eyes against further inquiries.

Steve Darley stood for a moment, took in the pallor, the freckles, that bright carroty hair that spiked out in all directions. Then he turned to Maddie.

"Haven't you learned by now that a traveling child shouldn't be indulged with all the sickly rubbish in creation, especially on a long, hot journey such as this one?"

Maddie blushed. Anger, pity for Skeet, and a sense of guilt made her prickle with antagonism.

"I don't need you to tell me what's best for Skeet, thank you," she replied coldly.

"I'm telling you what's worst for him, not what's best. If you know it already, why indulge him?" He turned, picked up the boy. "Come on, nipper. I'll take you to your room, and your sister can put you into bed. You'll feel like a new feller in the morning!"

Skeet gave a pale grin. His thin hands clutched at the broad, white-shirted shoulders. "You bet, Steve!"

Maddie's lips were pressed tightly together as she followed the bellboy in the wake of Steve Darley and her brother.

The room was large, shabby like the hall downstairs, but reasonably cool and comfortable. Double screen doors opened out onto a balcony above the street. Furniture was limited to the bare necessities—a couple of chairs, a wardrobe, a marble washstand, and two narrow beds.

Steve glanced around, then down at his watch.

"I'll see you downstairs in ten minutes," he said. "The dining room is on the left as you come down."

"Thank you, I'm not hungry." Maddie's voice was intentionally frigid.

"You'll be there, nevertheless. As I have it from Skeet, he was the only one who made free with the chocolates and suckers—isn't that so, Skeet?"

Skeet nodded agreeably. "Maddie never ate a thing, hardly, did you, Mad? She said she couldn't look at food. Sis is always like that when she's all steamed up about something, aren't you, Maddie?"

"That's enough, Skeet." She wrestled with his buttons, gave him a quelling look.

"Well, it's true," Skeet reaffirmed, not to be quelled on any account. "An' you are all steamed up—about this Yattabilla place and that man you said was so—"

"*Skeet!*" Her face was flaming. She gave him an urgent shake, none too gently. Skeet decided that he had really better get undressed pretty quickly, since Maddie appeared to be in one of her moods.

"I'll be down presently," she told Steve. "You needn't wait."

"A pity. And just when the conversation was becoming so interesting," he observed blandly. "Very well, Madeleine, I'll leave you to it. Ten minutes, mind."

She heard his steps retreating along the passage to a room farther down the corridor somewhere. Maddie clenched her teeth. Oh lord! Why did that wretched man have to turn up like this? And why did Skeet have to disgrace her by being sick the moment they arrived? And why, of all the people he could doubtless have chosen, had her father picked Steve Darley to be an executor and trustee of his estate? Not only a trustee, either, she was forced to remind herself. Maybe even a legatee, if Maddie couldn't hold out for her rights and stay at Yattabilla for the required time.

Well, she would stay, she and Skeet, come what may.

In fact, if the man only knew, his high-handed behavior had the effect of strengthening Maddie's determination rather than weakening it. She became more resolved than ever that nothing and nobody was going to stand in her way. Sydney was behind her, and so was London and the imports firm. She had burned her boats, come all this way, and she certainly hadn't done it for nothing. Maybe Steve Darley didn't know it yet, but she could be just as determined, as single-minded, as he. She was quite fit for his scheming ways and devious charm. She wasn't in the least taken in by his motives in meeting them at the train at Noonday, either. He would doubtless do his utmost to put her off at the very start—to present Yattabilla in the worst possible light. That's why he had come to drive them there, rather than let them find their own way.

Maddie waited for Skeet to brush his teeth in the bathroom along the passage, then saw him slipped between the sheets.

" 'Night, Skeet."

"G'night, Maddie." His voice was drowsy, indistinct with sleepiness. "Have a good dinner, Mad. I bet you need it, after eating practically nothing all day."

"Thanks, Skeet, I will." Maddie's reply was tender, in spite of herself. Mosquito, the pestiferous one, certainly did not make life any easier, but she loved him, all the same.

After making herself tidy she went downstairs, into the dining room on the left.

Steve was already there, sitting at a table set with cheap steel cutlery. He rose when she appeared, saw her seated, handed her one of the glasses he had brought in from the bar at the rear of the hotel.

"Gin and tonic," he informed her lazily, in answer to the unspoken query in her eye. "I thought the ice and a lemon twist might help to cool you down—that temper, too."

He was baiting her. Maddie glared at him repressively

and sipped her drink. It was very cold, and the lemon did give it a certain tart freshness.

"Why is this place called Noonday?" she asked, purposely ignoring that opening personal thrust. She was darned if he was going to amuse himself at her expense.

The broad shoulders in the white shirt shrugged carelessly. His sleeves were still rolled up, but Maddie noticed that he had buttoned the neck of the shirt and now wore a neat, striped tie.

"I guess the explorer had run out of inspiration by the time he arrived here. He named almost every landmark after himself on the way out—mountains, gaps, rivers, creeks, even the plains. This town is sited on a permanent waterhole in the river—a stretch that never goes dry. He'd have been pretty glad to see that waterhole, with the wilga trees scattered all along it, after a long hot slog across a waterless waste." He quirked an eyebrow at her absorbed face. "His diary records that he reached here at noon and pitched camp. Noonday it's been ever since."

"Oh, I see."

The train had come across that same waterless waste, too; chuffing slowly through the vibrant heat, bringing herself and Skeet with it. Maddie could realize what a welcome sight those trees and that stretch of water must have been to some weary, dry-throated, footsore discoverer of long ago. She had not yet seen the river, the trees, or the layout of modern Noonday, because it had been so dark when they arrived, but her imagination was captivated, all the same.

"You think it romantic, Madeleine?" Uncanny, the way he had read her mind. "You won't for long. You'll soon be immersed in harsh realities, my dear—and with only your stubborn little self to blame." He ground out his cigarette, as a woman appeared from the kitchen regions, carrying two plates of mutton stew and vegetables already served out.

"No oysters tonight, I'm afraid." Steve's gray eyes

were dark with irony. "Out here you eat what you're given, and no questions asked. You accept the cards that a sometimes unkind Fate deals out, too, and simply do what you can with them. You'll see just what I mean before long. Salt? Pepper?" He passed the cruet set, helped himself liberally after she herself had used it.

Was he warning her? Maddie glanced surreptitiously at the unrevealing mould of his weathered features. It was totally devoid of expression as he applied himself to his food.

Maddie determinedly did the same. He was trying to shake her, no doubt about that. She had thought he might do that—had almost been prepared for just these words. Even so, the little butterflies of apprehension had started fluttering alarmingly about once more inside her. She made a bid to control them and kept her eyes fixed on her plate.

No oysters? No, and no frills, either—not out here. And all that grandeur, the Blue Balcony, the gourmet menu, the wine and music, had in any case been purely incidental so far as Steve Darley's invitation to her had been concerned. He hadn't even bothered to change for dinner, had he? Not like he had for the Greek goddess, for instance. Maddie wished that that sophisticated, proud white vision would not keep intruding into her thoughts.

It was doubtless the sight of this big, powerful, teak-skinned man, exuding self-assurance on the opposite side of the table, who was responsible for the unwelcome image her mind had conjured up.

She would never be comfortable in his company again, Maddied decided now. Not after that! He had been bound to realize who it was that his lovely companion had alluded to so cattily. The only thing he didn't know was that Madeleine, too, had heard her. A pity she had not been able to catch his own murmured reply. If she had, she might have had a better chance now of knowing what he was really thinking when his eyes roved her face and finally came to rest on her rich, golden mane, just as they were doing right this minute.

"Pudding?"

Maddie shook her head.

"Cheese, then, and two coffees, please," he told the woman who still lingered after removing their dinner-plates. "How long is it since your mother died, Madeleine?"

The direct question took her by surprise. "Four years."

"That made Skeet six, and you 16, is that correct?"

"Yes, that's right."

"And you were left with the child on your hands. How did you handle it?"

Maddie's hackles rose. He made Skeet sound like an unwanted parcel, and he had never been that! He might be Skeet and pestiferous at times, but never un-wanted—never a burden. She wished she hadn't told Steve the mosquito bit, after all.

"I managed, thank you." She was brief, defensive.

"How?" he persisted, but not as if it really mattered.

"Well, I—I left school, went to a business college, and took a commercial course, that's how. The rooms I found were run by a nice woman who didn't mind a small boy around—she'd had a family of her own. In fact, she used to look out for Skeet when he came back from school in the afternoons and kept him going until I could get there myself."

The gray glance probed keenly. "She did that for noth-ing? Without expectation of payment?" Steve queried, drawing the familiar cigarette papers and tobacco from his shirt pocket, and pushing his chair back a little from the table.

"Not exactly for nothing." Maddie spread her fingers and regarded them closely. "I took a job four nights a week," she admitted with some reluctance. "It was shift work in a late cafeteria. I used to go once I'd put Skeet to bed. They paid the waitresses quite well."

Steve, too, was looking at her hands. Maddie put them quickly down out of sight, on her lap. They weren't really pretty hands. The nails were short and neat, because of the typing. No amount of nightly creaming could quite disguise the fact that they had had to be useful sort of hands. Unbidden, there came to Maddie a picture of other hands—the slender, tapering fingers, the polished oval brightness of the Grecian goddess's beautiful nails.

"And then?"

Maddie shrugged. "It was easier once I had a regular daytime job," she admitted candidly.

"In an importing business, I think you said?"

"Yes, it was quite a good job, really, although without the prospect of much advancement. It was safe and secure, anyway. I was thankful for that." She yawned, in spite of herself. The meal, the warmth of the night, the strain of his presence, were telling on her.

Steve Darley pushed back his chair and came around to hers.

"Come, you've had a long day. You'd better get to bed."

His tone was kind, quite gentle, almost as though she had been a child, scarcely older than Skeet.

Maddie blushed. His hand on her elbow sent an unwelcome little shiver through her whole body. He was towering over her, and his eyes were on her hair again. Remembering made Maddie draw hastily away, rather pointedly shaking off the supporting grasp that was guiding her toward the stairs.

"Thanks," she said more tartly and ungraciously than she intended, "but I'm not so tired that I can't go up alone."

The hand on her elbow was withdrawn abruptly, and she looked up to see that his eyes had fastened on her, unpleasantly. They were cold, dark, impenetrable slits, that glittered oddly. When he spoke, his tone was at variance with those angry eyes.

"What's the matter, Madeleine?" he asked, in an amused drawl. "Is something rattling you?"

She ignored that. All the same, her breath came quickly as she hurried up the stairs.

From the gloom at the bottom she distinctly heard a laugh—a brief, deep chuckle—but a laugh, nevertheless.

"Don't worry, Madeleine." The teasing voice followed her, lifting slightly as she gained the upstairs hall, so that she would be sure to hear what it was saying. "You needn't, you know. Cradle-snatching isn't one of my vices, and furthermore, my dear girl, you don't happen to be my type."

Maddie found that she was almost running along the corridor to the room she was to share with Skeet. She somehow made herself slow down and walk calmly, so that the man still standing in the hall below would not guess how badly her heart was behaving, thud, thud, thud, against her ribs.

For a moment, down there, she had been frightened—precisely why, she could not have said.

Skeet was sleeping soundly when she gained the bedroom. He had pushed away the sheet, and his small body was sprawled over, almost onto his face. There was more color in his cheeks, merging the freckles with its own faint flush, but his spiky carrot mop was as unruly as ever against the pillow. In his blue, striped pajamas he looked touchingly innocent, angelic in slumber.

Maddie touched her lips fleetingly to the freckled forehead and quietly undressed. For a while she sat, brushing her hair with long, calming strokes. When she switched off the light, she hesitated a moment and then walked over to the double screen doors and stepped out onto the Victorian-style balcony. Its wrought-iron balustrade reminded her of something. Something painful. The Blue Balcony. It was like the Blue Balcony, except that it wasn't all edged out in blue and gilt. Beneath it there wasn't the hubbub of milling city traffic. There was just a wide, silent, tree-lined street in a dark, silent, country town.

Maddie walked to the edge and peered up and down the deserted thoroughfare.

It wasn't quite deserted, after all. Across the street, almost opposite, she could glimpse a white shirt, a tall, dark form. Steve Darley was leaning against a post that supported the canvas awning of the shop over the way, quietly smoking a last cigarette before he, too, retired. Maddie could see the small puffs of smoke drifting lazily up toward the stars.

Cautiously she withdrew, closed the screen doors noiselessly and slipped into bed. Lying there listening to Skeet's even breathing, she felt curiously alone, curiously depressed. It had, she knew, something to do with Steve, standing out there under the night sky.

A pity they couldn't even be friends, she thought drowsily. Not that that was possible, as things were, because they both wanted the same thing, didn't they. They both wanted Yattabilla. And anyway, hadn't he stressed just now that she wasn't his type? Not that you had to be someone's type just to be friends with them, did you?

Maddie lifted her head, punched her pillow, and tried once more to compose herself for sleep. She, Maddie, wasn't his type, but the Grecian goddess was. And she, Maddie, could never be like the Grecian goddess. There wasn't a hope that she ever could!

On that forlorn note, Maddie drifted into restless slumber.

CHAPTER FOUR

Skeet was up and dressed long before his sister next morning. When Maddie saw the empty bed beside her own, she dressed hastily, plunged the striped pajamas and her own night things back into the canvas tote, and went downstairs.

No one was in evidence, although she could hear sounds of activity in the kitchen quarters.

Maddie went through the reception hall and stepped out into the street. Noonday was bigger than she had thought it to be. It was low and spreading, but with a neatness and order of planning entirely lacking in the angled jumble of thoroughfares in either London or Sydney. This was Maddie's first experience of a country town, and she was impressed by the serenity of it all—the wide straight streets, the shade trees that bordered them, and the spacious stores with their neat canvas awnings. The cars were big, modern and shiny. The gardens were colorful, and luxuriant, watered from the slow-running river, the stretch that never dried up. The dots of wilga trees were nearby.

Maddie walked a short way up the street, curious, critical. She liked what she saw of Noonday. There was no evidence of poverty or shabbiness. Every building, every car, looked as though it had a reason for being there—as if it were making its own individual contribution to Noonday's prosperity. It was a thriving, cheerful center, sun-washed and peaceful too.

Maddie felt her own spirits lift. You couldn't help feeling good in a place like Noonday. Its modernity, its cleanliness, its tranquility—all encouraged in her an optimism that she had not felt last night.

When she returned to the hotel, Skeet was sitting on

the bench by the wall looking idly over some leaflets he had picked from the pile on the reception desk.

Steve was there, too. He was standing with his feet a little apart and his hands on his hips, immersed in conversation with a younger man.

When he saw her, he stopped speaking, and summoned her over with the familiar imperious gesture. It was a gesture that Maddie resented. For two cents she would have ignored it, only Skeet hadn't even looked up from his reading, and anyway, there was something undeniably attractive about Steve's companion.

He had fair, straight hair, neatly parted; smooth, youthful features in a round, congenial sort of face; happy eyes and a tan almost as deep as Steve's own. The two men were dressed very similarly, in pale, tight-legged moleskins, khaki open-necked shirts, and fine leather elastic-sided boots with well-defined heels.

There, Maddie decided, the similarity ended. Steve Darley was of a more powerful build altogether, with an aura of authority that even his younger companion seemed to find slightly overwhelming. It was probably responsible for his obvious air of deference and respect. Maddie knew just how he felt! She had an instant, common bond with this nice young man, even before they had been introduced.

"Madeleine, I'd like you to meet Tom Simson. Miss Masterton, Tom."

Maddie found her hand grasped and wrung with refreshing enthusiasm.

"Hello, Tom." She smiled up into the boyishly flushed face. "My friends call me Maddie," she murmured invitingly, some devil inside her gloating at Steve's fleeting look of surprise.

"Do they, by Jove! Well, Maddie, I hope I'm going to be counted as one of your friends in that case," Tom laughed. "Thanks for getting me in on the ground floor, Steve. I reckon this one's going to set Noonday by the ears, don't you? The Noonday sheilas will have to look to their laurels!"

Steve quirked a brow at her reddening cheeks and jingled the change in his pocket impatiently.

"Tom's something of an authority on the local glamour, I believe," he informed her smoothly. "He's also the junior partner in our biggest Stock and Station agency—in which capacity you might enter those cast ewes for the sale next week, Tom. As I was saying, Hanson can drove them in. They'll be yarded by Thursday night for sure."

"Yes, of course, Steve. I'll make a note."

"Do that." Steve's drawl was dismissing. "Come, Madeleine. Here, Skeet, you'd better get some breakfast before we leave town."

Tom Simson moved reluctantly to the door.

"Maybe I'll be seeing you again, Maddie, eh? Will you be coming in next week—to the sale, perhaps?"

"Madeleine won't be at the sale, Tom." Steve answered for her. "She and her brother aren't staying at my place. They're going to Yattabilla."

"To Yattabilla?" Tom was perplexed. "Look here, Steve, you can't mean to *stay* at Yattabilla?"

"That's just what I do mean, though, Tom. Now, scram, like a good fellow, while we get some breakfast—and don't forget those ewes."

"Er—no, Steve. Well, so long, Maddie. See you."

"See you, Tom." Maddie couldn't keep a wistful note out of her voice. Noonday was fun! With someone like Tom, it might even have been more fun. And what would Yattabilla be like in comparison?

Tom had sounded sort of surprised that they were going out there, she and Skeet. He hadn't made it sound as if staying there would be much fun at all. Still, once there—once she was out of the masterful Steve Darley's clutches—she'd be her own boss and do as she pleased. There was nothing to stop her coming in to Noonday any time she liked, was there? And just because Steve's sheep happened to be coming in to a sale, that didn't mean that Maddie and Skeet couldn't come, too. It was a free country, after all.

"Yes, I'll see you, Tom," she called more loudly, more positively, and was rewarded to see the retreating figure turn and wave, quite gaily, to show that he had heard.

"Don't be too innocently impressionable, will you, Madeleine?" Steve's murmur grated on her ear as he stood aside to allow her to pass into the dining room. "There's a girl shortage out here, and the local lads are apt to go overboard for any imported talent that happens to show up."

Ungallant brute! thought Maddie sorely, not even bothering to acknowledge that she had heard him. That was all he thought of her, obviously—just another girl, in a little country town where scarcity value provided almost any girl with instant popularity.

Maddie remained silent through most of breakfast.

In spite of herself, her feelings were bruised. She was humiliated, for the second time in his presence. The first time, it had been the goddess. This time it had been Steve himself, quite deliberately. Just then, Maddie found herself longing to be free of his overbearing presence. It would be heavenly to say good-by to Steve and to be alone with Skeet once more, even if it meant being alone at Yattabilla. She longed for the moment when Steve would leave them and get out of her sight more than she had longed for anything in a good long while.

The hours dragged by. Roads, dust, and the accompanying flies were now the background to her unhappy thoughts.

Steve's big Chevvy was comfortably upholstered and well sprung. The engine purred quietly as it ate up the miles. They were monotonous miles, and there were long spells when the shock-absorbers shook and quivered unceasingly over the deep corrugations in the dirt road.

Skeet's piping voice, where he sat in front next to Steve, rose above the muted music from the car radio in an endless succession of questions.

"What are those birds, Steve?"

"The pink and gray ones? They're galahs, Skeet—a kind of parrot."

"And those ones there? There must be hundreds of them!"

"Parakeets, Skeet. They're colorful, aren't they? They often fly around in great flocks like that. We disturbed them, and when one is disturbed, the lot take off. Noisy little beggars, eh?"

"Mm, they sure are, Steve. But pretty. What colors! I never knew there were birds like that in the world, all colors of the rainbow almost. Can you get more than one channel on that radio?"

Long fingers flicked a switch.

"Two, actually, but this one doesn't have such good reception when we're traveling. Too many commercials, too."

The switch was returned to its previous position.

"Why's there a hole in that fence, Steve—the one ahead, where the road goes through?"

"That's not a hole, young feller. Well, it is in a way, I suppose. It's a ramp instead of a gate, you see. It stops sheep and cattle getting over. Saves opening so many gates, because the car just goes over it, whereas the livestock avoid it like the plague. You'll see when we get there."

They rattled over the sleepers on the ramp with a deafening noise that sent hundreds more of the little yellow and green birds whirring out of the gums along the fence.

"What's that, Steve? Quick, look! It—it's not a—a—*kangaroo*?" Skeet's voice was awed.

"It's a 'roo, all right, and a big feller, too. See him

bounding away into the scrub. He could go faster than this car's going right now, Skeet, if he wanted to." The man's deep voice was amused.

"Gee! Truly?"

"Truly, Skeet. I'm not putting you on." A pause. "Are you quite comfortable in the back ther , Madeleine? If you can't see the scenery properly, three can easily fit in front, as I said earlier."

"Thank you, I'm perfectly comfortable," Maddie replied stiffly.

He *had* suggested that they all ride in front at the beginning of the journey. When he had opened the passenger door and Maddie had seen that she was to be in the middle, she had hastily scrambled into the back, saying that she much preferred to stretch out.

She had a feeling, by the way that horridly expressive eyebrow lifted and the gray glint came into his eye, that Steve had not been deceived as to her motive. He had made no further comment. He had simply opened the rear door for her as she wrestled with the handle and saw her seated.

Now, although she could indeed stretch her legs, or even loll along the whole length of the seat if she chose, she had to admit that one could not see the scenery nearly so well from here. She had to duck her head into her shoulders to peer at everything upon which Steve passed comment. Furthermore, the back of his crisp, dark head, tanned column of neck, and wide, khaki-clad shoulders proved almost as unbearably close and provoking as if she had been sitting in the front seat, wedged between himself and Skeet.

When he pulled up in front of a gate across the road, the long trail of dust flying out behind the car caught up with them. It came flurrying into the car in a suffocating cloud that settled over everything and everyone.

Steve ignored it.

"Gate," he said, in an expressionless voice.

Maddie, startled, scrabbled at the door-handle.

"*Front* passenger. Leap to it, Skeet!"

"What? Oh—sure, Steve." The child scrambled out obligingly.

"He—he might not manage the catch, Steve. He's only little." Maddie was defensive.

"Not too little to learn, Madeleine." Steve's tone was hard. "You coddle him too much."

The child was wrestling with the gate, tugging at the upright iron bar. Steve leaned his head out of the window.

"Sideways, Skeet, not toward you. Take your time—really *look* at it and discover how it works." He stretched his legs clear of the pedals and started to roll himself a cigarette. Maddie hated the calmness in those fingers, and she hated the way he had spoken about Skeet.

The little boy was standing now on the bottom rung of the gate, working the bar this way and that in red-faced embarrassment. His carroty hair stuck out in all directions. He glanced, just once, despairingly, over his thin shoulders to the two people waiting in the car. Maddie just could not ignore the appeal in that glance.

"I said stay *here*." Steve's eyes had caught her movement toward the door. He leaned out the window again. "Take your time, young nipper," he advised Skeet once more. One could not but admit that he sounded much more kind and patient with her brother than he had with Maddie herself. "See what happens to the bottom of the catch when you pull the bar sideways. It releases, doesn't it? Well, try opening the gate at the same time, Skeet, and pulling the whole thing toward you."

The boy obeyed, and sure enough, the gate swung wide. He sent Steve a jerky wave of triumph, then stood on the bottom rung again and rode with it to its final position clear of the roadway.

"I did it, Steve!" he cried jubilantly, when the car had

gone through, and he had shut the gate and returned to his seat.

Steve ruffled his hair and let in the clutch.

"Sure you did, Skeet. That one'll never beat you again, eh, old cobber. Now we'll see how the next one goes."

There were quite a number of other gates after that, and each time Skeet jumped out. Now he was doing it excitedly, as if the challenge of opening that gate had suddenly become enormous fun.

"That's it, Skeet." Maddie tried to ignore the new rapport that had sprung up between the man in front and the eager boy. She tried not to feel, quite suddenly, out on the fringe. "That's it, feller. This one is called a parrot-catch, because it's shaped just like the beak of one of those pink and gray galahs you were asking about. That bit lifts up, right? It's like a cocky's tongue, in the middle of his beak, see?"

After a time of intermittent gate sessions and long dusty stretches of road in between, they passed a fork where a notch of ironbarks separated the track into two.

Steve jerked his head to the road on the left.

"That's the way to Bibbi."

"Bibbi?"

"Yes, my own place. It's on the other side of that ridge there."

This time, when Maddie looked out, she could see a long mountain range ahead of them rising out of the plains in the distance. It had the pretty mauve softness lent by heat waves off the plain, but it was clear enough to see the broken line of valleys denting its horizons into deeper color. Pale reddish escarpments, worn by the onslaught of wind and sand, made gashes in the farther end, where it finally crumbled away into the plain again.

"There's Yattabilla homestead now," Steve informed them without expression.

Maddie peered out anxiously. There was an inexplicable lump of emotion blocking her throat—a mixture of fright and longing. This was, after all, her homecoming. This was where she had been born, although she couldn't recognize a single landmark, or recall a solitary feature of the surrounding terrain.

"Is *that* it?" Skeet's voice was tremulous with disappointment, disbelief. Even Maddie blinked her eyes several times, as if by doing so she could wake herself up from what she could only wish had been a dream—a nightmare.

The homestead was a dissolute dwelling of creaking timbers, whose cracks were sufficiently wide in places to render it open to the prevailing weather. (Maddie could only pray that that weather might always be kind.) One end, that they walked around now toward the veranda, was made differently from the rest. It seemed to be laced together in some way with pieces of hard mud brick.

"Pise." That was Steve, still expressionless. "This is the original house. The weatherboard bit was a later addition."

Later? Maddie looked askance. How much later could it possibly have been, she wondered, frantically racking her brains for her scant knowledge of Australian history. Surely it must have been one of the first habitations since Captain Cook came ashore at Botany Bay.

Carefully she summoned her control, because she had a sudden hysterical desire to giggle. Somehow she managed to mask her expression and her thoughts, because Steve was watching her closely, through unrevealing, half-shut eyes.

They walked on, past the baked mud bit, to the veranda beyond. The weatherboard portion of the house was raised right off the ground. There were wooden steps up onto the veranda. The flooring was rotten, completely gone in places.

"White ants." The dispassionate toe of Steve's elastic-sided stockman's boot despatched a decaying piece of timber into what might once have been a yard. He placed the cases one by one on the veranda.

"So long, feller." He patted the top of Skeet's carroty head, turned to go.

"W-won't you stay for a—well, a cup of tea?" Maddie felt somehow driven to ask.

His smile was a little grim. "I don't think so, Madeleine, thanks. I'll leave you alone to your surprises. I'm sure that's what you'd prefer."

"Yes—well—er—" she extended her hand—"thank you for bringing us here. It was very kind of you to meet us in Noonday." She was secretly enormously relieved that he was going. She felt too shocked to keep up this pretense of calm much long. There was a lot to be said for being able to lick one's wounds in private.

"Kind?" The shrug of his broad shoulders negated her words. "If you ask Mrs. Lawrence down there in that hut, she'll give you some tips. Lal Lawrence is your overseer, actually, but at the end of the day, he's answerable to me. Please remember that, won't you, Madeleine? And try not to keep little brother wrapped in cotton wool, will you? He's tougher than you may think."

With a brisk and businesslike gesture of farewell, he was gone.

Maddie sat down hard on the edge of the rotting veranda and watched the dustball that was Steve's big Chevvy roll slowly away, back along the road to that fork in the track that went to Bibbi.

"Gee, Maddie! It's not much of a place, is it?" Skeet's voice came disparagingly, jolting her numbed brain into action once more.

She scrambled to her feet, picked up the cases, and trod warily in the direction of what she supposed was the hall.

"Not right now, it isn't, Skeet, but let's not be too disappointed. I'll make it nice, you wait and see. Bring the canvas bag, Skeet, and let's go in." Her tone was purposely bracing.

Inside was almost worse than out. It was dark and hot, with a stuffy smell of mustiness and disuse. The windows were small, and Maddie found them difficult to open when she tried to do so. The catches were rusty, and the putty had worked loose from their shaky frames. The floors were wooden—cypress pine, with a pretty grain, although dull with neglect. Maddie was relieved to note that their condition was somewhat superior to that of the decaying veranda. Some wax and her own elbow-grease might help. But that linoleum was beyond everything! It ran from the main hall right through to the kitchen quarters. It was buckled, cracked, and dry, breaking up altogether in numerous places. It did not take her long to realize that these were the places where the rain pelted in through the cracks in the weatherboard. It was obvious, too, from the expanse and position of the affected floor, then when it rained, a lot of water entered, one way and another. Maddie could only suppose that her father had either been too busy to keep mopping up the water, or else he had lost heart to the extent that he simply hadn't bothered. The water had lain there in ample pools until the heat of the atmosphere had evaporated it all again.

Maybe it did not rain all that often, anyway. Maddie opined to herself on a more cheerful note, remembering about the explorer and his hot, dry slog across the plains to Noonday, the only place hereabouts where the river didn't dry up. Maybe Yattabilla was a very dry place—the feed out on the plain certainly looked brown and uninteresting enough. Maybe it wouldn't rain at all—at least, not for the year she and Skeet would be here. She had read somewhere that in parts of Australia it did not rain for years and years, quite literally.

"Golly, Mad! C'mon and look in here!" Skeet had gone before her into one of the bedrooms. "Do we have to sleep in *here*?"

Maddie eyed the sagging, cross-legged stretchers with dismay.

Mice—or was it rats? Ugh!—had gnawed at the flock mattresses, dragging trails of kapok out onto the floor. The furniture was substantial, old-fashioned, but of good quality, under the concealing layers of dust. Cobwebs hung from the central light fixture, and in the corners of the window-panes there were whole cemeteries of dead blowflies which had been ensnared in the spiders' cunning filaments.

Maddie swallowed—hard. He might at least have had the place cleaned up for them, she thought, feeling anger mounting inside her. He must have known when they were coming. Mr. Opal must have told him which train they were booked on. That was how he had met them at Noonday. Maybe he was as busy a man in the country as he had been in the city. Maybe there was not much time, since he could only have arrived home yesterday himself, but you'd think he might have given instructions to someone—Mrs. Lawrence, perhaps—to clean the place up, especially as Lal Lawrence was responsible to him. Maybe men just didn't think of these things, though.

Looking around her, she could well believe he would prefer to have his cup of tea when he got back to Bibbi, rather than here.

Maddie's heart hardened and so did her resolve to stay here, come what may. It would take more than rotting boards and mouse-holes in mattresses, or spiders on the window frames to drive her away from her inheritance. Steve would soon find that out.

"I'll make it nice for us, Skeet, never fear," she vowed between clenched teeth. "Let's see if we can find some tea or something—I'm famished, aren't you?—and then you can explore outside while I get one of the rooms ready. We'll decide which one when we've eaten. In a day or two you shall have one of your very own."

There was a fuel range in the kitchen, some kindling wood in the boiler-room beyond. Maddie had never seen a stove quite like this one before, but she supposed that it worked just like an ordinary fire. She had the flames crackling at last and despatched Skeet outside to look for more wood, while she explored the cupboards.

Surprisingly, there was a healthy store of groceries laid in, all canned, even to butter, bacon and milk. Gingerly she opened a can of bacon, found one of beans. By the time Skeet reappeared with an armful of firewood, her face was flushed with exertion and anxiety. She had never seen canned bacon before, but she was able to set down two plates of hot beans and crisply fried rashers and a pot of tea on the table.

"Gee, Maddie, this is great!" She smiled at Skeet's enthusiastic pronouncement as she dug a hole in the milk can and poured it into a jug, added the prescribed amount of water, and stirred the whole vigorously.

Darling Skeet! He was really such a dear little boy, and he had not complained again, not since that last, surprised utterance about the bedrooms. His hair stuck out in spikes that seemed every bit as excited as his facial expression. Skeet, indeed, was obviously beginning to regard the whole thing as fun. At ten years old, Maddie supposed that that was natural. You were too young to realize what was at stake, to appreciate the difficulties that lay ahead. Just now, as she looked at Skeet wolfing down those beans and the hefty chunks of bacon with undaunted relish, Maddie felt as though a whole century of age and wisdom separated her from her jaunty little brother. Her shoulders felt old, stiff, and heavy with the weight of the responsibility that rested there—a weight made somehow more intense because Skeet could not appreciate it and couldn't be expected to share it.

Maddie, in fact, felt lonely.

Not only lonely—but *alone*, which was, if anything, one degree worse. As she sat there at the wooden table in the shabby kitchen at Yattabilla, she knew that she was more alone than she had ever been in her life, even though Skeet was sitting right here beside her.

After she had washed up the dishes and cleared away the remains of their meal, Maddie lit the water-boiler in the room off the kitchen. Once the water tank was hot, she set about scrubbing out the bedroom where they would sleep. That must have priority, she had decided, because Skeet by now was beginning to sound tired. The long journey was telling at last, and his voice was a little bit querulous, his laughter more shrill and strained.

Maddie recognized the signs in Skeet and renewed the vigor of her attack on the filthy room. She ground her teeth together as she swiped determinedly at the cob-webbed windows; shut her eyes as she placed her shoe squarely on the wriggling, fat bodies of a couple of funnel-web spiders that she dislodged. The floor she left till the end. Once the boards were washed and wiped as dry as possible, she found blankets and sheets. She made up the beds, first concealing the worn mattresses in clean calico tics that she unearthed in the linen closet.

She was so exhausted by evening that the thought of preparing another meal was almost too much for her. A can of soup, some toast, would suffice, and the inevitable pot of tea.

"Won't there be eggs, Maddie? There's hens down in the backyard there—white and ginger sort of speckled ones."

"You'd better leave them, Skeet. They might belong to the Lawrence's for all we know. You didn't actually take any eggs, did you?"

"No, but I saw some, and one of the hens wouldn't get off her nest. She's sitting on a whole lot. I could feel them under her. She pecked my hand. See!" Skeet held out a grubby paw for inspection.

"Yes, well, maybe she's meant to be sitting on them or something, Skeet. Maybe she's been set there, to hatch out some chicks."

"Chicks! Great!"

"We'll see in the morning."

"Chicks! Golly, Maddie, I hope they're our hens and not the Lawrence's, don't you?"

"We'll know in the morning, Skeet." She tried unsuccessfully to stifle a yawn, straightened her aching back, and took him by the arm. "Come on, darling—bed. I'm coming too."

"Maddie, what'll be do about school? Or won't I have any? Gee, it'd be great not to have any school. Maybe there isn't one, and I could play with those chicks all the time—I mean, look after them just so long as they're little and don't know what to do themselves."

"We'll find out in the morning."

Skeet began to pull off his clothes, throwing them haphazardly in the direction of the small cane chair by his bed. Even though one sock and his pants missed the chair altogether and landed on the still-damp floor, Maddie felt too worn to reproach him. It was simpler, tonight, just to pick them up herself.

"Can we go into Noonday again soon, Mad? I liked Noonday, didn't you. It's a stupid name, but I liked the place okay. How'll we get there, Maddie? Will Steve take us in his big car again? I can open every gate from here to Noonday now, Maddie. When can I do it again?"

"We'll see in the morning, Skeet. Go to sleep."

"I'm longing for morning, aren't you, Maddie?" Skeet's voice was drowsy, but enthusiastic.

"Yes, darling," she responded untruthfully, because she knew that that was what Skeet wanted her to say.

From her pillow, Maddie could see the ridge of hills out the window, across the plain. The ridge reared up against the night skyline, like some prehistoric monster. The clefts and scars, in profile, were like the scales on the monster's hide. The clumps of trees on the highest hill were his ears—or were they horns?

Odd to know that Bibbi was just over that ridge.

Thinking of Steve Darley made Maddie tense. Remembering those spiders, the clinging cobwebs, the

mouse-holes and the dead blowflies, made Maddie remember, too, that she hated Steve. It was a pity, she
mused blearily, but that was the way it was. Love for this
wretched, crumbling place couldn't make her stay at
Yattabilla, but hate for Steve could. That was the truth, if
she really was to be honest with herself.

Maddie would have to nourish that hate, because she
certainly intended to stay.

CHAPTER FIVE

It was almost mid-morning when they woke up next day. When Maddie went through to the kitchen, she saw that someone had left some fresh meat on the table. It was quite neatly cut up and covered over with a fine-meshed cover to protect it from the flies that were crawling over the wire, trying frustratedly to get underneath.

She brushed the flies away, took up the plate, looked helplessly at the ancient kerosene fridge that she had no idea how to work, then put the cover back on and replaced the plate on the table. Immediately the flies increased their demented buzzing and settled on the protective screen once more.

Maddie pressed her lips together and walked out the door, over the shaky veranda-boards and down the steps. When she reached the little, pink weatherboard cottage that Steve had pointed out, she rapped smartly on the door.

She could not pretend, even to herself, that she was taken with the woman who finally opened the door and stepped out, closing it after her in an unfriendly fashion. Mrs. Lawrence was a taciturn, gray-haired creature, with withered skin and shifty eyes. She wore a dirty, cotton apron and tattered slippers.

"Well?"

"Good morning, Mrs. Lawrence. I'm Madeleine Masterton. I came down to thank you for the meat."

"Mr. Darley said you was to be kept in meat. Lal took it up—it ain't *my* place to be waitin' on folks."

Maddie swallowed. The woman's attitude puzzled her.

"No—er—of course not. Well, please thank Lal for me, will you? And perhaps, if he has time later, he might come up and show me how to get the refrigerator working."

"He don't come home till sundown."

"I don't mind how late, Mrs. Lawrence, but I must have a refrigerator that works," Maddie replied firmly.

Mrs. Lawrence sniffed.

"You don't know much, do yer? You sure don't look much like Gerald Masterton's kid ter me."

"Possibly I take after my mother," suggested Maddie sweetly, but the woman's reply bested her.

"Yeah, her that cleared out on 'im. Maybe you do take after her, at that. Reckon you'll soon get sick of the life, same as what she did. You city types don't exactly fit in out 'ere, do yer?"

"Are those hens up there yours or ours, Mrs. Lawrence?" Maddie asked, deciding that the only dignified way to deal with the woman's insolence was to ignore it.

"They belong to the house. I've simply been keepin' 'em going on Mr. Darley's instructions, but you're welcome ter take over, seein' as you'll be getting the eggs. I seen yer brother out lookin' for 'em yesterday. He's not slow, is 'e, to be takin' what he don't even know is his!"

"Very well, Mrs. Lawrence." Maddie's voice was cold. "From now on, I shall look after the fowls, since they belong to the house. Please tell your husband that I shall expect him this evening, however late."

She turned on her heel and retraced her steps to the homestead, aware that her legs were trembling and her palms perspiring. It would be a long time before she went down to see Mrs. Lawrence again. She could only hope that the husband, Lal, might prove a little bit more friendly and helpful.

He did as it turned out.

When he came up that night, he was awkward, rather than taciturn like his wife—the quiet, inarticulate sort, but passably obliging. He had the fridge working and showed her how to fill the tray and soak the wicks. He also informed her that he would bring meat to the house twice a week and that Wednesday was mail day. Groceries could be ordered by telephone, or she could get her own supplies if she happened to be in Noonday.

"Is there a bus, Lal, that would take me in?"

"A bus?" He scratched his head, regarded her in perplexity. "There ain't no buses out 'ere!"

"But I can't drive a car. I don't know how to."

He shrugged. "Nor could she—yer ma, I mean."

"I—I could learn," said Maddie rather desperately.

"Yer could," Lal agreed dubiously. "The Buick's still in the garage, miss, but *I* ain't got time ter learn yer."

"No, of course not, Lal. I—I'll think of something. There must be a way." She brightened suddenly, as a new thought struck her. "There must be some sort of school transport, Lal? Perhaps I could get a lift on that sometimes."

Lal shook his head.

"There ain't no school transport, miss, excepting the one *in* at the beginnin' of the week and *out* at the end."

"In and out—to Noonday?"

"That's right, miss." His eyes slid away from Maddie's incredulous stare. "Well, I better be goin' now, miss. Anything yer want, just tell my missus an' she'll pass the word." Lal was evidently unaware of his wife's peculiar lack of cooperation. He picked up his wide-brimmed hat, clamped it on his head, and walked over to the kitchen door. There he turned. "By the way, go easy on the electric light, will yer? The one generator's gotter do the whole set-up here, and I ain't always around the place ter be chargin' her up. Any time I'm out on the back of the property for a coupla days, she'll run down, so keep yer lanterns handy."

"Lanterns?"

"Yeah, the lamps, the Tilleys. Through there in the pantry." He spat out into the darkness. "G'night, then, miss."

"Goodnight, Lal. And thank you for your help."

"Any time, miss." Maddie heard his slow steps clumping away over the hard ground outside.

She sat down in the chair beside the wooden table and put her head on her arms. She wanted to cry, more than anything, just then. Yes, she could wish for nothing more satisfying than to simply give way to her feelings—to sit there and sob her heart out with noisy abandon.

Instead, she got up out of the chair and went slowly to the telephone in the hall, turned the handle with resolution, and lifted the receiver.

"Can't you hear the line's engaged?"

"Pardon?" Maddie was startled.

"Sounds like a new voice, Gladys. Who are you, dear?" asked the nasal one again.

"Madeleine Masterton, from—er—Yattabilla."

"Oh, I see." The strange voice immediately became more friendly. "You're new here, aren't you, duckie? In that case, we'll forgive you for butting in."

"I'm sorry." Maddie was forlorn. It seemed to her that she could do nothing right. It was all so strange, even this present conversation. "I didn't mean to interrupt. I just wanted the exchange."

"Well, we won't be long, will we, Gladys, and then you can have the line. It's a party line, you see. And the rule is, listen first, and if no one's on the line, you can have it. Don't listen *in*, though. That's a different thing altogether, isn't it, Gladys?"

"Too right it is! It's the quickest way to lose your friends," agreed the more distant Gladys.

Friends? They were something Maddie didn't have, so she couldn't very well lose them, could she?

"I'm sorry," she repeated once more. "I didn't mean to listen in. How do I get the exchange when the line is clear, please?"

"One long ring, and they'll answer you. You're two

longs and a short if it's Yattabilla you're speaking from. The party numbers are all morse-code ones, you see. The numbers on your own line—that's our one too—can all be rung without bothering the exchange at all. You'll soon get used to it and remember the different rings. Just latch onto your own ring for now, and only lift the receiver if it gives two longs and a short—otherwise you'll be accused of eavesdropping."

"Yes, I see." Maddie was contrite. "I'm sorry I interrupted your conversation. I—I'll go away now and come back when the line is free."

"That's the idea," applauded her unseen helper. "So long for now."

"Goodby."

Maddie went back to the kitchen and made herself a cup of tea to steady her frayed nerves.

A good thing Skeet was in bed and couldn't see how shaken she was. To Skeet Maddie must always see that she appeared as a tower of strength, an unshakable pillar of wisdom, through thick and thin, come what may. That was what Skeet had come to expect of her. It would never do to let him become even the tiniest bit aware of the dread and doubts that assailed his outwardly calm and confident sister.

Back at the phone, the line sounded dead. Maddie gave a single long ring, and when the voice at the other end answered, heard herself say clearly, "Barron Creek 234D, please."

A moment's buzzing, and then the voice she was expecting. Steve's.

"234D here."

"Steve?"

"Is that you, Madeleine? How are you making out?" How deep, how reassuring, could be the voice of someone you knew—even if that someone was Stephen Gainsborough Darley.

"Quite well, thank you." She took a breath. "I wanted to ask you something. Is there a school nearer than Noonday—somewhere where Skeet can go?"

A pause. Then—"I'm afraid not, Madeleine."

Maddie sagged against the wall beside the phone. It was true then, what Lal had told her.

"But—but how will I get Skeet in each day? So—so far?"

"I guess you'll have to do what the rest do, Madeleine. There's a perfectly comfortable hostel in Noonday, especially laid on for out-of-town pupils. There's good food, supervision, and—" his voice was dry, "it has the added advantage of costing you nothing, not a cent. It's all from taxes, for the more distant pupils."

"But—" she was aghast—"you can't mean—*leave* him in there? Not—not *all* the time?"

"That's just what I do mean, Madeleine. It could be very good for Skeet. He might even enjoy it, and you'd have him home each weekend," Steve pointed out reasonably.

Home? Yattabilla, home?

"But in that case, I'll be here all alone, throughout the whole w-week." Her voice wobbled and tears stung her eyes. They were tears of despair. "I w-won't even have Skeet!"

"Not losing your nerve already, are you, Madeleine?" The sarcasm in Steve's tone had a curiously astringent effect upon his listener.

"Of course not!" she replied vexedly. How she hated that man.

"Well then, buck up and stop sounding like a mother doe relinquishing Bambi to the wolves. Are you still there, Madeleine?" His voice had sharpened. "Listen, I'll come over tomorrow. We'll discuss it then."

"That's not at all necessary, thank you, Steve."

"I'll be there, all the same." His deep voice was imperturbable. "I'd prefer not to talk about it over the party line, in any case. Good night, Madeleine."

"Good night," she replied woodenly, then she replaced the receiver and made her way to bed.

For a long moment she stood beside Skeet's sleeping form, striving to control the panic that had set in. Yattabilla, with Skeet, was bad enough! Yattabilla, without him, would be altogether insupportable.

Maddie recalled the crisp, taunting voice of Steven Darley and knew that she would have to bear the unbearable, all the same. She'd get through it somehow, even if only for the satisfaction of seeing that loathsome smugness wiped off his tanned, handsome face.

As she finally laid her head on the pillow, she thought how differently things might have turned out. If there hadn't been this legal rope binding her to Yattabilla, she could have settled in Noonday itself and found herself a job. Skeet could have gone to school each day in the town, and come home to her each night, like he always had.

Noonday was such a nice place—so cheerful and peaceful and prosperous. There were friendly people there, too—people like Tom Simson, for instance. Maddie could shut her eyes and still see the warmth and admiration in his glance, the friendliness in his youthful smile. Yes! A job in Noonday, near to Tom, could have been a very pleasant way out of things. Maybe, even now, she could work Steve Darley around to the idea.

On a more optimistic note, Maddie fell asleep.

When Steve appeared in the morning he took them by surprise. Maddie had been looking out from time to time to the approach-road that they had come along in the shiny gray Chevrolet. She would watch for a rolling dust-cloud in the distance. When she saw it, she would be able to brace herself mentally and summon her reserves for Steve's visit. She'd need to collect her wits before that dust-cloud resolved itself into a speeding sedan with a big, brown man at the wheel.

Instead, Steve simply walked into the hall where Maddie had gone down on her knees to polish some of the dull neglect from the pretty cypress-pine flooring. He threw his hat with a deft, spinning accuracy onto the table by the telephone.

"Oh!" Maddie scrambled to her feet and wiped a sticky tendril of hair from her perspiring brow. "It's you! I looked out just a moment ago, and there was no sign of a car."

"I didn't come by car. I came on horseback, over the ridge. It's quicker." A keen glance raked her. "What's the matter? You look all keyed up. Don't tell me you're nervous?"

"Should I be?" she countered with deceptive calm. "This meeting was your idea, not mine. I wasn't begging for company when I rang last night, if that's what you thought. I merely wanted some advice."

"Relax, then, infant." He grinned down at her lazily. "I've already told you, you aren't my type, so save the intensity and maidenly fluttering for someone young and impressionable." He sat down, stretched long legs in dust-covered riding-boots, and reached for tobacco and papers in his shirt pocket. "I'll have some tea if it's on the go, Madeleine—or could you possibly run to a beer?"

"No, I could not!" she replied tartly. "If you wait there, I'll bring tea," she added repressively and marched off to the kitchen, irritated beyond measure. Steve got under her skin at every turn. She had a feeling that he did it on purpose, too—part of the "get-her-out-of-Yattabilla" campaign? If so, he'd be disappointed.

"Where's Skeet?" he asked, when she came back with the tea.

"I sent him down to play at the creek. I thought it better that he wasn't around while his schooling is being discussed. It—it might make him feel insecure."

Steve eyed her over the rim of his teacup.

"There's not much chance of his feeling insecure if you handle it right. Kids like to be the same as other kids, Madeleine. Surely you've found that out by now? You might even remember it from your own childhood days—they weren't all that long ago."

"What do you mean?"

He shrugged carelessly. "Either he stays out here with you and gets his schooling by mail or some other, more unsatisfactory means; or he goes into Noonday during the week and feels himself to be one of the crowd, doing the same as they do. It's easy to guess which Skeet would prefer, if he could look at it objectively, without those sisterly but misguided little hands of yours playing jigsaws with his emotions all the time, so he doesn't know what's up."

"How dare you!" Maddie was incensed. "Are you suggesting that I won't do what's best for Skeet? That I'd put my own feelings before his welfare?"

Steve drew on his cigarette and regarded her through critical eyes.

"You said it—I didn't," he answered calmly. "If you want to prove your point, you'll let him go to the hostel in Noonday, just like all the other boarders. He can come out on weekends, just like they do too. It'll be the first taste of normality that he's had in his life for a while, I daresay."

Maddie bit her lip and dropped her eyes to her hands, that were clenched tightly in her lap.

"It's what I intended to do, in any case," she stated coldly, because she knew she was cornered. She ran her tongue over her dry lips and tried to coax some friendliness back into her voice. "Steve, there really isn't any reason why I couldn't stay in Noonday, too, is there, and come out on weekends with Skeet? What I mean is—well,

Yattabilla, Noonday—it amounts to almost the same thing, doesn't it?"

He laughed softly. To Maddie it was a thoroughly unpleasant sound.

"So you *are* losing your nerve. I thought as much. Or is it that you can't face the thought of not possessing your little brother for a whole seven days out of every seven? No, Madeleine, it is not the same thing. As you say, it's almost the same, but not quite. The letter of the law is inflexible where definitions of this particular nature are concerned. You either stay at Yattabilla, or you don't."

"But—" Maddie's eyes had filled with tears of sheer frustration—"But my father didn't know about Skeet when he made that stipulation," she pleaded.

"But you knew about him when you accepted it, didn't you?" Steve pointed out with characteristic ruthlessness. "Legally, I'm afraid that Skeet doesn't exist—not as Gerald's son. We've checked the birth register in the district in London where he was born. The paternity side is unfortunately a blank. Whether your mother was too bitter even to write Gerald's name, or whether she was simply distraught, is anybody's guess, but there's no doubt that it was hardly fair to Skeet."

Maddie opened her mouth to speak, but Steve's raised hand called for silence, so she closed it again.

"There is no doubt," he went on, "that Skeet is Gerald's child, please understand that. But legally—no."

"Oh-h." Maddie's eyes were round with hurt.

Steve shifted his weight in the chair. He too, looked grave—unhappy, almost, Maddie would have said as she found herself trying to analyze his expression.

"Look, Madeleine"—he leaned forward, toward her, persuasively—"why not be honest with yourself and with me. Admit that Yattabilla isn't what you thought it was going to be, and that you aren't prepared to see it through on Gerald's terms. I'll drive you back to town in time for the evening train. You can talk to old Opal and try to contest the will."

Yes, that would no doubt suit him all right, thought Maddie bitterly to herself.

She pushed back her chair with an oddly final gesture.

"Thank you for your suggestions," she said wearily, "but if this is the only legal way, then I shall take the only way that's open to me. After all," she couldn't resist adding acidly, "if the law is as inflexible as you say, there would be little point in contesting it anyway. I shouldn't have expected any helpful advice from the other involved party, in that case."

She rose from the chair, and Steve stood too. He seemed put out. Not just put out, but really angry for the very first time. She knew that she had flicked him on the raw with that last remark. Maybe he realized that his chances of getting Yattabilla weren't quite so bright as he had anticipated, in spite of the spiders, the blowflies, the worn, mouse-eaten mattresses, and the white ants in the timber.

Steve cursed softly. The next moment Maddie's shoulders were grasped in a hard hold. His hands were cruel, bruising the soft flesh under her shirt. There was a stormy glitter in his eyes as he looked down at her, and he even had the nerve to give her a fierce, brutal shake.

"Listen to me, Madeleine, and stop talking like that!" he told her on an oddly harsh, rough note. "Why can't you be sensible about the whole thing? God, do you think a man likes to go through what you're putting me through? Do you think it's pleasant for me to go on just as I always do, over there at Bibbi, over that ridge, with every modern comfort, every convenience, a plane, a car, a swimming-pool, air-conditioning—the lot—while you and Skeet sweat it out in this hell-hole of rot and filth and—"

"Don't tell me your conscience bothers you?" Maddie interrupted sarcastically.

"Enough of that, Madeleine!" he barked, so forbiddingly that she experienced a pang of pure fright. His expression told her that she just might have gone too far. "You know perfectly well what I mean You're city reared, even if you are Gerald Masterton's daughter. You're just a foolish, misguided, stubborn child, and—"

"And not your type," she finished for him, gazing pointedly at his hands on her shoulder. "Thank you," she continued, as he let her go and reached for his hat. "It's more than kind of you to be concerned, but I think you'll agree it's pointless to continue this discussion. We see things from precisely opposite angles. It's natural in the circumstances, wouldn't you say?"

Steve rammed his hat on his head, glared down at her furiously.

"And what in tarnation is that remark supposed to mean?" he demanded angrily.

"I'll leave you to figure it out on your way back over the ridge," she replied demurely.

"The hell you will!"

With a look that should have put her under the decaying floorboards upon which she stood he turned on his heel and clattered down the steps without a backward glance. It was obvious that Steve Darley was a very angry man indeed.

Maddie felt a satisfying spurt of triumph as she gathered together the empty cups and put them on the tray. She had won that round, no doubt about it.

She hummed a little tune to herself on the way back to the kitchen, there to be pulled up short by the sight of Steve once more. This time he was sitting long-legged in the saddle on a restive and powerful bay stallion. He was leaning out of the saddle, actually, and talking down to Mrs. Lawrence, who, still in her dirty apron and the carpet-slippers she always wore, was standing with a kitten wriggling in her arms. She must have been out looking for it as Steve was leaving.

Maddie put down the tray and crept to the window, listening unashamedly to see if she might hear what they were saying.

"—everything in the house when she arrived?" That was the end of a question from Steve.

"Yes, Mr. Darley, I left it like you said. Lal took up some meat, like you said, too. Everything was just the way you ordered."

"Right, Mrs. Lawrence. I'll see Lal on my way out just now."

He turned the stallion's head, and minutes later the horse and man were cantering easily away toward the ridge. With his broad-brimmed hat pulled well down over his eyes, and his lean body slanted to the stallion's gait, Steve Darley appeared rakish and satisfied, as if he hadn't a care in the whole wide world. He didn't look at all like a man who had just been vanquished.

Maddie suspected—more than suspected—that her victory had been a hollow one, after all.

She sat down in one of the rickety kitchen chairs. Just imagine! If she hadn't happened to come through just now and overhear that tiny snippet of conversation, she might never had known that Steve Darley had actually arranged the homecoming she had received, in advance.

The filth, the spiders and cobwebs, the dusty mattresses and unmade beds with the kapok tumbling through the springs(ugh!)—they had all been left like that on purpose. They were all part of the Discouragement Committee. Steve had actually stooped to connivance with that dreadful Mrs. Lawrence, so that Maddie would get precisely the reception that she had.

Maddie blinked in bewilderment and hurt. There were tears in her eyes, but she was hardly aware that she was brushing them away with the back of her hand before they could spill over. She felt dazed with disillusionment. She had known he was ruthless, yes. You could see a mile off that he was the sort of man who would let nothing stand in his way. But to sink to such deception as this. To stoop to this level! Maddie could hardly believe it, and yet what else was there to believe? She had heard it with her own ears—"I left it like you said, everything was just the way you ordered."

Oh, Steve!

Maddie supposed that this was one of the most painful lessons a human being could ever experience—the discovery that someone you had liked (well, not liked, not a bit, really—respected, that was the word) could do you down and stab you in the back when you were not even looking.

She couldn't ever trust him after this, she realized sadly. All those things he had said about feeling bad because she was here in this awful house, and he was over the ridge in his lovely modern one. They meant absolutely nothing, not a thing! They were just a blind.

Maddie scrubbed at her eyes with her knuckles. A righteous anger was beginning to supplant the hurt and disillusion. She would show him. She certainly would. And if "showing him" meant that she had to live at Yattabilla alone, without Skeet, for five whole days in every week, well, she could do that, too! The time would soon pass. She would keep herself extra busy on those days. At night she would make her mind an absolute blank, so that it would not dwell on the absence of her little brother's even breathing and comforting presence in the next room or, on the strange creaking sounds that the veranda boards made as they contracted in the evening air after the heat of the day. Sometimes, when they groaned in the darkness, it was almost as if someone, or something, was pressing them down with a stealthy tread. Someone such as a tramp, or a—well, a bushranger, if they still had those in Australia. Something such as a wombat, or one of those big kangaroos like the one that had bounded along beside Steve's car, or maybe even a snake. Maddie decided that she wouldn't be very frightened if it turned out to be a wombat noise or a kangaroo noise—but a snake? Ooh! Her slender shoulders shook at the mere idea.

Stupid! she chided herself. She must not let her imagination get out of hand.

Maddie took a grip on herself and went into the boiler room for some potatoes that someone—Lal, presumably—had dug up and put in a dented kerosene tin that served as a pail. She wondered where they had come from. Certainly not from the "front yard", where weeds were rampant, and the only recognizable surviving flowers were a few struggling geraniums and some sort of broad-leafed thing which she supposed might be a canna. More probably they had come from the plot down near the fowl-yard, where she had recognized the spindly remains of dying artichoke tops and a wandering patch of melons.

When Skeet came in, she had peeled the potatoes and put them to boil on the big, black stove. She had decided that she would form them into cakes and serve them with some more of the canned bacon. Maddie was not quite sure what to do with the meat that Lal had left. She was still far too upset by Steve's visit, with all its implications, to be bothered pondering over cuts of mutton just now.

Skeet was dirty. His face was covered with dust, and there were pieces of straw in his hair.

He returned her stare of disapproval with an undaunted grin.

"I've been down at the hen, Maddie—the one on the eggs. I'm sure we're going to get chicks!" He rubbed a sweaty palm over his forehead, leaving a grimy trail in the dust already there. "Gee, Mad, I wonder how long it'll be before we get them?"

"We might not, Skeet," she warned cautiously. "They might not be even fertile."

"Fertile?"

"Yes. You know, the right sort of eggs—ones with little chicken seeds in them."

He gave her a withering look.

"Don't be silly, Maddie. Of course they'll be the right sort. She wouldn't be sitting on them all this time if they weren't, would she? *She's* not silly! She's a very sensible hen. She even knows me now when I lie down beside her to look underneath. She doesn't even peck me any more, 'cos I've tamed her. Of course she'll know about the chickens. Hens just *do*!"

"Well, I hope so, Skeet." Maddie's ignorance of poultry was only slightly less abysmal than her brother's. She remained unconvinced, but secretly hoped that he might be right. Chickens would be fun. They would help her to pass the time when Skeet was away in Noonday at school.

Maddie felt a hollowness inside her. She would have to tell Skeet soon. It was no use putting it off. She opened her mouth and found herself asking instead, "What are you doing?"

Skeet, quite obviously, was scratching. Even as she watched, his efforts became more frantic. Tiny red blotches appeared on his neck and throat, on his bare arms and legs.

"Oooo—oh!"

Maddie pulled him over to the window to inspect him more closely.

"Why, Skeet, it's fleas or something. Little tiny red things. You're smothered in them!"

"So's Etta, but she doesn't seem to mind." The little boy's voice was muffled as he twisted around in an effort to reach his back.

"Etta? Who's Etta?"

"Henrietta. My hen. I call her Etta for short. She has them too, but they don't seem to bite her like they do me. Ow!"

"That's it, Skeet, that's what they are—hen fleas. I don't think they live long, but—" she watched his ineffectual scratching for only a moment—"you'd better have a bath, and a complete change of clothes. Come on, quickly!"

Maddie drew the pan of potatoes to one side of the stove and marched him off in the direction of the bathroom.

Skeet, for once, did not protest, although normally he hated baths. Over the sound of the running water, Maddie told him that he must not go near the hen again.

The little boy lowered himself into the bath and looked at her mutinously.

"Well, not quite so near," she amended, weakening at the sight of his forlorn expression and blotched body as he began to soap himself.

"No, not quite so near," Skeet hastened to agree.

"You might frighten her off the eggs, anyway, Skeet, and then you'd be sorry."

"Look, Maddie, haven't I told you, Etta an' me are friends. Anyway, she doesn't scare easy."

"Maybe not, but the chicks will."

"No they won't. And she'll be walking about when they come, Maddie, not sitting forever in that musty old hay. That's where the fleas are—in the straw. When the chicks come, we'll all go walking about together, and the fleas won't get me then."

Skeet stepped out of the bath and began toweling himself.

Maddie swallowed. Then she made herself say what she knew had to be said.

"On the weekends, Skeet. You can walk around with them on the weekends only."

"How do you mean, Maddie?" The towel was arrested in mid-air.

Carefully she explained about the school. She told him

about the bus in at the beginning of the week and the one out on Fridays, about sleeping at the hostel and playing with a lot of other children.

To her surprise—her chagrin?—Skeet accepted all she had told him with equanimity, almost, in fact, with actual enthusiasm.

"In Noonday? Truly? That'll be great. How many of us will there be on the bus? What time will it come?"

"I don't know, Skeet. I'll have to find that out."

"I like Noonday, don't you? I reckon I'm really glad the school's in Noonday. Can you come too, Maddie?"

She shook her head. "No, darling, I'm afraid not, but you'll have lots of playmates, so you won't really miss me. I'll have to look after the house here, you see. Someone will have to mind Yattabilla."

"Yes, and Etta, too. Someone'll need to keep an eye on Etta. It can't be me, not when I'm in Noonday. I'd rather it was you than Mrs. Lawrence, anyway, Maddie. I don't think she likes hens, do you?"

Maddie bit her lips as she patted calomine lotion onto Skeet's blotches. So much for her own misgivings. And so much for the loyalties of extreme youth. Skeet wasn't even going to *miss* her—not in the way she was going to miss him, at any rate. Why, he was going to miss Henrietta more than Maddie. He was going to miss a hen more than his very own sister. It hadn't even occurred to him how lonely and deprived Maddie was going to feel, all by herself here without him.

Steve's recent words rang in her ears like a jibe—

"It's easy to guess which Skeet would prefer—"

Skeet's thin shoulders shifted under her grasp.

"Ow, Maddie! Don't do it so hard."

Maddie came out of her trance to find that her fingers were indeed digging into Skeet's arm. Even the savage little jabs with which she found herself applying the pad of cotton-wool to the blotches were quite foreign to her gentle nature.

"Sorry, darling." Maddie hugged Skeet in compunction.

What was that Darley man doing to her, she wondered, as she bent to pick up the damp towel. She mustn't let him get her down like this. She might have to live at Yattabilla with Steve as a neighbor, but she was darned if she was going to let him have any further influence in their lives after this.

Maddie's cheeks were flushed and angry. When she returned to the kitchen, she found herself wielding the potato-masher with every bit as much energy and indignation as she had that pad of cotton-wool.

CHAPTER SIX

Maddie felt like crying when she waved Skeet off on the bus on Monday morning. She could not even hug him or anything like that, because of the other passengers in the dusty vehicle.

Three other boys and two little girls, all in clean cotton clothes, all with country-brown, inquisitive faces, leaned out the long back window to get a better look at the new pupil as he gave a jaunty wave and strutted independantly toward the waiting bus, clutching his small suitcase.

The driver, an elderly man with a mop of grizzled hair and leathery jaws studded with gray bristles, swung down the steps and shoved Skeet inside.

"Grab the hand-rail, that's it, sonny." He turned for a second before pulling the door shut behind him. "He'll be okay, miss, you betcher he will! Siddown, you lot at the back and get away from that winder—that's if yer don't want ter come a cropper on the ground out there!" The driver slid a conspiratorial grin in Maddie's direction as he added, "Maybe you *do*, though, eh? Maybe you'd all *like* it if I was to take yer to the 'orspital instead of the school, eh?"

"Yes! Yes!" chorused the children, giggling delightedly.

Maddie made herself smile. It seemed to take a long time for the bus to jerk away down the road, and her lips were stiff with the effort of keeping up that smile. She felt as if she had lost Skeet—really lost him.

All day she fought against the swamping tide of loneliness that engulfed her, but with little success. There did not seem much point in doing anything without Skeet. It wasn't even worth making proper meals without his eager little presence at the table. Maddie eyed the stack of fresh meat that Lal had brought in disgust. How could one person possibly get through that? How, indeed, could one person even be bothered to cook it?

At night the loneliness became worse. Not only were there all the snuffling, sighing night noises to identify, the groaning veranda boards to analyze, there was also this consuming anxiety for Skeet. How strange he must be feeling! Maybe even frightened. He had never slept away from home before. He wasn't used to country people and country towns, even if he had liked Noonday when he was there with Maddie. He was not used to discipline, either—not really—especially the discipline of a boarding hostel. They would have to be strict, Maddie was sure, because there would be so many children there all at once, and Skeet wasn't really accustomed to strictness. He would not cry, she didn't think. Skeet was good at being brave, at "not crying." But he might feel like crying and that would be awful.

Maddie turned her head into her pillow, and cried for him. She cried for the little brother she had tended and protected, the little boy who wasn't legally there at all, the little baby whose paternity had not even been stated on his registration form. And then she cried for herself—for the lonely, frightened girl she knew she was. When she opened her eyes and looked through her fingers into the dark, her tears made the prehistoric monster silhouetted on the ridge all wavery and strange. He looked as if his long, valley-scarred body was shaking with amusement.

The monster was laughing at her plight, and Steve Darley, over the ridge there at Bibbi, would be laughing, too.

Somehow she worked her way woodenly through the next day.

That night she had company, of a sort that Maddie would have preferred not to have at all. She was getting ready for bed when something made her glance out onto the veranda and there it was. A snake! Maddie had to blink her eyes twice to be sure. Even in that moment it began to slide silently away across the boards and over the edge of the veranda itself. The strangest part, for Maddie, was that its passage was utterly noiseless. Not a single creak from the rotting timbers gave away its presence.

Maddie made for the telephone in blind panic, hardly pausing to check that the line was free.

"B-Barron Creek 234D? S-Steve?"

"Madeleine? Is that you?" His voice sounded comfortingly close, gruff with surprise.

"Steve, there's a—a snake." Her own voice trembled, trailed off into nothingness. The relief of hearing him seemed to have rendered her temporarily speechless.

"Did it get you?" he asked in an odd, abrupt sort of way. Then, more harshly, "Madeleine, answer me! Were you bitten?"

"N-no," she whispered. "I'm all right."

"No harm done, then. Mind you, even if you had been, they've a comprehensive anti-venom now, you know." Steve's tone had altered subtly. There was almost a teasing note in it, she could swear. "It does for all types, which is handy, since one sometimes doesn't get a chance to identify them properly."

"You mean they can b-bite you without you even seeing them?" Her question was at treble pitch.

"Don't be silly, Madeleine. I didn't say that at all. Where's this one now?"

"It's g-gone. It slid over the end of the veranda." Heavens above! He couldn't think that she would be standing here carrying on a phone conversation with that snake still around, surely?

"What color was it? Did you get a good look?"

"B-black. It was black."

"Sure?"

"Of course I'm sure! It was black and horrible. Sort of sinister."

Steve laughed. He actually laughed—outright!

"Not to worry, Madeleine. The black ones aren't sinister at all. It might have made you feel rather off-color if it had bitten you, but that's about all, so cheer up. And remember, the poor brute's a lot more scared of you than you might think. All he wants to do, nine times out of ten, is to get out of your way. What you have to watch is that you don't tread on one by mistake." Silence. "Do you follow me, Madeleine? Snakes haven't very good eyesight, as it happens, and they might not see you until you're almost upon them. They go by vibrations more than actual sight, so it's a fair bet that you'd spot them before they spot you. If you don't, you can be unlucky." There was dry amusement in Steve's drawling voice.

"Unlucky! I think you—you're heartless!" Maddie mumbled.

"What did you say, Madeleine?"

"Nothing," she retorted crisply. "I'm sorry I bothered you over such a minor matter."

Steve chuckled. "No bother, I assure you," was his bland reply. "Any time at all, in fact. I enjoy these little chats in the middle of the night."

"You—oh!"

"Just one thing, though, Madeleine—and I'm being serious now—phone me promptly and speak a little more distinctly if one ever happens to get holed up inside the house, will you, there's a good girl?"

"Holed up?"

"Yes, holed up. Snakes don't care much for being cornered, you see. If they think their freedom is at stake, they're apt to get a bit—er—aggressive. So phone me without delay if it ever happens, won't you?"

Maddie found herself struggling for words.

"Won't you, Madeleine?" Steve's voice was insistent over the wire.

"No, I won't. I'll never phone you again, Stephen Darley, that's the one thing you may be sure of. I wouldn't phone you again if you were the last man on earth! Not even if there were 50 snakes holed up in this house! Not even if there were kangaroos and c-crocodiles as well!"

She slammed the receiver down right in the middle of his rich, deep chuckle. She was so furious that she had to restrain herself from actually tearing the phone off the wall. One could hardly blame the instrument, though, for that unfeeling creature at Barron Creek 234D.

Maddie was still seething with indignation as she clambered into bed. Not once did her thoughts turn snakeward again, and surprisingly, she slept almost immediately.

When Lal came up to the house in the morning, Maddie asked him about the car. She had wanted to ask him for days now, but he was always rather taciturn and came and went with scarcely a word. She had decided that Lal was essentially a man of action, because although he was so grudging with actual speech, whenever she asked him to do anything for her, he was quietly obliging. In manual activity, he was happy enough. Socially, he just couldn't be bothered. If she remarked that it was a nice morning, all she was likely to receive was a grunt of assent. A trite observation about the heat merited a similar acknowledgment. Already she had given up trying to make light conversation to Lal.

Every time she passed the Buick sitting in the garage, it presented a challenge to Maddie. What a boon it would be if she could drive! How it would improve her present state of dependence on Steve for almost everything. Why, she could even drive into Noonday sometimes and see Skeet during the week. Maybe she would even get to know Tom and some of the other young people of her own age in the town.

The more she pondered over it, the more it seemed almost essential that she should learn to drive that car, especially if she was to be here, virtually in solitary confinement, for a whole year. That thought gave Maddie the incentive to mention it to Lal.

"Can you drive, Lal?"

The man scratched his head uncertainly.

"I ain't got a license to, if that's what yer mean," he replied.

"No, but do you know how to drive? Could you teach me? Give me some lessons in the Buick?"

"Lessons!" Lal looked askance. "Stone the flippin' crows, miss! As if I got the time ter be givin' sheilas drivin' lessons! I got me work ter do."

"Not sheilas, Lal, just one sheila. Me. Couldn't you, Lal, please? Just sometimes, now and then?" Maddie persuaded.

Lal, however, was adamant. "No, I rakin' well couldn't. What d'yer think Mr. Darley'd do if I was ter leave off me work ter give drivin' lessons? 'E'd give me the boot, that's what. E's me boss, miss, and I'm answerable to 'im, don't forget."

Maddie had temporarily overlooked that fact, she had to admit. She turned away in defeat.

"Anyway, the battery'll be flat an' everythink after all this time," Lal observed dourly as he went down the veranda steps.

"Maybe I could teach myself, if you could get it right for me, Lal?"

"Maybe yer could, at that, if you was ter get one of them drivin' manuals or somethink. There's plenty of bleedin' space for beginners out 'ere, anyway." Lal gave a brief guffaw at his own joke and lumbered off.

His parting remark set Maddie thinking all over again. There was plenty of space around out here for learners. Perhaps she could indeed teach herself, with the aid of a book and a new battery. To get those, she would have to get into town somehow, into Noonday.

It was then that she remembered the sale. It must be on

Friday, mustn't it, because Steve had said his sheep would be in the yards on Thursday night. If only she could get into Noonday on Friday, she and Skeet might be able to come home together. That bus-driver had seemed a kind, friendly sort of man.

Maddie tackled Lal once again. Did he, by any chance, know how she could get into Noonday on Friday, short of walking? Was there anyone who might take her with him? Someone he knew who would be going to that sale, for instance?

Lal scratched his head again and finally came up with the obvious reply—the one Maddie had overlooked.

"Reckon Mr. Darley might take you in, if you arst 'im."

"Anyone *except* Mr. Darley," she amended hastily.

"Anyone *except* Mr. Darley?" echoed Lal, eyeing her firm expression in some puzzlement. "Well, let's see now. There's a stock lorry comin' in with a load of weaners from over at Barron Downs. I reckon she'll be passing the twin-fork to Bibbi soon after sun-up, if that's any use ter you."

"Soon after sun-up?" Maddie found herself beaming up into Lal's brooding face. "The very thing, Lal! Thank you! I'll try it."

Lal nodded.

"Ted Widmore's the cove who's bringin' 'em in. 'E's a contractor for that sort of thing, but 'e's a decent bloke, Ted." He spat neatly into the "front" jungle that had once been a garden, and walked away.

Maddie spent the better part of Thursday evening preparing for her trip to Noonday. She washed her hair, whitened her best shoes, and pressed her cotton two-piece. It was straw-colored, with a white collar and might have appeared drab on lots of girls, but Maddie had chosen it because not only was it well within her price range, but the neutral shade was a perfect foil for her pale complexion and golden hair. With it she would wear brief white nylon gloves. She did not possess a hat.

When she was getting ready, she kept her excitement in check by reminding herself that she might not get a lift at all. "Soon after sun-up" was a fairly vague attempt on Lal's part to pinpoint the precise time when the lorry might pass. It could be an hour either way, and she would have to walk to the twin-fork first. That must be a good two miles up the road and would take her at least half an hour, maybe even an hour. She had better leave the house while it was still dark to give herself a better chance of intercepting Ted Widmore. If transport was his business, then he probably would not mind transporting a girl along with his weaners, whatever they might be.

There was a welcome rustle of cool air amongst the gum leaves when Maddie slipped out of the homestead next morning. Only the pale mirror of color showed her where the eastern sky was. Down at the creek the frogs were still croaking harshly; the high, persistent song of the little green one interrupted every now and then by the sudden, base "gerrup" of a big mud-colored daddy toad. His deep voice would silence the trilling choir for half a minute at a time, and then the chorus would begin all over again.

Maddie was wearing her canvas casuals on her feet, and in her tote she had put her good white shoes, so that they would be clean and smart to slip on as she, Ted Widmore and the weaners were approaching the town. If the frogs could sing, so could she. It was a morning for singing, Maddie decided, because it was the morning she was going into Noonday—at least, she hoped she was. She must not let her pace slacken, because the mirror in the sky was spreading into a flame and rose-colored dawn. She must reach the turnoff to Bibbi by sun-up.

She waited there for perhaps half an hour, sitting on a log and admiring the changing hues as the sun crept up the horizon. Then she heard the grinding noise of a heavy vehicle's approach. When it was quite near, she waved it down and was gratified to hear the driver change down his gear and finally stop right beside her.

The rest was easy.

After a swift, appreciative inspection, Ted Widmore said, "Well, I'm jiggered!" and then he said simply, "Hop up," and opened the passengerside door for her. He even put out a large, rough hand to haul her up onto the running-board, from where she was able to slide into the seat at his side.

"A beaut day, eh?"

"Yes, beaut!" Maddie agreed enthusiastically.

Everything was beaut, because she had managed to hitch a lift into Noonday after all. When she returned to Yattabilla in the evening she meant to have a driving manual and a battery for the Buick. Then she would teach herself how to drive that car. Maybe, very soon, she would be able to get into Noonday and back to Yatta-billa under her very own steam. The idea appealed to Maddie enormously.

She chattered away to her companion, glad that she had kept her old canvas shoes on when each gate came along and she had to jump down into the dust to become the gate-opener. When Noonday came into sight, spread-eagled over the plain beside the brown waterhole with the wilga trees nearby, she put the canvas shoes into the tote and slipped on the white ones. Then she pulled on her neat white gloves.

Ted watched these operations with interest, one eye on the track and the other on his unexpected hitchhiker. It wasn't every day he struck it lucky this way—and to get the gates opened, too—

"I'll drop you in the main street, Maddie, if that's okay? There is really only one main one, so you can't get lost. The shops are mostly down this end, see?"

"Thanks, Ted—and thanks again for the lift." Maddie

jumped down and pushed the door shut. "Where do you go from here?" she called up to Ted.

He jerked his head in the direction of a line of tin-roofed buildings.

"Over there. That's the sale-yards. Sheep first, cattle after. Well—" a grin—"so long, Maddie. Do it again some time, will you? Any time at all's okay by me!"

"Yes, I will, Ted. Goodby."

She hoped she wouldn't have to, though, not again. Because, next time, she hoped she'd be driving herself. That way, she would not have to ask Lal if he knew of anyone passing. Neither would she have to ask Ted, although he certainly had not seemed to mind, but had been genuinely glad to have her company. Most important of all, she would not have to ask Steve. She never intended to ask Steve anything, ever again—not anything at all.

Preoccupied, Maddie turned and cannoned straight into the object of her thoughts.

"Oh!"

Steve steadied her and lifted his hat.

"Good morning, Madeleine. You seem to make a habit of trying to knock a chap over—one way and another." His voice was dry, but his gray eyes were alight with amusement. Then he frowned. "Where's your hat?"

"I haven't one," she replied defensively, nettled that he had hardly spared a glance for her pretty biscuit two-piece and neat white gloves. Just because he was sporting one of those rather battered, broad-brimmed stockman's affairs, he needn't make her own lack of a hat sound such a crime, need he?

"Then you get one right now," she was told. "You can put it down to the Yattabilla account. In fact, that's something I've been meaning to speak to you about, Madeleine. I hope you'll use that account for any necessities at all, quite apart from groceries and household goods. Don't go short of anything through stupid pride, will you? You're quite fit for it, in my opinion. Just remember that it's not to me that you'll be beholden, but to your own father's estate. In other words, it's no more than your due."

Maddie, for some reason, was touched—not by what Steve had actually said, but rather by the way in which he had said it. His voice was kind, and even his eyes had become gentle and smiling as he looked down into her own upraised face.

"Thank you, Steve. I'll get a hat, I promise."

"That's it! And always wear one, Madeleine. Every time you go outside, even at Yattabilla, be sure to have your hat with you. The Australian sun can be cruel as hell to your sort of fair English complexion."

"Yes, Steve." Maddie's voice was submissive. She had not thought he had even noticed her creamy skin. Maybe the man was human, after all. A dimple grooved her cheeks at that, and she peeped up to see if the human side was still in evidence. It wasn't.

"How did you come into town, Madeleine?"

Maddie told him about hitching a lift with Ted Widmore, and as she told him Steve's scowl grew fiercer and fiercer.

"I don't want you doing such a thing again, do you hear! It's most unsuitable, and you took a heck of a risk. Ted's a decent cove, it's not that, but it could have been anyone coming along an outback road at that hour. It's hardly the way for Gerald Masterton's daughter to get around, anyway, is it? You should have called me, and I'd have brought you myself."

"The last time I phoned you," Maddie could not resist pointing out, "you were hardly sympathetic."

"What? Oh! You mean about the snake?" Steve had the nerve to grin at the memory. "*Touché*, Madeleine. I'm sorry about that, but I was too far away to be of concrete assistance, and it was the only way to handle it. You'd had a fright and were badly in need of bracing up.

There's nothing like a spot of healthy indignation to put fear to flight, eh? Aren't I right?"

"Well—" Maddie gave an answering, reluctant smile, in spite of herself.

"Let's call it quits for now. You go and get that hat, and in return I'll promise to be more sympathetic next time. Okay?"

"Yes, Steve, okay."

He touched his brim in a gesture of farewell and strode off. Maddie watched him cross the street and walk in the direction of the tin-roofed sheds that Ted had pointed out. She watched until he had disappeared right around the corner of one of those sheds. Then she went to buy a hat.

It was a pretty, stitched cotton hat with a white-lined brim to match her collar. She also bought a cork toupee, to wear at Yattabilla, as the storeman assured her that that was what many of the country women favored. It was light and cool, as well as practical and sun-stopping. She got a small one for Skeet, too, and a pair of sandals, because she had noticed that that was what the other children in the bus had worn. She knew Skeet would want to be the same. In his ankle socks and laced shoes, he had looked odd, because the others had not even socks—just bare brown legs.

Kids like to be the same as other kids, Madeleine. Steve's words echoed in her mind as the man was wrapping the sandals in a piece of brown paper for her. Drat Steve! She wished she could forget all those nasty things he had said. They were all the more nasty because, largely, they happened to be true.

After Maddie had finished in the clothing store, she bought her driving manual and then crossed over the street to the garage to get the battery. She was quite horrified at the price! Her own purse would not run to such expense. Maddie spent a short while wrestling with her conscience. Could she mark it down on the Yattabilla account? Steve had said she must do that, for necessities. And you could say that that battery was a necessity, couldn't you? Without it the Buick would not go, and unless the Buick went, Maddie would be unable to teach herself how to drive it.

By the time Steve saw those accounts and studied the individual items on them, she would have achieved her purpose.

"Just mark it down to Yattabilla," she told the garageman calmly.

Maddie's next discovery was that batteries are not only extremely expensive, they are heavy, as well. Too heavy, that is, to carry about Noonday with one, until the school bus left.

Maddie was dithering as to whether she should persuade the garage man to deliver it to the bus, or persuade the bus driver to call for it at the garage, when a cheerful voice hailed her.

"Maddie? It is!"

Tom Simson shook her gloved hand enthusiastically.

"By Jove, it's good to see you! I wondered for a minute if I was dreaming. What are you doing in Noonday—I mean, here, of all places?" He cast an eye at their oil-stained surroundings.

"Well, as a matter of fact, I've bought a battery. I don't quite know what I'm going to do with it next." Maddie went on to explain just why she needed that battery.

Tom seemed highly amused at the whole adventure.

"And do you know what to do with it after you get it home?" he asked dubiously. "No? You hope Lal might?"

He stood a moment after Maddie had spoken, wrapped in thought. Then he smiled at her disarmingly.

"Look, Maddie, I've a much better idea. You're not going out on that bus this afternoon. I'll run you and Skeet home instead and tune up that car for you."

"But, Tom, it's 60 miles!"

Tom roared with laughter.

"60 miles, she says! Oh, Maddie, that's an English remark, if ever there was one. These aren't your narrow little hedge-bound lanes, remember, it's the wide open spaces. 60's nothing to Australians, especially country Australians. Goodness, girl, we'll go 100 miles to a dance and back and think nothing of it. No, I insist," as she started to protest again. "It'll be my pleasure, and anyway, I rather fancy myself as a mechanic."

"Tom, really—I don't know how to thank you." How kind, how warmhearted these country people were. And he wasn't only going to drive them home, he was going to get that car going for her as well.

"You can thank me by having lunch with me," said Tom firmly. "One o'clock at the Royal—that's it down there, the place with the green awning. It'll only be steak and eggs, but it's good steak. Will you?"

Maddie smiled warmly.

"I'd love that, Tom. I'll be there at one o'clock—and thank you again."

"On the contrary, thank *you*, lady," corrected Tom with mock gallantry, before he, too, went off in the direction of the sale-yards.

Maddie wandered around the town for a time. The day was getting hotter as it wore on. After her early start and the long trek to the twin-fork, she soon tired of walking about. After she had ordered a cool lemon drink in an Italian café, with a huge fan whirring softly above her head, she sat for a while enjoying a respite from the sun outside. Everyone seemed nice in this town. Many of the people had smiled when she passed them in the street, and some even went so far as to nod and say "G'day."

Maddie had known all along that Noonday was that sort of place. You could tell by the look of it, in some indefinable way. Here, in Noonday, people seemed to have time to think of other people. They were considerate and interested, without being actually inquisitive.

The café proprietor came over and leaned his forearms

on the formica table at which she was sitting.

"The drink's okay?"

"It's delicious, thank you."

"It's fresh lemon, see." He jerked his head toward the back of the premises. "Off the lemon tree. We gotta lemon tree out there, and always she has lemons! On a hot day, very good, eh?"

"It's really lovely. Thank you." Maddie smiled her wide, warm, spontaneous smile—the one that Skeet adored—and the Italian smiled, too.

"You come the nex' time," he said to Maddie when she rose up to leave, "And you get more lemon, eh? Always we have the lemons—the best in Noonday!"

"Till next time," promised Maddie in farewell.

"Sure, till the nex' time." The Italian showed his beautiful, white teeth in a big, broad smile. He seemed very pleased.

Out in the street once more, Maddie hesitated a moment, and then she, too, turned in the direction of those tin-roofed sheds. She could hear, even at a distance, the continuous bleating of large numbers of sheep. There seemed to be occasional shouting and a constant cloud of dust. Behind the sheds, Maddie found that all the sale activity was taking place in the open air. The yards consisted of a series of pens, strongly fenced, and on those fences sat a lot of men. Some were buyers, but a lot were simply looking on. When the auctioneer had sold the sheep in one pen, the men all got down off that fence and moved on to sit on the next one. Maddie thought she had never seen such a funny sight—rows and rows of men, all straddling the fences, all with those wide felt hats pulled down to hide their expressionless brown faces, so that you couldn't see their eyes at all. She wondered, indeed, if they themselves could see what the auctioneer was doing—or did they just listen to his voice?

She watched with interest, amazed at the speed of the auctioneer's patter. All sorts of unfamiliar terms rang in her ears—wethers, hoggets, two-tooths, broken mouths, sound mouths, cast for age, off-shears. To her it was an incomprehensible dialect, and she marveled that those rows of brown-chinned, broad-hatted, apparently eyeless men must know what it was all about.

Steve must have been one of the faceless figures sitting on the fence. Suddenly he was there beside her.

"That's a pretty smart hat. I'm glad you bought one."

"Thank you," she returned politely. "I'm pleased you like it."

She felt, quite suddenly, a little bit breathless, a little bit unsteady. Steve always seemed to have this effect on her, she realized irritably. She wished he didn't make her feel so young—so—so unsure. Standing there beside him, she felt dwarfed. There was no doubt he was a handsome creature, arrogant even when his lean brown face was caked with dust and sweat as it was at this minute. His deep, mahogany-colored tan only served to make his steady gray eyes a lighter color than they really were, with an attraction all their own. It didn't take away any of that keenness that made her feel so uncomfortable, though. It was the same with his teeth. They appeared white and strong, making a pleasant contrast to the browness, but they could snap shut with disapproval, too, just when you were hoping they wouldn't.

Right now, his lips were curling in a rather irresistible way.

"You'd better come out of the sun, Madeleine." He drew her into a small patch of shade near one of the sheds. "Watch from here; it will be cooler and less dusty. In a little while I'll take you for some lunch."

Maddie was taken aback.

"Oh! Well—er—actually I have already made arrangements to have lunch with someone else—with—with Tom, I mean. At the—the Royal, at one o'clock." Her cheeks were afire, and the words seemed to tumble out. How she wished she could control that angry blush.

Steve was watching her all the time she was speaking. His expression did not appreciably change, but his eyes narrowed, if anything, and they held that depth of intentness that made her feel so awkward. His strong brown fingers caressed his chin in a steady, imperturbable sort of way.

"I—see," he finally said, and Maddie didn't much like the way he said that, either. "You certainly don't let the grass grow under your feet, little one!"

"I—don't understand," mumbled Maddie.

"No? Ah well, perhaps not." He straightened, glanced down at his sweat-damp shirt and dusty boots. "In any case, I daresay young Simson's in a more fit state to take a lady out to lunch than I am!" He looked at his watch. "I'll take you home when school comes out, Madeleine. We can collect Skeet on the way."

She was now really scarlet with embarrassment.

"Well, as a matter of fact, I—I mean, Tom said he'd take us home, too, thank you. I—I mean, he offered. He—he wants to."

"I'm sure he does," drawled Steve adding in a murmur, "Youth will to youth, and it was ever thus!"

"P-pardon?"

"Nothing, Madeleine. A misquotation, merely, but appropriate in the circumstances. Off you go then and enjoy yourself."

"Thank you, Steve. And—er—thank you for telling me about the hat."

Steve's grin was sardonic.

"Noble of me, wasn't it? Just think, if you had died of sunstroke, Yattabilla would be mine!"

Before Maddie could reply, he was gone—just a faceless figure in a slanting felt hat, amongst all the other faceless figures sitting on the fence.

CHAPTER SEVEN

Maddie enjoyed her lunch with Tom, up to a point. But only up to a point.

She could not say exactly where her reservations lay, because, as Tom had promised, the steak was good, and so were the two fried eggs that went along with it. His company was amusing, too. She felt relaxed with him, so that was not the reason for this feeling of incompleteness, of anticlimax, either.

Maddie looked across to where Tom sat and saw his round young face change under her dreamy gaze. Suddenly the roundness had gone. It was replaced by leaner, tougher cheeks, with deep grooves beside the mouth. And the eyes weren't Tom's merry blue ones any more. They had become gray, grave and watchful. They seemed to be piercing right into her mind, trying to tell her something. Yes, they were Steve Darley's eyes, and they were trying to tell her just why she was not enjoying this luncheon with Tom as much as she had thought she would.

Maddie blinked and was relieved to see Steve's image fade. It was replaced by Tom's once more. She realized that she had almost dozed off because of the heat and a meal that was larger than she was accustomed to eating in the middle of the day.

What nasty tricks one's mind could play at times. How silly! As if she could possibly prefer that it should be Steve sitting there opposite. Her mind ought to know better than that. It ought to know that she loathed the very sight of Steve, and all that he represented. The man was a positive threat to her inheritance. That's what he was! Maybe that was why she couldn't stop thinking about him. Why his image had even come between herself and Tom, sitting here in the Royal having lunch.

"Ice-cream, Maddie?"

"Mm, yes, thank you."

"And some fruit salad along with it," her companion said to the waitress. "And a pot of tea." He turned back to Maddie. "We all drink tea out here, so I didn't bother to consult. Okay? Tea and beer—the national beverages, you might say."

"Yes, I've noticed that." Maddie smiled, remembering the happy, young crowd of Australians on the boat coming out. They had consumed vast quantities of beer, some brashly and noisily, others quietly and steadily, but they had seemed to want beer with everything they did, whether it was swimming and deck sports, or dancing and cards. The national beverage? Yes, Tom could be right.

"Cigarette?" When Maddie declined, Tom lit one for himself and leaned back. "Tell me, Maddie—and shut me up for an interfering fool if you like!—but wouldn't it be nicer for you to live in town during the week, when Skeet's at school and just go out to Yattabilla on weekends? From what I've heard, the house isn't—well, up to much, is it? No offense to your dad, mind you, Maddie, but one gets to hear things out in the bush, you know. Yarns sort of get around. I can't help feeling, from what I've heard, that you would be a good deal more comfortable in town. I could maybe even fix you up with a job, if you'd like that. My old man knows just about everybody hereabouts, and it wouldn't be hard to find you something to keep you amused."

How often had not her own mind run along just these lines! Here was Tom suggesting the very thing she had yearned for, and Maddie could not accept. She bit her lip in vexation.

There was nothing for it but to tell Tom about that binding legal clause in her father's will—about that "term of residence" that was already proving almost more than Maddie could cope with, now that she had to do it alone, without Skeet.

Maddie told Tom about the will, but only the bit that applied to herself. She could not say why, but some inner sense of caution and pride prevented her from even mentioning Steve's name in this connection.

"So you see, Tom, I'll have to stay there to comply with the terms. Of course I'd much rather be in Noonday, but there's no help for it. And anyway—" she brightened—"if I can only get that car going and learn to drive it, I won't feel nearly so lonely and cut off. You do see how important it is for me, Tom? How much it means to me?"

"Yes, I certainly do, Maddie." Tom gave her a warm look of undisguised admiration. "You leave that bit to me, eh? I'll get her going for you, like a bird, I promise. I'll tune her up, give you a few preliminary hints, and then I'll keep an eye on your progress whenever I get the chance. How's that?"

"Marvelous! Oh, Tom, thank you! You don't know what it means to have someone on my side."

He looked puzzled.

"On your side, Maddie? Lord, you must be out of your mind, my girl! I can't think of any chap who wouldn't want to be on your side, sweetie. My motives are purely selfish, I warn you. I'm merely trying to beat the others to it, to be on your side first." He winked at her, checked the time. "I'll have to go. Lunch-break is over, I'm afraid."

Tom stood up, reached his hat from the hook above his head, and guided her out toward the street. Outside, he nodded to two stockmen as they passed. When they said, "G'day, Tom," he replied, " 'Day, Jackie, Billy."

"Who are they?" asked Maddie, eyeing the retreating figures with interest. They wore open shirts—the striped variety that should have an accompanying collar attached to the neck but hadn't—khaki pants and heeled boots. On their heads they sported quite the most dilapidated felt hats that Maddie had ever seen. The older one had a tangled beard of a surprising and unexpected gray, wrinkled black skin, and ageless brown eyes.

"They're two of Steve Darley's stockmen," Tom informed her. "The older one's called Billy Sundown, a bit of a local character. He's supposed to be a descendent of King Billy himself. I'm surprised you haven't seen him around the place. I believe Yattabilla was pretty much undermanned when your father died, Maddie. Now the Bibbi men work the two properties together, more or less, for the time being. Decent of Darley, but he's that sort of chap—and anyway, he's a trustee or something, isn't he?"

Or something! Maddie swallowed, trying in vain to ignore the sinister portent of Tom's innocent observations. So that was what Steve was up to. He was so sure that he was going to get Yattabilla, that already he was working it along with his own place. He couldn't even wait a year.

He must feel very certain indeed. He must be very sure that Maddie would not manage to "stick things out." Well, she'd show him! His underhand connivings would only serve to strengthen her personal resolution to defeat his ends. She would stay at Yattabilla, no matter how awful it was. When the year was up, it would be hers. Hers and Skeet's, that is. And in the meantime, if she could only learn to drive that car so that she was able to get about a bit, that too would help to make life a little more bearable.

Decent, indeed! It was all Maddie could do to refrain from an indignant snort. If only Tom knew! Still, he was better not knowing that Steve was involved in any way, for such was Steve Darley's charm and influence that Maddie would not put it past him to go to work on Tom and win him around to his way of thinking. Maddie didn't want that to happen. She wanted Tom to be on her side. Most of all, she wanted him to help her to learn how to drive that car. If Steve found out about that, he would doubtless put a stop to it, as he would to anything that was going to make her life at Yattabilla more pleasant. It was necessary to keep absolutely quiet just now. Tom could think Steve was decent, if he liked—but she, Maddie know better.

"I'll see you later, then, Maddie." Tom was speaking to her. "You meet Skeet when he comes out of school and see that he doesn't get on the bus. Then you can both come around to the office. We'll collect the battery at the garage on the way out of town. Right?"

"Right, Tom." She smiled her gratitude.

"Down that sidestreet, then. You'll see the name, with "Stock & Station Agents" painted on the windows. You can't miss it. See you."

"See you, Tom."

When he had left her, Maddie wandered over to the park. There were pretty trees and flower-beds there; a narrow path along the river-bank, where walking was cool and pleasant. Further on, there was a shallow, walled wading pool, with a fountain in the middle.

She sat on a nearby seat, watching several tiny tots splashing water over each other while their mothers looked on patiently. When it was time for Skeet to come out of school, she stood and walked, more quickly now, in that direction.

Her heart was beating faster in the anticipation of seeing Skeet. How she had missed him, all this week! Maddie's pulse slowed again to a monotonous tattoo as she remembered all the other, similar weeks that were to come. There were a whole 52 of them in a year, weren't there? The only cheering thought was that some of the 52 would be school holidays, when she and Skeet could be together all the time.

He came out of school cockily, one of a number of small jostling figures, who called high-pitched farewells to the teacher at the steps, as they came rushing forth.

When he approached, Maddie saw that he had abandoned his ankle socks. Beneath his grubby knees his legs were bare, like the other children's—a sign that Skeet himself had already recognized the need to be like the others and had taken what personal steps he could to achieve this end. She was glad that she had bought those sandals. He could wear them to school on Monday, like all the rest.

Maddie felt that she was seeing Skeet in a new light.

They had never been apart before. Now, for the first time, she was able to take an objective look at her little brother. She could swear that he had actually grown during the past week. His spiky red hair was as unruly as ever; his freckles as profuse, but he seemed taller than she had thought—more self-reliant, too. He was spindly and maybe frailer-looking than these sturdy country-reared children. Of course, his skin wasn't the sort to take a tan. The thinness of his limbs had always worried her. Now Maddie was aware, for perhaps the first time ever, of an underlying toughness in Skeet's wiry frame. With surprise she realized that, far from needing her constant care and protection, her young brother was well able to take care of himself.

It appeared that he was already fitting happily into his new environment. There was a certain amount of good-natured scuffling and repartee with his friends before he even bothered to acknowledge her presence. When he did, t was with a rather unenthusiastic, " 'Lo, Maddie. Can't I stay a while longer? The bus doesn't go for ages yet."

"We aren't going on the bus, Skeet. Tom Simson's driving us home. If you come now, you can have an ice-cream before we leave."

Skeet hesitated, but his playmate's exclamation of "Lucky coot!" was enough to send him off with Maddie without further argument. He paused only to turn and make a hideous face at his small friend, who giggled as he walked away.

He regaled them with his week's adventures the whole way out to Yattabilla, stopping only to hop out and in when the gates came along. This time he had no hesitation in opening all the different catches. "He's not too young to learn, Madeleine." Maddie remembered Steve's reproving words. They had seemed tough and unfeeling at the time, but she was forced—very grudgingly—to admit that he had been right.

When they arrived at the homestead, Skeet leaped out of the car and ran to see Etta, his hen, in order to reassure himself that Maddie had indeed been attending to her faithfully, as she had sworn she would. Satisfied on that score, he reappeared to find Tom drinking a beer, and his sister making tea.

Afterward, he followed Tom out to the garage and watched with interest as he began to overhaul the car. Skeet had always possessed an innate curiosity about the workings of engines. It was pleasant to sit on a drum, feeling satisfyingly full of tea and cakes, watching Tom's greasy fingers following terminal leads, checking points and plugs. When the overhaul got to a certain stage, Tom reversed the car right out of the garage, and took Skeet for a run down the track.

When they came back, he lifted the hood, made a few more minor adjustments, and then sent Skeet in to get his sister.

For nearly two hours Tom put Maddie through her paces. He was a patient instructor, first explaining the basic movements of the gears, the action of the clutch and accelerator. After that, he made his pupil go through all the motions herself. Finally he started the engine, and, with Maddie at the wheel, they began to make hesitant progress over the tracks around the homestead.

It was dark by the time Tom said he must be going. A perspiring, but triumphant Maddie slid thankfully from the driving-seat and allowed her tutor to put the Buick away in the garage.

"Not bad. Not bad at all!" That was Tom.

"I'll practise like anything, Tom. I'll do it every day."

"Keep trying as much as I've shown you, Maddie, and

we'll do it again next week. How about coming in again on Friday, like you did today. I'll take you back."

Maddie hesitated, sorely tempted. There would probably be a truck passing the twin-fork again. At least some sort of vehicle was bound to pass if she arrived there early. It was only a matter of waiting and then hitching a lift. The thing that made her hesitate was her promise to Steve. Why a promise made to someone who was himself so unscrupulous should be so binding to her, Maddie could not really have said. Perhaps, if she were honest with herself, she would admit that she was just the least bit frightened of Steve. The thought of being caught by him, standing at the twin-fork waiting for a lift, when he had expressly asked her not to do it again, was enough to make her go weak about the knees and shake her head, more adamantly, at Tom.

"I couldn't, Tom. There's no means of getting in, short of chancing a lift. I—I didn't much enjoy doing that this morning. I felt—er—sort of nervous."

"Quite right, too," he approved. "I don't think you'd better do that again, either. Tell you what, Maddie, I'll come and collect you."

"Tom, you can't."

"Can't I? You watch me! It'll be early, but you won't mind that, will you? So long as I'm ready when the office opens, my time's my own, Maddie. I can't think of a more pleasant way of spending it, so positively no ifs or buts."

"I don't know what to say. It's much too kind. But maybe, after another lot of lessons, I'll be able to practise enough to get a license quite soon," she added hopefully.

"Sure you will. You're a natural!" he grinned. "Well, see you on Friday. Be ready."

"I'll be ready on Friday, Tom," Maddie called, waving to the retreating car, while Skeet yelled "Goodby" from his position on the top wire of the fence. With an answering toot-a-toot, Tom was off. Maddie and Skeet stepped carefully over the weak places on the veranda and went inside out of the darkness.

Maddie felt tired, but cheerful. She had actually managed to drive that car. It was simpler than she had imagined. Admittedly it had leaped around like a startled kangaroo at first, but by the time she had stopped, she had begun to get the feel of the wheel beneath her hands and the pedals under her feet. She was sure she could do it! It was only a matter of practice.

Maddie indulged Skeet hopelessly during the weekend making all his favorite dishes and some treacle toffee into the bargain. Suddenly life seemed worthwhile again, because he was back with her. Skeet was her reason for living, she had discovered—or at any rate, her reason for living at Yattabilla. His piquant little face hovering over the dinner made the cooking of it a pleasure. The sight of his skinny form squatting patiently beside Henrietta down in the fowl-yard gave Maddie herself a feeling of peace and stability.

When the time came to say goodbye to him again on Monday morning, Maddie found that she had not quite the same sense of deprivation that she had experienced the previous week. It was impossible to feel sorry for Skeet, strutting proudly over to the bus in his new brown sandals, looking extremely peased with himself. She felt sorry for herself! But that would not do, either, Maddie told herself determinedly, when the bus had rumbled out of sight. She must keep busy. That way she would manage somehow to stave off the loneliness that threatened.

At least there was something to be busy *at*, she reminded herself. That something was the car.

Maddie drove it at every opportunity throughout the week, uncertainly at first, and then with increasing confidence. She did not attempt to make turns, because Tom had not shown her how to do that yet. She practised the gear-changes, stopping, and starting. In the evenings she studied her manual, so that she would get to know her signals and traffic code. The thought of traffic caused Maddie to smile wryly. At Yattabilla there was not even a slope on which to try hill starts, let alone another car to contend with. She would have to learn about those things, to prepare for the time when she could drive into Noonday to get her license. Tom had said that he would help her to get a permit, and that he would accompany her into town when the great day came.

She was ready when Tom arrived to collect her on Friday morning. She had put on the same cotton two-piece as she had worn on the previous visit, because it was the only suitable garment she possessed. This time, however, she did not need her canvas shoes. There was to be no long walk to the twin-fork. Instead, she was able to step straight into Tom's comfortable car.

It was pleasantly cool traveling over the plain at that early hour, but, as before, the day's heat was beginning to make itself felt by the time they reached Noonday.

Tom surprised Maddie by taking her straight to his own house—"to wash off the dust," he explained with a grin. After she had done that, his mother took her out onto a trellised veranda. She insisted on giving her what amounted to a second breakfast, of grapefruit, toast, and deliciously refreshing China tea with lemon. Mrs. Simson was kind, welcoming, and uncritical, as the Noonday people all seemed to be. Maddie chatted to her happily, making her laugh at some of the innocent pickles which she had got herself into as a newcomer to Yattabilla.

Maddie managed to make it all sound fun—a big, humorous adventure.

She did not mention the loneliness, or the spiders when she had arrived, or the mouse-holes in the mattresses, or the dead blowflies, or even the snake. They were things that she did not want to remember, so she talked instead about the deafening noise the frogs made in the creek—how they had kept her awake at first, but now amounted to a sort of lullaby—about Etta, the hen, and Skeet's attempts at fishing, and her own at driving.

When Tom left to open the Agency office, he said that he would see Maddie again after school. This time he would not be able to have lunch with her. His father was away valuing a property, so he was holding the fort, but Mrs. Simson would love to have her for lunch anyway.

Maddie protested at such intrusions upon their hospitality, but they were jointly insistent.

"It's no trouble, my dear," Mrs. Simson assured her warmly, "and it will do me good to have some young company about the house. I've a daughter, too, you know—did Tom tell you about his sister? She's about your own age, Maddie, nursing in Sydney. How I miss my Jill, but it's something she always wanted to do ever since she was a little girl. One mustn't stand in their way. I suppose I'm lucky that Tom, at least, has decided to follow in his father's footsteps and won't ever be too far away, for that reason. When he decides to get married, he'll have to have a house of his own, of course, but he'll be in Noonday to be near the office."

Maddie helped her hostess carry the breakfast dishes in from the veranda and to wash them up. The house was modern, small, air-conditioned and delightfully cool. There were terrazzo floors in the kitchen and bathroom. Tiles on the veranda completely encircled the house. A bit different from the rotting planks at Yattabilla, thought Maddie wryly.

She enjoyed helping with the small amount of housework, and when she had done all she could, Mrs. Simson made another pot of tea, gave her some magazines, and told her to amuse herself on the veranda for a while.

"You were up so early, dear. I'm sure you could do with a rest. You must work quite hard out there at Yattabilla, Maddie, even if you do have some fun, too. It's common knowledge that Gerald didn't do a thing to that homestead for years. He lost heart once your—once he was on his own."

Once your mother had run out on him? Was that what Mrs. Simson had been going to say? That was what Steve had said, anyway. That was how he had put it.

"Oh, it's not too bad, really," Maddie heard herself defending the old place loyally. "The kerosene fridge works all right, once you get to know its little foibles. Most of the time there's electricity. And when the generator runs down, and Lal is away, we have the Tilleys."

"Oh, my dear!" Tom's mother looked so genuinely distressed that Maddie wondered if she had been tactless in mentioning it.

After lunch, Mrs. Simson suggested that they walk around to the shopping center together.

"I've just a very few things to order, Maddie. You'll be able to go on to the school to collect your brother from there. That suit you?"

"Perfectly, thank you. And thank you, too, for the delicious lunch and all your kindness. I've had a beautifully lazy day."

"And deserved it, too, dear, I'm sure. Why, hello, Steve!"

Steve Darley's fingers lifted the gate latch neatly back into place behind him. He raised his broad-brimmed hat respectfully to the older woman.

"Good afternoon, Doreen," he said to Mrs. Simson, then, looking past her to where Maddie had adopted a frozen stance, he added more coolly, "And to you, too, Madeleine."

"Do come in, Steve, won't you, and have a drink? Beer? A whisky?" Tom's mother suggested coaxingly. She seemed pleased and surprised to see Steve coming up her path, and made her delight at his visit quite obvious.

Maddie wished that she could share Mrs. Simson's pleasure at the sight of him, but she couldn't. Neither must she give way to the nasty sinking feeling that had suddenly assailed her stomach.

The sinking sensation eased a little bit as she heard Steve decline the invitation.

"Not just now, thanks all the same," he replied politely, standing in front of Mrs. Simson and smiling down at her. "I just came in to say that I'll be taking Madeleine and Skeet home from school when the children come out. I happened to come to town today in any case. I'm meeting Kareena off the plane."

"Oh, I see. Did you want me to tell Tom, Steve?"

"No need. I've already seen him," returned Steve coolly, still talking to the older woman and completely ignoring Maddie. They both were, in fact. Steve seemed to have that effect on people. He could possess their entire attention to the exclusion of everybody else. That was what he was doing now with Mrs. Simson. She appeared pleased and flattered that he had come to see her at all. The fact that he had high-handedly altered her son's and Maddie's plans without consulting either of them did not seem to be causing Mrs. Simson the same degree of pique as it did Maddie.

"I know Geoff's away on a valuation, so it will save Tom the run out later on," Steve was saying. "I called in at Yattabilla on my way in. Mrs. Lawrence said he'd taken Madeleine into town very early. I've told Tom I'll handle the return trip myself."

But what about my driving lessons, Maddie wanted to wail—only she stopped herself, because Steve must not know about those. They were her secret—hers and Tom's.

Oh dear! Why had Steve to come into Noonday today of all days? She had thought it an opportune time because there was no sale today and few country men in town. Of course she had not known anything about him coming in to meet somebody whose name was Kareena.

Now her visit to town seemed to have lost its purpose, except for her meeting with Mrs. Simson, that is. She had to admit that, up until the moment Steve had appeared, her day had been enjoyable. It was warming to think that she had made a real friend in Noonday. She could understand, too, that Tom had not wanted to make an issue of the drive back to Yattabilla. There were plenty of others days ahead. On their slender acquaintance, it would have appeared odd if he had protested too much when Steve offered to take her him, especially as Steve almost passed her homestead on his way to Bibbi.

Maddie knew that she could count on Tom not to have mentioned the driving lessons. Skeet, too, had been sworn to silence, because, as she impressed upon him, it would be such fun to suddenly surprise everybody. Skeet had giggled and agreed to say nothing to anyone."

When she and Mrs. Simson were walking together at the shopping center some time later, Maddie heard a deep droning noise up in the sky. Looking up, she saw a neat silver plane circle once at the edge of the trees and then gently descend until it was out of sight behind the houses. That must be the plane that Steve had come to meet, she supposed. It would be the plane with Kareena.

Maddie had been wondering about that, but up to his moment she had not liked to mention it for fear of being thought inquisitive. Now she asked as casually as she could, "Who is Kareena, Mrs. Simson? I suppose that will be her plane? I hadn't realized there was a plane service to Noonday."

"There isn't, dear," replied Tom's mother dryly. "Kareena always charters a plane especially to bring her. That's the way Kareena works, you see. If things don't suit her, she finds a way around them, or else she alters them until they do. She doesn't like trains, so she simply hires a plane whenever she wants to go any great distance from Sydney. It's as simple as that—to Kareena."

"But who is she?"

"Kareena? She's the niece of a very prominent grazier who had a string of properties starting on the west side of Noonday and continuing almost to the center of Australia itself. Her uncle's dead now, but he and Steve Darley's father were great friends—natural, I suppose, as the Darleys are in a big way out here too. Kareena still comes up for all the big events and often stays at Bibbi for them." Mrs. Simson adjusted the string bag she carried to a more comfortable position on her arm, declining Maddie's offer to take it from her with a smile. "No, it's not heavy, Maddie, it just kept catching on the clasp of my purse. That's better." She returned to her previous topic. "It's early for Kareena to be paying a visit, I must say. The next big thing on the social calendar is the Polo Carnival. That's not till fall. It isn't like her to come right in the middle of the summer heat. But of course—" Mrs. Simson looked momentarily coy—"there may be more to it than meets the eye. I mean, obviously Steve has asked her, hasn't he, when she has come out of season. We've all been wondering for some time now about those two. After all, he is a very attractive man, you know."

That was something Maddie didn't know. Attractive? Well, yes, in a way, she supposed he was. In a physical way, that is—if you cared for the tough, authoritative, insensitive type—which Maddie didn't. Unscrupulous, overbearing, domineering, autocratic. There was no end to the list of undesirable adjectives she could apply to Steve Darley, but of course she didn't say them out loud. It was more tactful to pass off Mrs. Simson's glowing statement with a noncommittal murmur, the sort that could be taken for agreement.

When they had finished their shopping, they went into the Italian café that Maddie had discovered on her previous visit. Mrs. Simson seemed to know about the lemon tree, because she ordered two fresh lemon drinks with ice and said to Maddie, "The most cooling drinks in town, these are. There's something about *fresh* lemons that a bottle can't capture, don't you think? Mm! Isn't that fan nice on one's face!"

She lifted her head to catch the breeze from the big circular fan above them and Maddie did the same.

It was very hot indeed today—a dry, intense, still heat that made one's clothes stick to one's body. Maddie knew that her little cotton outfit, that had started the day so crisp and smart, was now as limp as a rag. Thank goodness she did not have to go home in the old school bus. That was at least something to be thankful for, if Tom was not now taking her. There was no doubt that Steve's big Chev was fast, smooth, and comfortable.

When she had thanked Tom's mother once again and had said goodby, Maddie made her way slowly up to the school. By the time she arrived she was perspiring freely again. Her white shoes were covered with dust. Her cotton gloves were grimy, too. Ah well! Maddie drew them off resignedly and tucked them in her bag. They seemed to soil more readily than her nylon ones. It was better to wear none than to have dirty ones. Maddie had always been fastidious about nice, clean gloves.

The children had hardly run out of school, scuffling and pushing each other like the last time, when Steve's big car approached.

As it took a wide turn outside the building and drew up to face the direction from whence it had come, Maddie could see that Steve already had a passenger. Sitting beside him in the front passenger seat was an elegant figure in dark sunglasses and a sleeveless hyacinth-blue linen dress.

This must be Kareena.

Skeet pitched his school-bag unceremoniously into the back seat and scrambled in after it. Steve, who had come around to open the door for Maddie, hauled him back with an equal lack of ceremony.

"Ladies first," he rebuked sternly, then nodded to Maddie to get in, while he kept a restraining grasp on her brother's shoulder.

His nearness and sternness made her dithery. She slid past him into the seat and muttered a greeting to her fellow passenger. Kareena turned sideways to give a cool and markedly unenthusiastic reply.

It was only then that Maddie realized just who was hiding behind those dark glasses. She did not really need to see that perfect profile and feminine neck. She didn't need to see the beautiful, dark upswept hair, or the lovely slender hand that rested its manicured fingers on Steve's steering-wheel. The voice alone would have been enough. For Maddie there was no mistaking the clear, resonant, pure diction of the goddess herself!

CHAPTER EIGHT

"Kareena, this is Madeleine Masterton, and her brother Skeet. Kareena Powell, Madeleine."

The goddess removed her sunglasses for an instant and regarded Maddie with a curious, pale blue stare.

"Haven't we met before somewhere? No, it's obviously not possible." With an elegant shrug of her slender shoulders and a distasteful glance at Skeet, Kareena answered her own question. "Please don't put your *extremely* dirty sandals near my hat-box, will you, little boy?"

Her voice was husky and carried the sort of sarcastic adult humor that was completely lost on Skeet.

He mumbled "Sorry!" and became so red that his freckles disappeared altogether. He hastily tucked his feet in at a safer distance from the cream hide case beside them. Maddie felt overwhelmed with pity for her little brother's embarrassment, and indignation on his behalf.

Surprisingly, it was Steve himself who came to the rescue.

Maddie saw him watching Skeet in the driving mirror, and then he asked, "How's school, Skeet, old chap? I hear your soccer's coming on fast. You'll never guess who told me that!"

"Who, Steve?" Skeet leaned forward eagerly, his misery receding.

"Peters himself. He's the one who picks the team, isn't he?"

"Yes, that's right. Gee, Steve, did Peters really tell you I was getting good?"

"Certainly he did. I wouldn't be saying it right now if he hadn't."

"How do you know Peters, Steve?"

"I know his dad, that's how."

"He has a sister, too. Do you know her? Her name's Susan, and she's really the sissiest kid!" Skeet's voice was loud with disgust. "I think girls are all sissy, Steve—or most of 'em. Gosh, in school they cry for just about anything. They spend their whole time crying about something, even if it isn't anything much, don't you think, Steve?"

Steve's eyes in the driving mirror met Maddie's for an instant.

"I guess they grow up, Skeet," was his tolerant reply. "They all grow up, and then they'd rather die than be seen crying. Haven't you noticed that yourself, Skeet? You will, when you grow up too."

Steve's mouth was smiling, but his eyes weren't. Maddie could see that they were quite serious before he turned them back to the road ahead.

"I suppose so," returned Skeet more thoughtfully. "Maddie's grown up, and she never cries."

"Exactly," Steve said succinctly.

Kareena moved impatiently against the leather upholstery at her back. She seemed amused.

"Dear me, Steve darling, I'd no idea you could be so chatty with children. I'm seeing you in a new light, pet! So patient and sweet—quite avuncular, in fact."

"Maybe you don't know me quite as well as you thought, Kareena." Steve's reply carried a dangerous smoothness. "I've always liked kids."

If Maddie had been the other girl, she would have taken the note in Steve's voice as a warning to change the subject, but Kareena didn't seem to feel that way. Perhaps it was because she had known Steve for such a long time that she felt she could now rush in where Maddie would have feared to tread.

"Quite, darling. So long as they don't make themselves heard too much, I adore them, too. As for not knowing you, that bit fascinates me. I thought I knew you very well—very well indeed, in fact—but I like discovering new facets in people, don't you? I'd hate a man who withheld nothing of his character from me. I like a little mystery in my friendships. It makes them more challenging and more promising, I think."

"You always were a girl for a challenge, weren't you, Kareena?" Steve chuckled indulgently.

"Well, you know what I mean, darling. I don't care for obvious people. I lose patience with these naïve young things who fawn all over one—it becomes so boring. Of course it's fun at Madeleine's age—" Kareena turned her head again, to address Maddie herself—"That nice young Simson boy, for instance. I hear he's quite smitten with you. I'd encourage him if I were you, my dear. They're a good sound family. He's wholesome, if a bit ingenuous. I'd say you'd be quite well matched—even lucky to get him."

"How kind you are to be interested in my welfare," replied Maddie meekly, although she was burning up with fury at the other's hateful condescension. Her eyes were angry. She had managed to make her voice submissive and honeyed and was rewarded at the sight of Steve's lips twitching with a quickly suppressed smile.

"I think Madeleine would prefer to look after her own welfare, Kareena, without us offering her any advice, however helpful," he interposed calmly. "Tell me, how are the Harris family doing, since they moved to Melbourne? Do you hear?"

He had adroitly steered his companion onto a new course.

Kareena talked animatedly of mutual acquaintances in the major cities. It appeared that she and Steve shared a wide circle of friends, many of high social standing, by the sound of her conversation. Maddie and Skeet were effectively excluded, but Maddie could only feel relief at that. She knew that in Kareena's particular sort of barbed repartee, she would be hopelessly bested, so she was glad just to lie back only half-listening in her corner as the miles skimmed past.

Skeet had been lulled to sleep by the constant buzz of voices from the front seat, concerned only with topics that bored him. His head had fallen sideways, and his mouth was slightly open. When the first gate came, he was still asleep. Maddie acted fast, scrambling out in his stead.

She noticed that, this time, Steve didn't prevent her and insist on the front passenger doing it, as he had that other time. Maddie couldn't resist a smile at the thought of Kareena's face if he had done that. She lifted the latch, glad that she had already had some personal practice at gate-opening with both Ted Widmore and Tom. At least she wasn't making a fool of herself in front of the goddess, she thought acidly, as she flicked the gate back into position and returned to the car.

Steve made no comment at the time, but after the last gate had been opened and shut, he said "Thank you, Madeleine" when she got back into the car. Kareena, of course, said nothing at all, but then Maddie had not expected her to.

At Yattabilla Steve helped her out and woke Skeet up. He had stopped a short distance from the homestead. Maddie was secretly glad—not that Kareena would have got out, but from here it was improbable that she could even see the desolate front yard, let alone the dilapidated condition of the house itself. Maddie did not want any more of that patronization. For once she was grateful that Steve had seemed to read her mind, with that uncanny knack he had.

"Well, feller," Steve ruffled Skeet's hair, "have a good weekend and keep up that soccer. Goodby, Madeleine."

"Goodby. Thank you for bringing me home."

He grinned. "If I thought you meant that, I'd tell you it was no trouble at all," he replied blandly, before he walked back to his car.

Seconds later, Maddie heard him changing gears as he gathered speed along the road. There was no doubt that he and Kareena made a handsome picture, sitting together in that great big car. They all went well together—the car, and Steve and Kareena.

Maddie shrugged her shoulders irritably. The thought had made her feel oddly sore and miserable inside. She did not know why. Probably because she was tired, too hot, and had found their enforced company a strain, she supposed. She put all thoughts of them firmly out of her head and walked resolutely into the house.

The weekend was spent, generally speaking, in indulging Skeet as before. Maddie admitted that it was some weakness in herself that allowed her to do it, and that probably it was bad for Skeet in the long run. She also had the idea that he would only be young once, and that there were a lot of things lacking in his life—things like a father and mother, for instance, and a nice little home instead of this rambling and comfortless place. Maddie wanted to make up to him for the lack of all those things that she was powerless to acquire. At times she felt almost hopeless with an all-pervading sense of inadequacy and frustration.

After Skeet had returned to school again, she started to paint the inside of the house. She had ordered some white paint through the mailman. Now she began to cover the ugly caramel color that seemed to be everywhere she looked and that was depressing in the extreme. It was useless even to consider replacing the outside paint. It was in such bad condition that it would need to be removed professionally, she felt sure.

She started in the hall, and by the end of the week had worked her way through to the kitchen. The following week saw the completion of that and also the adjacent boiler room and the meathouse. Maddie was pleased with her handiwork. Skeet, when he came home, was encouraging, too.

"Golly, Mad! What a difference! It's beginning to look quite—*homey*, isn't it!"

Maddie could have hugged him for his choice of adjective, even if it wasn't the kind one found in recognized dictionaries. "Homey" was what she wanted to make this unloved, unlived-in homestead, above all else, and "homey" was what Skeet had said.

In between times she practised her driving, wishing that she had been able to have a second round of instruction from Tom. She realized that she had still a great deal to learn before she could be classed as proficient.

Tom had called her on the phone. She had had several long and entertaining conversations with him. His father had had to go away again, but when he returned, Tom would have more time to spare. The first thing he intended to do, he told Maddie, was to come out and see her again—unless she could get in to town? His mother had enjoyed her company and would love to have her for the day again at any time. She must just say when would suit her, and he would arrange it.

Maddie told him, in turn, about the painting, how much nicer the house was looking, and how Skeet had said it was "homey."

"Well, don't fall off the ladder, or something, Maddie, will you? I'll call you about the end of the week. So long, sweetie."

"So long."

When the telephone rang toward the middle of the week, Maddie put down her paintbrush carefully and went to answer. She naturally thought it would be Tom. However, when the operator said "Long distance calling," amid a series of buzzing noises, she realized that it couldn't be Tom after all. She was at a complete loss as to who could possibly be phoning her.

It was with the greatest surprise, and an unprece-
dented measure of delight, that she heard Robert's voice.

"Maddie? Darling, is that you at last? It's Robert."

"Robert!" She felt quite dazed at first. "Rob! Where
are you speaking from? It's so good to hear you!"

His voice was distant, but quite distinct. He sounded a
very long way away indeed.

"I've been in Brisbane."

"Brisbane?"

"Yes, Maddie, Brisbane. And listen, Maddie. I'll be
passing quite close to Noonday on our roundabout way
south again. We've a little job to do, and when I look at
the map I see you won't be far away at all. I thought I'd
stop off and see you. I'll only have a few hours, but it'd be
worth it. I just have to see you. There's something I want
to tell you, something important."

"Oh, Rob." Maddie was trying to collect her thoughts.
How could he possibly come out, if he only had a few
hours? "It's 60 miles from Noonday, Rob. It takes just
ages to get here."

Robert thought a moment.

"Well, could you come in and meet me? I know it's a
lot to ask, but there'll be two other men with me. I can't
take them so far out of the way. We're on a tight schedule, you see."

Maddie hesitated.

"I could try," she said dubiously.

"Yes, do try. It's important—to me, at any rate. If I
don't see you now, Maddie, it might be a whole year,
mightn't it, until we see each other again? Can you make
it the day after tomorrow?"

Maddie was thinking hard. She was remembering all
Robert's kindness, his steadiness and dependability, his
help when her morale had been so low, his interest in
Skeet, the lovely evening of dancing he had wanted to
give her, which had been spoilt by Steve's goddess.

"Yes, I'll come, Robert. I'll be there. At a place called

The Royal, in the main street. The day after tomorrow."

"Bless you, Maddie! 'Bye for now and be sure to be there, won't you? Don't stand me up!" he laughed, and Maddie smiled, too, at her end of the phone.

"I won't," she promised. "I'll be there."

But *how*? she asked herself, when she had replaced the receiver. How do I get there?

It was the same old problem, but this time it was more difficult to solve, because Tom could not help her out.

Steve? Maddie was reluctant to ask him, but in the present circumstances, she could think of no alternative.

"Of course I'll run you in, Madeleine." Steve seemed agreeable and willing. "I'm glad you asked me, if a little surprised that you did. You must want to get to town pretty badly."

Maddie flushed at his dry tone.

"I've to meet a—er—a friend for lunch," she said, "someone I knew in Sydney, who hasn't much time to spare and can't come out here. I'd very much like to see him, but he's just passing through. It would mean a lot to me to see him, Steve. This is my only chance."

There was silence at the other end of the line. Then Steve's deep drawl came through again.

"I see," he said, in that way that made Maddie feel too transparent for words. "Well, in that case, Madeleine, I'm at your disposal. As a matter of fact, Kareena can use a trip to town, too, so we'll make a day of it."

The receiver clicked down.

Maddie stood by the wall and sighed. Another journey with Kareena was not an especially attractive thought, but she'd put up with anything to repay Robert for some of his kindness to her.

When the time came, she found she could not wear her little two-piece again, because there was a mark, like a grease stain, near the hem. She would need to use a solvent to remove it. As she had none at Yattabilla, there was only her emerald shift—the one she had worn the very first time she had met Steve in Mr. Opal's office.

She felt an an immediate disadvantage when she reached the car and found Kareena there, impeccably turned out in an expensive shantung outfit, with crocodile bag and shoes. She was perfect, she really was! Maddie admitted the fact to herself in a generous spurt of honesty. There was absolutely no flaw visible in either Kareena or her attire. Maddie reflected on the imbalance of a Fate that could endow one person alone with so many enviable qualities. It was hardly fair! The odd thing was, though, that even with all her many advantages, Kareena did not seem to be a happy person. Her lovely mouth pouted more than it smiled, and her eyes chose to be cold and critical more often than to be warm and friendly. Or perhaps it was just because of Maddie's own presence that she chose to be so petulant. No doubt she regarded Maddie as a nuisance. But she might have acted a little more graciously, since Steve had said that she, too, could use a trip into town.

Beyond a coldly formal greeting, Kareena said absolutely nothing to Maddie the whole way into town. Steve, too, was strangely silent, except to say "Thank you, Madeleine" when she opened the gates, as he had the last time.

Steve insisted on her having some morning tea with them upon arrival. After that she was thankful to escape, excusing herself by saying that she had some shopping to do.

"We'll meet here again about five o'clock, then, Madeleine, if that's all right with you? I promised Mrs. Farrell, my housekeeper, that Kareena and I would be back for dinner."

"Yes, very well, Steve. I won't keep you waiting."

Kareena and I—for dinner. What a pleasantly intimate sound that had! Maddie tried to imagine what Bibbi must be like and what Mrs. Farrell would prepare for her sophisticated guest for dinner. Steve's house sounded so modern and luxurious that perhaps they even dressed for dinner. She could visualize the scene: Kareena statuesque, in one of those deceptively simple dinner-gowns that accentuated her faultless figure; and Steve dark and awesome, suave in his dinner jacket. Maddie found the picture a singularly disturbing one. In fact, she wished that she had never begun to think of it at all. It was no business of hers, anyway.

She bought herself a bottle of cleaning fluid to remove the grease mark from her suit and then wandered about, at a loss, until it was time to meet Robert.

When she saw him standing waiting for her outside The Royal, he looked so dear, kind, and familiar that Maddie ran across the street and right into his arms. She found herself hugging him like a long-lost brother.

"Oh, Rob! I am glad to see you!"

"Maddie!" He held her away from him. "I was hoping you'd make it. Here you are, as lovely as ever. No, a little on the thin side, darling, but gorgeous, all the same. It's a wonder you haven't melted dead away in this climate, if you ask me. Is it always as beastly hot as this in Noonday?"

Maddie laughed gaily. It was exciting to see Robert again, here, of all places, so unexpectedly.

"It has been like this ever since I came. You get used to it. Take your jacket off, though, Rob. Everyone else has. Look! Nobody even bothers to wear them for eating out here."

"Yes, that's certainly better." He hung his coat on one of the hooks and placed his hat over it. It was a pork-pie sort of hat, natty and citified, and looked somehow out of place beside the rows of wide country felts on either side of it.

"Now, what will you have?" Robert asked her across the table.

"There is only one thing," Maddie informed him, "and that's steak and eggs. But it's good steak!"

"Two steaks and eggs, please," Robert said to the waitress. "I'm told it's good steak, too."

"It's beaut," agreed the waitress laconically and went off to get it.

"Now, Maddie, tell me all you've been doing since you left. How is Skeet? And how are you managing to get along at Yattabilla?"

As they ate, Maddie told him all the things that had happened to her and Skeet since they had come out here into the country. She didn't make it all sound quite so funny as she had to Mrs. Simson, because Robert knew her so well that he would have seen through that sort of bravado. As she talked, his eyes became more grave. There were signs of tension in his expression.

"I hate to think of you there all by yourself, Maddie," he said wretchedly. "In your letter you didn't even mention that Skeet had to live away from home most of the time. I've been missing you and worrying about you as it is. Heaven knows, I'd have been ten times more miserable if I'd known you hadn't even your brother for company. It's a good thing I came by on this trip, or I might never have found out."

"There didn't seem much point in saying anything, Rob," Maddie shrugged. "After all, there's nothing you could have done about it, any more than I could myself. It's just the way things turned out. How did you come by, anyway? I do hope you haven't come a long way off your route just to see us?"

"No, I haven't. It was unbelieveable luck, as it turned out. The firm has a government contract for several water schemes they're starting. One was up near Brisbane. The other, for a dam, is only 50 miles or so north of here. We were to survey it on our way back. It seemed a heaven-sent opportunity to see you."

"I see. Does that mean that you'll be coming back again, then?"

"Not me, no. The construction men will be next on the scene. We've done our part, and they'll act on our findings."

Maddie spooned the remains of her ice-cream neatly into her mouth. "And what have you done with the other men who are traveling with you?"

Robert smiled. "They've gone for a swim, of all things. It seems there's a beaut waterhole down in the river here. They reckoned it was a good chance to cool off. They'll be hanging around here later in the afternoon—I pointed the place out. I thought you and I could go for a walk somewhere, maybe—somewhere where we could talk. Is there anywhere shady around here?"

She thought for a moment.

"There's a lovely park, where it's nice and cool. We wouldn't have to walk very far, and there are seats under the trees."

"Splendid." Robert collected his jacket and put on his hat as they came out into the sun. This time he did not put on his coat, but slung it over one arm. He took Maddie's own arm with his free hand.

Together they strolled over the lawns in the park, down among the trees where the little wading pool was. There were some ducks there today. Several children were feeding them with crusts of bread that they had brought. It was pleasant watching the tame birds snapping the water as the pieces fell near them and hearing the children's shrill laughter and exclamations.

Afterward they found a seat and talked spasmodically. Robert seemed to be preoccupied. Maddie was content to leave him to his thoughts. The afternoon heat, the buzzing of bees in the flower beds behind them, the distant voices and floating laughter of the children, all had a soporific effect on her.

It was Robert who finally broke the silence.

"Maddie, you said a while ago at lunch, that there was nothing I could do about you having to live there at Yattabilla all alone. And, if you remember, I had already told you on the phone that I had something to say that was important. Well, the two things are directly linked. There is something I can do, and it's something I want very much—something that I hope you will want as much as I do. I want you to marry me, Maddie."

Maddie looked at him, drawing her breath swiftly. Her eyes felt as if they must be as round as a couple of saucers.

"Will you, Maddie? Please? I can see I've taken you by surprise, but I've given it a great deal of thought. It's what I want to do most in the whole world. I've missed you dreadfully since you left, and it would solve your problem for you, too."

She gazed at him in a dazed fashion. Such a thought as marriage had never entered her head. Here was Robert, asking her to enter that very state.

She liked Robert—liked him enormously. Why, then, was she not feeling breathlessly ecstatic at his proposal? What was the matter with her? Why couldn't she fling herself into his arms and say "Yes, yes, yes, oh, Robert, yes, please." That's what Maddie would have liked to do. That's what she wished she could do, only something was holding her back. She couldn't understand what was happening inside her, but it was as if a great truth was crystallizing itself somewhere in the region of her heart. Maddie could not tell what the truth was going to be, just yet. She would have to wait for her heart to send a message to her mind. A sort of translatory message, it would need to be to tell her what this torn, unhappy, incredible feeling could mean.

What was she to say to Robert? Dear Robert, sitting there watching her in the most puzzled, uncertain way.

"But, Rob," she heard her shaken voice utter doubtfully, "one can't get married just to—well, to solve a problem."

"Maddie! It isn't only that! That's only a part of it—a very small part." Robert took her hand, looked down at her fingers curled in his. "I love you, you see. I thought I could wait a year, and now I know I can't. It's impossible, knowing you're there alone at that miserable Yattabilla. I had meant to wait, I'll admit that. I meant to wait until my prospects improved, so that I could offer you and Skeet much more than I can at the moment. The fact is, Maddie, that almost anything will be better for you than what you have now. Come back to Sydney with me—you and Skeet. Throw up this crazy residence thing and come back with me. Let me take care of you both. Marry me, please, Maddie?''

Robert was so humble, so persuasive. Maddie felt dreadful, because she knew she was going to have to hurt this person whom she liked very much. The blinding force within her had taken control of her actions, even though it had not yet identified itself to her. It was making her say things she didn't really want to say at all.

"Rob, my dear, I can't. I am so very sorry, but I can't.''

"Why not?''

"Because—I—I—don't know why, but I just know it wouldn't work out.''

"I'd make it work out," insisted Robert confidently.

"No, Rob, you couldn't, and neither could I. It wouldn't be right from the very beginning. I can see that now. I—I don't love you in the right way, Robert.''

He took her other hand, patiently.

"Darling, that would come," he told her gently. "I don't expect you to feel the same as I do, not at first, but you would grow to love me. Loving someone is a sort of togetherness, really. We'd be together all the time, and your love would grow.''

"No, Rob." She was sad, but adamant.

"Maddie, *why?*''

"Dear, I've told you. I've done my best to explain.''

Robert looked at her thoughtfully.

"And I can't accept your explanation, Maddie. It's too negative. There's no positive reason why—" He broke off, tensing suddenly. "Maddie, there's no one else, is there?" he asked anxiously. "Is there someone else?"

"No, of course not, Rob!" said Maddie, but even as she said it, even as she looked straight into Robert's dear, kind face and said those words, she saw his features change. The eyes she was gazing into were not Robert's at all. They were clear, gray, penetrating eyes, that could be uncomfortably intent one minute, infinitely tender the next. They were fine, steady, proud eyes. The black brows above them could draw together quickly into a quite terrifying scowl, or they could lift satirically, or quirk with humor. Steve! Oh, *Steve!*

"Maddie? Darling, are you all right? You look as if you'd seen a ghost, you're so pale!" Robert was back. He was sitting on the seat beside her, shaking her gently, anxiously.

"I'm—all right," she managed to falter.

A ghost? If only Robert had been right.

To be haunted by a ghost presented no problems—at least, not when you compared it with being haunted by a real, live, virile man, who not only lived on the very next property, but was the trustee of your father's estate as well.

Maddie was thoroughly staggered, utterly aghast at herself. How could she love Steve, when she knew that she hated him? Love? Hate? How closely allied those two emotions must be she was only now discovering. Maddie had known for the last few minutes what the great, secret truth was that her heart had been harboring. That truth was that she loved the very man that she had thought she hated. She loved Steve Darley with every fiber of her being, with an all-consuming dedication that was as hopeless as it was unrequited.

Oh Steve!

"My dear, we'll have to go." Robert glanced at his watch, pulled her gently to her feet. "I've kept you too long as it is, in this heat. Between that and the surprise, you've been knocked sideways." He stood looking down at her, still patient and considerate. "We won't say any more about it just now, not if it upsets you. But think about it, darling. I want you to think about it very carefully and then write to me. Will you?"

"It's no good, Robert," she said dully.

"Do it all the same, will you? For me? I'm not going to give up as easily as all that!"

"I'll—I'll try," she agreed weakly.

"Promise?"

"Yes, I promise."

"You're still awfully pale. We'll walk back slowly. You've been doing too much—all that painting and everything." He sounded stern and disapproving.

Maddie stumbled along at his side, too miserable and confused to talk.

As they neared the Royal, two men in a parked car gave a signal toot. They were waiting there to collect Robert, obviously. Farther down the street, on the same side, Maddie could see Steve's big Chev. He and Kareena were sitting in it, but when he saw Maddie coming, he opened his door and got out, stretching in a leisurely way in the hot sun.

Maddie dragged at Robert's sleeve.

"Let's say goodby here, Rob," she whispered a little desperately. She held out her hand.

Robert took her hand. Then, before she knew what he intended to do, he had pulled her into his arms and was giving her a quick, fierce kiss.

"I love you so much, Maddie," he muttered into her hair. "Promise to think about what I said?"

"Oh, Robert." She found she was clinging to him with a mixture of guilt and compassion, hardly knowing what she was doing. "I'll write, I truly will."

"And try to make it yes." He kissed her again, briefly and gently.

The next moment Robert was getting into the car with his companions, and Maddie was walking numbly toward Steve, standing nonchalantly beside his rear passenger door. He opened it for her, and she felt his eyes boring into her uncomfortably. Maddie found that she couldn't look at him—she just stared fixedly ahead of her, at nothing.

When he took her upper arm in a firm grasp, she shook herself free almost frenziedly.

"Take it easy, Madeleine, and get in there, for God's sake," he drawled softly right into her ear. "It's a heart-rending farewell for you, no doubt, but you don't want to make a fool of yourself right here in the street, do you?"

Maddie was aware that she was still standing there woodenly. A glance at Steve's closed face was enough to set her scrambling into the car with almost hysterical haste.

His gray eyes, which could sometimes surprise her with gentleness, were as cold and forbidding as she had ever seen them.

CHAPTER NINE

The next few days were rainy ones.

It wasn't even crisp, refreshing sort of rain, thought Maddie sourly, as she went about the house mopping up pools of water and placing basins at strategic intervals beneath the worst of the drips. Rather it was a steady, dismal drizzle—as dismal as her own thoughts. It kept Skeet more or less confined to the house on the weekend. When the school bus called for him on Monday, it came churning up the track in a flurry of black mud. Maddie was amazed at the way that arid, hard-baked plain could soften into dark mudpans when it became soaked with water. She waved goodby to Skeet, standing clear of the spray as the bus's wheels spun aimlessly for a moment, then took a grip of firmer ground beneath them.

By the next morning the sky had cleared, and things began to dry up. Maddie, who had been painting away at those awful, flaking, caramel walls all the time she had been indoors, was glad to see a pale, sultry sun struggling through once more. Steam rose off the flat down near the creek, and there was a strange tangy smell from the rain-soaked gum leaves.

In the afternoon, she thought she would practise driving the car again. Carefully she reversed it from the garage. She was always thankful when that bit was safely over and took a few tentative turns around the homestead. Gaining confidence, she headed down the track a little way. There was a wide turning place about half a mile down the road, where she could sweep right around in one go without having to do a three-point turn. Tom had not taught her how to do that yet.

Maddie was never sure, afterward, just what went wrong, or how she slipped into that skid. One moment she was accelerating confidently, with her front wheels aligned perfectly with the road ahead. The next, one tire seemed to drop into the mud-soft earth shoulder at one side and was being dragged off the road. When she tried to steer her way back, she only gathered speed as the car lost control.

Too late, she recollected that one is supposed to drive *into* a skid. She saw the bunch of trees looming in front of her, but was powerless to alter her course. Even as she spun the wheel frantically right into the line the car was taking, she realized that she had acted too late. She would have been better to brake and stop altogether, because the Buick was headed dead on course for those trees and was going quite fast when it hit the nearest one.

There was a sickening crash. Maddie felt herself flung into the air and for some panic-stricken moments seemed to hurtle through an endless space. Then there was an explosion of pain in her head. After that, total darkness.

She had no means of knowing just how long she lay there. It might only have been minutes; it could have been hours.

Her first awareness was of the wrecked car, some yards off, and then of the steamy sunlight beating down on her. Gingerly she moved her legs, one after the other. They seemed all right, although her whole body felt bruised and battered. When she came to move her left arm, though, pain brought perspiration to her brow. She lay back, quite still, not daring to stir again until it had receded.

Lying there, collecting herself, Maddie became aware of something she had not noticed before. On the skyline, up there on the ridge, was the silhouette of a horseman, just behind the two clumps of trees that were the monster's ears. Both man and beast were completely motionless. The rider's form was leaning forward against the animal's neck. They must have been there for some time, and Maddie thought to herself that it could only be Steve.

She had never known she could be so relieved at the

knowledge that another human being was around. She needed help, no doubt about that, and even Steve would be a godsend right now. She'd have to try to attract his attention.

Painfully and slowly she raised herself to a sitting position and waved her right arm. She was stiff and sore. Movement brought unwelcome jabs of pain in its wake, but it was necessary, all the same. She waved again, and still the profiled figure remained immobile. It didn't even wave back. Then, to Maddie's horror and disbelief, she saw it begin to move away—not down this side of the ridge, the Yattabilla side, toward her, but in the opposite direction!

She struggled to her feet, mindless of the stiffness, and waved and even shouted, but the dark figure only got smaller and smaller. The next moment it had dropped down out of sight on the other side of the horizon.

Maddie stared at the place where the horse and rider had disappeared, trying to take in the fact that they had gone. Steve had gone! He had actually gone away and left her, lying—or rather, sitting—in the mud beside a bashed-up car. Maybe he had actually left her here on purpose, to die. If she were dead, he would get Yattabilla, she thought grimly. And what a nice easy way in which to get it. You simply rode off and left your adversary to *die!*

Indignation, sheer rage enveloped Maddie. She was far from dead, as he would soon find out. A little bit hurt, maybe. That arm was a bit of a bother. There was a swelling on her temple where she had hit her head, but neither was the type of injury that was likely to kill anyone. Poor Steve, he would soon discover that he was out of luck, if that was what he hoped.

Maddie began to make her way slowly homeward. She shuffled along, aching in every joint. It took her an interminable time to reach the house. She staggered over the veranda and into the hall, then lurched along to the bathroom, where she made a half-hearted attempt to remove the mud from her bare legs. Her cotten dress was torn and stained. The face that gazed back at her from the mirror was paper-white, except for the dust that had mingled with perspiration in grimy streaks, and the blood-caked contusion at the side of her head.

Maddie supposed it *must* be her face, since there was nobody else here at Yattabilla homestead who could be looking into that mirror. It looked pretty awful, but it would have to wait. She felt too shaken and and exhausted to do more just now. Indeed, it was with the greatest measure of relief that she gained her bedroom and lay down gingerly on top of her bed.

She smiled bitterly to herself. She was for all the world like a wounded animal that crawls back to its lair to nurse its injuries alone.

She drifted into a state of semi-shock, almost of stupor, to be aroused a short time later by the sound of heavy footsteps outside. They took the veranda steps in a couple of bounds and came quickly into the hall. The next second Steve had burst into the room.

"Madeleine? Are you here? Well, thank God for that! I've been searching everywhere!" His face as he approached the bed was pale and stern beneath the tan. His eyes snapped with a mixture of anger and relief.

"I'm here, and I'm all right," she mumbled. "Please leave me alone."

"You're not fit to be left alone—in more ways than one!" he barked irately. "What the hell do you think you were playing at, trying to drive that ramshackle old car when you haven't even a clue how the thing works?"

He sounded unbelievably furious, and Maddie was stung to life.

"I *have* a clue," she retorted with spirit, "and I *do* know how it works. Tom gave me some lessons."

"I thought as much," Steve ground out, between

clenched teeth. "The senseless young idiot! He might have guessed you'd try it out alone!"

"I've been practising for weeks," she told him indignantly. "I'm getting quite good at it, too. It was only today that something went wrong."

"Wrong! You hit that tree with one hell of a smack, by the condition of the wreckage. How do you think I felt, hunting around out there with not a sign of you anywhere? You might have killed yourself. As it is, you seem to be all in one piece, thank heaven!"

He bent over her, and Maddie could have sworn that there was anxiety in his intent look—that is, if she hadn't already known that he had ridden away on purpose and left her to die. The hypocrite, she thought confusedly, because his nearness was bringing on a sort of mental panic.

"Let's see what damage you've managed to do, all the same."

Steve put out a hand, and Maddie shrunk away. Unaccountably, she had begun to shiver.

"Don't you touch me, Steve Darley!" she shrilled through teeth that chattered. "Don't you dare!"

Her eyes defied him, halted him momentarily in his intentions. He just stood there looking down at her thoughtfully, and then he tried again. There was a new, patient note in his voice this time.

"Come on, Madeleine," he said reasonably. "I'll be gentle, I promise, but we have to know, don't we? Maybe you do know already. Maybe you could just tell me, eh?"

His deep, coaxing tone was almost too much for Maddie. It brought tears to her eyes and a wobble to her own voice.

"What do you care?" she quavered almost unintelligibly. "You rode away."

"I—what?" He sounded incredulous.

"You rode away. You went *away*, on your horse. You left me!" She was almost crying, she was so distraught.

"Maybe you didn't think I saw you up there on the ridge, on your horse. You were looking right down on me, so you must have seen me, too. And then when I waved, you went away. I waved and waved, I even called, but you rode away!"

Steve stared down at her all the time she was speaking. His face had been expressionless all that time. Not even a single, flitting pang of guilt crossed his features for a moment. Only when she stopped did a shade of warmth enter his eyes. Slowly, to her amazement, she watched it spread into a look of great kindness and compassion.

He shook his head slowly, and a small smile lifted one corner of his grim mouth.

"I didn't ride away and leave you, Madeleine," he told her very gently. "The man you saw up there on the ridge was Billy Sundown. He's one of my stockmen, although I can't expect that you'd have realized that. When he saw you move beside the wrecked car, he came home to tell me. That was the right thing for him to do. He knew it was something for his boss to handle. I didn't come over on horseback myself. I came in the car, because I had a feeling it would be needed. It's just outside." He paused, leaned over her. "*Now* will you let me inspect the damage?"

Maddie was beyond words, but in any case Steve didn't wait for a reply. She closed her eyes as she felt his hands moving quickly over her bruised limbs, as expert and impersonal as any doctor's.

"That's fine." Satisfied so far, he held up her right wrist. "This has had a nasty wrench. Let me see you move your fingers."

Maddie wiggled them obediently in his own hard, work-toughened ones.

"No break there," he said on a note of relief, "although we'll have it X-rayed just in case. The main trouble seems to be this other arm."

He lifted it gently, but even that cautious movement

made Maddie gasp with pain. She seemed to be drowning in that unpleasant sensation. Steve's face hovered above her, dimmed and receded, as she drifted off on a pain-racked cloud.

When she came to, there was a welcome feeling of coolness about her face. A deep voice spoke very near her hair.

"Lie still, darling," it said. Or rather, that's what Maddie imagined that it had said. She must still be drifting in that cloud of semiconsciousness to even think such a thing.

She opened her eyes to find that Steve was wiping her face, very gently, with a soft, cold cloth. He was wiping away the blood and dust marks. The pain was gone, and her left arm was in an improvised sling, strapped firmly against her body.

"Better?" Steve's own face was pale and set. It seemed an effort for him to summon up the faint, reassuring grin he gave her. "You've broken your collar-bone, Madeleine. I'm going to take you in to the hospital to get fixed up. After that you're coming back to Bibbi with me."

Maddie stared. She still felt vague, and it was difficult to take in what he was saying.

"I can't," she reminded him in a husky whisper. "Don't you remember, Steve? I can't. I have to stay at Yattabilla. That's what Mr. Opal said."

Steve looked impatient.

"My dear girl, Mr. Opal would be the first to agree that the legal aspect be held in abeyance, under the circumstances," he told her tersely. "I'm not leaving you here alone in your present condition, so let's call a temporary truce, shall we? I'm going to get you a small cup of tea and a couple of tablets I have in the car. From then on you'll do as I say. I'm in no mood to argue, so be warned."

Maddie respected that warning.

As she sipped the tea he brought her and obediently swallowed the tablets, she could see that it would be dangerous to oppose Steve in his present mood. Gone was the gentleness that she knew she had not dreamed, even though that tender "darling" had been a figment of her imagination. Now there was only impatience to be gone—that, and the physical frustration that enforced inaction at a sickbed can cause in a big, active man like Steve.

Impatience and frustration were in every movement of his powerful frame as he walked about the room with his hands in his pockets while Maddie drank her tea. He was like a half-tamed tiger, resentful of its confinement. When she had finished her drink, he took the cup from her, set it on the bedside table, and pulled open the drawers in the dressing chest. Then he took her dressing-gown from the hook behind the door and began to fling things into the canvas tote with masculine abandon.

"You can tell me if I miss out on any essentials," he said grimly. "You don't need much. Pajamas? Nightdress? Whatever it is, where is it?"

"There's a clean one in my bottom drawer, and my cosmetic bag is in the bathroom," Maddie replied with meek apology, aware that he was anxious to be gone. She felt a dreadful nuisance and a bit of a traitor, too. Steve hadn't ridden away and left her, after all! It had been Billy Sundown, the grizzled stockman she had once seen in town, who had watched her on the ridge and who had then gone away to tell his boss. She hoped it was not that she had accused Steve of riding off and leaving her that made him look so grim and tense just now. She was sorry she had misjudged him—she really was. Sorry and glad. She was glad that her suspicions had turned out to be unwarranted.

Maddie slid her legs over the end of the bed and found herself caught neatly by Steve and lifted carefully into his arms. She was thankful to rest her head against his shirt, because nausea had suddenly assailed her at the movement of her bruised body when she stood up.

"Stubborn little thing, aren't you?" Steve's voice chided her. Then, as he took in the whiteness about her mouth, he put his head down closer, adding, "I'm sorry, Madeleine. I'll try not to jolt you."

Maddie felt his lips brushing her forehead; his face was so near to hers. Of course it was a purely accidental contact, because when she raised her eyes his expression was as unrevealing as usual. That meant he had not even been aware that his mouth had brushed over her brow with a touch as light and fleeting as a butterfly's.

He put her gently into the back seat and placed a cushion behind her head.

"Would you rather lie right down? No? Hold tight then, for a quick trip into town."

Steve hardly spoke the whole way into Noonday. As they passed the smashed Buick, leaning crazily up against a stout apple-gum, you could have cut the silence with a knife. Soon after that Steve groped in his shirt pocket for the makings and rolled himself a cigarette. Maddie, from her half-reclining position in the back seat, admired the dexterity with which he managed to do that and at the same time maintain a steady driving speed.

When he left her at the hospital, he smiled at her. It was the first real smile he had given her since the moment he came storming into her room to find her.

"Well, Madeleine, here goes. They're going to keep you in overnight just to make sure there's no concussion. They'll see you get a good rest, too. I'll come in the morning to take you home."

Home? Home to Bibbi, he meant. *His* home, certainly, but one that could never be hers. The thought was so painful, her longing and love for him so great, that Maddie wondered how she was going to be able to bear being there at Bibbi, with Steve. And with Kareena. She had almost forgotten about Kareena.

She smiled in return, gamely.

"Thank you, Steve. And thank you for bringing me here. I—I'm sorry," she said inadequately. What she really meant was that she was sorry for thinking he had ridden off to leave her to die, when he had instead been kind, efficient, and even quite gentle in between his bouts of anger and exasperation.

Steve glanced down at her wan face, at her pluckily smiling mouth. He grinned and ruffled her hair in the same way he sometimes did with Skeet, just as if she had been a child.

"I'll be back in the morning, Madeleine."

He walked out of the ward then, with that long easy stride, leaving Maddie to the ministrations of the doctor and nurses.

When he returned the next day, Maddie was sitting in a chair beside her bed, waiting for him.

Even in his faded moleskins and khaki shirt, and carrying that battered wide-brimmed hat, he looked carelessly handsome. Maddie could smell a clean shaving-lotion smell as he bent to pick up her bag.

"I can walk today," she assured him quickly. "I'm feeling much, much better. A bit stiff and sore, but it will soon wear off. I—er—I can't see any real need to come to Bibbi, Steve, can you? Couldn't you just drop me off at Yattabilla again?"

"No, Madeleine, I could not," he replied firmly. "I've had a report on you from the doctor. You're to take things easy for the next week. There's a distinct possibility of delayed shock. He advises bed most of the time, with increasing exercise as the days go on. Okay?"

Maddie sighed. "Okay," she agreed resignedly.

She was treated to a penetrating stare.

"What's the matter? You'll like Bibbi, I promise you. I'll even keep out of your way if that will make you feel happier. Oh yes, I've noticed how you go to the most extraordinary lengths to avoid my unwelcome presence."

"It's not that," she muttered miserably, with heightened color.

"What, then? If it's the legal side that bothers you, I've been in touch with Opal and put him in the picture. Will you accept my word on that?"

"Yes, of course!" she said in quick distress. She knew, too late, that she could trust Steve. She could trust him with anything, even her life. It hurt her to think that she could ever have doubted him when she loved him so overwhelmingly.

"Right-o, then. Stop looking as though you're going off to the guillotine and buck up, there's a good girl. Mrs. Farrell is longing to have someone to nurse and spoil!"

Maddie followed him in silence to the car. She offered to open the gates when they came to them, but was unsurprised when Steve would not permit it.

It was strange not to be taking the right-hand fork when they reached the turn-off to Yattabilla; stranger still to be running along the west side of the mountain ridge.

Maddie could see Bibbi homestead from a long way off. It crouched on the plain ahead of them, backed by ornamental trees and lawns, succored by a pumped water supply from the nearby Barron Creek. The house itself was white, in the old colonial style with handsome pillars at the front, and creeping vines of wisteria and bougainvillea. There were so many other buildings of varying sizes around about it that to Maddie's innocent gaze it looked more like a small village than a station homestead. All the outhouses had white corrugated roofs. On the far side, away from the rest, was a low, more recent building with a windsock drooping motionless nearby. That must be the hangar where Steve kept his plane, she supposed.

The avenue that they now drove along was lined with several different species of pine and the odd pepper-tree.

Momentarily, as they encountered the deep shade of the overhanging boughs, the house was lost to view. Then suddenly they were upon it, with the lawns that she had seen from the distance now on either side of the sweep of gravel. Flowerbeds made gay borders wherever she looked.

Maddie thought that she would remember forever her first view of Bibbi homestead, but Steve appeared to be oblivious to the magnificence about him. He helped her out, and introduced her to the kindly Mrs. Farrell, who had come down the steps to meet them. Then he took her case to her room, while she and the housekeeper followed more slowly.

Soon she was tucked between hem-stitched linen sheets in a cool, airy bedroom of palatial proportions. Her windows looked out onto boxes of petunias. Beyond those the trees and lawn stretched in a green and peaceful backdrop.

Maddie spent the first few days drowsing pleasantly and reading the magazines that Mrs. Farrell had put at her bedside. She made herself walk about her room and into the adjoining tiled bathroom, knowing that action was the only remedy for her strained and aching muscles.

Steve came to see her every day, politely inquiring after her health. Apart from that, he left her alone. Maddie supposed he must be with Kareena. She had not seen Kareena at all, but she knew that she was there, because Mrs. Farrell sometimes included her name in the conversation. Miss Powell, she called her.

When Friday morning came, Steve told her that he had arranged for the bus to leave Skeet off at Bibbi instead of Yattabilla.

Maddie protested. "I think we should go home," she said. "I can't go on trespassing on your hospitality like this. I feel a fraud."

Steve smiled kindly.

"You've no need to feel that way. Mrs. Farrell is enjoying herself enormously. You'll stay until next Friday, and then, if you like, you can go back to Yattabilla in time for Skeet's bus."

"I'm perfectly recovered. Truly." She wanted desperately to get away from Bibbi. Why, with Skeet here too, they'd be almost like a family! It hurt to even think of it.

Steve came closer. Just for a moment he cupped her face between his palms and inspected the bump on her temple. He ran his fingers over the swelling with a touch that was incredibly light for such large, masculine hands.

"Not perfectly," he corrected. "Not yet. But I'll tell you what. From tomorrow you can live more normally, to the extent you're able with that arm supported like that. Mrs. Farrell will still help you to bathe and dress, but you'll take your meals with Kareena and me. That will be nicer for Skeet, too."

Skeet certainly seemed to enjoy himself that weekend. Steve took him swimming in the pool and helped him to catch several small carp in the creek with the aid of a homemade line. The child made friends with the Bibbi hens, too. When he told Steve that he was worried about Etta, Steve laughed and said not to be, that he had told Mrs. Lawrence to look after the poultry again in the meantime.

Mrs. Farrell welcomed Skeet, too, as warmly as she had his sister. She treated him with just the right balance of firmness and maternal indulgence. Skeet responded to this approach.

"I like Mrs. Farrell, Maddie," he confided. "Even when she's angry with you, she doesn't really get snarky, an' she always tells you *why*—not like Kareena," he added darkly. "She's angry all the time, I think. Even when she smiles, her eyes don't, not like Mrs. Farrell's that go all laughy. I hate the way Kareena looks at us!"

Maddie knew just what he meant. She was surprised at Skeet's perception, but she could not help agreeing with what he had said. Kareena did not seem to like Skeet any more than she cared for Maddie. She made no effort to hide the fact from the two people concerned.

At meal times she gave her attention to Steve alone, careful to keep the conversation on topics upon which neither Maddie nor Skeet could add so much as a sentence. Personal things, between herself and Steve. She would use all her considerable charm and attraction to hold his full attention, as if he and she were in an intimate little world of their own, choosing for the most part to ignore the other two. When Steve did attempt to draw them into the conversation, Maddie couldn't help noticing how quick and skilful she was at creating a diversion and making herself the central figure of interest again.

Once she said to Maddie, who had been telling something that was making Steve laugh, "Will you please tell your dear little brother to keep his feet to himself when he's at the dinner table?"

She said it with an exaggeratedly bored patience, as though it were a nuisance with which she had been putting up in silence until it was no longer bearable. Maddie could guess, from the indignant pout on Skeet's red face, that he had done nothing at all—or if he had, that it had been a purely accidental contact.

Another time, Skeet had splashed her linen dress as he came out of the pool, and she exclaimed, "Look what he's done! You nasty little boy! I'll be glad when you're back at school."

"So will I," confessed Skeet morosely to Maddie, after that incident. "I don't like it here with her, even if the rest of the place is terrific."

"Never mind, darling. You'll be off again in the morning, and next weekend we'll be back at Yattabilla."

Maddie herself was secretly longing for the day. Here she was under a continual mental strain, frightened that by word or deed or look, she might give away the secret that she carried in her heart: her fruitless love for the owner of Bibbi.

That her latent fear had indeed been justified was borne out the day before she was to leave. Maddie was reading in bed before switching off her light for the night, when a brief knock sounded on her door. Before she could even call "Come in," Kareena had opened it, slipped into the room, and shut it softly behind her again.

She came over purposefully and sat down on the end of Maddie's bed, beautiful beyond description in an aquamarine nightdress and matching negligée, a froth of lace at throat and wrists. Her dark hair fell free beneath her shoulders, and her smooth skin looked like warmed honey in the glow of the bedside light.

"You're leaving tomorrow, aren't you?" she asked without preamble.

"Yes, in the morning."

Maddie blinked. What a strange thing to ask, at this hour, when the whole household had retired for the night. She herself might just as easily have been fast asleep as reading a book. Surely Kareena would not have gone to the length of waking her to say that?

It soon became clear that Kareena would go to quite extraordinary lengths to say what was on her mind.

"I thought so," she said calmly. "That's why I chose to come tonight. You may feel embarrassed at what I'm going to say, Madeleine. We'll find it easier on both sides if we don't see each other in the morning. I shall make a special point of sleeping in." She permitted herself a faint smile.

Maddie felt a chill of premonition playing over her spine. "Yes?" she prompted, wide-eyed, inwardly steeling herself against the unpleasantness she guessed was to come, although she could not even hazard what form it might take.

"Don't be tempted to go out of your depth, my dear, will you?" begged Kareena; then, on an insipidly kind, it's-for-your-own-good sort of note, "About Steve, I mean," she elucidated, taking in the other girl's blank stare. "I know that older, experienced men like Steve can have an almost fatal attraction for young, untried girls like you, but you'd never be able to cope. Madeleine, take it from me. Experience requires experience, you know. I can only urge you to stick to those other nice young men you have—Tom Simson, for one—I don't think I ever knew the other's name, did I?" She gestured vaguely.

Maddie was horror-struck, agonizingly embarrassed and outraged. She put her hands up to her burning cheeks.

"But I—I've *never*—" she began protestingly, when Kareena stopped her.

"Madeleine, there's no need for pretense with me," she interrupted firmly. "A woman always knows, especially about another woman's feelings. I can see you're deeply infatuated with Steve. You've been going about like a lovesick adolescent all week. There are all the signs, and I know I'm not mistaken. Just one little point, though, may help you to rid yourself of this ridiculous adulation, and that is—" she paused, regarding her painted nails with interest, knowing that that pause would lend added weight to what was to follow—"that Steve doesn't happen to be on the books. He's committed already, you see. You don't think he'd have invited me up here out of the social season if he hadn't wanted to ask me something rather special, do you?"

"I—I hadn't thought about it at all," Maddie heard herself stammer miserably.

"Well, it's time you did," returned Kareena tartly, "It's high time you did think, Madeleine. You really are being thoughtless and selfish about the whole thing, aren't you? I mean, Steve didn't ask to have a—a sort of ward foisted on him, did he? That's all he regards you as, you know—a responsibility. One he can't get rid of for a whole year. Being a gentleman, and loyal, Steve wouldn't put it as bluntly as that to you, but I feel *I* must, because, quite frankly, you are holding up our personal plans. Until Steve relinquishes that wretched trusteeship we can't get married. I intend to have a long honeymoon, perhaps even a trip around the world. Six months, anyway, at the very least. We can't do that until this tiresome Yattabilla affair is settled. Surely it's a bit much, if, in addition to this inconvenience, you intend to embarrass us by a rather distasteful display of quite unwanted and stupid youthful affection."

"Please go," Maddie said coldly. She must keep her dignity at all costs. "Please leave now, Kareena. You've said quite enough."

Kareena rose gracefully, a tall, willow-slim, elegant goddess.

"I intended to, in any case." She walked to the door. "Think over what I've said, won't you, Madeleine?"

Maddie heard the soft click of the knob, and Kareena was gone.

CHAPTER TEN

Think it over, Kareena had said.

Maddie did indeed think it over! In fact, she tossed and turned miserably right through the night, unable to think of anything else.

It was heartbreaking to find yourself in love with a man who regarded you as little more than an inconvenient responsibility—a sort of debt of honor to a dead friend. It was much worse, much more humiliating, to realize that your secret had been discovered by a ruthless type like Kareena, who would not hesitate to use her knowledge for her own ends.

She had been antagonistic to Maddie from the very start, antagonistic and patronizing. Now her feeling had developed into one of cold hatred that she did not attempt to conceal from Maddie herself, although she was skilful enough at keeping it from Steve. Kareena obviously realized that an open declaration of war would place Steve in a compromising position with his—what was the word Kareena had used?—his ward.

As the hours wore on, and Maddie sweated out her present mental agony, one thing became increasingly clear to her. That was, that under these new circumstances, she could not suffer to stay at Yattabilla any longer.

What, after all, did the future hold for her there? Supposing she did manage to stick out her year's residence under this dreadful situation—so close to Steve, who could hardly wait to get rid of his responsibility to her, whom she loved with quite shattering singlemindedness, and who was himself betrothed to Kareena Powell.

Even if Maddie stayed and acquired the Yattabilla property as her inheritance, how could she possibly live there to witness Kareena as the new Mrs. Darley: the mistress of Bibbi, the love of Steve's life? They would be too tantalizingly near for Maddie ever to begin trying to mend her broken heart. All the time she would have Kareena's subtle enmity to contend with, as well.

No. To remain at Yattabilla would be unendurable, as well as foolish. It would, in fact, be utterly impossible!

"You'll have to go-away, go-away, go-away," trilled the bird in the yard outside Maddie's window. Dawn was breaking, and she had not managed to snatch even an hour's sleep. Her mind was in a turmoil, seething with uncertain plans for the future. What would she do? Where would she go—she and Skeet? Back to Sydney, obviously, to some dreary, ill-paid job. Thank God she was at least able to support them, after a fashion. She was still independent. That was something to be thankful for! Stenography could hardly be termed as a glamorous career, but its rewards had always been adequate to keep herself and Skeet.

Skeet! Dear little Skeet! He was at the root of her unhappiness when she thought about the alternatives. He was going to be a sufferer, in so many ways. For the first time in his life, he had tasted a seminormal existence; with the security of a home behind him, even if that home was a decaying dwelling like the Yattabilla homestead. Maddie knew that, in time, she could have made it nice. The white paint was already helping to do that. Hadn't Skeet himself declared it "homey!" She had had plans to dig up the ground at the front and plant some shrubs and flowers in the fall.

Now it looked as if they would soon find themselves back in some sort of humble lodgings in the city, two young individuals lost in the impersonal hurly-burly of urban life. It was a quelling prospect, but one that Maddie knew she must come to terms with.

She had to drag herself out of bed, weary beyond belief. When she looked in the mirror to brush her hair, she saw that her face was a dreadful parchment color, making the fading bruise on her forehead stand out in liverish contrast. Her eyes looked back at her, bleak and shadowed.

In the dining room Steve was breakfasting alone. True to her promise, Kareena had not appeared. That was something about which to be relieved, Maddie supposed bleakly.

Steve rose to his feet and put her into her chair. He was newly shaven, and his hair was slicked down tidily, still damp from the shower. Maddie caught the familiar whiff of his after-shave: a masculine aroma that had a curious mixture of tobacco and horses about it, since he was in his everyday, working garb. His muscular, brown forearms, with their thick covering of springy hair bleached almost gold by the sun, came down on the arms of her chair on either side and pushed it nearer the table as she sat down.

Steve took his seat again and favored her with a keen regard.

"You don't look well," he remarked abruptly.

"I'm fine," she replied with synthetic brightness.

He put out a hand, felt her brow.

"You've been overdoing it. Possibly there's a delayed reaction to the accident, too." He studied her afresh. "I think you'd better remain here a few days yet, Madeleine. I'll fetch Skeet from the bus. He can have another week-end here."

The mere idea was enough to send Maddie into an almost hysterical panic.

"No, no," she cried. "I have to get back! I *must* get back, today!"

Steve's mobile brow lifted expressively.

"Dear me," he murmured, "I'd no idea you were so fervently attached to the place. So be it, then, if you're fretting to be gone."

That made her feel ungracious.

"It's—not that," she said unhappily. "You've been so kind, more than kind, and so has Mrs. Farrell. It's not that I don't appreciate all you've done for me, it's just that—well, I left in such a hurry, so unexpectedly. I'm feeling perfectly well again and anxious to—to return, that's all."

Her eyes pleaded for understanding.

"Don't take on too much too soon, then, Madeleine," he advised her seriously. "Young bones mend readily, I know, and there's no reason to believe yours will be different, but your whole system has had a shake-up, obviously. You look on the point of collapse, if you want the blunt truth—far worse than you did at the time!"

Maddie smiled. It was a wan effort, quite unlike the lovely transforming smile that Skeet so loved.

"I'm all right, truly. I promise I won't do too much."

I won't do anything, in fact, she thought grimly—*except our packing!* There was no point now in going on with the painting or the yard, or even those driving lessons.

When she returned to Yattabilla, the first thing Maddie did was to clean all the paintbrushes and put away the paint and ladder. Her right arm was back to normal. She removed the left one from its sling and used it cautiously, without causing her collarbone any discomfort.

She had decided that she would say nothing to Skeet until he came home for the weekend. (Funny how she was thinking of Yattabilla as "home," she thought, with bitter irony, just when they were going to have to leave it.) She intended to be absolutely ready to leave when Friday came. They would catch the day train on Saturday morning. That way, Skeet wouldn't even have long in which to think about it. The break would be made, cleanly and swiftly—and permanently!

Maddie knew that she could count on Tom Simson to help her to get to the station. He had been a kind and understanding friend. Since he was young and eager to please—without that domineering, autocratic streak that Steve had, for instance—it would be easy enough to work him round to cooperating with her plans. If he could not come for them himself, Maddie would ask him to hire a car on her behalf. She had enough money to pay for that and their second-class fares to Sydney, and a little left, over and beyond, for their first week or so in the city.

She was going to miss Tom and Noonday, she realized with a sad little pang. Tom had been like an elder brother to her. Straight away she had felt for him the kinship of youth. He was fun to be with when she went to Noonday. The town itself had been so peaceful and friendly, too.

The week was spent mending and washing her own and Skeet's few belongings. She polished their shoes, ironed short and shirts, and packed everything neatly into the two shabby cases and the canvas tote.

On Friday she switched off the kerosene refrigerator and removed the fuel tray, emptied the lamps and trimmed the wicks. Looking about her, she could not help contrasting the shining cleanliness everywhere with the discouraging filth on her arrival. At least she had struck a blow for poor old Yattabilla, she thought wryly. It had been her father's house, after all—the place where she herself had been born—and it was the richer, rather than the poorer, for her short stay in it. She felt she had made a positive contribution, however slight, to its preservation. From now on, it would be for Steve to take over. Perhaps he would even depute Kareena to arrange for something to be done with it, although Maddie could not imagine the future mistress of Bibbi bothering herself with such an unglamorous assignment.

After she had done all the last-minute chores in the house, Maddie called Tom.

She was fortunate to get him at the office. She knew that with Tom alone she could cope, but not with the added complication of maternal distress and disapproval that Mrs. Simson would be sure to voice.

Even Tom himself was difficult. It took all Maddie's

not inconsiderable persuasive powers to make him even think of doing what she wanted. She found herself actually begging desperately, with tears in her voice, before he finally and reluctantly conceded.

Maddie put down the receiver. She felt limp with the effort. Thank heaven she only had to go through it all once! Soon she and Skeet would be away from here. Then she would have to set about pulling herself together and making some sort of new life for them both.

She had a bath, then washed her hair, awkwardly, because doing so necessitated holding her arm at an odd angle. It took a long time, but in the end she was satisfied that the golden strands squeaked with cleanliness. She brushed it out into a polished curtain, prepared herself a quick snack for lunch, and then sat down and wrote a letter to Robert.

Maddie had known all week that she was going to have to write that letter, because she knew, finally and irrevocably, that she could never marry Robert—not when her heart was already given to Steve.

She could not compare the two men, even hypothetically, as prospective husbands. She trusted Robert, respected him and liked him, but she did not love him—and no marriage at all was better than one without love.

She could never give herself to Robert's arms while, in her heart, she longed for the strong, muscular ones of Steve Darley about her. She could never again put her lips to Robert's without remembering the butterfly brush of Steve's firm, cool ones against her damaged brow. In her heart of hearts, Maddie knew that she could never love again. Steve's place there was for always—however futile and hopeless.

Maddie found Robert's a difficult letter to write. She intended to mail it in Noonday in the morning, because she did not mean to get in touch with him again in Sydney—or not for a long, long time. He was so kind, so responsible, that he would feel the need to take care of them and keep an eye on them. He might even use their situation as a pressure point for an early marriage. Maddie did not wish to burden him with the knowledge that she and Skeet were once more on their own. She felt that would be unfair to Robert. If he really did imagine himself to be in love with her, it would be kinder to keep right out of his way. Maddie was sure that he would soon forget her and find some other more rewarding romance, if she did that.

She simply explained that she could never marry him, but that she valued his continued friendship and left it at that. She sealed the envelope, licked a stamp, put it on the corner, and then went to her bedroom and placed the letter carefully in her purse, so that she would not forget to mail it in the morning.

Out of her bedroom window Maddie caught sight of a dust-cloud. It was away along the track, about the place where the wrecked Buick had been. It certainly could not be the Buick, because that vehicle was roadworthy no longer, alas! In any case, Steve had had Lal tow it into one of the sheds. Neither could it be the school bus, which was not due for another hour or more.

Maddie watched the dust-cloud in a fascinated way as it moved along fast, nearer and nearer to the Yattabilla homestead. When it was quite close, she drew in her breath sharply. Her knees became so weak and wobbly that she had to clutch the window-sill to support herself.

It was Steve's car, the big Chevrolet. He was alone.

Maddie saw him get out, slam the door behind him with unnecessary force, and come striding quickly up the path. Then she heard his stockman's boots clattering over the veranda. The screen door banged.

"Madeleine?" He sounded breathless.

Maddie smoothed her newly-dried, shining hair with fingers that trembled and went into the hall to meet him. They faced each other across the bare stretch of pine flooring.

Steve's face was grim, the grooves at the sides of his mouth deep and taut, pulling his lips into a compressed, forbidding line. His gray eyes were dark, smoldering with anger.

"What's this ridiculous nonsense I hear from Tom Simson, about you leaving Yattabilla?" he asked, without further hesitation.

Maddie stiffened. "It isn't nonsense at all." She did her best to sound cool. "In any case, it was between Tom and me. He had no right to tell you."

"He had every right," Steve contradicted tersely. "For once the young ass did the right thing where you're concerned. He was worried and got in touch with me."

"It has absolutely nothing to do with you," she protested.

"Oh yes, it has. It has plenty to do with me! I'm your father's trustee, which young Simson fortunately seems to know. He also knows that if you go away, you forfeit your inheritance. I suppose you told him the legal angle at some point, and luckily he took it in."

"Luck doesn't enter into it either way." Maddie steeled herself into calmness. Now, if ever, she had to test her powers as an actress. "I realize that by leaving I shall forfeit my right to Yattabilla, and it doesn't worry me in the least. What's more, it's nobody's business but my own."

Steve's jaw hardened.

"You mean you're serious?"

Maddie nodded. "Perfectly serious. I'm leaving tomorrow, by the day train, with Skeet, of course."

Steve's probing glance became incredulous. The incredulity was swiftly banished by suspicion. His eyes narrowed, more keenly penetrating than ever.

"Madeleine, why?" A few strides brought him right to her side. "Why the sudden change? Heavens, it's not more than a few weeks since you were digging in your toes, cursing me to hell, and telling me you'd see the thing through at all cost. What's happened to knock the stuffing out of you?" His voice deepened in concern. "It's that blasted accident, Madeleine. You haven't given yourself a chance to recover properly. Don't do anything hasty while you're still feeling under the weather. Come back to Bibbi for a little while, and you'll see things differently. I knew you weren't fit. I shouldn't have allowed you to persuade me that you were. A week or two more and you'll have your fighting spirit back. It's one of the things I admire about you, that spunk! I'll fix it with old Opal."

Maddie swallowed a lump in her throat. When Steve was as near as this, looking down at her with almost tender persuasion, she found it difficult to be strong. But she *must*!

"No, Steve." She shook her head. "My mind is quite made up."

He was silent for a moment.

"There has to be a reason," he said at length. "Why are you doing this, Madeleine? What's changed your mind for you?"

Maddie blinked, stared woodenly at the middle button of his khaki shirt that was on a level with her own eyes. Yes, Steve was right. There had to be a reason. She had to find a reason. Any reason at all would do, so long as it wasn't the right one!

She blinked again, muttered a silent prayer for inspiration. As if in answer to her prayer, inspiration came.

"Robert has asked me to marry him."

Steve's eyes locked with hers. He stood incredibly still.

"Is that true?"

"Absolutely." It wasn't a lie, anyway, she told herself a little desperately. Robert *had* asked her to marry him. She was only *implying* that she had accepted, after all.

"Yes, that figures." Steve was speaking almost to himself. "You did look pretty shaken when you had to leave him that day. I wonder why I didn't think of that!"

"One doesn't like to make things too obvious, does

one?" suggested Maddie demurely. "I mean, one doesn't like to wear one's heart on one's sleeve."

What an actress she was turning out to be! She had had no idea that she would be capable of bringing so much conviction to her role.

"No, that's right." Steve's voice was oddly strained. He walked abruptly to the window and stood there looking out. In profile his stern features were expressionless and still, save for a small muscle that jerked somewhere near his jaw. When he turned to her again the stormy look had left his eyes. They were composed, almost bleak. His face beneath its deep tan had the alabaster pallor of the Sphinx itself.

"Very well, Madeleine, I accept your explanation." A pause. "I can only hope that you'll be very happy."

"You, too, Steve," she whispered, with tears in her eyes.

You and Kareena, she wanted to say. I hope you and Kareena will be happy, too, Steve, because I couldn't bear it if you weren't happy, even if it has to be with her.

"I'll leave it to you to tell Mr. Opal," she said. "From now on, it will be for the two of you to arrange. Goodby, Steve."

She put out her hand formally, felt it taken in a firm grasp. She wanted to cling to that hard brown hand, to beg him to feel a little bit for her what she was feeling for him just now. But she couldn't, of course. Anyway, what was the use? She was no more to him than a tiresome and inconvenient responsibility, of whom he would soon be rid. Then he could go right ahead and marry his Kareena.

"I'll say goodby to Skeet for you. I think it would be better if he didn't see you again."

The ghost of a smile twisted Steve's set mouth.

"Do that, Madeleine. For once I agree with you about what's best for Skeet, it seems."

Those were the last words he said to Maddie. He didn't look back when he reached the car, not even to wave farewell. Maddie was watching, hoping that he might, but he started the engine and left without a backward glance. She stood at the fence until his car was right out of sight.

Telling Skeet proved almost worse than telling Steve. At first he could only blink disbelievingly. Then, as he saw that Maddie really meant every word she said, the freckles began to stand out as his face lost color.

"But why do we have to go, Maddie? Why? I like it here, and I thought we had to stay for a year. I don't want to go, Maddie!"

She sighed, squaring her thin shoulders.

"We have to leave, Skeet, for reasons that you're too young to understand. Some day, when you're grown up, I'll tell you all about them. Then you'll see that it was the only thing. I promise you there's no other way. You'll just have to trust me to look after us both, darling. It won't be so bad. I thought you quite liked Sydney?"

He stared at her mutinously.

"I like Noonday best. I like the school there, too. It's the most fun I've ever had." His small face brightened as a thought struck him. "Maddie, couldn't we stop in Noonday if we have to leave here? I could stay at school, then, and you could get a job. You like Noonday, too. You love it, same as me, I know you do! Gee, that'd be great!"

Her heart turned with anguish, because she knew she was going to have to drive that eagerness right out of Skeet's wiry little frame. Noonday? And see Kareena and Steve even more often than she would here at Yattabilla? Impossible!

"No, Skeet, I'm sorry, it's out of the question. We have to go right away. But I'll make it up to you, pet. We'll have good times down there in the city, once we get settled somewhere. You'll see!"

Skeet shook his head. Without replying, he got up and left the room. A few minutes later Maddie saw his disconsolate form wandering aimlessly outside, kicking a pebble in front of him with the toe of his new brown sandal. Later still, she spotted him walking with more purpose toward the fowl yard.

When she went to make the tea, her mind was still on her own problems and the unpleasant things she yet had to do: like trying to explain to Tom, for instance, when he took them to Noonday in the morning. She was totally unprepared, therefore, for the hysterical sound of sobbing that reached her ears as she was pouring boiling water into the teapot.

Maddie put down the kettle quickly and rushed outside. Skeet was leaning up against the veranda post, crying as if his heart would break.

She knelt down beside him and drew him into her arms, feeling his small body, wracked with distress, shivering against her.

"Skeet darling, what is it?" She stroked the ginger spikes of hair, smoothing them down with a soothing touch. "It won't be as bad as all that, Skeet, truly it won't. I wouldn't do it if I didn't have to, but I'll make it up to you. You wait and see. We've always managed to have fun, haven't we, even when things were at their worst?"

"It isn't that." The words were strangled.

"What then?"

"It's Etta."

"Etta?"

He nodded miserably, trying to control himself.

"What about Etta, Skeet? She's fine. I've been looking after her for you, the same as always. She was all right this morning."

"*She's* all right, but—Maddie—" his voice quavered all over again "—she's left her nest, Maddie, an' she's broken all the eggs. I saw her! It wasn't that I was disturbing her or anything, honestly, I promise. She just suddenly stood up as if she was terrible angry. She scratched about as if she'd gone mad an' she broke every one." He sobbed afresh. "There's no chicks in them, Maddie. We're not going to get chicks after all. They're just a lot of rotten old eggs! Rotten! *Rotten!*"

He kicked fiercely at the veranda post. A bit of timber that the white ants had attacked went flying off into the weeds where the yard had once been.

It only needed this! Maddie told herself, distraught for her little brother. It only needed this!

"They weren't the right sort of eggs, Skeet," she comforted him sadly. "They couldn't have been, could they? Nothing's right for us here, darling. We thought it was going to be, but nothing's right! Things will be different when we go. We'll put it all behind us. We'll forget all about those rotten old eggs and—and—everything." She took his hand. "Come on in. I've made the tea. Scones, too."

Skeet ran his sleeve over his tear-stained face and came.

In the morning, Maddie laid out his clean things for him to put on for the train and dressed in her emerald shift. She knew she would get hot and sticky on the journey. She must keep her cotton two-piece with the white collar to wear in Sydney when she was job-hunting next week. It was essential to appear neat and well-groomed when you were an ordinary sort of shorthand-typist—unable to boast the devastating speeds of efficiency that some of her colleagues at the business college had achieved!

She found herself hampered scarcely at all by the sling now. In fact, she was using her arm quite normally and only bothered to tuck it into the supporting fold of cloth when there was nothing else she wanted to do with it. She would see a doctor about a final clearance when she had found somewhere for herself and Skeet to stay. That was the first priority.

When she and Skeet had breakfasted, she carried the suitcases and canvas bag onto the veranda, locked the doors, and took the keys down to Mrs. Lawrence—not that there was a likelihood of anyone using the house, but it seemed an appropriate and responsible gesture.

Mrs. Lawrence looked her over curiously when she handed in the keys.

"I ain't surprised at you clearin' out so quick. Some might be, but *I* ain't. I said you was like your ma all along," she said, nasal and unfriendly as ever.

"Please tell Lal that we don't need any more meat, Mrs. Lawrence," Maddie returned evenly. "And I'd be grateful if you'll keep an eye on the hens, too."

"It won't matter to you, will it? You'll be gone see. And anyway, it's Mr. Darley that gives me my orders. If Mr. Darley tells me to look after the poultry, I'll look after it."

Maddie felt there was nothing to be gained by a response. She turned and walked back to the house. Not long after that, Tom came to collect them.

It was easy enough to discourage a post-mortem of her decision with Tom. She hated herself as she did it, but she simply raised her eyebrows, glanced meaningly in Skeet's direction, and whispered, "Not *now*, Tom. Don't say anything in front of *him*, please."

Maddie knew she was safe in saying that, because Skeet would be with her all the time from now until the moment when they boarded the train at Noonday station.

Skeet jumped out eagerly when the first gate came. Maddie felt her heart contract when she remembered who had taught him how to open it and all the others, on that very first trip out to Yattabilla. Steve's voice echoed in her ears—patient, amused, and firm in alternating degrees. He had always been kind to Skeet, she had to admit that—kind, almost fatherly, even though he had approached her with that astringent cynicism that had the effects of making her brace up inwardly, determined to fight her own battles.

Maddie could have done with some bracing up right now. There was not much fight left in her. She was feeling something of a failure. Tom's worried face and slightly resentful silence served only to add to her sense of guilt and hopelessness.

The plains, today, were at their most beautiful, with that oddly stark, contradictory splendor that dry, sun-drenched country sometimes has. Away to their right, the ridge reared up, a freak of nature, majestic in a purple haze of distance against the pale, cloudless sky. Maddie took her last long look at that ridge, tried to forget that Bibbi lay on its western flank.

"Goodby, old monster," she murmured under her breath, but the monster slumbered on, impervious to her farewell just as he had been oblivious to the mortal comings and goings about him ever since prehistory.

When they arrived in Noonday, Tom carried their bags onto the platform. Maddie took Skeet to the news agency to buy some reading material, a bottle of lemonade, and some sweets. She also bought a bag of apples and several oranges, recalling her brother's biliousness on the journey out. Steve had been right about that, too. It was true that she had indulged Skeet freely with all sorts of sickly rubbish which he had pointed to on the confectioner's counter at Sydney. This time, she was firm.

On the way back to the platform, she mailed her letter to Robert. It would have the Noonday postmark on it, so that he would never need to know that she was no longer at Yattabilla. She would not contact him again until she had achieved a measure of security and independence for herself and Skeet in Sydney. At the present moment she felt too vulnerable to trust herself, and realized that, out of sheer weak relief at the thought of a masculine arm to lean on, marriage to Robert could become a very real temptation. It would also be a mistake. One that she intended to avoid, at whatever cost to herself just now.

There were few travelers on the small train this morning.

"It doesn't take on more carriages until it reaches the big junction in the wheat belt," Tom explained. "That's where most of the Sydney-bound passengers get on. If they live as far out as this, they often use planes, you see, Maddie."

When the whistle blew, Maddie received Tom's shy, rather fumbled kiss in silence. What, indeed, could she say that would not sound hopelessly inadequate after his goodness to her? As the train moved slowly away from the platform, her final glimpse was of him standing there, in his white, open-necked shirt, holding his wide felt hat in his hand, and looking after them with a sort of puzzled, fond bewilderment.

Maddie could not blame him. She still felt a certain bewilderment herself.

CHAPTER ELEVEN

Maddie decided that she must put that first awful two weeks back in Sydney right out of her mind.

It did not do to dwell on the past, even the very recent past, she told herself firmly. She remembered all the miles she had walked searching for the type of accommodation that she could afford, recalling all those fruitless interviews with every employment agency she could find in the telephone directory.

The trouble arose over the question of hours. She had hoped for permanent work for a certain period each day, so that she could be at home to welcome Skeet when he came in from school. It was depressing enough for him to have to return to the dingy room that they were occupying, without finding that room empty.

The landlady did not care for children. In fact, when Maddie had confessed to possessing a small brother, she had almost snatched the lease right out of her prospective tenant's hand.

"I don't hold with kids," she had said censoriously, as if she herself had plunged straight from the cradle into adulthood, escaping that tiresome juvenile state altogether. "They don't care a fig for other folk's property, especially boys, I've always found. Ten's about the worst age of the lot, if you ask me! I don't really think I can take you, after all. If I'd known about *him* from the start, I wouldn't even have considered it."

Maddie had had to plead. She was footsore, pale, and desperate. Maybe her own appearance had something to do with the landlady's final capitulation. Maddie felt it a matter of necessity to keep Skeet under constant surveillance. If she was not there when he returned from the school each day, she quailed to think what pranks he might get up to in her absence. For the same reason, she did not dare to take on supplementary employment in the evenings. She had been able to do that in London only because of the landlady's motherly cooperation in keeping an eye on Skeet for her.

Because she could not work after three o'clock and not at all on Saturdays, Maddie's salary was pruned accordingly. She could not argue with the fairness of that, but it meant that she was earning barely enough to pay for the room and to keep herself and Skeet in any sort of comfort. She went without even the tiniest luxury for herself and sometimes without necessities as well: giving Skeet the biggest helpings of food when it came to mealtimes, because he still had a lot of growing to do, and mending her clothes as they became threadbare. Grimly she realized that she could afford no replacements at present. Nostalgically she found herself remembering those vast piles of butchered meat that Lal used to bring up to the homestead twice a week, and the Yattabilla account Steve had urged her to use without hesitation if she should need anything. These were changed days now!

Summer turned to fall. The weather changed to cold, windy days and blustery nights when a thin mist of rain blinded the small top-floor window of their shared bedsitter.

Maddie was soaked one day returning from work. Although she changed her clothes immediately, she succumbed a few days afterward to a bad bout of flu. The doctor, grudgingly summoned by her landlady, insisted on a whole week in bed and another of convalescence.

Maddie wrote a postcard to her employer, apologizing for the inconvenience her absence would doubtless cause, and asked Skeet to mail it. When she received no reply, she began to fret. Perhaps no news was good news, but it could also imply her pending dismissal. In her present physical state she wondered how she could possibly go through the wearisome procedure of finding employment all over again.

"You did mail the card, didn't you, Skeet?" she croaked the question huskily from her bed.

"Yes, Maddie, honest I did. I put it in the mailbox at the corner."

She passed her hand over her aching brow.

"Maybe they just haven't acknowledged it. Or maybe they're going to fire me. I won't know till I go back. Anyway," she smiled into her little brother's suddenly anxious face, "I don't like it much there, Skeet. It's not much of a job. I'll easily get something better!"

He appeared reassured, to her own relief. She must not let Skeet see how worried she was. He had been so sweet and helpful while she was in bed, and even before that, too. A new closeness had sprung up between them. Both realized how completely interdependent they were upon each other for comfort and what little happiness they could find in this new, rather grim phase of their lives. She would not mention it again.

By the middle of the second week, Maddie realized that the doctor had been right to insist on an additional period of convalescence. She was not picking up as quickly as she had hoped. Certainly her limbs no longer ached with those influenza pains, and her sore throat was quite better, too, but she felt curiously languid.

She was glad to remain in bed in the mornings. In the afternoons she would wander listlessly about the room in her dressing gown, knowing that she would have felt warmer under the blankets, but appreciating the necessity of getting her strength back with the help of some exercise. The coins she put in the slot for the gas fire didn't seem to make it hot for very long. She had worked out a daily ration of money for that purpose—more than she could afford, really, but it barely served to take the chill dampness out of the air.

She was doing just that—wandering about the room, tidying up Skeet's coloring books and crayons that were still where he had left them before school this morning, flicking a duster half-heartedly over the few pieces of furniture, when there was a knock at the door.

Maddie hesitated. It was too early for Skeet, so it must be the landlady. As always when she had a visit from the landlady, she felt a small knot of anxiety and apprehension tightening her stomach muscles. Some day she was bound to be given notice to leave, and maybe that day had arrived. Skeet had been in a boisterous mood last night, restless because the weather had stopped all outdoor games in the school playground, bored because Maddie could not even take him out for a walk in the rain. He had made more noise than he intended. The landlady had complained.

She went to the door and opened it. When she saw who was there, she froze where she stood, wide-eyed, clutching the folds of her shabby dressing gown closer.

"Madeleine?" It was half-question, half-statement. "Aren't you going to invite me in?"

"Steve." She could hardly breathe his name. "Why have you come?" she managed to ask huskily.

Steve's white teeth flashed in his wet, brown face, but his eyes were oddly serious. The banter in his voice did not quite ring true.

"Looking for Madeleine Janet Masterton, that's why I'm here." A mock sigh. "I seem to have spent a good deal of time looking for Madeleine Janet Masterton, do you know that, Madeleine? First in London, and now in Sydney. The trouble is—as soon as I find her, she sort of slips away."

Maddie continued to stare. She was swaying on her feet.

Steve, characteristically, did not wait for that invitation he had suggested, since it did not appear to be forthcoming anyway. He took her firmly by the hand, propelled her inside, and shut the door behind him. He was wearing a gray city suit, but not the one he had worn the first time, all those months ago. This one was equally well-cut, but of a heavier weight. Maddie could see that his broad shoulders were dark with rain; it glistened on his lean, tanned cheeks as he stood there just inside the door, looking down at her strangely.

The bantering tone wasn't there any more when he spoke again.

"Come clean, Madeleine." He gave her a little shake. "Why did you do it? Why did you run out on me? And don't try any more of your nasty little inventions on me, either! You won't get away with it a second time, I'm warning you—especially not here!" He made a gesture of distaste that somehow encompassed the whole of the shabby set-up that surrounded them, his eyes taking in his environs in a single disparaging sweep before they came to rest on her once more. "You're shivering. I forgot that you'd been ill. We can talk just as well sitting down. Get into that chair."

She sank into it in wordless obedience.

"You haven't even a fire!" he condemned tersely, kneeling down in front of the gas affair in the hearth. "How does this damn thing work?"

"With coins." Maddie found her voice. "B-but I've run out of change," she lied weakly.

There was a muttered oath from the man squatting at the fireplace. He stood up, sorted through a handful of money from his slacks pocket for the appropriate coins, jabbed them into the slot, and turned the switch.

"You could do with a good spanking," he told her repressively, as he took the chair opposite her own. "And if you hadn't just had flu, that's what you'd get, make no mistake about that!"

One part of her brain registered the cold, suppressed fury in the way he spoke those words, while another bewildered part grappled with the puzzle of just how he could possibly know she'd had flu.

Was the man psychic, or something? He certainly was behaving very oddly. He looked, in fact, not only capable of beating her as he had threatened, but even of boring right into her mind to see what she was thinking if his psychic powers should fail him. Steve Darley was sitting there, big, menacing, and much too large for that flimsy wicker chair, looking as if he might be capable of anything.

"Well, Madeleine?" he suggested in a carefully controlled voice. "Let's have your story—and no more flights into the realms of fancy this time. I won't fall for it twice!"

Maddie swallowed on a peculiar constriction in her throat. She couldn't think of a single thing to say, just then.

"H-how did you find out where I was?" she asked, after a painful interval spent groping wildly for some safe topic.

A little grimly, Steve reached into the inner pocket of his jacket.

"I had a letter," he informed her, taking out an envelope. "From Skeet."

"From *Skeet*?" Maddie sat bolt upright in surprise.

"From Skeet. Like to hear it?"

Without waiting for her assent, he withdrew the folded sheet and read:

"Dear Steve, I hope you are well." He paused. "It's dated just three days ago, by the way, and the address is your present one."

"Go on," she whispered. This was dreadful!

"I hope you are well. I am writing to you in class, because we are learning how, and the teacher says if we write a letter real good we can mail it. Her name is Miss Sparrow and she has got a stamp. We can even lick it ourselves and put it on so as we will know for another time. Your address is the only one I know except for Maddie. It would be silly to write to her when we live in the same room, anyway, so I hope you don't mind. Maddie has had flu and was awful sick but the landlady brung drinks twice and I got tea. I got boiled eggs two nights and another time I got beans. We have got a stove. You use matches to light it. Maddie might lose her job but she doesn't care because she says it isn't very nice anyway."

A small, involuntary sound from Maddie made him look up.

"Do you want me to go on?" he asked in level tones.

She nodded. "You may as well finish," she agreed lamely.

"I was sorry I couldn't say goodby when we left Yattabilla because I would have told you that Etta's eggs was rotten, the whole lot, and there was no chicks inside after all, so we got nothing. Maddie said there was nothing for us there anyhow, but I reckon there could have been chicks only there wasn't. She said they weren't the right sort of eggs. I hardly cried at all. With lots of love from Skeet."

In silence he folded the page carefully, put it back into its envelope, and returned it to his pocket.

"Well?"

Maddie stared at the floor, twisting her hands together nervously. She wished she could think of something to say, but there seemed to be a temporary paralysis of her mental processes.

"Why did you do it, Madeleine?" Steve's voice was deep, insistent.

She shook her head, shrugged helplessly.

"I don't know." It sounded weak.

Steve must have thought it sounded weak, too, because he walked over and put his hands on her restless fingers. He drew her purposefully to her feet to face him.

"Of course you know," he contradicted her gently. "There had to be a reason, didn't there, Maddie?"

He used the contraction of her name without seeming aware of it. His eyes were searching hers, but there was a tenderness softening their gray depths. His mouth was kind, just above her own.

Maddie stared at that mouth, mesmerized.

"There had to be a reason, hadn't there?" His lips murmured the words, against her ear. "Will you give me the right reason this time, Maddie? The honest one?"

Maddie felt his hands relinquish their grasp on her fingers and move to her back. Then she felt them drawing her toward him until she was right up against him, so that her eyes were on a level with the middle shirt button of his neat, pin-striped shirt. Steve's square-tipped brown fingers tilted her chin upward so that she had to look at him.

"Maybe this will help to give you a clue," he whispered huskily. Maddie watched his lips curve, in the merest hint of a smile. Then they came down gently onto hers.

Steve's kiss was restrained at first, and then Maddie felt his arms crushing her to him as passion took over. He was kissing her now with a swift mastery and possessiveness that brought such a heavenly weakness to her limbs that she could only cling to him. And then she was returning his kiss, with all the love she had bottled up secretly for so long.

Presently he straightened, put her away from him and watched her. There was a curious expression on his face, a mixture of triumph and relief.

"So two and two appear to make four after all," he murmured obliquely, in an oddly shaken voice. He took her shoulders and gave her a reproving shake that was somehow an endearment as well. "Now we know the truth, don't we? We know the reason, don't we, darling?" he persisted, as she continued to feast her eyes on him in wonder.

"Yes, Steve," she whispered.

"You didn't intend to marry Robert when you went away, did you?"

"No, Steve."

"You just said that to push me off. You didn't intend to marry *anyone*."

"No, Steve."

"You were running away, weren't you, Maddie?"

"Yes."

"Who were you running away from, Maddie?" he asked, with laughter in his voice. "From me?"

"I suppose it must have been. I don't know." She dropped her eyes. She was shy of this new, unfamiliar Steve.

He gave a deep chuckle.

"Yes, you do. We both know now, don't we? You ran away because you'd found out that you didn't hate me any more. You'd fallen in love and wanted to escape, because you didn't know, you silly little darling spitfire, that I'd fallen in love with you, too."

"How *could* I know? How could I guess?" she defended herself, still in a state of dreamy unreality at the turn her life had taken in this past half-hour.

Steve's eyes devoured her.

"No, Maddie, I'm sorry." He was sober all at once. "You couldn't have guessed, little one—not even if you'd had far more experience of such things than I can tell you've had. I didn't intend that you should know. I loved you from the moment I set eyes on you in old Opal's office—that wonderful hair and creamy skin, your brave little independent spirit that defied me from the start. What a combination! I knew right then and there that one day I meant to have you, but at that stage you hated me. Oh yes, you did!" He dropped a kiss on the point of her chin. "Remember what you said the day we said goodby at Yattabilla, Maddie—about not wearing one's heart on one's sleeve?"

"Yes, Steve, I remember every word we said that day."

"Well, by God, that shaft went home, because that's precisely how it was with me. I couldn't wear my heart on my sleeve. If I had, I'd have scared you off. You'd have thought I was simply after Yattabilla, and you wouldn't have believed me anyway."

He passed a hand over his eyes. Only then did Maddie notice how pale he was. There was an unfamiliar tremor in the usually capable fingers that passed themselves across his forehead as if trying to erase some painful memory. Just for a moment, he was the old, grim Steve, not the tender, loving one who had been kissing her a short while ago.

"I thought I had a year, you see, Maddie. I thought I had a whole year, but dear heaven, how wrong can a man be? I meant to wait until Yattabilla became yours, and then, I thought, I'd take it slowly from there. At first I wanted you to leave that wretched homestead. It was torture thinking of you battling away there on your own. I really did think you might stand a chance of getting the place some other way. And then I realized that if you tried it and failed, I'd have lost your trust forever. It was an unenviable choice, but in the end I reckoned you'd be better to stay and see the thing through. The only way I could help you to do it was by rather brutal means, I admit—jibing at you when I felt you might be losing your nerve, making you angry when your courage faltered, and so forth. It was hell! Anyway, I began planning what I'd do once the year was up. I'd give you time, lots of time, so that gradually you would learn to trust me. Once you trusted me I knew I'd have the battle half won, and that I could make you love me the way I loved you."

"Oh, Steve!" There were tears in Maddie's eyes, tears of love, joy, and incredible wonder that Steve could be saying these things to her, when all the time she had thought he and Kareena—"I didn't know."

"Of course you didn't," he took her hand, sat down in the upholstered chair that Maddie herself had occupied, and pulled her onto his knee. From the haven of his arms she went on listening. "I nearly gave myself away, just once. It was only when I got Skeet's note and started thinking things out that I realized things just might have been different if I had revealed my feelings after all."

Maddie nodded.

"When I had the accident?"

"You knew?"

"I thought I was dreaming. You called me darling! Oh, Steve, did you really call me that? I didn't dream it, after all?"

"I really did." He held her close. "I was demented with worry. By the time I had searched and couldn't find you, I was nearly out of my mind. I hardly knew what I was saying—but I also knew what I *mustn't* say! It just slipped out somehow." He grinned, self-mocking. "I didn't think you'd heard."

"I *think* you said it twice."

"Probably I did. I was having a pretty tough time keeping my feelings under control at all." A pause. "And then you went away. You told me you were going to marry Robert, and suddenly there was not a future that included me at all. There was no reason for planning what I'd do in a year, because you'd gone away." He passed a hand over his eyes in a replica of that former painful gesture, unaware that he did so. "They were unpleasant weeks, Maddie, those ones after you left. I wondered how the hell I could go on living! I put Kareena on a plane. Then I came to grips with Opal about the property. I've had it transferred from my name to Skeet's, by the way. It's in trust for him. He'll come into it when he's of age."

"Oh, *Steve!*"

"Well, darling, he is Gerald's son. He had a greater moral claim than anyone else to it, and I must say I felt a little better once I'd done that. It takes a while for these transfers to be properly drawn up, of course, but the lawyers would have tried to contact you as Robert's wife in order to let you know. We'd have found out then that you had not married him at all! I'd have been out of my mind,

Madeleine,"—he regarded her reprovingly—"because none of us would have had any idea where to find you. I'd have tracked you down somehow, be sure of that, little one. You wouldn't have escaped me for long, but thank the lord Skeet wrote me when he did! He saved me one hell of a frantic search. He's a great little cobber, is Skeet."

His arms tightened, and they kissed again. This time Steve did it with gentleness and understanding, in a way that told her she need not worry any more. They trusted each other at last. They had found each other.

"I can hardly believe it, Maddie, that your feelings have changed to this extent. It was either very sudden, or you've been a damn good actress for a very long time. Which?"

"It happened a long while ago," Maddie replied dreamily. "I realize that now. I thought I hated you, because I didn't know what the symptoms meant, that's all. I've never been in love before—not properly, not this way. I can see now that I was awfully ignorant." She touched his tanned cheek with one finger, ran it down the groove beside his mouth. "I think I did hate you at first, Steve. Well, maybe hate's too strong a word. It was dislike, because you made me feel all shaken and peculiar inside. I didn't know why. You disturbed me, and I resented it. I only really hated you just once. That was when I found out that you'd conspired with Mrs. Lawrence to scare me off."

"When I *what*?" Steve was startled.

"When I heard her telling you she had left the house just like you said—out the kitchen window. You rode over on your horse, remember, and we quarreled about Skeet's schooling. You met her as you were leaving, near the garden fence, and I heard."

He sighed exaggeratedly.

"Maddie, my girl, try to make a little sense, will you,

darling? I'm afraid I simply can't see why my speaking to Mrs. Lawrence should make you hate me!"

She flushed.

"You do remember speaking to her?"

"Certainly I do. I asked her if she had left everything in the house the way I had said. She replied that she had. What harm is there in that, you little goose?" His tone was teasing.

Maddie pulled herself away from him indignantly.

"Steve Darley, I'm afraid I don't think it was funny! I didn't then, and I don't now." Her eyes glittered at the memory. "Steve, how could you! All those cobwebs and the dirt and grease; the mice in the mattresses; all those dead flies in the windows—*hundreds* of them, even if they were dead! Anyway, those big fat spiders weren't! They were alive, and I had to shut my eyes when I—"

"Hey, steady on." He had stopped smiling. His eyes narrowed, and the warmth drained away, leaving them cold, like slits of ice. "Just what are you trying to get across?"

Maddie's eyes locked with his, hers still defiant, his increasingly thoughtful. He put her firmly off his knee and stood up, tall and very forbidding, with his back to the flickering gaslight.

"I admit I checked with Mrs. Lawrence that day to see that she had left things as I said," Steve told her carefully, "and what I had told her was this. I told her to clean up that hell-hole of a homestead, to scour it from top to bottom, with carbolic if need be, to see that the kitchen was spruce and the rooms shipshape and the beds made up, and to make sure that—"

Maddie's giggle halted him. It only began as a tiny one, but it somehow took possession of her until she shook with uncontrollable, almost hysterical mirth.

"Maddie, stop it, for heaven's sake!" barked Steve. "It's I who am not amused now! Listen to me, Madeleine." He took her by the shoulders, "are you trying to tell me that that house wasn't like I ordered? Are you saying that—" He could only shake his head helplessly. Words appeared to have failed him.

"I wish you'd seen it!" Maddie wiped tears of laughter from the corners of her eyes. "The kapok was strewn all over the floor, and the mice, or rats, or whatever they were, had—"

"You needn't go over it all again, Maddie. I get the general idea." He began to stride restlessly about the tiny room, grim-faced. "My God, I'll have her hide when I get back! The scheming witch! I'll get to the bottom of it and find out what goes on in that woman's mind. I'll have the truth, and before heaven, she's going to regret it!" he muttered savagely.

"Darling." Maddie ran to him and put her hand on his sleeve. "It doesn't matter now, Steve, can't you see? It doesn't matter any more, now that I know you weren't involved. She can't hurt us now, even if she tried. She was never nice to me, the whole time I was there. She looked at me with real hatred the very first morning and told me I wouldn't stay long. She said I was like my mother."

"Did she, by Jove! I'm beginning to wonder just how much she had to do with *that* breaking up, now I think about it. She's nothing much better than a malicious mischief-maker! Obviously she has a grudge against her own sex. There *are* people like that. The fact that butter wouldn't ever melt in her mouth with either myself or Gerald bears it out. Anyway, Maddie, you can forget about her. You won't need to see her again. Lal's one of the best station-hands there is, but he'll be retired by the time Skeet takes on the running of the place. Mrs. Lawrence will be out of the way."

Steve pulled her into his arms, kissed her roughly.

"No one can ever come between us now, little one," he told her on a strange, harsh note. He looked at her. "Are there any more misunderstandings, I wonder, floating around it that indignant little mind of yours? Have you been nursing your wrath over anything else? If so, we'd better have it out right now."

Maddie's eyes fell away. She hesitated.

"There is just one thing," she admitted, "although there's no question of wrath entering into this one!"

"We'll deal with it, then. What is it?"

"Kareena." Steve swore softly as she said that name. "It's just that I thought—well, what I mean is, I thought—"

"I can imagine what you thought, Madeleine," Steve interrupted her ineffectual mutterings dryly. "I worked out just what you must have thought; what you may even have been *led* to think when I found out from Skeet's letter that you hadn't married after all. You'd simply run away. I went back over everything, trying to pick up some clues. I remembered the look in your eyes, at the break-fast-table, that last morning at Bibbi. A sort of trapped look, it was, of pure desperation. You'd made up your mind to clear out that morning, hadn't you, Maddie? Am I right?"

She nodded silently.

"Sit down again, and I'll tell a little bit about Kareena."

He put her back into her chair, took the cane one again, and began to fashion himself a cigarette. When he had done that, he stretched out his long legs, leaned back, and gave her a level regard.

"Kareena's what you might call an old family friend—the family's, rather than mine personally. Her uncle and my own father were very close all their days. They both had the same pastoral interests and were active politically. A couple of tough old pioneers, you might call them. Kareena used to come up often to stay as a child, and so we saw a good deal of each other, I being the older by only a couple of years. When my parents and her uncle died, she seemed to want to keep coming. I didn't try to stop her, because of the old associations. I sometimes do things like that for friendship's sake, Maddie. I'm beginning to find out that it can land one in all sorts of bother!" He paused, grinned. "Look where my friendship with Gerald Masterton landed me, for instance—in the role of the big bad wolf, my one desire to oust his lovely daughter out of her rightful inheritance and take his property to myself! Ah, well!" He pulled on his cigarette, exhaled, continued. "Kareena has had an understanding that she doesn't need to wait to be asked up. I can't keep my eye on the social calendar, I've better things to do. Usually the phone just rings, and it's Kareena to say she'll be up for the polo, or the winter ball, or the spring meeting, or some such goddam' thing—I never really thought about it much. This last time, though, there was nothing on socially, nothing at all. That rather puzzled me, for a start. I remember now that I had told her a bit about you when I took her out that time in Sydney. Even then, I was a little bit in love with you, my darling, and it was a temptation to talk about you, I'm afraid. I know I didn't say much, beyond the fact that you were a lovely young girl and that you'd be at Yattabilla for a year, so that the place could become yours legally. You know the sort of thing. I thought nothing more about it."

He looked about him for an ashtray, reached for the cheap tin one on the table behind him. It had a beer advertisement running around the sides. A boy at school had given it to Skeet last week.

"I didn't even connect that conversation with her recent visit to Bibbi; not until yesterday, when Skeet's letter arrived. I began to go over everything in my mind. I knew that I intended to fly down to Sydney right away, because I just had to find you, but I wanted to square Kareena first. I phoned her and put a few questions to her. She beat about the bush for a while at first, but actually went so far as to admit that she had recognized you the moment she saw you in Noonday as the girl who walked past us in the nightclub one night. I'd already told her about taking you for a meal in the Blue Balcony. Then I let you walk straight past our table that night without a hint of recognition. To Kareena it could add up to only one thing, so she decided to stay on at Bibbi to do a spot of meddling, I suspect. She said a lot of things to me, then, Maddie, that I won't bother you with and would prefer to forget, accused me of hiding things, of a sneaking regard for you and so forth. I've no doubt that from the moment she had these suspicions, she started scheming to keep us apart. Poor Kareena!" He sighed. "She was certainly livid when I told her on the phone that what I felt for you was much more than a sneaking regard, and that I was coming to Sydney to ask you to marry me! She hung up on me. I don't think Kareena will ever trouble us again, darling, because she knows she's overplayed her hand."

Maddie smiled. "But you didn't, Steve," she murmured, dimpling.

"Didn't what?"

"Didn't ask me. To marry you, I mean."

"My God, I don't believe I did!" Steve was out of his chair and across to hers, pulling her up into his arms again. He cradled her head against his chest. "You will marry me, won't you, Maddie?" he said, into her hair. "I want you for my wife, darling, quite desperately. Will you?"

"Of course I will. I mean, yes, *please*."

He kissed her fiercely, as if he could never let her go. Maddie felt herself melting against him in that divine state of ecstatic half-reality.

Steve put her from him with a groan.

"Let's make it soon, darling. There's nothing to wait for now, is there?" He sounded shaken, hoarse. "Dear heaven, I'd never have lasted that year out, anyway!" He laced her fingers through his, looking at her with tenderness. "We'll get a license tomorrow, Maddie. We're going home to Bibbi as man and wife, do you hear?"

"Yes, Steve," was her submissive reply.

The banging of the front door announced Skeet. He stood just inside the room, staring for one incredulous moment at the tanned, tall man who still held his sister in his arms. Then he threw down his schoolbag and hurled himself at them, whooping with sheer joy.

"Sh! Skeet, the landlady!" Maddie's warning was automatic.

"Golly, Steve! It's good to see you! Wow, it is!"

Steve mussed the ginger hair into spikes, smiling down at him.

"Did you get my letter, Steve, the one I wrote from school? Did you reckon it was a decent letter—well, I mean, fairly decent?" Skeet qualified modestly.

"I reckon it was *very* decent," Steve assured him earnestly. "In fact, Skeet, I'd go so far as to say it's the most welcome letter I've ever had in my whole life."

"Really, Steve?"

"Sure thing, feller," was Steve's oddly serious reply. "I'm going to keep that letter for the rest of my days."

Skeet wrinkled his freckled nose.

"I'll have to tell the teacher. I didn't know it was as good as all *that*! Where's the tea, Maddie? Are we having some 'cos Steve's here, or do we still have to stretch things out?"

"Skeet!" She blushed, reproving him.

"Well, that's what you're always saying. You have the fire on full, too! Where on earth did you get the money, Mad?"

"*Skeet!*" she choked. "I'll get the tea."

Steve chucked Skeet softly under the chin.

"It's a special day, Skeet, that's why we're not waiting till later to eat those biscuits—if biscuits there are? We'll eat the whole lot now and anything else that's around as well. Then you'll put on your best pants, and your sister will put on her prettiest dress. We'll all go out on the town. We'll have the biggest meal you ever ate in your life, because we're celebrating this very special day, all three of us!"

"What are we ceb—celebrating?" Skeet stumbled on the word.

When Steve told him, his eyes got round with wonder, and excitement brought vivid spots of color to his cheeks.

"Gee! You mean, we'll be living at your place? At Bibbi?"

"That's right. When you're grown up you won't, of course. You'll be living at your own place instead, at Yattabilla, but it will be right next door. In the meantime, you'll live at Yattabilla, though. Billy Sundown and I will show you how to do all the things you'll need to do some day for yourself on Yattabilla."

"Golly!" breathed Skeet. Then a thought struck him. "*She* won't be there, will she, at Bibbi? I don't think Maddie an' me will like it much if *she's* there."

"She?"

"Kareena." Skeet uttered the name with supreme disparagement.

Steve shook his head positively. "There'll just be the three of us, Skeet, you and Maddie and me. And Mrs. Farrell, of course."

"And Etta? Can't we have Etta?"

Steve's lips curled into an amused grin.

"I suppose we could have Etta, too," he conceded. "We'll bring her over from Yattabilla easily enough if you particularly want her, but there are lots of hens at Bibbi, if you remember, Skeet."

"But will there be chicks?" Skeet asked anxiously.

"There are hens sitting on eggs right now. One or two of them at the very least," Steve assured him, "so you can count on chicks, too, I reckon."

"But will they be the right sort of eggs? Will the hens

know if they're the right sort of eggs, Steve? Etta didn't."
Skeet sounded worried.

"The Bibbi hens will." Maddie heard Steve's deep
voice, grave and unsmiling, as she placed the cups on the
tray at the other end of the room. "The Bibbi hens will
know all right, you can take it from me. Bibbi knows
what it's doing. You'll find out all sorts of exciting things
there, Skeet. It can teach you so much, because it's been
there for so much longer than you or I, since the beginning of time itself, probably. Bibbi always knows just
what it's doing. You needn't worry any more about anything, Skeet old feller, because Bibbi *always* knows!"

TOWN NURSE — COUNTRY NURSE

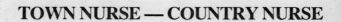

TOWN NURSE—
COUNTRY NURSE

Marjorie Lewty

Kate was dismayed when her dental surgeon boss suggested she help out Ben Holland, a colleague of his in a small country town. Yet she couldn't refuse.

Kate had gone to considerable effort to change herself into a city girl. After a disastrous love affair, she felt she never wanted to see the country again. London was the place for her!

Yet strangely, the thing she resented most about Ben Holland, attracted though she was to him, was his assumption that she was a London girl who could have no place in his life.

It was too late now to tell him that she was a farmer's daughter!

CHAPTER ONE

Lady Benton was our final patient on that summer Friday afternoon. Dr. Hartington waited until I'd escorted her to Manchester Square and her chauffeured Rolls and had come back to start tidying up the office, before he dropped his bombshell.

After a morning of operations in hospital, he'd had four fairly complex consultations that afternoon. Now, with a weary grunt, he stretched himself out on the white contoured dental chair, placed both hands behind his elegant gray head and said calmly, "Kate dear, how would you like two weeks in the country while I'm away?"

He wasn't to know it was a bombshell, of course. He's rather a dear and wonderfully easy and considerate to work for. He must have imagined that by sending me into the country in June, in the middle of a London heat wave, he was doing me a favor. I couldn't very well tell him that ever since yesterday evening, when Hugo called to say he was back in England, I'd been busy fabricating exciting plans for the coming two weeks. He didn't know that sending me off to the country was just about the worst thing to do to me.

"You see," Dr. Hartington went on, without looking at me, "this wretched girl just walked out at a moment's notice—something to do with her boyfriend, I gather—and there was poor old Benjamin high and dry with his appointment book bulging and no help of any sort in the office. He was bewailing his fate to me on the phone yesterday evening, Kate, and then I thought of you and how you'd be at loose ends while I was away."

Loose ends! I'd planned to spring clean all the cupboards and the equipment, go through the linen, bring the drug order up to date, check the cards. Also, to be strictly honest, I'd hoped to get away early in the afternoons if Hugo had the same kind of idea that I had about our seeing a lot of each other.

" . . . and you can travel up there comfortably first class on Sunday afternoon. Accommodation's no problem—all fixed up, in fact. It's a couple of miles out of Lambton itself, on the main bus route from Stratford. I've written down the address and phone number and the address of the practice in Lambton. You'll find them in the top desk drawer. It's very good of you, Kate. You'll be doing me a favor as well as saving poor old Benjie's sanity."

I opened my mouth to say that I hadn't said I'd go. Then I closed it again. I knew my chief. When 'Uncle Geoffrey' arranges something it's as good as done; and in organizing all this in detail and then telling me about it afterward, he was using the technique he always uses for apprehensive patients: "We've arranged for you to go into the hospital on Monday, Mrs. Carruthers. Here's a note for you to give to Matron when you arrive, and here's a list of things to take in with you. I'll pop in to see you on Monday evening when you're installed, and we'll get your little job done early Tuesday morning. . . ."

And Mrs. Carruthers goes without a murmur. Oh yes, I knew the routine. It works like a charm, especially on susceptible females.

He levered himself out of the contoured dental chair with a deep sigh. "Lucky Kate! I could just do with a couple of weeks in Lambton myself. Why did they have to arrange this wretched conference in June? Rome will be an inferno. I can't even persuade my wife to come with me. But Lambton—leafy, green Warwickshire—glorious! You love the country, of course?"

For one crazy second I toyed with the idea of telling him the truth, of saying, "I wouldn't mind if I never saw the country again, except from the inside of a train traveling through it at 80 miles an hour. I'm a city girl now, and that's how I want to stay."

But I couldn't do it. I simply couldn't tell anybody, in cold blood, that I didn't love the country.

"Oh yes," I heard myself murmur. "Of course."

"Good. Good. I'll phone them later, then, and tell them to expect you Sunday afternoon."

He'd taken off his glasses when Lady Benton left, and now he was wandering around the surgery looking for them. I found them, polished them and helped him into his jacket, thinking that for such a brilliant man he was singularly helpless in some ways.

He smiled kindly and vaguely at me and wandered away. With that particular expression on his long, intelligent face he suggested, quite falsely, that he was completely out of touch with most of what is going on.

"You old fraud," I said helplessly to the closed door. "I don't want to go to your beastly leafy Lambton to work for your beastly old Dr.—" I consulted the paper he'd left in the desk drawer "—your beastly old Dr. Benjamin Holland, and I hope you fry in Rome, and—"

I stopped since it was no good moaning about it. I had a wonderful job; I was fantastically lucky to have it. In a job like mine these were the sort of challenges you had to be prepared to meet, so I wasn't in any position to refuse.

Neither could I stay away from the country forever just because the thought of cows grazing and turf soft under my feet, hit me like a blow in the stomach.

All right, Dr. Benjamin Holland, I'll come and do my best for you for two weeks. And as for Hugo, well, if he's really keen on our getting to know each other better, two weeks won't make any difference. And if he isn't, then surely it would be more sensible if we don't even begin.

That, I felt sure, was the way my cousin Louise would view the matter. Louise was my blueprint for pretty well everything—had been since I came to London three years ago.

Complimenting myself on this sensible solution, I finished putting the office in order and made my way along the quiet, carpeted corridors to the reception office. Louise presided over a huge desk furnished with three phones, an intercom, a library of appointment books and a bowl of yellow roses.

For some years, before I came to London, Louise had been receptionist at the practice in Manchester Square. Six bronze plates on the front door discreetly announced the august names of the consultants who had their rooms at that address.

Louise is 26, four years my senior. Everyone says we are alike, but I can never really believe it myself. Louise is tall, willowy and elegant with beautiful fine bones and the kind of sculptured pale hair that somehow never gets untidy in a wind. I have the same kind of straight little nose and there's not much to choose between the quality of our skin, but there, I think the resemblance ends. My hair is fawn-colored and I wear it shoulder-length (tied back during working hours). I'm smaller than Louise, and although I try to remember my posture, nobody would call me elegant or willowy. Just an ordinary girl, that's me. My best point, I suppose, is my eyes. I never knew my mother, for she died when I was a baby, but Daddy always told me I had my mother's eyes: green-gray with long, dark lashes.

Louise's father and my father were the kind of brothers who think the world of each other and never drift entirely apart. Even when my father chose farming and Uncle Humphrey went into business in the city they never lost touch, right up to the time that Uncle Humphrey was lost in a plane crash.

When I was little my father and I used to visit my aunt

and Louise at their home in Epsom quite regularly. Louise sometimes spent her school holidays with us at the farm.

When Louise was 20 and had already started work as receptionist in Manchester Square, her mother married again and went to live in Scotland. I think my cousin was lonely for a while, though she wouldn't admit it, and she came more often to see us than before.

So perhaps it was partly gratitude that made her offer to share her apartment with me when my world cracked up around me three years ago, and I came to London to start training as a dental nurse. We were so different—Louise the smooth city girl and me, literally, the country cousin—that I don't think either of us expected that we should be together very long. But as things turned out we got along pretty well, and I've been with her ever since. She has been the model for everything I made up my mind to become myself—poised, elegant, confident, with the kind of resilience that stops short of toughness but can manage to stand up to a few knocks without showing any dents.

Sometimes I thought I was succeeding in making myself into a new personality from the naïve little 19-year-old I must have been when I came to London. Sometimes I wasn't so sure. But I knew that I had Louise to thank for a great deal, including my job as nurse-secretary to Dr. Geoffrey Hartington. I'd had it for eight months now, after working in a large partnership practice in Chingford.

I never ceased to feel grateful to her. I tried to make it up to her in little ways, like doing a bit more than my share of the cooking and cleaning.

I waited now while Louise took an incoming call and made the necessary entry in one of the appointment books. Then I told her my news.

She put down her pen and made a sympathetic face at me. "Poor old Kate, what a bind! And just when Hugo has come home too!"

"I know, that's what makes it so maddening. But you know what Uncle Geoff is like when he sets his mind on something. You find yourself going along with him. I can't even let Hugo know about my change of plans."

"Oh? Why not?"

"Because I don't know where he is—except that he's in Bournemouth. When he phoned last night he said he had to go straight down there to report to his father, and it was going to take him the whole weekend to work through all the stuff he'd brought back with him."

Hugo was the son of Alexander Whipple of Whipples' Tours Limited, and he'd spent the past two months in Europe, traveling around inspecting hotels for his father's agency.

"Couldn't you phone his office and see if they can tell you where Pa Whipple is staying in Bournemouth?"

I said doubtfully, "I suppose I could, but I don't want to make too much of a thing of it. We didn't make a definite date because Hugo didn't know when he'd be free. He just said he'd call again as soon as he got back."

Louise looked at the bowl of yellow roses. "Mean a lot to you, Kath?" She still called me Kath sometimes. I'd always been "Kath" at home, but somehow Kate seemed more Londonish, so I'd altered it.

"No. Yes. I don't know yet," I said idiotically.

Truly, I didn't know. I'd only met Hugo once, the day before he left for Europe. I'd gone with Louise to a party given by one of her friends. I didn't know anybody there and I'd lost Louise for a moment; I was feeling rather out of it when I saw this man standing beside the bar, his brown eyes lazily searching the room. They met mine, stopped, held for a moment and then he came across to me and said, "I'm Hugo Whipple, who are you?"

"Kate Moorcroft." I smiled coolly at him, the way I'd learned from watching Louise.

"Hullo, Kate," he said.

He asked me if I wanted another drink and I said no; then he took my arm and led me across the dimly lit room with its weaving couples and throbbing rock music, saying, "All this is rather juvenile, isn't it? Let's go somewhere else."

We'd walked down to the river and over Hammersmith Bridge to watch the lights from the South Bank, and he told me about the travel agency and his proposed trip. We'd drifted into the second half of a guitar concert at the Queen Elizabeth Hall, eaten hot dogs at a street stand afterward and then Hugo had hailed a taxi and driven me home.

"Much too early," he said regretfully, and he kissed me goodnight without showing any tendency to linger, "but I have to be up at the crack of dawn tomorrow to catch my plane. Why didn't we meet before? Never mind, Kate, we'll make up for it when I get back home again. And I'll send you some postcards."

And that, I'd thought, was that. *Finis*. But actually he had sent me three postcards from Italy, Greece, and Yugoslavia; fabulous hotels standing on pine-trimmed hillsides, or against a backdrop of snowy peaks, with incredibly blue lakes in the foreground.

He hadn't said much on the postcards, merely witty gibes about the hotels themselves. The professional approach, I decided. To me any one of them looked like heaven.

After the postcards arrived I began to think quite a bit about Hugo and wonder if he meant what he said about our seeing more of each other when he returned home. Then, last night, he'd phoned.

And that was all. How could I possibly answer Louise's question?

"Ah well," I said lightly, "I'll just have to hope he won't find someone else while I'm away among the sheep and turnips."

Louise gave me an odd look that made me wonder if she read below the lines of my flippancy and guessed how I felt about going back to the country. I had a feeling that she did; she doesn't miss much.

"Who is this man you're going to work for? Do you know anything about him?"

"Not a thing, except that his name is Benjamin Holland, and he's a buddy of our revered Uncle Geoff. Same vintage, I presume. Anyway, they go fishing together, the old darlings. Well, I'll be getting back to the apartment now to sort out my clothes and see what I have that'll be suitable for the country. You coming?"

Louise glanced at her watch. "I'll be another half hour at least. I'm waiting for a call from St. Mary's about one of Dr. Fitzgibbon's patients. Don't wait for me."

I collected my things from the cloakroom, walked to Oxford Street and took a bus along the Bayswater Road. In spite of what I'd said to Louise about sorting out clothes I didn't feel like going straight back to the apartment; it was a perfect afternoon for a walk across Kensington Gardens.

At that time in the afternoon, most people were still at work and the Gardens were quiet. Old folks sat with their eyes closed and their faces turned to the sun; nursemaids pushed carriages or gossiped while the children played around them; tourists with guide maps and cameras slung over their shoulders wandered about.

I kept to the grass and walked slowly, as if by hanging back I could somehow avoid the memories I knew I had to face. I'd shoved them away so often in the past few years. I suppose in a way I'd built a wall between one life and the other. But now I had to climb the wall and go back, and I mustn't go unprepared. Making myself remember was a kind of defense.

It had been a hot June day like this, except that in the heart of Warwickshire the trees had no dust on them, and the sky was bluer than it ever was in London. My father had just taken delivery of a new tractor, and he and Denis were going down to the Lower Field to try out its paces. I remembered how their boots clattered across the yard, and how I called to them from the dairy as they went past saying I'd bring tea down to the fields for them.

They called and waved back and I stood watching them till they were out of sight, the two men who made up the whole of my world. Mentally I hugged myself because I was so happy. Lucky me, I thought, when so many people are lonely, to have not only one man I adored, but two.

That was what I thought as I stood looking after them: that I had everything in the world any girl could want.

When I reached the Lower Field an hour later, I had nothing and nobody.

I didn't know that day that I had lost them both. All I knew then, through horror and shock, was that something had gone wrong with the tractor, and in struggling with it, Daddy had revealed a heart condition that neither he nor anyone else had suspected.

It wasn't until a week later, two days after the funeral, that I found I'd lost Denis too.

He tried to put it in a roundabout way, I suppose to spare my feelings, but that only made it worse.

At last I got the message, and at first I couldn't believe it. "But, Denis, are you saying that you only wanted to marry me because Daddy was going to make you a partner in the farm?"

I spoke blankly, because even then I thought there must be some mistake.

But he flung away from me angrily, and I knew then that it was no mistake. "Gosh, Kath, do you need to make it sound so bloody awful? It wasn't like that at all. I'm awfully fond of you, always will be, but—well, you see, I simply have to be practical. It's my whole life that's at stake. My whole future."

Louise had told me that men always put their careers first, but until that moment I don't think I'd really believed it.

"If only your dad hadn't had this enormous bank loan!" Denis ran his hand through his reddish hair and looked dreadfully unhappy. "You see, I could never take on the running of a farm this size on my own, and anyway the bank wouldn't play ball with me. Mr. Rogers as good as told me so when I went in to see him about the account the other day. I'm too young and don't have the experience. So when this offer came from that fellow I met at the exhibition to go to Australia, it seemed as if it was meant to be."

There was an awkward silence then, because we both knew that he could have said, "Come out with me, Kath. Let's get married and go together."

The silence went on until I couldn't bear it any longer. Through the great hard lump that had lodged in my throat I said, not looking at him, "Of course you must go. As you say, it's your whole future. I'll be all right."

The relief I saw in his face made me wince, but I knew dimly that he didn't mean to be cruel. At that moment I think I felt years and years older than Denis.

He told me what a wonderful girl I was, and he talked on about making his way in Australia and sending for me to go out to him when he had a home to offer me. I wasn't listening very hard because I knew it was all over. I gave him back his ring, he stayed for a few more embarrassed moments and then he went.

When everything was settled and the solicitor had told

me how little was left, I went to see Miss Lang, the principal of my old school, and asked for her help.

She had my graduation marks on the desk in front of her as she asked, "What would you like to do, Katherine?"

I said promptly, "I'd like to train to be a nurse. That's what I'd have done if—"

If I hadn't expected to be a farmer's wife at Christmas.

She studied my results, pursing her mouth thoughtfully.

"Leave it with me for a day or two," she said, "and then come and see me again."

When I returned she told me that general nursing was out. I didn't have good enough marks in the right subjects. There might be a way around this by what she called a "back door" examination, but it all sounded rather time-wasting, and I desperately needed to begin training for something straight away. Knowing how to make butter, feed hens and clean eggs wasn't going to get me very far in London—and that was where I was going. As far away from the country and my old life as I could go.

"Would you consider dental nursing?" Miss Lang asked me. "I've been into this with our guidance counselor, and she tells me there is always a demand for trained dental nurses. With your marks you could probably get into a course at one of the dental hospitals, which would likely give you a chance of a better position than you could get if you started training in a private practice."

"Oh yes, I think I'd like that," I said. It felt like a lifeline. Something definite to do.

Miss Lang gave me a look of approval. "As a matter of fact we've been in touch with St. Matthew's—one of the hospitals that runs a course for dental nursing—and we have arranged an interview for you next Monday, with the idea of your starting training when their new term begins."

"Oh, thank you," I said, and began to cry. I used to cry rather a lot around that time—whenever people were kind to me.

But all that was three years ago, and now, walking across the grass toward the Round Pond, watching the sun glinting on the water and the children tossing bread to the ducks, I didn't feel like crying, not even at the black memory of that time. I never cried these days. I was nearly 23 and could stand on my own two feet. I loved London and my job. I wondered if I was going to find myself loving Hugo too.

Certainly, I thought, I was going to remain clear-eyed about it all. Romantic love was something that happened when one was young and had a childlike trust in the world and in the goodness of people. I didn't think I was cynical or bitter—I hoped not—but certainly I wasn't childishly trusting any more.

But Hugo was exciting; he was fun; and any girl would be an idiot not to feel thrilled and flattered when the junior partner of Whipples Tours Limited singled her out for attention.

I sighed. It was really too bad that Uncle Geoff was banishing me to the country.

A big red ball suddenly rolled to my feet. I picked it up and threw it back to the chubby imp who was tottering unsteadily after it. I smiled at him, and he stood in front of me clutching his ball and surveying me with a wide, unblinking stare. Then he turned and veered toward his mother's arms.

I was still smiling, for he had looked so touchingly secure, cocooned in his own tiny world, as I walked on toward the apartment, resolutely turning my mind to the clothes I needed for the country.

CHAPTER TWO

On that Sunday afternoon, Paddington Station had an atmosphere of drowsiness. When I asked for my ticket, the clerk in the booking office yawned hugely as he pushed it, together with the change, in my direction. I consulted the departures board and found my platform. The empty train was standing there, but the barrier was closed, so I dumped my suitcase down and waited. After a while an elderly couple joined me; then a stout mother with a baby in her arms and a whiny toddler hanging despondently onto the edge of her skirt. Gradually a few more hopefuls drifted along and lined up behind.

A diesel engine came nosing slowly along the opposite platform, snaking its train of coaches behind it around the bend. At the same moment a ticket collector shuffled up and opened the gate. I moved forward hopefully, but he lifted an official hand and mumbled something that I took to mean that our little line-up must wait until the incoming train had emptied itself of passengers.

Doors flew open, people climbed down and began to filter slowly along the platform.

Something was actually happening, trains really did come in and out of Paddington on a Sunday afternoon. I laughed to myself and wished I had somebody to share the joke with.

A tall man in a light corduroy jacket and stylishly cut slacks was walking toward me from the incoming train. I found myself absentmindedly admiring the way he walked—gracefully, like a dancer. He carried a pale leather holdall; altogether he looked rather exclusive, like one of those fashion photographs in *The Times*, showing what the modern young man-about-town is wearing.

I went on gazing idly at him as he approached. He seemed to be looking back at me.

We recognized each other at the same moment. I saw his bored expression change, his mouth lift, and I could feel my own face suddenly stretching into an incredulous, delighted smile.

"Katy!" cried Hugo, and he enveloped me in a hug that wouldn't have been noticed in Paddington Station at any normal time, but on Sunday afternoon must have provided quite a light relief for the line behind me.

"Well, well, well—!" Hugo detached me neatly from my place at the front of the line. "But this is fantastic. How on earth did you know?"

I simply couldn't believe it yet. I stared up at him. Two months in Europe had given him a devastating tan. "You look so well—I didn't—" I began. I pulled myself together. "How did I know what?"

"That I'd be on this train. I didn't know myself until half an hour before I left Bournemouth. Kate—you haven't been waiting—?"

Suddenly I saw what he was getting at. "Hanging about on the off-chance that I might meet you? Hugo dear, you didn't really imagine I was that sort of girl, did you?" It was quite surprising how like Louise I sounded as I said it.

He grinned. "Not really. Well then, why? And where?"

I said, "Believe it or not, I'm on my way into the wilds of Warwickshire as a temporary assistant for two weeks. This was wished on me after you phoned on Thursday." I sighed. "It's a fearful nuisance, but I'm afraid I couldn't get out of it."

He stared at me in mock horror, still holding both my hands. "Kate, you can't! Not when I've just got home."

This was very flattering and encouraging. I said, "I know it's awful, but I'm afraid I must. Orders are orders, and Dr. Hartington didn't leave me any choice. He's off to Rome for a couple of weeks and that left me free. I was planning to spend the time stocktaking on materials and so on, getting in late and leaving early and having a beautifully lazy time. Then he told me he wanted me to go to Lambton and help out this colleague who has a dental practice there and has lost his office nurse."

"Well, I think it's damned inconsiderate of him." Hugo stuck out his lower lip. He looked sulky and rather sweet.

Over his shoulder I noticed that the passengers in my line were filing past the barrier. I glanced despairingly up at the gadget that serves for a clock at Paddington and said in a small voice, "I ought to be getting on the train."

"Oh no, you don't!" Hugo picked up my case and took me firmly by the arm. "You don't imagine you're going to get away from me as easily as that when we've only just found each other again, do you? I'll tell you what we're going to do; we're going to pick up my car at home and drive out of town to have a meal together. There's a good place I know near Aylesbury. Then I'll deliver you to this spot in the middle of nowhere—what's its name?"

"Lambton."

"Oh yes, I know it; it's a small town not far from Stratford. I'll get you there okay, I promise."

"But, Hugo," I demurred, not very convincingly, "surely you don't feel like driving all the way and back, do you? It must be 60 miles or more. And I've bought my ticket." I held it out.

He took it from me and began to ferry me toward the taxi rank. "We won't let that little matter worry us. What's the good of being a travel agent if you can't fiddle a little thing like a railway ticket for a friend?"

We were both giggling as we piled into a taxi. Paddington Station, as we drove away, had changed subtly and was looking quite gay.

The taxi deposited us at a small, expensive-looking house in St. John's Wood.

"Come in while I dump my gear and wash up," Hugo

said. "The parents are both in Bournemouth, so there won't be anyone here, but we could make some tea or coffee—whichever you like—before we leave."

Inside, the house was all the outside had suggested. Gorgeous colors and shapes and designs. Sumptuous deep chairs; pale satiny wood; Swedish glass in jewel colors of crimson and indigo and amethyst.

Hugo put his bag in the hall. "Look, you make yourself at home in the kitchen while I go and clean up. I always feel lousy after a train journey. There should be milk in the fridge; the daily takes some every day for herself even if we're not here. I expect there'll be something to eat if you look around."

The kitchen was a dream. There were seven varieties of tea in hand-painted caddies on a white shelf. I chose Darjeeling and explored for biscuits. I found a box of *petits fours* in the cupboards, and milk in the fridge. I was carrying the tray into the living room as Hugo came downstairs looking combed and damp and smelling mintily of toothpaste.

"Better?" I inquired as he took the tray from me.

"Improving rapidly." He put down the tray and came over to me. "I like that yellow suit, Kate. You've got good taste in clothes." His eyes, looking down into mine, were very dark and bright. "This," said Hugo, "could be the start of a beautiful friendship. Yes?"

I wondered how Louise would answer that one. For a moment I felt rather out of my depth.

I smiled. "Perhaps," I said, and sat down beside the table. "Milk and sugar?"

He grinned, so I knew I'd said the right thing. He was civilized and adult—not the callow, grabbing kind.

It was lovely having tea in that beautiful cool room instead of trundling along in a noisy train. We took our time and Hugo told me some stories about his trip. He talked very amusingly. In the end it was nearly six o'clock before we got up to leave.

I said, "I suppose I ought to phone these people I'm staying with to let them know I'm going to be later than I thought. There's probably only the one train and they would be expecting me to be on it."

Hugo said, "The phone's over there by the window; help yourself. I'll be getting the car out. Come along to the garage when you're ready."

I found the slip of paper with Dr. Hartington's directions, and really read it for the first time.

There was the address of the practice: Benjamin J. Holland, B.D.S. (Lond), 14 High Street, Lambton, Tel. Lambton 340. Underneath was written: Mrs. Garrett, Summerfields, Little Tressington, Tel. Lambton 876.

Obviously it was this Mrs. Garrett I had to contact. I dialed the operator and waited for the call to pass through its various junctions. At last the ringing tone sounded— and sounded. Brrh-brrh, brrh-brrh, reflecting back to me.

It went on and on. Mrs. Garrett was evidently not at home.

I contemplated trying the number of the practice but there didn't seem much point in that, so, hoping that Mrs. Garrett wasn't too much of a stickler for punctuality, I gave up and went out to look for Hugo.

The traffic in town was heavy at first, but once we left London, Hugo's white car leaped on the miles and devoured them with a kind of satisfied, purring sound that I imagined a panther would make.

I'd never ridden in a luxury car like this before so I sat back to enjoy it watching Hugo and wondering what it was like to be born with a silver spoon in one's mouth. Hugo seemed to have everything—money, good looks, an exciting job. He simply oozed confidence; you couldn't imagine him failing at anything.

We had a gorgeous meal at a small hotel that Hugo knew about between Aylesbury and Bicester and then we headed for Warwickshire.

It was a beautiful June evening; the cars had thinned out and the scent of early summer was all around us. It was so peaceful and so nostalgic—the thrusting green of the corn, the cows grazing, the great spreading trees. Yet I didn't feel so shattered by memory as I might have done. Perhaps it was because Hugo was there beside me.

We'd consulted the map at dinner and decided that Little Tressington was south of Lambton itself. Soon we began to look for the turning.

"We can't be far away now," Hugo said at last, "but I refuse to deliver you just like that. When we turn off the main road we'll park, smoke a friendly cigarette and say our goodbyes in the proper manner. Ah, this looks like it now." He slowed down to read the signpost. "Yes, Little Tressington it is."

It couldn't have been Hugo's fault. He took the corner quite safely, but the accident was unavoidable. The motorbike came roaring around the blind turn in the lane, straight at us. Hugo wrenched the wheel over; the brakes's squeal mingled with the thud of something hitting the car. Something dark and solid seemed to fly past the car window; we lurched into a ditch. There was a ghastly silence.

I suppose I was numb for half a minute. I seem to remember wondering if Hugo was hurt and feeling a wave of thankfulness when I saw that he was pulling himself up. Thank goodness for seat belts, I thought fervently, seeing that we were both held tightly.

Hugo was fumbling with his buckle. "That's just about done the car in. Blasted young fool, coming around a corner at that rate! Looks as if our radiator was pushed in. You all right, Kate?"

"Yes, I'm all right. Hugo, where is he? He must have hit us somewhere—I heard it. He might be—"

"Dead? I shouldn't think so. It's the pillion passengers who get killed, poor mutts, not the crazy drivers."

The car was sloping at an acute angle and Hugo levered himself out, holding on to the doorpost. He held out his hand for me, but I said urgently, "I can manage. You go and look for the boy."

We found him several yards away, lying half on the roadway and half on the grass. He was alarmingly still, one leg sticking out at an awkward angle from his body. There was an ugly cut high up on one cheek and blood was running down to the collar of his leather jacket. His crash helmet had been pushed sideways, but mercifully was still on his head. He looked about 17 or 18.

I leaned down and reached for his wrist, but before I could find the pulse he had come around and started to moan.

Hugo said, "What had we better do? Do you know anything about first-aid?" He was very white and I saw his hands shake as he lit a cigarette.

At that moment I'd have given anything I possessed to be a real nurse. But at least I knew enough not to do any harm.

I said, "You try to stop a car on the main road and as them to phone 999. That'll bring an ambulance."

He hesitated. "Ought we to move him or anything?"

"No, I'm sure we shouldn't. If there's a rug in the car give it to me and I'll cover him up, that's all we can do. Have you got a first-aid kit?"

He shook his head. "Afraid not. I always meant to get one, but—"

"Clean handkerchief, then?"

He found one, gave it to me and brought a rug from the car.

"Go quickly," I said, and pressed the wad of linen against the wound on the boy's cheekbone.

Hugo returned to say he had flagged down a car. It didn't seem long after that before we heard the whine of an ambulance, closely followed by a police car.

The ambulance men jumped out with their stretcher.

"You haven't moved him, have you, miss?" the leader asked me and seemed relieved when I said I hadn't.

"So many people will move an accident case," he said. "Even lift 'em off the road. All with the best of intentions, of course, but so often it makes the injury worse, if it doesn't finish the poor blighter off altogether."

The boy in the leather coat was groaning and moving his arms.

I said, "Is it—do you think he's very bad?"

"Don't know, miss." The ambulance man was adjusting the blankets on the stretcher and in a matter of minutes the injured boy was safely on his way to hospital.

Then it was time for the police to do their stuff, and this wasn't quick at all. I didn't seem to be needed at this stage so I sat down on the grass to wait while Hugo went over and over the details of the accident and the policeman wrote in his notebook. The sun began to go down behind the hedge. Dark clouds blew up and the rear of the white car, suspended over the ditch, took an unreal and rather frightening aspect. In fact, everything began to seem unreal.

I suppose it was delayed shock and having nothing to do, that made me feel very cold and dizzy. Suddenly I shivered and put my head down in my hands—

"There you are then, that's fine. Feeling better now? You did flake out, didn't you?"

I blinked dazedly and found I was lying flat on my back gazing up at the sky. A girl with dark hair was bending over me.

"Feel like sitting up now? There, that's better."

Groggily, with her help, I pulled myself up. I had a tweed jacket wrapped around me. There was a man standing a little way back and I guessed the jacket must be his.

"He went with the policemen," the girl said, reading my mind. "They were going to drop him off at our local garage so that he could arrange about towing this car in and hiring another one. I promised to look after you until he came back."

"I see," I murmured, trying to sound as if I were in full possession of my senses. But all I could think of was that I wished Hugo hadn't gone away and left me with strangers.

The young man spoke for the first time. "I don't think we ought to hang about here waiting, Chloe," he said to the girl. "Bates may be out, or he may not have a car ready—you know what a drifter he is. I'll go back to get Flossie out, then you can drive the girl home for some good strong tea. She looks as if she needs it. I'll wait here till the chap gets back and bring him along with me. Okay?"

He wasn't speaking to me, and anyway I felt too awful to argue about anything. So he went back along the lane and the girl and I sat together on the grass. She chattered on, but I couldn't concentrate on what she was saying. Something about going to the bus to meet visitors but they hadn't turned up.

Soon the man returned, driving a large, ancient, open car. This shook me a bit because it was exactly like the old car we'd had at home; the one my father used for odd jobs of fetching and carrying around the farm. Her name had been Sarah, not Flossie, but they might have been twins.

The man jumped out and helped me to my feet and into the car. His hands were strong yet quite gentle.

I murmured shakily, "This is really awfully good of you." He said with a grin, "Think nothing of it. Just something my sister and I do regularly before supper, isn't it, Chloe?"

The girl climbed behind the wheel and we drove away

with a jerk and a rattle. "Won't be long," she sang out cheerfully over the noise. "Our house is only at the end of the lane."

I sat back and closed my eyes, so that I didn't get a look at the house until the car stopped. I had an impression of a solid, oldish building of rosy red brick with a creeper trailing over the front porch.

"Come along in." Chloe took my arm and led me into a large, comfortably furnished room. It seemed to me a welcoming room; flowered curtains and chair covers, a big copper jug filled with delphiniums in the fireplace. "Now you relax in this comfy chair and I'll have some tea made in a jiffy."

She was staring at the skirt of my yellow suit. "Oh, look, its got grass stains on it. What a shame! You must let me wash them out as soon as we've had tea. If you leave 'em to dry they're hopeless, aren't they?"

She was kind and warm and friendly and I was a stranger. You don't get that spontaneous approach in London—or if you do I hadn't encountered it. I felt tears prick at the back of my eyes.

Chloe went off and I could hear her clattering about at the back somewhere, whistling cheerfully. Very soon she was back with a big brown pot of tea and four cups and saucers.

"Very strong," she said, "and I've made lots of it for when the men come back." She ran to the window as the sound of a car's tires crunched over gravel outside. "Good, here they are now."

Hugo entered first and walked straight across to me. He was frowning and still looked very pale.

"I'm sorry I had to leave you like that, Kate. I couldn't think of anything else to do. But I've managed to hire a car, so we can leave as soon as you're fit again."

The girl Chloe said, "But you'll have a cup of tea first, won't you?"

She was standing by the table, the teapot in her hand. I looked at her properly for the first time and saw a slight figure in old, faded blue jeans and a short-sleeved cotton shirt. She had a nice but unremarkable freckled face with a cheerfully tilted nose and a wide mouth under a mane of dark straight hair. But what struck me again was the warmth and friendliness that seemed to come right out to meet you.

But Hugo scarcely glanced at her. "Thanks, no," he said. I was sorry he sounded so offhand. It seemed a poor return for kindness, but of course he didn't really know how kind she had been to me, and I got the impression that he was irritated that I'd come to this house at all.

"I think you should, you know."

The words, spoken very quietly, came from the doorway, and I saw Hugo's eyebrows lift. It was only very slight, just the faintest bristling of one male animal resenting another male animal's assumption of authority. Hugo wasn't a man to be dictated to by anybody, least of all by a country boy.

I looked toward the door and saw that I'd been altogether mistaken. This wasn't a country boy. He wasn't a boy at all, he was much older than I'd taken him for out in the lane—probably 30 or a little over. He was leaning against the doorpost, both hands stuck nonchalantly into the pockets of his gray slacks. His face was long and rather thin; his mouth was thin, too, and mobile. His eyes were very clear blue and direct; his dark hair flopped sideways over a bony forehead.

When Hugo didn't reply he shrugged. "Please yourself, of course, but it would pull you together if you've much farther to drive today. These accidents can shake you more than you realize."

To my surprise Hugo changed his mind. "Well, thanks, I will then." Rather belatedly he smiled at Chloe and took a cup of tea from her.

"Do you have to press on straight away?" Chloe looked from one to another of us. "You could stay here and relax for a while—we wouldn't bother you. And I was going to try to get the grass stain out of your—Miss—. Gosh, isn't it stupid? We don't even know each other's names."

Hugo said, "I'm Hugo Whipple and this is Kate Moorcroft."

The dark man detached himself from the doorpost and strolled across the room.

"Really?" he said. "Then perhaps you won't have any farther to go after all. May I introduce us? This is my sister Chloe—Mrs. Garrett. And I'm Ben Holland." He turned to me. "Welcome to Summerfields, Kate. Uncle Geoffrey phoned me that you were coming today. We've been expecting you all afternoon. I thought you'd decided not to come."

He held out his hand to me, but he didn't smile, and the eyes that met mine were narrowed assessingly.

Altogether, I thought with a sinking feeling inside, not a very promising way to become acquainted with my temporary chief!

CHAPTER THREE

"I don't get it at all," Hugo said plaintively. "I mean, why couldn't old Hartington have told you the score? Why did he have to make you believe you were coming out to the country to work for some ancient buddy of his?"

We were sitting in Hugo's hired car. I'd come with him to the end of the lane to help him perform the dismal job of transferring everything from the damaged sports car to this small family sedan. We'd spent the last quarter of an hour emptying the lockers and pockets and trunk of the white panther, now looking very forlorn in the dusk.

I stared at one of the rear wheels, stuck up in the air, while I thought about Hugo's question. Actually I was feeling rather the same as he did about, it, but you had to be fair.

"I suppose," I said slowly, "that he didn't really make me think that. I just jumped to conclusions. But that's like Uncle Geoff—he always leaves you to find things out for yourself and make up your own mind."

"Well, I don't like it at all. I don't take to this fellow Holland. He's an overbearing type and I'd be willing to bet he'll work you to death; he's the sort that expects the earth—I've met his kind."

Hugo was looking deliciously masterful. "It's only for two weeks," I soothed him, encouraged by the fact that he seemed to be worrying about me. "He probably won't present any problems I can't handle."

"I believe you rather like the guy," Hugo said darkly.

"After five minutes in his company? I'm not so easily bowled over as that. Actually, I thought he was rather rude."

I was beginning to feel quite kindly disposed toward the

arrogant Dr. Benjamin Holland for lighting up this delightfully possessive streak in Hugo.

He slid his arm along the back of the seat and pulled me close to him, tracing the outline of my chin with his finger. "You're sweet, Kate. You've got smoky eyes like a gorgeous cat and smooth skin and a delicious mouth." He touched each in turn.

I grinned. "Do go on, this is wonderful."

"Seriously," said Hugo, "you're the sweetest thing I've seen for two whole months and I've got to leave you behind with the peasants. Come back to London with me, Kate," he urged suddenly. "We could have such fun and get to know each other properly."

I didn't ask him exactly what he meant by that. As always, in a new situation, I asked myself how Louise would cope. She'd play it light, I guessed.

"No can do," I smiled. "I have my job to consider, Mr. Whipple."

"To blazes with your job," said Hugo. He bent his head and kissed me rather angrily and went on kissing me.

I heard the footsteps behind us in the lane and pulled away. We sat there while Ben Holland passed the car, looking neither to right nor to left and turned in at a field gate opposite the car and disappeared.

I really don't know why I should have felt angry and at a disadvantage. There was no earthly reason why Hugo and I shouldn't be "saying our goodbyes in the usual manner" as he himself had put it. Nevertheless, there was something in the tall straight back and the set of the dark head that annoyed me.

I sighed. "You'd better go, Hugo," I said.

"Damn the fellow!" said Hugo, exasperated. He kissed me again, but the mood of the moment had changed and we both knew it.

He said rather grumpily, "I may as well push on. I don't suppose this jalopy will do better than 40."

"Poor Hugo, it's a shame," I said. "And all because you were nice enough to give me a lift up here. It's my fault really."

I shouldn't lose any sleep about that," Hugo said, but he was looking at the rear of the wounded white panther and not at me.

I slid out of the car. Everything was going wrong and I could have wept.

Hugo put the car into gear. "'Bye, Kate and sorry about everything. I'll call you."

"Yes," I said. "That would be lovely." I wondered if he would.

He lifted a hand in salute and the little family car buzzed away down the lane. I stood watching it until it turned the corner into the main road. Then I walked slowly back to Summerfields.

The sitting room was empty, but Chloe must have heard me come in, for her voice came cheerfully from the back regions, "I'm in the kitchen, cutting sandwiches. Come here."

The stone-floored kitchen was enormous, about half as big again as the front room. Great cupboards and a dresser were all along one side of the wall. There was an electric stove and a washing machine, but the table where Chloe was shearing neat slices of bread off a huge cottage loaf was the solid white kind that needs scrubbing every day.

She looked up and smiled. "Primitive, aren't we? John's going to convert the kitchen for me one day, when there's time to get around to it. You know, tiling on the floor, stainless steel sink, formica tops—the lot. Meanwhile I don't mind battling like his mother and his grandmother did; it's fun really. Just so long as I don't have to continue when the family starts to come along."

Her eyes were suddenly soft as she buttered a slice of bread in a manner that could only be described as dreamy. I wondered if the family was already, so to speak, in the offing. If so, it wasn't obvious. Chloe was thin to the point of little-girl skinniness. In fact, although she was probably a year or two older than me, there was something very ingenuous about her altogether.

She remembered I was there. "Have you seen your friend off? Poor dear, he did look fed up about having to leave you behind. He's terribly good-looking, isn't he?" She stopped suddenly, bread knife poised in mid-air. "Oh dear, I'm so frightful, the way I natter on and on. Ben says I'm the worst chatterbox in the world. Just tell me to shut up if I say anything I shouldn't. I never mind."

She grinned ruefully at me and I smiled back. It was refreshing to meet someone absolutely natural and genuine. I'd have staked my life on Chloe Garrett being both.

I said, "I think Hugo's rather good-looking too, as a matter of fact," and we both laughed. I had the delightful warm feeling that I'd made one friend at least at Summerfields.

Chloe turned back to her sandwiches, saying, "I sent Ben out to find John—my husband, that is—and bring him in. Oh, I can hear them now. Good!"

There was the sound of men's footsteps on the tiled floor of the hall. A deep voice called triumphantly, "Chloe, where are you, love? Elsie's just produced her calf and it's a bouncing boy; mother and son are both doing well."

Chloe responded to this whimsical announcement with a whoop of delight and ran straight into the arms of a giant of a man with russet brown skin, deep-set eyes with crinkles at the corners, and graying hair that stood up from his head like a brush.

It was then that I realized, with a feeling that I'd been punched hard in the middle, something that I suppose I might have guessed before if I hadn't been so wrapped up in my own affairs. John Garrett was a farmer and Summerfields was a farm. I was going to have to spend the next two weeks in a place even more painfully nostalgic than I'd expected.

Chloe was chattering away about the new calf. I gathered that Elsie, the mother, had been giving everybody cause for alarm, and that this was what happened each time she calved. We'd had a cow at home called Clementine, who—

Stop it! I told myself. There was simply no sense in letting everything remind me of a way of life I'd put behind me for good. I was a London girl now and cows and their calves held only a marginal interest for me.

Chloe had evidently come to the same conclusion by a different route, for suddenly she spun around and said, "Kate must be frightfully browned off with all this farm talk. This is my husband, as you'll have gathered. John, this is Kate Moorcroft, Uncle Geoff's nurse. She only arrived a little while ago. She came by car and they had an accident at the end of the lane—a boy on a motorbike—"

John Garrett took my hand firmly. "Ben's just been telling me about it. It was bad luck; must have shaken you up. These young motorcyclists are the limit sometimes; they seem to go mad when they get on their bikes. At first I had a nasty feeling that it might have been Bobby Farnham, who's a pupil of mine on the farm here, but Ben told me he left some time ago, so it couldn't have been. Lucky for me—we're very busy just now with haymaking."

I liked John Garrett straight away. I guessed that he was quite a bit older than Chloe, but from the way he looked at her I thought she was a lucky girl.

"Where's Ben now? Shall I make the coffee and not wait for him? You must be simply starving, Kate." Chloe was stacking crockery onto a tray. "Let's be civilized and have it in the sitting room tonight, as we've got a visitor." She flashed me a smile.

From the hall there sounded the ping of a telephone

receiver being replaced. Ben Holland appeared in the doorway, his face grim.

"Bad news, John," he said. "I've just called the hospital. It seems that Bobby was hurt. I managed to speak to the casualty doctor, but he couldn't tell me much yet. They were just about to X-ray. He seemed pretty sure there was one fracture of the leg, possibly two. So it looks as if Bobby will be out of circulation for some time."

Chloe made an exclamation of dismay and moved nearer to her husband, who put an arm around her. "Poor Bobby, how awful for him! But John, I don't understand how he could have been there when it happened. He left here ages ago; he said he was going home for the evening. How could he have got only as far as the end of the lane? And he's usually so careful on that bike, not a bit wild or crazy like some of the village boys."

John Garrett shook his head worriedly, "Yes, he is a careful lad. I can't understand it either."

Ben Holland said nothing, but he was looking at me. I fact they were all three looking in my direction, and suddenly I felt guilty; it almost seemed as if they thought I was responsible for running down the boy. I knew quite well, of course, that they couldn't really believe that. All the same I felt, or imagined I felt, this faint prickle of hostility about them. It was the old "them" and "us". The city people versus the country folk. I remembered it so well, and I knew how easy it was to fall into the habit of reacting that way—often quite unjustly. But always before I'd been on the other side of the fence.

I felt my cheeks go hot and I wanted to say, "I'm on your side. I'm one of you." But instead I heard myself say defensively, "He did seem to be coming around the corner much too fast."

Ben Holland's clear gaze swept across my face and passed on to his brother-in-law. "Shall we drive over to the hospital, John, and see for ourselves what the score is? But we'd better eat first."

"Yes, of course." Chloe picked up the tray and carried it into the front room. Perhaps she guessed a little of my feelings, for as she passed me she stopped and whispered, "Don't worry, dear. It couldn't possibly have been your fault, anyway," and gave me her warm, quick smile.

We sat around informally on chintz-covered chairs to eat sandwiches and cakes and to drink coffee. But the atmosphere was anything but informal. The Garretts tried to be polite and make conversation. They asked me about London and my work, but it was obvious that the accident was very much in the front of their minds. Ben Holland didn't even try to make conversation, and didn't look in my direction until he took my cup to be refilled.

It certainly wasn't a very promising start to my two weeks in the country, I thought dismally, as the two men finally went out to the car.

Chloe gathered the plates together. "I'll take these into the kitchen and then I'll show you your room. I should have done that before, I know, but somehow everything got a bit out of hand. Please forgive me. We're all very fond of Bobby—he's such a nice boy. Plus it's going to make a big difference to John, not having his help just now when it's a busy time. Oh well, I suppose we'll manage somehow; we always seem to," she added philosophically. "And Ben will lend a hand when he has time. He's very good like that."

Following her up the narrow staircase, bending my head to avoid the low beams, I inquired, "Does your brother live here with you?"

"No, not permanently. He's staying with us at present while all the alterations and decorations are being done to the apartment above the practice in Lambton. Then he'll move in there."

She didn't say whether he was married, or about to get married; it sounded rather probable, I thought.

"Is it a new practice, then?" I asked, trying to get the general feel of things.

"Oh no, it's quite old and a very busy one. But the man who had it before was getting on a bit. By the time he retired the whole place needed doing over. Ben's had quite a time of it, trying to keep the practice running smoothly, with workmen in and out all the time. And then this girl he's been training as office attendant just packed up and left without notice. Something to do with her boyfriend leaving the district—you know how it is. It was a stroke of luck when Uncle Geoffrey said he'd ask you if you would stand in for a couple of weeks until the new person Ben has engaged could start. He's very grateful to you for coming."

Was she being nice to me to cover up for her brother's ungraciousness? I wondered. I had to admit that he certainly hadn't looked particularly pleased to see me.

Chloe led the way into a small, pretty room; painted white, with flowery curtains and a blue cotton spread on the plump bed.

"I do hope you'll be comfy," she said, suddenly rather shy. "I expect you find it all rather cottagey after being used to living in London."

It was so very like my little room at home, the room I'd spend my childhood in, that I was feeling pretty shattered. But I managed to say, "It's a delightful room and it will be heaven after the noise of the traffic in the city. I'm sure I'll never manage to wake up in the morning."

"Oh, I'll wake you," Chloe said, "and bring you a cup of tea. About seven, will that be all right? Ben will drive you into Lambton with him—he usually leaves about a quarter past eight. It's only a few minutes' run, but he likes to get in early while the workmen are there."

She lifted my case onto a chair and folded up the blue bedspread. "Now I mustn't natter any longer or the chores won't get done downstairs. I always prepare for breakfast the night before—we get up so early. You have to, on a farm," she explained.

I nearly said, "Don't I know it?" but stopped in time. These people naturally thought I was a city girl, and I didn't want to start talking about my past life to any of them.

I said instead, "I think I'll turn in now, if that's all right with you. It's been quite a day, one way and another."

"Yes, you must be dead tired. I do hope you're comfortable and sleep well. The bathroom's just opposite, and there's always lots of hot water, so have a bath any time you feel like it."

She said goodnight and insisted on taking my skirt away with her to try to remove the grass stains. When she had gone I had a leisurely bath, put on a cool nightie and began to feel more relaxed. It would have been easy to slip straight into bed, but there was something I had to come to terms with first.

I switched off the light, pulled back the curtains, threw the casement window wide open and let in the warm night air.

It was quite dark now. The sky was black velvet and the stars were huge and brilliant. They seemed to be much nearer than they ever were in London. There was the smell of damp grass and, when you listened, you could hear the pulsing and ticking of myriads of tiny living things; the night noises.

It was all peaceful and beautiful, something that had been so deeply part of me until I deliberately cut it out. And now that I had come back to it I felt an outsider. Something that was probably self-pity caught at my throat and brought tears flooding into my eyes.

An own hooted quite near and I saw the lights of the car coming along the lane toward the house. I drew back from the window as the car pulled up below me and the two men got out.

John Garrett's voice said, "Thanks for coming along with me, Ben. I'm glad we went."

"It looks as if it might be a long job. A fractured femur takes quite a time to mend." That was Ben's voice, lighter and more incisive.

I shouldn't have stayed to listen, I know, but I wanted to hear more about Bobby's condition.

All John Garrett said, though, was "Are you going to put the car in tonight?"

"No, I'll leave her out, I think. I want to start in good time in the morning—that is if Uncle Geoff's treasure comes up to scratch." I could imagine the twist of his mouth as he said the words. "I can't imagine she's feeling exactly joyful about moving out among the hayseeds. I can only hope she'll unbend enough to be of some use to me."

A match flared as John Garrett bent his head over his pipe. Then he said mildly, "Oh, come off it, Ben. I thought she seemed a friendly, capable sort of girl."

"Did you? Well, she may be—in her own surroundings. You haven't seen Uncle Geoff's set-up in London, have you? Very, very plushy! Wait until she catches sight of my office—she'll probably get the next train back. No, it's not a very promising prospect for me; I would much rather have battled on alone, but it was just like Uncle Geoff's high-handed way to insist on sending her."

They were going into the house now. I heard John Garrett's rumble of laughter and I suppose he was trying to cheer up his brother-in-law. Whether he succeeded or not I couldn't manage to care very much.

Somewhere farther away, in the darkness, the owl hooted again and this time he sounded even more desolate than owls usually sound. Not more desolate than I felt, though.

At that moment I'd have given a great deal to be back in the Kensington apartment, with all my familiar and comforting things around me, looking forward to an evening out with Hugo tomorrow. Instead I had the prospect of finding my way around in what was undoubtedly an elderly and probably rather out-of-date practice, working for a man who, if not actually hostile, certainly didn't want me there.

I stood beside the window for quite a long time, seriously turning over in my mind the idea of confronting Dr. Ben Holland with what I'd just heard, and saying, "As you don't want me here any more than I want to be here, surely the most sensible thing is for me to go back to London straight away?"

Two things, however, stopped me from taking that tempting course. Or maybe three.

The first was that I've always thought it rather weak and contemptible to promise to take something on and then give it up without a reasonable trial.

The second was that I happen to have a most regrettable streak of pride, or cussedness, or something, which popped up now and made me yearn to see the arrogant Dr. Ben Holland eat his words.

And I suppose the third was that I didn't fancy facing Dr. Hartington when he knew I'd gone against his wishes.

I got into bed and pulled the covers over my ears—a childish gesture but somehow comforting.

Two weeks, I told myself. *Just 14 days. I'll stick it out.*

CHAPTER FOUR

"That's the practice, that house over there with the blue front door," Ben said, indicating it with a sweep of his left hand. His right one pulled the wheel of the car around to park diagonally within the white-lined area in the middle of High Street.

I didn't miss the note of pride in his voice; in spite of what he'd said last night to his brother-in-law, he certainly wasn't going to make any apologies for the practice to me.

While he locked up the car I stood and looked around in the morning sunshine. Lambton was a typical small country town: a long High Street, straggling away up a gentle hill, a supermarket, a Boots' drugstore, a W. H. Smith's bookstore, and the usual assortment of butchers, groceries and bakeries. From the crest of the hill a square church tower rose up into the pale, cloudless sky. The skeleton of a row of stalls just beyond the parking lot indicated that a street market was held here on some day in the week.

I followed Ben across the road to the blue front door with the new-looking bronze plate on it announcing: Benjamin A. Holland, B.D.S.(Eng.)

He threw open the door, letting out a strong smell of paint, and stood aside for me to enter first.

The hall was carpeted and had a door leading off on either side. "This is the waiting room—" he nodded toward the door on the right "—and this is the office."

I peeped inside. I don't know quite what I had expected after what I'd heard him say last night; probably something like the office I remembered being taken to in Warwick when I was a small girl, with a dark brown leather chair, an old-fashioned foot-engine, and pattern-ed lace curtains covering the windows.

But this office was nothing at all like that. It was large, light and airy with a modern dental chair and cream-colored unit and cabinet. It was quite different from what I'd anticipated, but I could hardly say so, nor could I admire it without sounding horribly patronizing. After all, both of us knew all about Dr. Hartington's luxurious set-up in Manchester Square, and to compare this office with that one would have been like comparing Ye Olde Tea Shoppe with the Ritz.

Ben said briskly, "I'm afraid all I can offer you by way of cloakroom, rest-room, lunch room and everything else is the kitchen, because the decorators are working up-stairs; everything is chaos and confusion up there. You can just about get into the bathroom; it's on the left at the end of the landing, and mind the ladders."

He led the way to the kitchen, which was undoubtedly just as the previous owner had left it—stone floor, stone sink, sad green paint, and an enormous coal range, the kind that needs blackleading every day.

"This part hasn't been altered yet," Ben Holland told me, and added drily, "as you will no doubt have noticed. But I have ideas for it. There's a pantry through that door which will make an excellent darkroom for developing X-rays. This room I plan eventually to divide into two for a recovery room and a small second surgery. There's plenty of space to build on at the back as well."

I glanced up at him and saw that his eyes were shining. Enthusiasm certainly improved him, I thought. He was a different man this morning from the dark rather dis-agreeable person of last night.

He said, "Have you brought a white coat with you? We should have some put away somewhere if you haven't, but I'm afraid I don't know what the last girl did with them before she left."

"Yes, I have one of my own, thank you," I said.

When I'd dressed this morning I'd reckoned that it was going to be a very hot day, so I'd decided to wear a sleeveless dress in a thin white silky material, which I'd judged to be simple enough to be businesslike as well as comfortable. Over this I'd put a navy-blue jacket. Now I took the jacket off and hung it over the back of a chair, unfolded the surgery coat and shook out the creases.

Then I noticed Ben Holland. He was standing watching me get through this routine. What startled me—just as it had done last night—was the frosty sparkle of those very blue eyes.

It was quite absurd to feel a shock wave running down my back. I tried to look away, but I couldn't. I felt as if I were being charged by an invisible battery. Now I knew why Hugo had tamely changed his mind and accepted the cup of tea he had previously refused. This Ben Holland had magnetism—loads of it.

Something had to break the current—and something did. There was a clattering and a thumping outside the window and a male voice, thin and high, sang out, "Dump 'em there, George, there's a good lad."

George dumped whatever it was with a loud thud. Then a tenor voice raised itself into a hymn, "Beside the Syrian Sea," it warbled, and at the same time a cheerful tattoo sounded on the back door.

Ben Holland's eyes crinkled into a smile. He looked quite different when he smiled—much more ordinary and human.

"The men," he said, "have arrived. Both of them." And he went across and unlocked the outside door.

In the opening appeared one of the largest men I have ever seen. He seemed to fill the whole of the doorway, in width as well as height. He wore a decorator's coat, boiled to the final degree of whiter-than-whiteness. On top of all his snowy expanse was fixed a head that seemed much too small, and on top of the head a little cap that might have fitted a grade school student.

The flutey voice issued from the buttonhole of a mouth. " 'Marnin', all," it said amiably.

Ben gave me a warning glance; he must have noticed the corners of my mouth beginning to twitch.

"This," he said, "is Mr. Pill, who is doing the painting and decorating for me."

Mr. Pill the Painter. It was almost too much, but somehow I got control of myself and held out my hand. "Good morning. Mr. Pill," I said.

"Miss Moorcroft will be helping me in the office for the next couple of weeks," Ben said, "and I'm sure she'll make your tea if you'll send George down when you want it."

"Of course I will," I said, as my hand was grasped and shaken heartily.

"Thank you," said Mr. Pill, peering at me with his eyes half-closed, as if I were a new shade of paint that he wasn't quite sure of. "You from hereabouts?"

"No," I told him. "I'm from London."

"Aah!" Silence while he regarded me pityingly. Then, "I've a sister lives in London. Married a fellow keeps a grocer's in Shepherd's Bush." He shook his little head sadly. "Never been the same since she went. It's her bronchials, you know. I told her, I said, 'Cissie, you don't want to exchange God's fresh air for that filthy, fumey stuff they call air in London.' But she went, o' course, and now look at her! In and out of 'ospital for years she's been."

He heaved a long sigh and then suddenly became very businesslike.

"We'll be on to the front bedroom today, Dr. Holland. The lad's brought the paint. George! Where's that lad? Jump to it, now!"

A diminutive boy, also clad in a dazzlingly white coat,

appeared, a tin of paint in each hand, and scuttled across the kitchen across after the mountainous form of Mr. Pill.

Ben smiled. "A sterling character, our Mr. Pill, and a quick worker in spite of his bulk. But I'm afraid you'll have to live down coming from London. It's his pet hate, especially the fumes—as you'll have gathered."

I almost forgot myself far enough to say that it wasn't only with Mr. Pill that I should have to live down coming from London. I wondered how he would have reacted if I had. From the glint I'd just seen in his eye I suspected that he might have a sense of humor of the kind I'd go along with, but you couldn't be sure.

The next moment I was glad I hadn't risked it, for his voice was quite formal again as he said, "Will you go to the office when you're ready? I'll see Mr. Pill started and then join you there."

The office proved to be as uncomplicated as it had looked at first glance. Fortunately the unit was the same model as one I'd been familiar with in my first job, so it held no surprises for me in the way of hidden switches or unfamiliar gadgets. I gave it a good polish with a duster I found in the cupboard under the hand-basin. I filled the sterilizer and switched it on. It was odd to be dealing with an ordinary steam sterilizer again after the modern autoclave that Dr. Hartington used, but somehow rather nice and homey.

I explored the drawers in the cabinet and located all the usual instruments and materials, trying to memorize their positions as I went along.

By the time Ben Holland came into the office I had everything ready for the first patient.

He stood in the middle of the room looking around at the gently steaming sterilizer, the clean towel on the hand-rack, the pile of bibs on the trolley and the inspection instruments laid out on the bracket table.

"I think I've found where most things are kept," I said. "And I opened the laundry parcel. I hope that's all right."

"Of course," he said coolly, and added, "You don't have to ask me what to do, you know. I assume you know your job. I'm afraid the last girl I had was a dead loss; she couldn't have cared less. You'll probably find dirty towels tucked away in corners, and the chrome on the unit hasn't been polished for days."

"It has now," I said, and was suddenly uncomfortably aware that I sounded smug.

He gave me a level blue look and merely said, "Good."

I helped him into a clean white coat and said, "I've been looking for the appointment book, but I can't find it."

He went out into the hall and came back with an appointment book.

"On the telephone table," he said. "Have you any better ideas about where to keep it?"

I hesitated, not sure whether he was needling me or whether he really wanted to know, but he didn't seem to be expecting an answer.

His head was bent over the book. "I see we've got Mrs. Cartwright coming in at nine-thirty. She's the wife of one of my brother-in-law's farm workers. Last time she came she brought three small children along. It's tough going while it lasts, I warn you. You won't find it in the least like Uncle Geoff's Top Patients."

I said rather shortly, "I expect I can cope. I haven't had Top Patients to deal with all my working life, you know."

"Haven't you? I thought you might have had. Uncle Geoff didn't tell me. He doesn't communicate much, does he? Or perhaps he does with you?"

"He certainly doesn't. He takes it for granted that everybody will rush to do just as he wants them to. Why, he didn't even ask me—" I broke off, suddenly appalled at what I'd nearly said.

The blue eyes were regarding me with what could only be called malice. "Go on, what didn't he ask you?"

To my confusion my cheeks began to burn. "It doesn't matter." I turned away and began to open the drawers in the cabinet, checking again where the instruments were kept.

He came and stood behind the cabinet and leaned both elbows on the top and regarded me quizzically. "We might as well get this straight, right from the beginning. Should I be right in thinking that you were very reluctant about the whole idea of helping me out, and that it was only Uncle Geoff's high-handed tactics, or fatal charm, or whatever, that made you come at all?"

I stared down uncomfortably at a row of shiny elevators in the top drawer. Had I really seemed as ungracious as that? Then I looked up and felt unable to tell the little white lie. I had the strangest feeling that I would always have to tell the truth to this man. He had that effect on me.

I said, "I'm sorry, I didn't think it showed. But it hadn't anything to do with you, or the practice."

"Well, that's something on the credit side. On account of leaving the boyfriend?"

"Aren't you being rather personal?"

He said wryly, "I have very recent experience that that's the way these things go."

I didn't particularly relish being put in the same category with the last girl who'd been a "dead loss."

I said stiffly, "As a matter of fact Hugo's been away in Europe for two months and I thought it was a bit hard to be whisked away just the very day he returned."

"Fair enough. I get the point. But if you felt so strongly about coming, why did you agree? You didn't have to come."

"Because I—well—because—" I broke off in baffled exasperation. "I suppose," I said finally, "I could have refused. But Dr. Hartington—your uncle—*is* my employer, and I have a duty towards him. Oh dear, that sounds awfully pompous, and it's only part of the truth anyway. I think it was mostly because when your uncle wants something done, you just do it, that's all."

He nodded and there was a gleam in his eye that might have been amusement. "I know what you mean. And by the way, he isn't my uncle, he's my godfather, but he's been *in loco parentis* to Chloe and me ever since our parents died when we were both kids. He's a very positive person."

"Very," I agreed, mentally adding, *Just as you are yourself*. Probably Ben Holland had acquired his air of authority from his godfather. It was a pity, I thought, still smarting from his recent remarks, that he hadn't also got the charm that goes with authority and makes it acceptable.

He tugged his white coat straight on the shoulders and buttoned it up. His movements were quick and economical, and he looked, I had to admit, quite impressive with his deeply sunburned face and forearms and his thick dark hair.

"Well," he said briskly, "I'm sorry you're here against your wishes, but it would be most inconvenient to send you back now. The woman I've hired can't start for two weeks and there isn't time for me to look for anyone else to fill the gap now. As it's only for a couple of weeks perhaps you can bear it."

I began to say that it wasn't really like that, and I wouldn't dream of letting him down if he wanted me to stay, but I could see that for him the matter was now closed. He'd gone across to the filing cabinet and was leafing through a wad of blue cards, frowning.

"These are in a shocking muddle," he said. "The last

girl seems to have been playing Rummy with them. See if you can get them into order when there's a spare moment, will you?"

Obediently I went across to the filing cabinet. The personal exchange was evidently at an end and our relationship for the coming weeks defined. That suited me fine, I thought. The less I had to do personally with Dr. Ben Holland the better.

At twenty past nine a bus trundled past the window; a few moments later the front doorbell rang. On the doorstep I found a dumpy woman in a tight blue dress. A couple of toddlers, boy and girl, were busy running up and down; she carried a baby of two or three months in her arms.

"Mrs. Cartwright?" I said.

She gave me a really beautiful smile—milk-white teeth in a round, pleasant face—and said, "That's right, love. I'm not late, am I? Such a game I had getting them all ready to catch the bus. Frederick! Rosemary! Give up now, and come in to see the dentist. If you're good and quiet Mommy'll ask him to give you a ride in that lovely chair again like he did last time."

Rosemary, a delicious brown morsel in a pink dress, stopped immediately and came and stood beside her mother, eyeing me solemnly. Frederick, establishing his superior masculine status, took two more jumps before he obeyed and lagged behind the rest of the party into the waiting room.

Mrs. Cartwright collapsed into a chair with a heavy sigh, jogging the baby, who was beginning to grizzle. Rosemary placidly possessed herself of a comic from the pile on the table, and immediately this was the one and only comic that her brother also wanted. He made a grab at it; his sister's mouth wobbled but she hung on gamely. Mrs. Cartwright delivered a smart slap to her son's bottom, with orders to, "Give it over, do. Rosie got it first."

Frederick opened his mouth to howl, thought better of it, and directed a glowering look toward his little sister. I had a horrible feeling that the slap was due to be passed on down the line at the first possible moment.

I stood in the waiting room doorway and looked at them all. How, exactly, did one cope? In Manchester Square the problem of a patient turning up with three pre-school children simply would not arise. There were nursery schools; there were au pair girls. Even in the first practice where I'd worked in London there was always somebody free to keep an eye on a toddler while his mother had treatment. But here there seemed to be only me.

"Will you wait a moment, please," I said, playing for time. "I'll see if Dr. Holland is ready for you."

Back in the office I found Ben Holland making adjustments to the high-speed drill. "Mrs. Cartwright is here, with three children," I said. "How do we manage? Does she bring them all into the office with her?"

He didn't lift his head. He merely said, "That's what I hoped you'd tell me."

So the ball was in my court. I was the trained surgery attendant. I was Uncle Geoff's "treasure", and I could jolly well demonstrate my resourcefulness.

"Very well, Dr. Holland," I said smoothly, reminding myself of my training. "A good dental nurse considers the comfort of the patient equally with the needs of the operating surgeon." I could almost hear the lecturer's voice.

I whipped the bottom drawer out of the desk, emptied it and lined it with two thick hand towels and wad of paper napkins. "That," I said, "will do for the baby."

In the waiting room Frederick and Rosemary were sitting side by side, eyes glued innocently to their comics. Too innocently! Even before I could breathe a sigh of relief Frederick's chubby leg swung sideways and caught his sister on her ankle. Tumult!

When peace had been restored I said to Mrs. Cartwright, "Will you come in now please? I've made a little cot for baby and we'll put him where he can see you all the time. Perhaps the other two will be happy here for a while?"

She stood up and glared sternly at her two eldest. "Now, mind you behave, Fred and Rosie, or I'll give you what for."

She padded into the office. "Good morning, Dr. Holland. I'm ever so sorry I've had to bring them all along with me again, but what with Mr. Garrett being short-handed and their dad so busy, he couldn't look after them for me. There now, lovey, isn't it a clever nursie to make such a nice little nest for my sweetie? You lie there and be good while Mom has her teeth done."

She climbed into the dental chair, cooing at the baby, who seemed to take quite kindly to his new surroundings, his eyes wide open and traveling with a baby's vague wonder around everything they could see.

I tied a bib around Mrs. Cartwright's plump neck and retired behind the chair to wait instructions, wondering how much was expected of me. Working with Dr. Hartington I knew exactly and could put each instrument into his hand as he needed it, without a word from him. But every dental surgeon has his own routine and method of operating, and I wasn't familiar with Ben Holland's. On the whole, I decided, it would be better to hold back than to be too eager, when perhaps I'd be more of a hindrance than a help.

He picked up a mirror and probe. "Now, let's have a look. These are the ones we filled last time. How many more to do, Nurse?"

I consulted the card. "Four." Left upper six and seven, both occlusal. Right upper seven, distal. Right upper eight, M.O.D."

He nodded. "We'll do the right upper today. Xylocaine, please."

He was evidently expecting top service from me. I found an ampule and began to fit it into a syringe.

To the patient his voice was pleasant and reassuring. "We should be able to finish off in one more visit, Mrs. Cartwright. I'll get the two biggest fillings done today and that will leave the other two, the scaling, and polishing for the next time. That suit you?"

"Just whatever you say, Dr. Holland." She was evidently the perfect patient—placid and amenable. "I leave it to you. But I'll be thankful to get them finished. We're that busy just now, what with Frank working overtime every day. It was a pity about that young Bobby having an accident, and old Mr. Rykes is getting on a bit now and can't do what he used to. Mr. Garrett works too hard himself, Frank's always saying."

Ben nodded. "I agree, but what can you do? It looks as if the day of the small farmer is coming to an end, doesn't it?"

"Aye, that's what Frank's always saying. Not that we'll ever have our own farm, o'course. Not a hope of that. But if Mr. Garrett was to join up like with one of the other farmers hereabouts—Mr. Croft of Broad Meadows, maybe—it would mean more security for everyone, wouldn't it, sir?"

She looked anxiously at Ben, perhaps afraid that she had spoken out of turn, but he said pleasantly, "I expect you're right," and took the syringe from me, holding it up to test for air blocks and meeting my eyes as he did so.

"My temporary nurse is from London," he remarked, "and I'm sure she's bored with all the farm talk around here. She must think we have one-track minds, don't you, Nurse?"

I didn't smile. I knew quite well that this kind of remark in the surgery meant nothing at all, and was merely in the interest of diverting the patient's attention from the work in hand, or quelling the more talkative ones like Mrs. Cartwright. Nevertheless, jokes of that sort were something I just couldn't take. If he thought I was being sulky and defensive, well, he would just have to think so, and that was that.

Evidently he did think so. I saw the corners of his mouth go down and his eyebrows go up. So the "treasure" was touchy as well as superior, was she?

Suddenly and ridiculously I could have wept. Not that it mattered in the least what Dr. Holland thought about me, of course. It was the general falseness of my whole position here that was getting me down. I wished now that I'd said, right at the beginning, that I was a country girl, born and bred. Just for a moment I toyed with the idea of saying it now. But of course I didn't. Instead, I moved to the cabinet to measure out amalgam for the fillings.

I watched him do the injection and very impressive it was too. Even Dr. Hartington could hardly have done it more skilfully. The way he handled the high-speed drill was a masterpiece of delicacy and precision. I couldn't help thinking that, with a technique like his, he could rise to the top of his profession very rapidly in London. Where there was to rise to in Lambton was quite another thing.

"Now, just a little bit more here—and here—that's fine—" He mopped out the cavities, dried them with the warm air jet, began on the lining.

Every movement was deft and confident, and as I handed him the various instruments and took the ones he had finished with, I felt at once that we could work well together. It's something you can feel right at the start; a kind of sympathy that makes a good team of surgeon and nurse.

I felt my spirits rise a fraction. At least, I thought, I should enjoy working with Ben; perhaps he'd stop needling me after a while and we could spend a peaceful two weeks in double harness after all.

I leaned forward to look at the size of the cavities and hazarded a guess about the amount of amalgam that would be necessary.

He said over his shoulder, "Two units, please," just as I'd begun to mix two units. And at that moment there was a loud thud and a louder yell from across the hall.

Mrs. Cartwright, mouth gagged with cotton-wool rolls, uttered an agonized "Uh!" and her eyes, wide with alarm, appealed to me.

No time to ask Dr. Holland's permission. I just plonked down the pestle and mortar on the cabinet and fled across the hall and into the waiting room.

A chair was overturned on the floor. Frederick lay partly underneath it, crimson in the face and making noises like a baby sea-lion. His sister was watching him with detached interest.

Deciding that, from the noise he was making, Frederick was not badly hurt, I picked up the chair and lifted him to his feet.

Surprised by this sudden action, Frederick stopped roaring and glared at me.

"She pushed me—" He pointed an accusing finger at Rosemary.

I was wholly on Rosemary's side. We girls must stick together, I thought, and besides, she really did look angelic in that little pink dress.

"Oh, I'm sure she didn't mean to," I said unwisely.

"She did. She did. I hate her!" roared Frederick, in a passion.

He made a sudden lunge at Rosemary who fled to the other side of the table, tripped over and fell full length to the floor, with her brother sprawling on top of her.

It was just as well that I'd had some slight experience with small children. Most of our farm workers at home had large families and didn't hesitate to bring them along when their mothers wanted to go to town to shop. I seemed to remember that there is always a short period of dead silence between falling down and the first howl, and that if you can step in at that moment and do something to divert the child's attention you may manage to cut short the howl.

As both children were squirming into a sitting position, mouths wide open, I grabbed the pile of magazines and comics from the table and threw them up in the air in all directions.

"Look," I cried. "A snowstorm!"

It worked. They were both on their feet in a flash, picking up the falling magazines and hurling them into the air again, chuckling with wild delight. "Woosh!" exulted Frederick, pudgy arms waving. Rosemary lisped, "Thnow! Thnow!" and joined enthusiastically in the fun.

But this couldn't go on. Somehow I must quieten them down and get back to the surgery as quickly as possible to help with the fillings. A scraping noise from the room above gave me inspiration. Mr. Pill—of course! He looked so benevolent; he simply must be the father of a large family, and probably a grandfather as well.

I picked Rosemary up and tucked her under my arm; she was as light as a bundle of goose feathers.

"Come upstairs and see what I've got to show you," I tempted Frederick, and up we went, Rosemary crowing with laughter, all her shyness of me gone, her brother scrambling up the stairs behind.

Mr. Pill was on his trestle, painting the ceiling in the front room. He made a magnificent sight up there, wielding his flat brush, slapping swaths of emulsion paint across the ceiling and crooning in his inappropriately high voice—still the bit about the Syrian Sea.

He looked down at our entry, swaying slightly on the trestle and for one dreadful moment I thought that he was going to overbalance, but of course he was far too much the professional for anything like that to happen. He straightened again with dignity.

"Please, Mr. Pill," I gasped, setting Rosemary on her feet, "could you possibly be an angel and keep an eye on these two for a few minutes? Dr. Holland's doing some fillings for their mother, and I ought to be in the surgery helping him."

Blessed Mr. Pill, his face broke into a beam above his huge white body. "Rosie! Freddie! What have you two rascals been up to, eh? Something bad, I'll be bound."

He began to climb down the ladder. "You get along miss, and I'll keep these two in order for you."

"Oh, thank you," I breathed and escaped downstairs, one hand to my dishevelled hair and the other trying to straighten my creased white coat. The chaos in the waiting room would have to wait until the main part of the exercise was completed in the surgery.

Then I stopped in my tracks, for just inside the door of the waiting room stood a tall, fair girl in jodhpurs and a cream silk shirt.

Charming, I thought bitterly. Another patient, the waiting room converted into a snowstorm, and me looking like an orphan of the storm!

But of course it couldn't be another patient. The front doorbell hadn't rung. Then how—?

Cool gray eyes looked me up and down and a cool clear voice said, "You must be the new girl from London?"

There are certain people you dislike at first sight. Most unreasonable, but there it is. For me, this girl was one of them.

"I am from London, yes." I turned the answer into a question.

"Don't be alarmed," she said smoothly. "I haven't broken in; I came the back way." Her glance took in the chaos in the waiting room and returned to me. "I take it Dr. Holland's busy?"

"He has a patient in the surgery," I said. To another sort of person I might have explained the condition of the waiting room, but not this one.

"I see. Will you tell him that I'll wait until he's finished."

"Certainly. Who shall I say it is?"

"Just say it's Val." She sauntered past me toward the back of the house, flicking her riding crop as she went.

I stood looking after her. There was no doubt she was very much at home in Ben Holland's establishment.

Well, and why not? It had nothing at all to do with me.

All the same, as I patted my hair straight and went into the surgery I had the feeling that, whatever Ben Holland's shortcomings, he didn't deserve a girl like that.

CHAPTER FIVE

Ben Holland had finished mixing the amalgam and was beginning to tackle the fillings by himself when I entered the surgery. I hurried and took the amalgam gun from his hand and he gave a little grunt, which I took to be of relief. To cope with an amalgam filling without an assistant to "feed" is about the most irritating and time-wasting operation a dentist can attempt, added to which is the danger that the amalgam may begin to set before the filling is finished and the contours trimmed up.

However, on this occasion I had returned in the nick of time and all went well.

"That's it, Mrs. Cartwright. Now, just give a last rinse out, please."

She obeyed, dabbed her mouth, and twisted her head round to me. "What happened? Are the kids all right?"

"Perfectly all right," I reassured her. "I left them upstairs watching the decorators at work. I'll go and bring them down when you're ready."

Frederick and Rosemary were having a marvelous time stirring the paint, closely supervised by Mr. Pill, who evidently had a firm but benevolent hand with children, as I had guessed.

"Time's up and Mom's ready for you," I told them. "Just one more stir each and then we'll go downstairs again. Perhaps Dr. Holland will give you a ride on the big chair."

Rosemary had her stir and then held out her thin little arms to be carried down again. I picked her up and cuddled her close; she was an angel, no doubt about that at all.

Halfway downstairs the angel turned into a demon, as angels will. I'd thought my hair was already in a mess, but it must have looked too tidy for Rosemary. She proceeded to bury both small paws in it and reduce my precious set to a bird's nest, crowing with glee.

"Stop it, you little wretch!" I was giggling helplessly, trying to extricate myself with one hand without dropping her down the stairs.

I heard the surgery door open and was aware dimly that Ben was standing there surveying the scene, but I could do nothing about it. It was, I realized, hardly the kind of calm and unflurried atmosphere so necessary in a dental practice. Somewhere along the line I'd failed badly. Oh well—

Mrs. Cartwright came out then, pounced on her daughter, scolding enthusiastically and lifted her out of my arms. At the same moment Frederick hurtled down the stairs demanding his right on the dental chair.

Ben took charge then, and it was positively masterly the way he coped with the two children without even raising his voice. Such is the power of authority, I thought weakly.

Peace and quiet reigned while he planted each child in turn on the chair, pumped it up high and then let down like an elevator. This had to be repeated three times in all, but when he said definitely, "Last turn now," neither child whined or argued. Five minutes later the whole Cartwright family were seen off the premises by me, in good order.

The family was in good order, that is, but certainly not me! From my point of view the first appointment in the Holland practice had proved more taxing and exhausting than a whole morning's work in the hushed and impressive consulting rooms in Manchester Square.

I went to the mirror over the mantelpiece and was horrified to see my flushed cheeks and shiny nose. My lipstick smeared and my hair was standing up in spikes. Rosemary had done her work of devastation very thoroughly; the result was far from the image of an assured and competent dental nurse.

I fished in my handbag for a comb. From behind me Ben Holland's voice remarked coolly, "Well, I warned you, didn't I?"

I felt hot and sticky and not in any mood to be needled. I said shortly, "I wasn't complaining."

He stood behind me and I saw his reflection over my shoulder in the mirror. I began to tug the comb through my hair.

"Rosemary has left you a keepsake," he said. "Hold still a minute and I'll remove it."

I felt the touch of his fingers on my neck and it was so unexpected that a shiver passed down my spine. I spun around as if I'd had an electric shock.

"What—?"

"Here you are." He held out a feather, a speckled hen's feather. "Rosemary carries a supply of these around in her pocket. She made me a present of one last time they came. You can consider yourself honored. She only presents them to people she likes, so her mother told me."

I took the feather from him, feeling my poise oozing farther and farther away every moment. I couldn't find it in my heart to blame Rosemary for putting me in the ridiculous and humiliating position of having feathers extracted from my hair, because Rosemary was undoubtedly a poppet.

Ben was smiling now, his maddeningly superior smile. That put the finishing touch to my indignation.

"I assure you I do feel honored," I said, and, with some horror, heard myself add, "It's always pleasant to know that somebody appreciates one."

The smile disappeared. "Don't be childish, Kate. I thought we agreed to tolerate each other for a couple of weeks, so we might as well keep on terms of truce at least."

He turned his back on me and walked away. I tucked the feather away in my handbag and finished tidying my hair with hands that weren't quite steady.

At that moment the door opened and Val Whoever-it-was appeared. The way she looked at me gave me a shock—just as if someone had pointed a gun at me. Oh dear, I'd forgotten all about her, waiting out there. She wouldn't like that one little bit.

She flashed a smile at Ben. "May I come in? I heard your patients leave."

"Val! Of course, come in. Delighted to see you. Is this a professional visit or just to brighten my day?"

"Both, I hope." She dimpled at him. "I've brought you a note from Daddy about that patient you referred to him—Mrs. Barber. He says he'd like to have a chat with you about it. Also he's had the information through from the hospital about that Nurse Marsh he found for you. He'll tell you about her himself, but he thinks she'll be quite suitable for you. She hasn't had any dental experience, but she was S.R.N. before she gave up nursing so she should soon pick it up. I mean, there's not all that much to learn about dental work, is there?"

Ben pulled a wry face. "You might be surprised if you knew how much. Wouldn't she, Kate? This is Kate Moorcroft, Val. You remember I told you she was coming from London to help me out temporarily. Kate, Val Deering. Val's father is our local medico and my very good friend."

"How do you do," I said politely.

Val Deering gave me a brilliant smile. "So lucky you could come to help Ben out! I'm afraid you'll find us very rustic after the big city. We haven't even got a movie house. I hope you won't be too bored."

Ben turned his blue gaze on me, eyes narrowed, a faint quirk at the corners of his mouth. "Will you be too bored, Kate?"

It wasn't fair, I thought, to take advantage of Val Deering's presence to score off me. But I wasn't going to give him the satisfaction of knowing that the shot had gone home, so I said composedly, "I'm sure I shall enjoy being here very much."

I heard him draw in his breath quickly and I had time to think, "This is turning into a fencing match," and then the telephone rang and I escaped gratefully into the hall.

"Good morning, Dr. Holland's practice," I said in my best receptionist's voice.

A masculine voice replied mockingly, "Good morning, Mr. Hugo Whipple's residence. How are you, Katy love?"

"Hugo!" I breathed. "How did you—"

"You left the phone number here, all written out carefully on a piece of paper beside the phone. Careless of you, sweetie."

"Oh," I said. From his tone I knew that he thought I'd left it here on purpose; he was no doubt quite accustomed to feminine ploys of that sort. I wasn't going to argue about it.

"I've only just dragged myself out of bed," Hugo said. "I thought I deserved to sleep in after all the fun and games yesterday. You all right, Kate?"

"I'm fine," I said. I didn't know what to say next. Hugo, in his elegant house in St. John's Wood, seemed to be speaking from another world.

"Good. Now I'll tell you my plans. I've been on to that garage and they've promised to have the car ready for me by Friday, so I'll come up and collect it then. I've got some people to see in Stratford about a tour, so I can stay overnight and work that in at the same time. That'll leave us free to hit the high spots together on Friday night. How does that strike you?"

"Lovely," I said. Out of the corner of my eye I could see the door beside me open a fraction and I caught a glimpse of Ben's white coat. I wondered how he would view a nurse who chatted to her boyfriends during surgery hours.

"Sure you're all right?" Hugo said. "You don't sound very full of joy."

"Of course I am. We've just finished a rather hectic appointment, that's all. My head's still whirling around."

"That fellow's putting too much on you," Hugo said darkly. "I told you he was the slave-driving type. Look, Katy, shall I come up and rescue you? You've only to say the word. There's nothing to make you stay there, you know. You can put it right with old Hartington when he comes back. Say the country gave you hay fever, or something."

I laughed. "Oh, I really don't need rescuing, thanks all the same, Hugo. But I'll look forward to seeing you on Friday."

I heard him begin to say something about my being an elusive little something or other; then the surgery door opened wide and Ben appeared with Val. Simultaneously the front door bell rang, and I had to say goodbye hurriedly to Hugo and hang up.

I hoped he wouldn't think I'd been lukewarm about his invitation, but there wasn't time to worry about that until later. The man on the doorstep, in farm-worker's clothes, had a swelling like a tennis ball on his lower jaw; obviously his need was of greater importance than my private affairs.

Chloe was tying up the clematis that trailed over the front porch when I arrived at the farm late that afternoon.

"Hullo," she greeted me, draping strands of raffia across her shoulder. "Where's Ben? Didn't he drive you home?"

"I took the bus," I told her. "Ben asked me to say that he's gone to Dr. Deering's and he probably won't be in for supper."

Chloe climbed down the ladder. "Damn," she said, distinctly and forcibly. She glanced over her shoulder, pulling a face at me. "Sorry, don't take any notice. You'll know by now that I'm one of those awful people who don't stop to think before they speak. Well, come along in, supper's all ready. There'll just be the two of us; John's still working in the fields."

As we went into the house together I asked her if there was any news from the hospital.

"Yes, I drove over this afternoon and they let me see Bobby for a few minutes. He's feeling very sorry for himself, poor boy, but at least there doesn't seem to be any damage that won't mend in time. He's got lots of bruises, a cut on his cheek and his leg is fractured. They won't keep him in hospital longer than they need to; then he'll go back to his home in Chipping Norton and wait for the leg to heal."

I said, "I'm awfully glad it wasn't any worse; I've been feeling badly about it."

Chloe shook her head. "You don't need to. He told me that he knew it was entirely his own fault. Apparently he'd been to see a girlfriend after he left here and he was speeding—whether from the sheer joy of life or so as not to miss his supper at home I wouldn't know."

We parted at the kitchen door and I went upstairs to wash and tidy up after the day's work. When I came down again Chloe was piling two healthy-looking servings of ham and eggs on to our plates.

"You don't mind eating out here 'as family'?" she said as she drained the potatoes. "No, of course you don't. You're the sort of nice person who fits in, although you're so elegant and city-civilized." There was laughter in her voice.

"Am I?" I sat down at the big table, spread with a blue cloth. "Am I really?" I suppose it was what I'd been working at for three whole years—becoming what Chloe called city-civilized, I mean—but until I came back to my country roots I'd never known whether I'd really succeeded or not. It seemed now that I had, though I wasn't even sure whether I was glad.

"Oh yes, of course you are. Your clothes, your hair, the way you speak, everything about you! Oh, I know the country life isn't as 'cut off' as it used to be, but even these days there's a big difference. I think Ben was a little apprehensive about expecting you to work for him, after London, but I told him not to be idiotic, that anyone could see that you weren't a bit snobby." She sighed and set dishes of peas and new potatoes on the table. "Men are such kids, aren't they? They always have to be worrying about their poor little pride."

I glanced at Chloe's freckled face. Uninhibited she might be, perhaps too much so, but there was something very endearing and attractive about her frankness. There was a good deal of realistic common sense, too.

"I certainly want to fit in here," I said. "And I'm glad you think I do."

"I meant it. I knew straight away you were the sort of person I could be 'easy' with, and I felt so thankful. I hate having to stand on ceremony with people. You know?"

I couldn't help thinking of Val Deering. "Yes," I said, "I know."

Chloe was uncharacteristically silent for a few moments and I wondered if she, too, had someone special in mind.

Then she pushed the dish of peas across to me. "Help yourself—all grown on the premises. Now, tell me what you thought of Ben's practice and how you got on together—"

We'd finished our supper and were lingering over our coffee when John Garrett entered the kitchen, hot and tired and smelling of hay; saying that he must eat something before he could do another stroke of work. The two men were willing to carry on until the light failed, he said, so long as they could have some food.

Chloe jumped up immediately and began to slap slices of cold ham between great hunks of bread. I finished my coffee and left them packing it all into a basket to take out to the fields.

All this was such a familiar routine to me, especially at hay-making time, that I went up to my room assailed by the nostalgia that was beginning to form a kind of permanent background to my stay. I hadn't relished the idea of returning to the country, but I hadn't thought it would be quite so bad. Everything reminded me of things I had decided to put out of my life for good.

I wrote a long letter to Louise, stamped it, and decided to walk to the end of the lane, where I'd noticed a mailbox.

There was nobody downstairs, but as I went out of the house I saw Chloe in the distance, engaged in what looked like shutting up the hen-houses for the night. She saw me, waved and I waved back.

The mailbox was attached to the telegraph pole, at the point where the lane joined the main road. I mailed my letter and paused, wondering whether I should go for a brisk walk before bed to make sure that I was tired enough to fall asleep immediately. But there were no footpaths on the main road and I didn't fancy walking against oncoming traffic in the quickly-gathering dusk, so I turned around and retraced my steps along the lane.

Quite soon I came to a gate. To a country-born person a field gate is always a temptation. You simply must go and lean on it and see what there is to see on the other side.

On the other side of this one I saw a flock of sheep. Some had already settled down for the night. Others were still tucking in to their never-ending meal, moving lazily as they munched.

The evening air was warm against my cheeks; even the rough wood of the gate felt warm after the long hours of sunshine. I stood there listening to the soft ruminative thud of chewing, letting my thoughts free-wheel, the damp grass licking coolly at my ankles.

The noise beside me was only a slight rustling in the hedge, but I jumped, smothering a cry. One country thing I'd never learned to love is a rat. I was just about to make a bolt for it when I heard another noise that certainly wasn't made by a rat. The sound was a faint, plaintive bleating.

A sheep stuck in the hedge. Well, that was quite a different matter and one that I could deal with. From the lane side of the hedge I could see nothing, so I climbed over the gate, landed in soft earth and peered down into the thick base of the hedge.

As I had thought, it was a sheep—or rather a fairly large lamb. The poor stupid thing must have walked into the hedge as innocently as a fly will enter a spider's web and found it just as impossible to get out again.

"You old silly," I told it, giving it an encouraging pat on its rump, which was toward me. "Now keep still, will you, while I see what's holding you. What could your mama be thinking of to let you get into a pickle like this?"

Oh, for a flashlight, I thought, and wondered whether it was worth going back to the farm to get one. Exploring gingerly, I thrust my hand into the base of the hedge and found that the lamb's front legs were held fast in a twisted mass of branches and roots.

"We'll just have to try to pull you out," I said, standing astride him and putting my arms round his woolly body. "Now—heave!"

No good. The legs didn't move. But the lamb was bleating and struggling now, very frightened indeed. I couldn't leave the poor thing now that I'd begun—I'd just have to get him free somehow.

"Never mind, pet," I encouraged him. "Let's have another go."

I circled his body again and pulled as hard as I could.

Suddenly there was sharp crack beneath me as the undergrowth snapped. The lamb came out backward and I shot forward over his back into the hedge and lay there, gasping.

I could hear the lamb galloping back across the field to his mother, bleating wildly. "Beast!" I called after him. "You might at least have stopped to say thank you!"

Painfully I crawled backward out of the hedge and heard a voice calling me. I recognized it as Ben Holland's.

"Kate! Are you there?"

"Yes, I'm here, in the field."

A thump as he vaulted the gate and landed on the other side. I looked up to see a dark form looming above me. "What for Pete's sake do you think you're doing there?"

Impossible to be dignified while grovelling on all fours in a hedge.

"Salvage operation," I explained briefly. "Lamb stuck in hedge. He tossed me over his head when he shot out. No doubt a Spanish bull in some previous existence. Ow!" I winced as he grasped me under the arms and pulled me to my feet. "That hedge is good and thorny."

He took my hands and peered at them in the dusk. "Good lord, girl, you're bleeding. You crazy child—fancy thinking you could yank a great sheep out of a hedge all on your own. Why didn't you come back to the house for help?" He sounded angry.

"He wasn't a great sheep, he was a middle-sized lamb," I retorted, slightly nettled by his tone. "And he was bleating," I added.

He ignored that. "You must get these scratches attended to straight away. Never ignore scratches when you're in the country. That's what you city people do, and then you wonder why you get poisoned fingers—or worse."

I began to simmer gently. Insufferable, I thought. Superior. Patronizing. You city people, indeed!

"Of course I won't ignore them," I told him stiffly. "I

may be only a moronic city girl, but at least I have that much intelligence."

He made a small exasperated noise. "Chloe asked me to come and look for you," he told me. "She saw you leave and wondered if you'd got lost. Look this gate's padlocked. Can you manage to climb over?"

The words were considerate, but the tone he spoke them in wasn't. He swung his legs across and stood on the other side of the gate, holding out his hands to me. "Steady now, don't go twisting your ankle."

It was the final straw. That I, Kate Moorcroft, who almost before I could walk had been climbing gates, and apple trees, and hay-stacks, and everything else around a farm that could be climbed, should be subjected to such indignity! Twist my ankle, indeed!

I ignored the hands he was holding out, swivelled my legs over the top of the gate and jumped.

Unfortunately I'd forgotten that climbing gates is a thing you need to keep in practice for. I'd also forgotten that I was still wearing the shoes I'd worn all day, and that they had heels; not very high heels, but high enough to throw me off balance as I landed.

I staggered, clutching wildly at the nearest thing to hand, which was, of course, Ben. I heard him mutter something and his arms came around me very strong and firm. I leaned against him, trying to get my balance. His body was firm, too, under his light shirt. For a moment we stood together like that. I heard his quick intake of breath and had the craziest notion that he was holding me against him on purpose; that in a moment he would bend his head and kiss me, that it was all inevitable and meant to be.

How absurd can you get? He let me go; he almost pushed me away. "That," he said, "wasn't clever at all."

I think part of me must have landed on a stone because my left foot was hurting like mad. The scratches on my arms were hurting too. But what was hurting most of all was my pride.

Without a word I turned and stalked ahead of him up the lane to the house.

In the kitchen he examined my arms under the light. "Good lord, you *have* made a mess of yourself! Stick your arms under cold water and I'll go and get a first aid kit and bandage you up."

I did as he told me. The water was icy cold as it ran over my bare arms and hands—as bracing as Ben Holland's tone of voice had been.

I smiled grimly, watching the earth being washed away from the long red scratches on my wrists. Why, I wondered, did Ben resent me so much? Why did he take every opportunity to "get at" me? It couldn't be simply because I was (he thought) "city" while he was "country". He surely wasn't as childish as that.

Ah well, I thought, I'd never know him well enough to find out. It was no good letting myself be bothered about it. I couldn't change Ben Holland's attitude to me, but I could, I decided, resolve not to be stung into resenting it.

That, I was sure, was how Louise would react to a similar situation (although Louise, of course, would never be stupid enough to get herself into such a situation!). That was how I was going to react from now on.

So do your worst, Dr. Ben Holland! You will not break inside my defenses again.

But oh, roll on Friday, and Hugo!

CHAPTER SIX

I got the impression that Chloe had been up for hours when I arrived downstairs at a quarter to eight next morning. The kitchen floor was washed; there were fresh creamy dew-spangled roses, in a blue bowl on the windowsill; a wonderful yeasty smell came from a huge brown crock, covered with a cloth, that stood near the stove.

I sniffed appreciatively. "Don't tell me that you bake your own bread! It smells gorgeous."

Chloe nodded, eyes dancing. "Twice a week. John's mother gave me a recipe that cuts out all the hard work and you don't have to knead it at all. But I don't always do it that way," she added. "I rather enjoy kneading when I have time. There's something very satisfying in digging your hands into lovely warm dough. Childish, I suppose. What do you fancy for breakfast, Kate? There's cereal, bacon and egg, toast and marmalade, and coffee or tea."

"Just toast and coffee, please." I remembered our huge breakfasts in the old days at home. Then I thought of the apartment in London and how Louise and I padded around in our dressing gowns nibbling thin wisps of melba toast. Louise never had any appetite for breakfast and somehow I'd managed to lose the one I'd brought with me from the country to London three years ago.

Chloe's mouth rounded into an O of maternal concern. "You ought to have more than that. You shouldn't work all morning without something inside you. I didn't press you yesterday because you'd been upset with the accident and everything, but I wish you'd have something more than just toast today."

"Don't worry the girl, Chloe. Kate hasn't got a country appetite, you know." Ben's voice came coolly from behind me and I turned to see him coming from the scullery, wearing rubber boots and an old tweed coat. He'd evidently been up early helping with the outside jobs.

What an infuriating man he was! He could make the simplest remark sound like a biting criticism. Or was I being stupidly defensive and lacking in a sense of humor?

He sat down opposite me at the table. "Good morning, Kate. Any coffee left?"

"Good morning. Yes, plenty." I sat up very straight and poured him a cup of coffee in a businesslike way, endeavoring not to look in the least like one of the pallid little London bed-sitter girls that John Betjeman's poem brought to life so marvelously. That was obviously the impression that Ben had of me.

He thanked me absently and glanced across to his sister at the sink. "John's having trouble with that water bowl again."

"Oh dear, is he? I'll go and see if I can help." She was drying her hands hastily. "Look, Kate, I've cut your sandwiches for lunch. They're on the hall table, with a bag of apples. Forgive me if I dash out now, won't you? John's a bit pressed without Bobby. Don't work too hard, the two of you."

She gave us both a brilliant smile and disappeared through the scullery and back door at a run.

"Chloe," remarked Ben, finishing his coffee and standing up, "is the nearest thing to perpetual motion that I know. You nearly ready to start, Kate? We'd better get going as soon as we can. The cleaning woman comes in this morning and she usually gets there about half past eight. You'd better let her do the cleaning jobs in the surgery today if your arm feels at all sore. How is it this morning?"

"Fine," I said. "It's nothing at all, really."

"Let me look."

I pushed up the sleeve of my thin white blouse. He took

my wrist firmly in his hand and examined my arm. "H'm, I'm not so sure. It looks a bit red and angry around the edges of the bandage. You'd better see Dr. Deering as soon as you can this morning; he'll probably give you a shot of penicillin or some such."

"Oh, I'm sure there's no need to worry about it," I said, drawing away from his touch.

"I'll give Val a call and arrange it as soon as we get to Lambton," he said just as if I hadn't spoken.

Again that calm assumption of authority! Just like his godfather, I thought sourly.

Then common sense took over. After all, he was acting in my interest, wasn't he? And a tweak of cynicism added that he wouldn't want his temporary nurse to be laid up and unable to work.

"Very well, if you think it best," I said meekly. That should be submissive enough even for Dr. Benjamin Holland, B.D.S. But he didn't reply. He was pulling off his rubber boots with his back to me. Ah well, there were some people you just couldn't please!

In silence I went upstairs for my coat and purse.

The silence continued as we drove along the lane and turned into the main road, five minutes later. It was a marvelous summer morning; already a heat haze was shimmering over the fields and the sky was a deep blue with not a single cloud to be seen. Later on it was going to be very hot.

I glanced up at Ben's profile. While he was driving I had a chance to study it without his noticing. It was a strong face, I decided: the deep-set blue eyes, the well-shaped nose, the firm, independent set of the mouth and chin. It was the face of a man who would never be pushed; who would always want things his own way.

Somehow, though, it didn't seem to me the face of a man who would treat an employee the way he was treating me, which I considered petty and unfair. I wished I knew why.

I cudgelled my brain for something to say and at last found it. "Do you think," I said, "that it would be in order for me to send Bobby something next time any of you goes to the hospital? He wouldn't take it amiss?

The dark eyebrows lifted a fraction. "I imagine he'd be delighted," he said drily. "Why should he take it amiss?"

I hesitated. "Well, I was in the car that he crashed into and I thought perhaps—"

"That he would be projecting the blame onto you in some way? Oh no, Bobby's not that sort. He knows quite well it was his own fault and he faces up to it. He's a good kid."

"That's fine then; I must admit I've been feeling badly about it ever since it happened. I suppose you always wonder, when you've been involved in an accident, if there was anything at all you could have done to prevent it. Not that there was," I added quickly. "Hugo's a marvelous driver."

"I'm sure he is," Ben said.

He didn't remove his eyes from their straight-ahead stare at the road. Silence seemed about to fall again and I pressed on, "I wonder what he'd like? Chloe took fruit, I know, and I expect his family keep him supplied with things to nibble and flowers and so on. Do you know if he has any special hobby?"

He negotiated a sharp bend carefully. "Yes, as it happens, I do know. He's very keen on bird photography."

"Oh, good, I'll remember that. Perhaps there's a book I could get for him."

After that the silence did fall and I couldn't think of anything else that would break it. So I sat and watched the fields and hedges gradually merge into the outskirts of Lambton, where modern houses were spreading farther and farther out into the country, as they are in most small towns. Somehow these didn't seem out of place; there was nothing brash about the mellow bricks and the well-trimmed lawns with their newly-planted shrubs and infant weeping willow trees.

All the houses looked very expensive, I thought. Perhaps Ben was right in choosing to practice here, in a developing small town. But I still wondered why he wasn't heading for the very top of his profession in London. I had no doubt at all that he could get there if he wanted to. Especially with Uncle Geoffrey Hartington behind him!

It was one of those days that worsens as they go on. Mrs. Bates, the cleaning woman, turned up 20 minutes late, began her work in the kitchen, for some reason, and was still polishing the waiting room floor when the first patients arrived. This, I thought, was very poor organization. When I was showing the first patient out and Mrs. Bates was still on her hands and knees doing the "surrounds" in the waiting room I touched her shoulder and whispered, "Would you come out into the hall for a moment, please?"

She struggled to her feet, breathing hard, wispy hair dangling over a thin, harassed face.

When she had trailed out after me I said briskly, "Look, Mrs. Bates, leave what you haven't finished in the waiting room, now the patients have begun to come in. Is there anything else you could do instead?"

She put on that particular mulish expression that said, without words, Who does she think she is, ordering me about?

"I always do the rooms in that order," she announced huffily. "I've been doing for Dr. White for nine years, and he's never said anything in all that time."

I smiled at her hopefully. "Yes—well—just for this morning, change them around, there's a dear."

Her lips were pursed, her pale cheeks had a spot of red in each one. She was evidently taking umbrage in no uncertain manner. For one awful moment I thought she was going to make a scene. But she thought better of it and retired haughtily to the rear quarters, grabbing her tin of polish and her bedraggled dusters as if she would defend them with her life. I thought of the squad of cleaners that moved into Manchester Square and whisked through their work as soon as we'd finished for the day. I felt, for once, quite sorry for Ben Holland if this was the best domestic help he could muster.

I went back to the waiting room.

"Mrs. Fellowes please," I said, and two women rose immediately to their feet. One was short, plump and cheerful-looking in a rosy linen suit. The other was tall, beaky and tweedy.

"I think," said the beaky one, in a "county" accent "that there is some mistake. My appointment is for nine-thirty. I always have the nine-thirty appointment." She proffered an appointment card, just as the plump one was doing the same thing, saying, "My name is Fellowes and my appointment is certainly for nine-thirty. My husband is outside in the car and has to be in Warwick on business by half-past ten, so I can't keep him waiting on any account.

I took the cards, one in each hand. There was no doubt about it—both appointments were for nine-thirty on Tuesday June 15th. This, then, was what Ben had meant when he said that the last girl was "a dead loss."

"I'm very sorry, but I'm afraid there's been some mistake," I stalled. "If you'll excuse me for a moment I'll check the appointment book."

I went back to the surgery and showed the cards to Ben. "Two appointments for the same time," I told him. "One's for a Mrs. Fellowes and the other—" I consulted the cards "—for a Miss Ponsonby-Foster. They both look ready to give battle."

He took the cards, drawing in his breath between his

teeth. "That girl! I'd like to— Oh well, what's the use?" He examined both cards, frowning. "Ponsonby-Foster's the uncrowned queen of Lambton and a holy terror. Runs the whole place—everyone's terrified of her. Fellowes is the wife of a managing director—oozing with money and influence. I can't afford to antagonize either of 'em, and I don't want any fur and feathers flying about either."

It was my job, not his, to straighten out bungled appointments, even though I hadn't been responsible for the bungling. "I'll do the best I can," I said and, with a sinking heart, returned to the waiting room.

I was going to need every bit of the tact I'd learned in Manchester Square, but somehow I had to cope.

I'd already decided that the plump Mrs. Fellowes had first claim—morally, at least, as her name was entered in the appointment book—so I hustled her into the surgery and returned to try to placate the dragon.

Miss Ponsonby-Foster was standing as stiff as a flag-pole. The way she looked down her beaky nose at me would have made me crumple a year ago. But not now.

"Dr. Holland is most upset about this, Miss Ponsonby-Foster," I said in my best Manchester Square voice. "The mistake was made by the previous surgery attendant, and he hopes very much that you'll forgive him. He had to take Mrs. Fellowes first as her name was in the appointment book and the preparations for her treatment had already been made. Also," I added, wondering whether I was, perhaps, laying it on too thickly, "I think he knew that you would understand and make allowances."

The implication being that Mrs. Fellowes wouldn't.

I was taking a chance and I knew it. Miss Ponsonby-Foster would have been perfectly justified in resenting my method, if she recognized it for what it was. But when you're used to dealing with what Ben Holland had called Top Patients you begin to learn a thing or two about human nature; to recognize which are the really big people and which ones have to be reassured all the time that they are big. Somehow I guessed that the dragon was in the latter category.

Fortunately for me I was right. The dragon flicked a speck of imaginary dust from the lapel of her tweed coat looking so much like a picture of a mythical animal with its scraggy claw raised that I had to suppress a terrible urge to giggle.

"Naturally I understand," she said in a very superior tone and sat down and picked up a copy of *The Countryman*.

"Would you care for a cup of coffee while you're waiting?" I suggested, deciding that dealing out V.I.P. treatment to Miss Ponsonby-Foster was probably of more importance at the moment than helping in the surgery.

"Thank you, child, but no." She inclined her head in gracious dismissal.

Breathing a huge sigh of relief, I went back to the surgery. Ben had got Mrs. Fellowes into the chair and I fetched a bib and fastened it around her neck. Over her head his glance met mine and his eyebrows rose questioningly. I smiled in reassurance and raised my two thumbs.

He nodded, let out a deep breath, and began Mrs. Fellowes's treatment.

I had a moment of triumph. One up for Uncle Geoff's "treasure", I thought with a hidden grin. Perhaps I was being some use to him after all. Perhaps he'd even tell me so. ("I must admit I was wrong about you, Kate. I thought you'd consider yourself too superior to wade into the chaos and confusion of a practice like this. But you've been wonderful, and I don't know what I'd have done without you.")

Ben glanced over his shoulder, roughly in my direction. "Porcelain silicate, shade 8," he said crisply.

So much for daydreams! I braced myself, deciding that

Uncle Geoff must have spoilt me, with his ready word of appreciation, his graceful little compliments. I certainly wouldn't get either from his godson. Satisfaction in a job well done must be its own reward here, I thought pompously, and went about mixing the filling material.

Pride, of course, still comes before a fall, just as it always has done. We'd finished Mrs. Fellowes and Miss Ponsonby-Foster. I made tea for Mr. Pill and George upstairs and coffee for Ben and myself. When I carried it into the surgery, he was looking dark with annoyance.

"I've had a complaint from Mrs. Bates," he said.

"Mrs. Bates? Oh, the cleaning woman."

"Yes, the cleaning woman. *The* cleaning woman," he added with heavy meaning. "The one and only cleaning woman it's possible to get." His brows drew together grimly. "I've no doubt that in London getting a cleaning woman presents no problems—always providing you can afford to pay her—but in a small town like this it's a very different matter. I simply can't afford to lose Mrs. Bates, so please try to be a bit more tactful, will you?"

I could feel myself bristling. Tactful! When I'd just soothed an infuential dragon with a perfectly legitimate grievance! Tactful! I was being kept on the run from chairside to front door to telephone to waiting room and back again, doing at least two people's work, if not three—and managing to keep pace with it.

My blood began to simmer gently. "Really, I do think—" I began hotly.

There was a tap on the door and Val Deering's face appeared around it. Her prepared expression of diffidence changed into one of cosy intimacy when she saw that there was no patient in the chair.

She came into the surgery, very businesslike today in crisp blue linen, two shades darker than her eyes. "Hullo, Ben, is it all right to come in? Daddy asked me to bring this report over to you."

She handed him a paper and for a moment her pale eyes rested on me. "Oh yes, and I nearly forgot, he can see Miss—er—your nurse now, if you can spare her. He was sorry he couldn't manage it when you called earlier but he had an urgent call."

She smiled at me very sweetly. "It's just along the road—you'll see the plate on the railings. Go straight in and knock at the surgery door. My father's expecting you."

In the hurly-burly I'd forgotten all about Ben's threat to send me to see Dr. Deering. He must have phoned while I was coping with the dragon.

He nodded to me in dismissal. "Run along then, Kate. Val will have your coffee and you can make another cup for yourself when you get back." He offered her one of the two cups I'd just brought in on a tray. "Sit down, Val. I've got a few minutes before the next patient. And thanks very much for arranging for your father to see Kate. Very kind of you."

"Kind? When you asked me? Oh, Ben!" There was nothing cool about her now; she was all warmth, with a laugh hidden in her tone of voice.

I left shutting the surgery door behind me.

Dr. Deering was a big, hearty man with a booming voice. He welcomed me in a friendly way, examined the scratches on my arm and took a benevolent and amused interest in my account of how I had acquired them.

"And how are you making out in that tooth-puller's establishment up the road?" he inquired jovially as he slapped a new dressing on my arm. "A bit of a change after London, eh? We're all glad to have a young man there, I can tell you. It was getting too much altogether for poor old White. He carried on for five years longer than he should have. The whole place was in chaos when he finally collapsed and Ben Holland took it over. He's done wonders with the place in a couple of months but there's still a lot to straighten out. Still, he's a bright lad and he's got ideas; I think he'll make a good show of it."

It was pleasant to be spoken to like a human being and an equal. I warmed to Dr. Deering. "It does seem a very busy practice," I ventured.

"Aye, there's room for two dentists in Lambton; it's expanding quickly. A partnership practice is the thing these days and that's what it may come to in the end; but it's early yet and Ben's got a lot to make up his mind about." He scribbled a prescription and handed it to me. "Take this along to Farthings; that's the drugstore on the corner by the traffic lights. That should take care of any possible infection, but come in and see me again if you're in any doubt."

He smiled kindly at me as I left.

After that friendly little interlude it was quite a letdown to see Val standing on the doorstep with Ben and realize how easy it was for a nice man to have an absolutely awful daughter.

As if to reproach me for my dark thoughts she waved gaily when she saw me coming. "There you are, Kate. Did you find the place all right and did Daddy fix you up?" She was all sweetness and light now, for some unknown reason. "What a nasty thing to happen, but it was very noble of you to rush to the rescue of one of John's precious lambs. Ben's just been telling me all about it."

I can imagine, I thought tetchily. And no doubt they'd had a good laugh together at the expense of ignorant city girls who make fools of themselves in the country. That, I suppose, was why Val Deering could now afford to be patronizingly affable to me. Oh dear, I was in a bad mood and I was being a cat about the girl. I must snap out of it.

Murmuring something vaguely polite, I hurried past them into the surgery to prepare for the next patient.

The day got hotter and hotter and more and more hectic as it went on. The ten-thirty appointment was a quarter of an hour late and we never quite made up the time. Then, just before the end of the morning session, a waitress from the White Hart turned up with toothache that meant emergency treatment. Finally we both had to eat Chloe's sandwiches standing up so that we could begin the afternoon list of appointments on time.

That was how it went all day. Patient followed patient. Beneath my white coat, my blouse clung damply to my back. The soles of my sandals kept sticking to the rubber mat that surrounded the dental chair. I worked like one of those speeded-up old films: mixing fillings, clearing up, sterilizing, waiting on Ben while he operated, washing glasses, attending to the patients, answering the phone, making appointments—

After I'd shown the last patient to the door I sat down at the desk, facing the formidable pile of cards and forms needing attention. My head ached with weariness and my feet felt about three sizes too large for my shoes.

Ben had worked imperturbably through the day. If he felt the heat he hadn't said so or showed any reaction to it. Now he was quietly making minor adjustments to the X-ray machine.

In similar circumstances I knew what Dr. Hartington would have done. He'd have flopped into the dental chair and said, "Kate love, that was one hell of an afternoon. How about a cuppa? Look, you relax and I'll call Withers to rustle one up for us." Withers was the caretaker and general factotum at Manchester Square.

Tea would have arrived on a tray. There would have been an atmosphere of harmony and a word of appreciation. All my tiredness would have evaporated in a few minutes and I'd have been ready and willing to start all over again to work through another such afternoon.

But then of course Dr. Hartington was a human being.

I looked over at Ben's straight back and the dark hair that fell forward over his wide brow, which was creased into a frown of concentration. All of a sudden I longed wickedly to say something that would get underneath his guard.

"That," I said, "was the last patient."

He glanced briefly towards me. "Yes."

"It's been a busy day," I said.

"Very busy."

"Hot and tiring," I continued doggedly.

His eyebrows went up a little, but he didn't rise to the bait. "Very," he agreed, and picked up a mini-screw-driver.

Well, I had very little to lose.

"Dr. Holland," I said, "may I ask you something?"

He did look faintly surprised at that, but he went on with his unscrewing. "Go ahead," he said.

I wished there were time to pick my words but I had to plunge ahead now. "I've worked here for two days now. The practice, and you, and everything, is quite new to me. I think the least you can do is to give me some idea of how I'm doing—whether I'm giving satisfaction, I think the term is."

There was a nasty little silence. Then he said, "I'm not sure I like your tone, Kate. Are you trying to pick a quarrel with me? I thought we agreed to tolerate each other."

"If we did," I said, "then I don't think you're doing your part. I don't expect praise and encouragement from you. Anyway it's fairly obvious that I wouldn't get it if I did. But I do think you might at least give me something to go on—tell me if I'm doing all right. Apart from my *faux pas* with Mrs. Bates, that is."

He shot me an exaggeratedly ironic look. "Oh yes, you're doing all right. You're doing simply magnifi-cently. You've demonstrated at every turn just what may be expected of a fully-trained, experienced, resourceful, efficient dental nurse. The kind of dental nurse, in fact, that my godfather can afford to employ. That was the object of the exercise, wasn't it?"

I said crossly, "You're talking in riddles now. I'm tired and I've had enough. I'm sorry if it's going to let you down, but I think I'm going back to London tomorrow.

He said calmly, "That's fine with me."

"I should never have come in the first place," I said, deflated in spite of myself.

"No, you shouldn't. I quite agree. Ah well, it's a bit hard on you, I must admit, but if you take on someone else's dirty work you must be prepared to accept the consequences, you know."

"Someone else's dirty work?" I stared at him, absolutely incredulous. He went on with his screwing very carefully. "What in the world are you talking about?"

He stopped then, and looked straight at me. I saw contempt in his eyes and I didn't like it at all. "As if you didn't know," he said.

I took a long, unsteady breath. "I assure you I don't know. I haven't a clue what you're talking about. I think the least you can do after making such an atrocious statement is to explain it." Funny how stilted you can sound when you're really hurt.

Up to then he had hardly seemed to be taking me seriously, but now he was. Deliberately he put down the screwdriver and came over to where I was sitting—rather limply, and humiliatingly close to tears now I'd aired my grievances.

"You mean—that Uncle Geoff didn't put you up to all this?"

He spoke very slowly; in contrast to my somewhat childish display he seemed to be keeping tight hold of himself.

I felt my body drooping. It no longer seemed any fun to

try to get my own back on Ben Holland. "Nobody," I said exhaustedly, "put me up to anything. I've just been doing my best to help you, as I said I would. I don't know what you're talking about."

There was a long, long silence. I supposed he was wondering whether to believe me or not. By that time I didn't care much either way.

Then the phone rang in the hall. Instinctively I moved to get out of the chair, but he gently pushed me back into it.

"I'll get it," he said.

I don't know how long he was away. I could hear his voice in the hall but I didn't listen to what he was saying. I was wondering how I could get to Leamington in the morning to catch a train to London. And I was thinking longingly of the apartment, Louise's cool reasonableness, and of Hugo, who treated me like a woman.

Ben returned. "That was Chloe on the phone," he said. "It seemed the Vicar's wife's fallen off a chair and hurt her leg. Chloe has to go around there to help because she's got three small children, so there won't be any supper for us tonight. She suggested I might take you to the White Hart to eat. They have quite decent food. Will you come, Kate? I'd like you to."

I looked up at him helplessly. He was smiling at me now, crinkles fanning out beside the deep-set, brilliantly blue eyes. To be on the receiving end of a smile that packed so many volts was very disturbing.

"Come on," he said and took both my hands to pull me to my feet. "Come and sample the White Hart's *scampi suprême*. Just," he added, "to show you've forgiven me."

And that, I thought, was all the apology I was likely to get. Ben Holland wasn't the type to grovel—not that I'd have wanted him to.

I could feel my mouth relaxing into a grin. "Scampi?" I said. "Truly?"

"Cross my heart. And I'll stand you a champagne cocktail to pep up your appetite."

"What is this?" I said, "a bribe?" I felt suddenly gay and lighthearted. I suppose that's the reaction you get when you meet with friendliness after hostility.

Suddenly he was quite serious. "I prefer to call it reparation," he said. "I've been very stupid. Will you come?"

"I've never been known to refuse scampi when offered."

"And you'll change your mind about going back to London tomorrow?"

"If you want me to stay."

He pulled a rueful face. "You bet your life I want you to stay," he said. "I never wanted you to leave, really, only I'm an independent cuss and I thought—oh, well, never mind about that now. I'll explain it all some time if you're interested. Meanwhile, you're the best dental nurse I'm ever likely to have around the place, Kate. I'll keep you here for your full two weeks, even if I have to bribe you with scampi every day."

"I'll get my things; I won't be long," I said.

It was pleasant to be appreciated, even if only for one's efficiency; it was even more pleasant to find that Ben Holland was human after all. As I swilled my face with cool water in the newly-decorated bathroom, renewed my make-up and brushed my hair loosely behind my ears, I wondered what Ben had meant about being "an independent cuss", and why it should have affected his treatment of me.

I straightened the collar of my thin white blouse. If I'd known about going to the White Hart for supper I'd have put on something more interesting this morning. Still, it wasn't really a social date, so it didn't matter.

I leaned nearer to the mirror and applied pale apricot lipstick with great care. I didn't really need that champagne cocktail to make me feel bubbly inside; for the first time since I returned to the country on Sunday I felt my spirits rising, up and up like a toy balloon into a blue sky.

I've always hated misunderstandings and anything that leads to a jarring atmosphere. I hoped that Ben would explain why he had misjudged me, but even if he didn't it wouldn't matter too much.

We were friends now, and that was the important thing. I intended it should stay that way for the remainder of my time here.

After all that, it was more than a little disappointing that the first people we should see when we entered the lounge of the White Hart were Val Deering and her father.

CHAPTER SEVEN

"And so you all had supper together at the White Hart?" Chloe asked as she set up the ironing board, an hour and a half later.

I nodded. "We met Dr. Deering and his daughter in the lounge. As they were having a meal there too, they suggested we should join them."

As soon as we got home from Lambton Ben had changed into working clothes and disappeared outside to help John. I'd offered to cope with the accumulation of dishes while Chloe, just back from helping at the Vicarage, was tackling the ironing.

Now she unfolded a shirt and spread it out thoughtfully. "What do you think of Val Deering?"

There was something in her tone that told me this wasn't an idle question. She really wanted to know what I thought, which made it tricky for me.

I dried a cup before I replied. "She's very pretty," I answered cautiously.

Chloe giggled. "I don't like her either."

When we'd both finished laughing she went on, "I don't know what it is about her; sometimes I feel a beast for criticizing, but I can't help it. She's always very sweet and amiable to me, but when she comes here she has a way of looking around. You're immediately aware that there are crumbs on the carpet, or one of the dogs has left a bone under the table, or you haven't put enough salt in the potatoes."

"Yes," I said, "I know exactly what you mean." I warmed to Chloe anew. "I thought it was just my rotten nature, but I felt like that about her from the very first moment I saw her yesterday."

Presently Chloe put down her iron and said abruptly,

"You know, Kate, I'm so afraid Ben means to marry the wretched girl. I'm sure she's not right for him. Oh dear, I shouldn't be saying this, I suppose, but I must tell somebody, and John wouldn't be interested. Men aren't, are they? He'd say I was exaggerating or imagining things. But it's been on my mind for ages. You don't mind me letting off steam, do you?"

"Of course not. But they're not engaged, are they?"

"Not officially. But unofficially—I'm not sure. She has an acquisitive look in her eye when she's with him. She plays up the old feminine charm."

I nodded. I'd had lots of it during supper at the White Hart. It had almost put me off my scampi.

"And he—" Chloe went on.

I waited to hear how Ben felt, or how his sister thought he felt.

"I don't think Ben's made up his mind. But the trouble is that she's so darned suitable. A country girl, born and bred, and a doctor's daughter as well. Pretty, dresses well, knows everybody around. Who could fit better into Ben's great plan?"

"Plan?"

"Oh yes, Ben has a plan for his life, all cut and dried. He's the kind of person who knows just what he wants. And one thing he's always been determined to have is a country life. He simply can't exist in a city. We were brought up by our godparents who lived in Hampshire and when Ben had to go to London for his training he was awfully deprived; he used to come rushing back every weekend. Of course Uncle Geoff had ideas about Ben going into partnership with him eventually, but Ben doesn't take to the idea. So when this opportunity appeared at the practice in Lambton he simply jumped at it. I think it seemed to him that Fate was taking a hand. Everything fitted in so well. John and I living so close and so on—" She frowned, and her small, freckled face looked quite distressed. "It was all so lovely and so right until Val Deering turned up and set her sights on Ben. Oh well, let's hope I'm wrong, or he doesn't fancy her. You never quite know with Ben, he's deep."

We worked in silence for a while. Chloe seemed busy with her own thoughts, and certainly she had given me something to think about. I was putting two and two together and wondering if I had at last solved the mystery of Ben's hostility.

Uncle Geoff wanted him to go into partnership in London; Ben wanted a country life. Impasse. The irresistible force and the immovable object! But Uncle Geoff never met opposition head on, and he'd doubtless been using as much subtle persuasion as he could muster. I, in my small way, seemed to have been part of the persuasion. I was just a carrot being dangled in front of Ben to lure him to London. Here, Uncle Geoff was saying in effect, is a really competent dental nurse, my boy; you won't be able to command that sort of surgery help in your horse-and-buggy town. All very flattering to me, no doubt. In a way I appreciated the compliment, but at the same time it made me rather angry to think that I'd been used.

Or were we both misjudging Uncle Geoff? Had he been just as innocent about the whole thing as I had. Was Ben making a mountain out of something even smaller than a molehill? It was nicer and happier to look at it like that. That, I decided firmly, was how I would look at it unless I had real proof to the contrary.

A long sigh from the direction of the ironing board broke into my thoughts. I looked around in time to see Chloe sinking into a chair, looking rather pale.

"I'm okay," she said in a small voice as I hurried over to her. "I get a bit lightheaded now and then. It's nothing. Just Junior starting to make his presence felt, I expect."

So there was a family on the way!

I gave her a glass of water, and when she felt better I insisted that we move into the sitting room so that she could lie on the sofa with her feet up.

She grinned at me gratefully. "But you mustn't encourage me to take this seriously," she said. "A farmer's wife takes a little thing like having a baby in her stride."

"When is it?" I asked.

"Oh, ages, not until around Christmas. Arranged cleverly for the off-peak season, you see."

I did see. Farmers's wives, like doctors's wives, are permanently geared to their husband's activities.

"Please don't get the wrong impression," Chloe said hastily. "John looks after me marvelously. He's always fussing, trying to get me to rest. But I think having a baby's a natural thing and it's silly to worry about it, so I just go on and try to forget about—"

She stopped. Then she shot me a rueful glance and added, "You see, this is our second attempt. I lost the first one early on in the process, but I'm sure it's going to be all right this time."

She sat up straight, suddenly alert. "There's John now. I don't want him to see me lying down here or he'll start worrying; he's got enough on his mind as it is. Don't tell him, there's a dear."

I promised I wouldn't, and I didn't. But all the same I felt faintly worried myself. Chloe's attitude was gallant and she might be right, of course, believing that worry might be more harmful than hard work on these occasions. And yet. . . .

I decided to have a word with Ben about it tomorrow. Dentists always have some medical knowledge in a general sort of way; he might be able to keep an eye on his sister without alarming her unduly. She had looked rather rotten out in the kitchen a few minutes ago.

John came in then. He'd pulled off his boots outside

and padded in in stockinged feet and sank into a chair.

"Jiminy, it's hot out!" He mopped his forehead with a handkerchief. "We'll have a storm before the night's out, I shouldn't wonder."

"Oh, John, what about Elsie and the calf? You remember we had a storm last time she calved and—"

"There, love, don't worry, I'm probably wrong and there won't be a storm at all." He leaned forward and patted his wife's hand. I thought again that this was a kind man, this giant with the brown skin and the laughter lines beside his eyes. Kind, thoughtful, and strong.

But even a strong man can get tired, working all the daylight hours, as I remembered very well. Daddy used to come in from the fields dead beat, just as John Garrett looked now, at sowing, haymaking, and harvest time. At any time, in fact, for the demands of a farm never seem to stop.

"I'll make us some tea," Chloe said, starting to get up, but John pushed her gently back.

"You stay there, lass. I'll do it."

Ben appeared in the doorway with a tray. "While you two are arguing about it, it's done," he said, and put the tray carefully down on the table. "Kate can pour, and that'll make it a joint effort. Kate and I work very well together, did you know?"

I knew it wasn't an idle remark. He was, in his own way, acknowledging to Chloe and John that things had been wrong between the two of us and that they were now right. I saw from Chloe's quick upward glance that she'd taken the point even if John hadn't.

And Ben was doing more than just that. He was subtly including me as "one of the family." I was no longer an outsider; it was a happy, warm feeling. Like coming home.

I picked up the big teapot in its yellow knitted cosy, and as I did so my eyes met Ben's and he smiled. I smiled back. The coming two weeks (minus two days) were going to be much more pleasant than I'd dreamed of.

The storm started at exactly four a.m. I awakened with a jump—I expect it was the lightning that actually woke me—just in time to hear the thunder begin to growl in the distance. I switched on my bedside light to look at the time, then switched it off again and lay, fascinated, watching the sky—the blackness sliced across by jagged streaks of white.

I've never been afraid of thunderstorms; perhaps it was because I was brought up by my father and I don't think he was afraid of anything. As the thunder came nearer and nearer, roaring and rumbling, rising and falling, I began to feel the old sense of excitement.

If there was a thunderstorm in the night Daddy used to steal into my room to see if I was awake. "It's grand, Kath, isn't it?" he'd say. "Better than fireworks." He'd wrap me in a blanket and carry me downstairs.

Sometimes, if there was a new foal or any of the cows had calved recently, he would throw his old waterproof cape around both of us and take me to the barn with him. When the storm was over he'd make cocoa for us both, pat me on the back and say I was a good scout and a proper country lass. I'd swell with pride at his praise.

It couldn't have been easy for him, I thought now, to bring up a child alone, as he had done. I began to remember again his kindness, his gentleness and understanding, and how much I had loved him. All the old bleakness and loneliness began to creep back. I felt desolate and couldn't lie there remembering any longer.

I slid out of bed, pushed my feet into my slippers and threw my fluffy blue dressing gown around my shoulders. I opened the bedroom door quietly—although I could hardly have been heard above the shattering noise of the thunder—and crept downstairs.

It's always strange to be wandering about someone else's house in the middle of the night, but I saw nobody. The lights were on in the kitchen and the back door was swinging open. Evidently John Garrett was out looking after his stock, just as Daddy would have been.

I stood in the open doorway and peered into the darkness. The thunder was receding for the moment, but the rain was gathering strength. In the radius of light from the kitchen I could see the great drops hurling themselves against the paving stones of the yard and bouncing back with their own force.

There's a certain smell in the country when it rains after a hot day. I'd forgotten about it, but now it came back to me as the cool air blew against my face. And then nostalgia really had me in its grip. The tears welled into my eyes and I began to shake all over uncontrollably.

I turned blindly to go back upstairs to my room and hide myself away, but at that moment I heard footsteps outside in the yard. A man appeared in the doorway in rubber boots and a yellow oilskin, with a sack thrown over his hair and falling to his shoulders. At first I thought it was John Garrett; then he pulled the sack off and I saw Ben's dark hair rough against his wet forehead.

We stared at each other for a moment—me in my blue dressing-gown, my hair loose round my face; he dripping water all over the kitchen floor.

Then he said wryly, "The ducks seem quite happy anyway, but it's no night for humans, or even for cows and sheep."

"But they're all safe?" I asked quickly.

"John thinks so. He's out with the new calf—the mother's restive. Chloe's with him."

"And the hay?" I said. "They'd just begun to carry, hadn't they?"

He shot me an odd look and I remembered my role as a city girl. "I mean, I noticed the stacks, or bales, or whatever, still out in the field by the main road," I said, feeling a fraud. "Won't it get spoiled?"

He shrugged and spread out his oilskin over an old wooden wringer in the corner. "That's what farming's about, isn't it?"

Suddenly there was a vicious flash of lightning and nearly at the same moment a shattering thunder-clap seemed to split the air into fragments and struck the ear-drums with an almost physical pain.

"Phew, that was close!" I gasped when the noise had rumbled away into the distance.

Ben came over and stood looking down at me. "Frightened?"

"No, not really."

He smiled. I could see he didn't believe me.

"I'll go back to bed now," I said, turning to the door.

"Hang on a minute, I'm going to make some tea —Chloe's orders. She caught the habit from our grand-mother, who brought us up. Any crisis, major or minor, must be an occasion for making tea."

He filled the kettle at the tap, carried it back and plugged it in. I saw his hand go to the switch, and then everything happened at once. There was a vicious flash of lightning, an ear-splitting crack of thunder, and simul-taneously every light went out. I heard the clatter as the kettle dropped to the stone floor. Then there was a black, terrifying silence.

I was petrified. I don't know what I imagined had happened; I just stood rigid and unable to think.

Then I heard a sound that was like music.

"Blast!" exploded Ben. "What the hell did I do?"

Another flash of lightning showed him to me, a dark solid form below a white face, blessedly alive and in one piece; not crumpled up on the floor as in my imagination.

I groped for a chair and sank into it, my knees shaking, and then I began to giggle out of sheer relief.

I heard Ben groping for the kettle and parking it somewhere. "So much for our cuppa," he growled, and, as I went on giggling, "What's so funny?"

"N-nothing," I managed to force out through chattering teeth. "Just for the moment I thought you'd elec—electrocuted yourself—"

"Yes, that would have been somewhat hilarious, I see that. As a matter of fact I wasn't too sure myself that I hadn't. Where are you, Kate?"

He'd evidently found his lighter. I heard the scratch of the flint; the tiny flame flared. He came over to me, holding it high, and his arm went reassuringly around my shoulders in a hard grip.

"Well, we're all right," he said, "but I'm wondering about John and Chloe over in the barn across the yard. There's sure to be emergency lighting over there, but I'd better go over and see what I can do—if I can find my way, that is."

I said, "I noticed two hurricane lamps hanging in the scullery. I saw them there yesterday."

"Did you now? That was bright of you, Kate."

His arm around my shoulder tightened into a squeeze and I warmed to the praise in his voice.

"Come on, then, let's see what we can find. We'd better stay in harness."

He held me close against him and we stumbled across the kitchen together, knocking into chairs as we went, linked like a couple of carriage horses. Finally we found our way through the door into the scullery.

Here it was more difficult. The small room was stacked with boxes, crates, sacks and other oddments.

I said, "The lamps were hanging up on the wall, just to the left of the back door—I'm almost certain."

Ben's lighter was called into action again. Sure enough there were the two hurricane lamps, just where I'd remembered seeing them. I held the lighter while Ben reached up for them.

"Let's hope John keeps 'em filled with oil." He shook

them gently before putting them down on the stone floor. "Yes, I think they're filled. Can you hold that light nearer, Kate? I can't see how the darned things open."

The lamps were just like ones we'd used at home. I'd been familiar with them since I was a small girl, especially since it was only during the last couple of years we were there that the outside buildings had electricity.

Ben was having trouble though, and after a few more minutes fruitless struggle he sat back on his heels. "I'm blowed if I can find out how the wretched thing works."

I said tentatively, "I think there should be a catch right at the top. If you release that the whole outer cover lifts off."

More fumbling. Then, "So it does, by jiminy," he said in an amazed tone. "Why didn't I know that? Let's have the lighter, Kate."

The lamp glasses were smeared and dusty, but they produced enough light to give the kitchen and scullery a more reassuring aspect.

Ben wrapped the oilskin around himself. He picked up one of the lamps and handed it to me; then he took the other and said, "I'll go over and see how they're managing. You'll be all right on your own?"

It wasn't really a question and I didn't answer. The opening of the door into the yard let in a sheet of rain, and after Ben had gone out I stood shivering for a minute. Then I carried the lamp up to my room and dressed hurriedly, thankful that at the last moment I'd decided to include slacks and a thick green sweater in my luggage.

The storm seemed to have retreated for the moment. Through my window I could see the horizon of rolling farmland flickering whitely with summer lightning; thunder still growled from the distance. The rain had settled into a steady downpour.

Downstairs again I put my lamp on the kitchen table and wondered if there was anything I could do. I filled a pan with water and put it on top of the stove, which was banked up for the night and quite warm. I found cups and saucers and set them on the table. Then I wandered around restlessly, unable to relax in the faintly eerie atmosphere of the empty room full of dark shadows; the only sound the smack of the rain as it loosed its fury against the windows and door.

When I couldn't stay alone any longer I found an old raincoat in the scullery; with this draped over my head and tightly clutching my hurricane lamp, I let myself out into the streaming yard.

In three years I had grown accustomed to city rain. Rain that was, so to speak, tamed and disciplined, with gutters to flow along and grids to gurgle into. But here in the country, the rain was part of nature itself, and just as wild. Water was turning the yard into a river and lapped coldly over the tops of my shoes as I waded toward the light that showed under the door of the barn, 20 feet away.

The big wooden door creaked as I pushed it open. Inside there was the warm, familiar smell of straw, cattle food, and clean, well-tended cows, that I remembered so well.

Chloe was alone there, sitting on an old-fashioned milking stool. An oil lamp swung from a hook overhead and in its light she looked forlorn, her elbows resting on her knees. Her head dropped forward so that her dark hair covered her hands.

She heard me come in and pulled herself up quickly.

"Kate! You've managed to swim over here! Ben said you'd been disturbed by the storm, but he thought you were keeping warm and dry in the house. What a night! The electric generator's gone phut; I suppose it's because of the storm. The men have gone to see if they can do anything to get the power back. They left me to keep an eye on Elsie." She nodded toward the stall where Elsie, a huge red cow, lay with her new calf.

"John thought the thunder might upset her," Chloe

went on. "Elsie's always been a problem cow. Most people think cows are all calm and placid, but some of them have funny tempers, just like some people, I suppose. When she gets in a paddy she kicks out with her hind legs. But her milk yield is so superb we just have to get along with her. And of course she's even more tricky while she's got her calf with her."

I drew nearer and looked down at the tiny calf nestled against its mother's great body. It was so small and so perfect that I couldn't stop looking at it. "It's always a miracle, isn't it?" I said softly.

"Yes, I think so too." Chloe knew what I meant.

I turned and looked at Chloe, then, and I said, frowning, "You shouldn't be here, Chloe. You should be in bed."

"Because of my interesting condition?" She smiled wanly. Then the smile disappeared. "As a matter of fact, Kate, I think you're right," she said uneasily.

"You're not feeling too well?" But I hardly needed to ask; I could hear the twinge of fear in her voice.

"Not too well," she agreed reluctantly.

I put my hand firmly on her arm. "Back to bed with you, then. I'll come with you."

But she shook her head. "Sorry, Kate, it may be silly of me, but I can't. John asked me to stay. If anything happened to the calf—"

"Isn't there anyone else?" I asked. "A cowman?"

She shook her head. "Old Dave Rykes is our cowman, but he's getting past it; he'd never come out on a night like this and John wouldn't expect him to. Bobby was acting as his second in command, and Bobby's in hospital, of course. So you see—" she spread out her hands.

I did see. I knew that if Elsie stopped being placid, if she really became nervous and started to thresh around in the stall, her offspring might be injured. All the same, I argued to myself, the welfare of Chloe and her coming baby was more important than that of any calf, however valuable.

"Please, Chloe," I pleaded, "go back to bed. You know you're feeling rotten. Admit it, and give up."

But she shook her head stubbornly. "Officer left in charge on the bridge. I couldn't let John down."

"Did John know you weren't feeling well?"

She shook her head.

"Look, girl," I said briskly, "have some sense. Who do you think John would put first—you or a calf?"

She began to laugh weakly and I knew I'd won. I wrapped the old raincoat around her and gave her the lamp I'd brought in with me. "I'll keep watch on the bridge," I said. "I daresay Elsie and I will get along fine." I opened the barn door and gave her an encouraging pat on the arm.

"I don't know if I should," she said hesitantly. "But anyhow, thanks, pal."

She looked so small and forlorn as she waded through the puddles outside, the lamplight shining through the rain as she went, that I felt a tightness in my throat and sent up a silent prayer that she'd be all right. I waited until I saw the house door close, then I went back into the barn. I sat myself down on the milking stool and began to talk to Elsie, patting her gently and rhythmically on her huge rump at the same time.

I always talked to the animals at home. Daddy used to tease me and say I'd never make a real farmer because I couldn't help making pets of the animals. But he used to talk to them too, and undoubtedly he had his favorites. I once caught him secretly giving Old Bessie an extra little ration of dairy cake at bedtime.

It was very peaceful in the barn. Elsie was awake—I could hear the soft thud of chewing—but she was quiet, and the calf was asleep beside her.

It was quiet outside too; the thunder seemed to have finally gone away.

"Good Elsie—good old girl," I crooned. "Lucky old Elsie, aren't you, with a gorgeous little calf all of your own—"

I wasn't thinking about what I was saying. I was thinking about Chloe and worrying in case she lost her baby. In the dim warmth of the barn I think I must have been half-asleep as I patted and crooned.

The thing that disturbed me first was a feeling of cool damp air blowing on my cheeks. I looked around to see Ben standing just inside the barn, his hand on the door catch. I wondered how long he'd been there listening to me talking rubbish to a cow and felt slightly ridiculous.

"Hullo," I said. "Chloe had to go in and—"

At that moment the trouble really began. Through the half-open door lolloped one of the farm dogs. I heard Ben mutter something under his breath as he tried to head the dog off, but it was too late. It was a large, blundering pup, obviously untrained. It was joyfully mistaking Ben's efforts to catch it as an invitation to play. Finding itself awake, surprisingly, in the middle of the night and with humans apparently willing to entertain it, the puppy was certainly going to make the most of the situation. It bounded around the barn, barking joyfully; to my horror it approached Elsie's stall.

The mere sight of a dog to a cow with a new calf will send her nearly mad, and Elsie reacted according to pattern; worse, being Elsie, she over-reacted.

"Get the dog away!" I yelled to Ben as the big cow lumbered to her feet, swaying clumsily and kicking out with her hind legs. I told myself that she was actually trying to protect her calf, but she was so terrified that in another minute she might trample on the little thing by accident.

Hardly knowing what I was doing, I pushed myself between the lurching body of the cow and the side of the stall, grabbed the calf and somehow half lifted, half pulled it out of the zone of its mother's flailing legs.

I dragged the milking stool well away, and, sitting myself down on it, held the trembling calf between my knees, soothing it. Ben chased the pup and finally managed to corner it and pick it up.

"I'll dump this somewhere safe and come back," he said to me, shouting above the bellow that Elsie was putting up.

"Can you manage to hang on?"

I nodded and he tucked the dog under his arm and carried it out of the barn. By the time he returned things were getting back to normal. Elsie had quietened down and stopped kicking and was turning her head first one way and then the other, no doubt missing her calf.

"Should I put the calf back, do you think?" I said to Ben. "She seems to be calm now."

I saw his worried frown and wondered just how much experience he'd had with farm animals. Not much more than I'd had myself, I guessed, mine was pretty rusty. But he took the decision straight away."

"Yes, let's do that," he said. "It seems natural."

The calf, thoroughly awake now, went to its mother as if drawn by a magnet, nuzzling up to her udder and sucking away hungrily. Elsie's head stopped swaying and she was suddenly as quiet and placid a cow as you could have seen anywhere. The panic of the last few minutes might never have happened.

Ben let out a long breath of relief. "Phew! That was quite a performance while it lasted. That blasted pup! John only bought her a couple of days ago. She must have broken out of the toolshed; that was where he was bedding her down for the present. I suppose she was frightened by the thunder." He put a hand on my shoulder. "You look all in, Kate: you must get back indoors."

I shook my head and explained briefly about Chloe while Ben listened worriedly.

"Everything seems to be getting more complicated by the minute," he said at last. "John's still struggling with the generator, but he doubts if he can get it going tonight. He'd better know about Chloe straight away. Silly girl not to tell him what was brewing."

I heard the affection in his voice and sensed the feeling there. I wished, not for the first time in my life, that I'd had an older brother myself. Perhaps one rather like Ben. Overbearing he might be, and was, but he had a kind of calm, reassuring strength that could be very comforting when you needed it.

He was looking up at the lamp that hung from a beam. "This darned thing's smoking; can you smell it?" He stretched up to adjust the wick and the yellowish light fell onto his raised face. His dark hair was wet and tousled, his chin shadowy with early morning growth.

"Afraid I'll have to leave you here while I contact John," he said, with arms still raised. "Can you hold the fort for a few minutes more, Kate?"

"Of course I can,' I said.

He'd fixed the wick and his arms dropped to his side. He turned and looked down at me. Then he put both hands on my shoulders and said, in a puzzled voice, "Quite a girl, aren't you, little Londoner?"

And he was gone from the barn before I'd recovered from my astonishment.

CHAPTER EIGHT

John didn't, after all, manage to start the electricity again that night. The gray light of dawn was creeping into my bedroom when I finally arrived there, yawning hugely and stupid with fatigue. I can just remember dragging off my water-soaked shoes, falling onto the bed and pulling the covers up to my chin. Then I must have passed out within seconds.

The sun was pouring in when I awakened again to see Ben standing beside the bed. Shaved, groomed, and dressed ready for surgery, a mug of tea was in one hand with a plate of butter, toast and marmalade in the other.

"I did knock," he said. "Shall I put these down on the table? I'm afraid there won't be time for a proper breakfast; we let you sleep in."

I wriggled myself up, blinking against the sunlight. "How's Chloe this morning?"

"All well at present. John rang Dr. Deering earlier and he came over himself about half an hour ago. She's to stay in bed for the present and rest."

"Oh good, that's a relief." I gulped some tea and felt more like a human being. "Thanks for this, Ben, but you should have woken me up earlier. I meant to get breakfast for all of us."

"We've coped reasonably, I think. And you've done quite enough for us already. Acting as assistant unpaid cow-hand wasn't in your brief, you know."

"I rather enjoyed it, though I was sorry about Chloe. And I was glad to help—that is, if I did help."

"You helped," he said quietly, looking down at me, which made me realize just how awful my hair must look. He glanced at his watch. "I'm afraid we ought to get started in about 20 minutes. Can you make it?"

"Yes," I said, and he nodded and left the room.

Even in my schooldays I don't think I'd ever crammed down breakfast and dressed more quickly. I felt as if I had an electric charge inside me; odd because I'd missed several hours of sleep.

On the way downstairs I hesitated outside Chloe's bedroom door, but I thought John might be with her. In any case perhaps it would be better not to disturb her. Who, I wondered, was there to take over the housekeeping and cooking while she was in bed? I remembered only too well just how much there was to do in a farmhouse; doubtless there would be some outside men to feed as well as the family.

I hesitated, but came to the reluctant conclusion that there was absolutely nothing I could do about it. My job was to help Ben in the surgery and I couldn't be in two places at once. I ran down to join him in the car.

As I was clearing up after the last of the morning patients Ben said, "I'm afraid there's no packed lunch for us today. There wasn't time to make sandwiches. I suggest you go along to the Brown Teapot and have a snack. I'll wait here until you get back; we can't both be out at once."

The Brown Teapot was a bakery and restaurant farther along the High Street. It looked pleasant enough, but all the tables seemed full and there was a smell of chips which I didn't find very appealing just then. So I bought some sausage rolls and maids-of-honour, stocked up with tomatoes and green peppers at the greengrocer's shop next door and started back to the practice. On the way down the hill I noticed a bookstore on the other side of the road and remembered that I'd intended to buy a book for Bobby in hospital.

I was lucky. The assistant was helpful and told me that a new book on nature photography had just arrived. It looked fascinating to me, with lots of splendid color plates. I hoped Bobby would like it. I had a sudden quick memory of a boy in a leather jacket stretched out on the roadside with a gash across his cheek. Could it have been only four days ago? It seemed like weeks.

When I got back to the practice Ben was in the kitchen. He'd taken off his white coat and put on a thin cashmere pullover.

I dumped my purchases on the table. "I brought some food back for both of us. It seemed a better idea than staying at the restaurant to eat."

"Oh!" I thought he seemed faintly put out. "Oh yes, good idea. But I'm afraid I'll have to leave you to eat alone. I've promised to go along to the Deering's. Val rang up—she wants to see me about something."

I pushed back a feeling of disappointment. I knew now that I'd been hoping that over a shared lunch he'd explain about Uncle Geoff, his own suspicions of me, and my motives.

"Pity," said Ben as I put out the sausage rolls on a plate. They looked delicious and I supposed they were the reason for this expression of regret. "Ah well, I'll be back before two."

He left me alone with the sausage rolls. I surveyed them gloomily for about five seconds; decided that, after only half a slice of toast for breakfast, I really was very hungry indeed. I put the kettle on for coffee and settled down to enjoy myself.

I hadn't seen Mr. Pill all morning (we'd been too busy to stop for morning tea), but I'd heard vague thumpings from the floor above. Now his large form appeared in the kitchen doorway, a fat book of wallpaper patterns tucked under his arm, followed by George, his diminutive assistant.

"George and me's going off for our lunch now, miss. I'll leave her here for Dr. Holland to look at."

"Her" was evidently the book of patterns. He put it

down on the end of the table and patted it lovingly.

"I can leave her with him for today," said Mr. Pill, "but I'll want to know by morning so as I can get me order in."

"Yes," I said. "Does Dr. Holland know all about it?"

To my surprise Mr. Pill burst into a cackle of laughter. His laugh was high pitched, like his singing voice. "Aye, he does that. Keeps putting it off till the young lady can come around to do the choosing, but we can't wait any longer. Tell him, will you?"

I nodded. "I'll tell him," I said, and Mr. Pill went out.

What a pity, I thought, spearing a sausage roll somewhat viciously with my fork, that Mr. Pill hadn't brought the book down a few minutes earlier. Then Ben could have taken it with him to the Deerings'.

Chloe's forebodings were evidently only too true. If Val were choosing the wallpapers for the apartment it looked more than likely that she would soon be sharing it with Ben. Poor Ben; he deserved something better.

He returned at a quarter to two, as I was washing my plate and coffee mug.

"There's plenty of food left," I said. "Or have you had lunch?"

He glanced at me absently. "Yes, I had a bite with the Deerings. I want to have a word with John before I start the two o'clock appointment. See if you can reach him on the phone, will you, Kate? I might catch him in the house about now if I'm lucky."

John answered himself. I called Ben and retired to the kitchen, but I couldn't help hearing his side of the conversation that followed.

"John? Look, I've just been having a talk with Dr. Deering. I thought I might get a bit more out of him about Chloe. . . . Yes, he said he was going to look in and see her again this afternoon. How is she? . . . Yes, well I suppose that's more or less what one would expect. . . . Yes, he said that, he was most particular about keeping her quiet. . . . Yes, I know it's difficult, she's always been a bit of a worrier. That's why . . . yes, that's what I wanted to speak to you about, John. Val Deering's offered to come over and look after things while Chloe's in bed. She says she'd love to take it on, and her father can do without her at present. He's got Miss Archer; she's prepared to sleep in while Val's away. What do you think, John? It seems a solution to the problem, doesn't it, or had you anyone else in mind?''

I turned the tap on hard to drown the remainder of the conversation. The only thought in my mind was that if Chloe's place at Summerfields was going to be taken by Val Deering, then the best thing *I* could do would be to move out as soon as possible.

So when Ben came back I said, "I've been thinking, would it be a good idea if I got a room at the White Hart for a few days, until Chloe is up and about again?"

He frowned. "Why?"

I couldn't very well explain my antipathy to Val Deering. It was too unreasonable and absurd. So I just said, "Well, I thought it would be easier all around if there was one less in the family just now—for the rest of the week, at any rate. I'm expecting to go back to London for the weekend—if that's all right with you, of course," I added.

He had his back to me, searching for something in the big cupboard, and he didn't answer immediately. In fact, the silence lasted so long that I was almost wondering if he'd heard what I said. He found whatever it was he'd been looking for, reached it, and turned around to me.

"Yes, well, perhaps you're right and it would be better. I'm more sorry than I can say that all this has happened—it's the last thing I would have wished. After all, you agreed to come here to help me in the surgery—not to get involved in all the chaos and confusion of farm life. We must have given you a very poor idea of the country," he added, with a hint of a return to his former stiffness.

"Oh no, it's not like that at all," I said. "It just seemed the obvious thing to do. I'll go and call the White Hart, shall I, and see if they can fix me up."

There wasn't any difficulty about renting a room. The receptionist sounded friendly and pleasant as she took my name.

I went back to tell Ben and he said, "Good, that's that then," quite briskly. The thought struck me that perhaps Val Deering disliked me as much as I disliked her and that she'd told Ben so. It was all rather depressing.

Mr. Pill came back from lunch just before the first of the afternoon patients was due to arrive. He patted his book of wallpaper patterns, which still lay on the end of the table. "Did the young lady tell you, sir?"

Ben said, "Tell me what?"

Mr. Pill repeated his requirements and Ben looked horrified. "Choose a paper for the living room? Must I?"

Mr. Pill beamed indulgently. "I'm afraid you must, Dr. Holland, if you want everything finished on schedule. I'll want to know by first thing tomorrow morning, if you'll be so good, sir. Just leave a note of the number with the book, then I can send young George off with the order as soon as we get here. I can get the rolls delivered ready for starting on Monday."

"But—" began Ben.

The front doorbell rang at that moment. I left them to argue it out and went to admit the two o'clock appointment. But it wasn't the two o'clock appointment. A girl of about my own age or a bit older stood there, a girl with short straight fair hair, wearing a plain blue dress with a white collar. I was accustomed to meeting professional nurse maids in the Manchester Square practice. My first impression was that she was one, come to make an appointment for one of her charges.

But I was wrong. Her eyes widened slightly as they fixed themselves on my white coat. "Oh," she said, on a note of confusion, "I thought—"

She paused, smiling shyly, and went on, "I think I'd better introduce myself. I'm Celia Marsh. I've just arrived in Lambton, and I came here straight away. I thought—I understood when Dr. Deering contacted me—that Dr. Holland was without any help in the surgery and might be glad if I could start work earlier than arranged, but if he's already got help—"

Of course, I realized, Ben's new surgery nurse.

I opened the door wide. "Won't you come in? Dr. Holland hasn't started afternoon surgery yet, so you could have a word with him now. By the way," I added, as we walked together down the hall, "I'm only temporary. I was sent down from London to stand in until you could start."

Oh, I see." She sounded relieved. "I thought he might have changed his mind. But the letter I had from Dr. Deering this morning sounded so urgent that I couldn't understand—"

Ben appeared in the kitchen doorway. I introduced them, left them together and went into the surgery to get a 'try-in' ready for the two o'clock appointment.

I took the articulator, with its pink wax model, out of the cupboard and set it on the cabinet. I wondered what Celia Marsh meant about having a letter from Dr. Deering this morning to the effect that she was needed here urgently, straight away. Why, Dr. Deering knew quite well that I was helping Ben out for this week and next. Why should he have—

But the front doorbell rang then and there was no time for any more speculations as we waded into the heavily-booked afternoon list.

It was one of those afternoons when everything goes smoothly. We kept up to time with appointments and even had time for a snatched cup of tea at four o'clock. The final appointment of the day was the trickiest—an impacted wisdom tooth belonging to the local church-warden. It was a difficult job and Ben coped with it very skilfully, I considered. I couldn't help thinking that for a similar operation Uncle Geoff would have had the patient in a nursing home for a couple of days!

Ben was drying his hands as I came back from show-ing the churchwarden out. "Did he seem all right?"

"Perfectly," I said. "Trotted off as chirpy as a cricket. It was rather a brute, wasn't it?"

Too late I realized that I hadn't got Uncle Geoff on the other side of the surgery. Ben and I weren't on terms where we chatted about his work, I didn't know how he would take my remark.

To my surprise he agreed with me. "Yes, it was a brute indeed. It didn't look nearly as bad on the X-ray as it turned out. Funny how thin little men like that are so often the toughest propositions." He threw the towel on the rail and added, "You were a great help, Kate. It's really quite something for me to have you on the other side of the chair when there's a tricky job."

"Oh," I murmured, somewhat shattered. "Thank you."

"And by the way," he went on, "that girl Celia Marsh. I'd understood she wouldn't be available until Monday week, but as she seems to be free now I've arranged with her to come in regularly from tomorrow, so that she can get the hang of things while you're still here. I hope you won't mind putting her in the picture? You know the way I like things done."

"No, of course I don't mind. But—" I hesitated. "But didn't you say she is a registered nurse?"

"Yes, she is, but she's never done any dental work. It's quite a different field altogether. She should pick it up quickly, though. She seems bright."

But I still had doubts. To start giving instructions to someone whose qualifications were far superior to my own might, I thought, be rather awkward.

Ben evidently saw my difficulty. "Don't worry," he said. "I don't think you'll find her snobby. This is entirely her own choice. She's given up general nursing because she has an invalid mother on her hands and needs a job with settled hours. She won't get as much money with me, but that's her affair, isn't it?"

That seemed to take care of my doubts. "I see. And of course I'll help in anyway I can."

Ben smiled enigmatically. "That's your speciality, isn't it, Kate?" he said, and disappeared to pack up the afternoon's crop of models and impressions for mailing to the dental laboratory.

He was sticking down the final strip of sealing tape when I joined him a few minutes later.

"You ready, Kate? We'll go back to the farm first so you can pack up your gear while I see how things are going on. Then I can bring you back to the White Hart any time. Val is going over to Summerfields this afternoon in her own car." He stopped and looked at me seriously. "It's too bad this had to happen. I'm very sorry and I know Chloe will be too, but there it is."

Under his scrutiny I was suddenly assailed by a dreadful shyness. Then my eye caught the book of wallpaper patterns and I said thankfully, "Hadn't you better choose that paper before we go? Mr. Pill will be dreadfully put out if you don't."

He groaned. "Oh lord! Oh, well, I suppose I'd better." He began to flick over the pages impatiently. "How about this one?"

I kept my face straight with difficulty. "This one" was a fabulously expensive embossed paper in a tobacco brown color. It would have looked in place in the smoking room of an exclusive men's club.

I pretended to consider it. "Um. Just a bit conservative, don't you think?"

"I don't know," he said helplessly. "I'm no good at this sort of thing. Look, Kate, you choose for me, there's a good girl. Will you?"

I began, "But surely—" I meant that surely this was Val's province? But she'd gone off to Summerfields. I had the horrid feeling that, if left to himself, Ben might pick on something even more inappropriate than the tobacco brown one. "I will, if you insist," I said doubtfully. "But—"

"Oh, I do insist."

"Then I think I'd better see the room it's for, which way it faces, the light and so on."

"Certainly," he said. "Let's go up."

The new living room was bare and echoed to the sound of our footsteps. It must have faced south-west, for the afternoon sunlight was pouring in through the two windows, making the new white paint look like icing on a wedding cake. Or perhaps that was just the way my mind was working, thinking of Val Deering.

"It's a beautiful room," I said impulsively. "What a view—!"

From the downstairs room one could see only the neglected back garden. But from up here the countryside stretched out into a rolling panorama of green, brown and gold patterned fields. Here and there cottages cuddled into folds of the land; feathery clumps of trees drifted along the far horizon, silhouetted against the pale blue sky.

I drew in a deep breath. It all looked so peaceful and gentle with a kind of reassuring timelessness.

Ben joined me at the window and we stood together looking out.

"What do you think of my place here, Kate?" He

sounded so offhand that I guessed that he needed approval—from me, or anybody else.

"I think it's splendid," I said. "You seem to have everything here—an up-and-coming practice, a splendid position in the High Street, a lovely apartment to live in. And," I added with a wave of my hand, "a view like that to look out on."

"A bit different from Manchester Square, though?"

"Just a bit," I smiled.

He pushed both hands into his pants pockets and stuck out his jaw like a defiant small boy. "I expect you, being familiar with both, would consider me stark staring crazy to choose a place like this when I could have inherited the Kingdom—in the shape of Uncle Geoff's practice?"

"Is that what he wanted?"

"Oh yes, he wanted it. Very understandable really; I must be a big disappointment to him. Hasn't he ever mentioned it to you?"

I shook my head. "Never. I didn't know a thing about you when he asked me to come here. I expected to find a courtly gray-haired gent of his own generation." I smiled faintly. "Did I have a surprise!"

Ben said ruefully, "You must have done. I wasn't even courteous, let alone courtly. And consumed with beastly suspicions into the bargain. I wonder you didn't walk out on me."

I wasn't going to rise to that. I said, "Did you ever consider coming to Manchester Square?"

He paused to think. "No. No, honestly I don't think I ever did. I suppose I was a bit dim not to realize that that was what Uncle Geoff expected of me. But I had ideas of my own. I expect I'm horribly self-centered. And, quite frankly, I never saw myself as specialist material."

"Oh, but you are!" I said impulsively.

He slid me a meaningful glance. "No ulterior

motive? No, all right Kate, I believe you. So"—he grinned—"you must really mean it. Thanks for the compliment. But even supposing you're right and I could have made the grade to the top, I wouldn't have fancied the Manchester Square set-up."

He leaned both hands on the sill and looked out across the peaceful fields. An old man from one of the cottages was strolling along beside a hedge, puffing at a pipe, a dog at his heels.

"I just love the country and the country life, always have done," Ben said. "I wouldn't change it for London, however brilliant the prospects, professionally. You have to choose; you can't have everything."

I nodded. "Chloe told me you pined away in the city. Would you have liked to be a farmer?"

"No, not a bit. I wouldn't like to make my living off the land. That would spoil it for me. I don't want to exploit the land, I just want to enjoy it for its own sake. Am I sounding awfully involved?"

"No, I think I see what you mean, that there's a certain danger in using something you care about as a means of providing bread and butter and cake. Like a professional musician, or an artist. The two things might tend to get mixed up—the money part and the other part."

"You put it very well," he said. "But if it hadn't been for Chloe I might have missed my own particular boat. I was, as she told you, pining away at the end of my hospital stint in London. Uncle Geoff was beginning to put on the pressure. I could almost see the shades of the prison house closing down on me. Then Chloe came here with a girl friend for a walking holiday. She met John, they fell in love and were married in a couple of months. This practice was up for sale. I came to look at it, saw the possibilities. And that's it. Except," he added wryly, "that the extent of my debts for equipment and every-thing else sometimes keeps me awake at night."

"All dentists have to start like that," I said. "And dental equipment is fantastically expensive. I read all the glossy ads that come by mail," I added with a grin.

He laughed aloud. "I see you're well-informed about the ins and outs of the dental profession. Oh, I shall get my head above water eventually, I'm confident about that. There's plenty of work in and around Lambton and I'm not afraid of work."

"So," I said, "you know just what you want and you're all set to achieve it. You're one of the lucky ones."

"I suppose I am," he said soberly, "though it's not quite as straightforward as it sounds. I feel a heel about disappointing Uncle Geoff. He's always been very good to Chloe and me. I suppose it was feeling guilty about that angle that made me touchy with you when I thought he was using you. I'm sorry, Kate, I misjudged things. But the old boy is inclined to be crafty about getting his own way, as I expect you know."

"I certainly do," I said feelingly. "Still, he's a dear, and I couldn't imagine him pushing anyone into doing anything they would hate. He's much too nice a person for that."

He pulled a face. "Don't rub it in!"

"I'm not trying to do that. And I'm full of admiration for the way you've got things worked out the way you want them. Country life. Country practice."

He smiled. "That's the ticket!"

I couldn't resist asking it. "Country wife, too?"

There was a fractional silence. I felt as if I dropped a pebble into a deep well, and it was taking a long time to reach the bottom.

Then Ben laughed and turned away from the window. "It'll have to be, won't it—to complete the pattern?" he said dryly.

I wasn't quite sure whether I'd been snubbed or not, but I was humiliatingly certain that I deserved to be.

Why, I thought, couldn't I stop myself from blurting things out and then being sorry afterwards, instead of thinking before I spoke? Louise, I was sure, would never put herself in such a position.

Miserably I sank down on my heels on the floor, murmuring that I'd look through the wallpaper book, while Ben went out to see how Mr. Pill was getting along in the other rooms.

He was back very soon. "Found one you like?"

I hadn't had time to make a proper choice, but he had his impatient look now; I didn't dare say I needed more time.

From the three "possibles" I hastily picked out the one I liked best.

"This one, I think, then."

The paper I'd chosen had a rough, off-white background, with an irregular design in fine black line. There were abstract forms in deep blue and scarlet with a touch of limey yellow.

"I like it," I said. "It's fresh and lively. What do you think?"

"Fine," he said. "Write down the number quickly."

He tore a sheet from his notebook. I made a note of the number and tucked it inside the book. I got the feeling that he had hardly noticed my choice of paper. In fact his gaze was directed at me and his blue eyes had a speculative look in them.

I could have kicked myself for asking that stupid, inquisitive question just when we were getting along so much better. I scrambled to my feet, brushing my skirt down. Before either of us could reach the door there was a sound of light footsteps tapping on the uncarpeted staircase, and Val's voice cried gaily, "Hullo! Anyone at home?"

She appeared in the doorway, immaculate in powder blue, and walked straight past me to Ben. "I thought we might drive to Summerfields together, Ben. I'd hate Chloe to think I was just walking in and taking over. I thought if you were with me—" She put a hand on his arm and smiled up at him with pretty deference.

Ben said, "Of course, though I'm sure there's no need to feel like that about it, Val. We're all very grateful to you. We're just about ready to leave, ourselves. Kate's been helping me to choose some wallpaper—I'm hopeless at that sort of assignment. How do you like it?" He gestured to the book.

That, I thought, took the prize for masculine tactlessness. I felt almost sorry for Val as I saw her flush crimson.

But you had to hand it to her; she carried it off very well. She sauntered over to the wallpaper book, lying open on the floor by the window, and stood looking down at it judicially, one finger against her mouth. Perhaps because I didn't like her I tried to be specially fair and admitted that she really did look very attractive with shiny fair hair, curving body and her peaches and cream complexion.

"Ye-es, quite effective," she decided finally. "But, Ben dear, don't you think it's just a tiny bit—well, not in quite the best taste for a country house? Just a little—er—showy?" She turned to me, prettily apologetic. "I do hope you don't think I'm trying to criticize your choice, Miss—er—"

"Not Miss anything," Ben said, smiling. "Kate."

"Of course. Kate, then. I'm sure it would look lovely in—where is it you live? Paddington?"

I smiled sweetly. "The other side of the Park. Kensington. Do you know it?" Childish of me to rise to the bait, and I felt ashamed of myself.

Val Deering ignored it. She was leaning down, turning the leaves of the book. Now she stopped with a little squeak at one of smudgy, yellow roses. "Oh, I do like that. Yes, that's lovely. And it would look so right in this room, don't you think so, Ben?" She looked up at him over her shoulder, prettily inquiring.

"Don't ask me," Ben grinned. "I'm only a plain working dentist. All I want is to get the place finished."

Val trilled with laughter. "Dear Ben, we'll never make an artistic type out of you, shall we?" she teased. She threw her arms wide. "This room could look marvelous—I can see it when it's all furnished. You know, you can pick up some lovely old stuff in the sales—there's often one of the big country houses coming up for auction. I'll have to keep my eyes open, shan't I?"

I didn't wait to hear Ben agree. I had a sudden vision of the room as it would be, with wishy-washy roses on the walls and pieces of "good" period furniture arranged on a suitably faded carpet. I expect I was being catty, but I got the impression that Val wouldn't choose it because she had an affection for beautiful old things, but because it was the safely correct and tasteful way to furnish a house in the country.

"I'll go down and get my things," I murmured, "and join you in the car."

I'd left my purse and light coat in the kitchen. As I was collecting them I heard the other two come downstairs and then the front door open.

I turned to follow them, but Val Deering was standing just inside the kitchen doorway, her face very pale.

"How dare you?" she said softly. "How dare you have the insolence to choose the wallpaper for the apartment? I didn't trust you from the first moment I set eyes on you, but this is altogether too much. I can see quite well what your game is, Miss Whoever-you-are. I can tell you that you're wasting your time if you think you can catch Ben Holland with your smooth London ways. Ben doesn't care for sophisticated girls, didn't you know?"

I could feel myself slowly stiffening with amazement at

this extraordinary performance. Embarrassed, too, that a girl could make herself so cheap.

I suppose she took my silence for guilt, for she lifted her chin even higher and stared down her nose at me. "Just remember, my good girl, that you're here in a subservient position; if you're looking for a husband it's not the slightest use looking in Ben Holland's direction."

And she swung around and swept out of the room.

I stood there, conscious that my knees were shaking. Pure aggression, however childish, always has that effect on me.

"Well!" I breathed aloud, picking up my bag from the table. "Well!"

Ben's voice called from the front of the house. "Kate, are you ready? Val's going on ahead in her own car."

"Coming!" I called back. As I joined him in the hall I thought once again what a merciful thing it was that I was moving to the White Hart. Summerfields would certainly not hold both Val Deering and myself just now.

CHAPTER NINE

I went along the landing and tapped at the door of the front bedroom that was John's and Chloe's after I'd packed all my things in my suitcase. Ben had gone to see John in the dairy before he drove me back to the White Hart, and I reckoned I'd have a short time to spare.

In answer to my knock Chloe's voice said, "Come in," in a muffled tone. I went in to find her sitting up in bed poring over a piece of white knitting. She looked small and rather pathetic propped up against the pillows in the middle of the big double bed. The room was like Chloe herself, warm and friendly with its gold carpet, flowery curtains and air of comfortable untidiness. Just now it had a shadowy appearance. The windows, like all the others of the old farmhouse, were small and deep-set; light had to filter through the branches of a huge pear tree just outside.

She looked up as I went in and broke into a smile. "Kate! How lovely! Come. Sit down and talk to me. Isn't it just murder keeping me here like this? I'm completely browned off already. And you taking yourself away, and that awful Val Deering coming here! It's too horrible to contemplate. Promise you'll come back the minute I'm up and about again."

"Of course I will," I said, to cheer her up, though I had reservations about it. I sat on the edge of the bed. "How are you feeling now?"

"I feel fine, that's the silly part of it." I caught an echo of Ben's impatience in her voice. "But I do wish you weren't leaving, Kate. Must you go?"

"I think I must," I said gently. "I should only be in the way if I stayed—one more mouth to feed—and I couldn't help here, having to be out at the surgery all day. Anyway," I added wryly, "Val and I wouldn't hit it off at all."

She gave me an old-fashioned look. "I'm not surprised. But the doctor said a couple of days in bed, so you could come back on the weekend, couldn't you?"

"Well, I'm planning to go to London on the weekend. Hugo has to come to London to collect his car from the garage; you know, it had to have repairs done after the accident. He's asked me to return with him."

"Oh, I see." Chloe seemed to be making rather heavy weather of her knitting, biting the tip of her tongue in childish concentration.

There was a short silence until she said suddenly, "Kate, are you going to marry him?"

I was getting used to Chloe's straight-from-the-shoulder approach, but even so, the question, fired at me like that, took my breath away.

"I—I don't know. I'm not sure—"

I think I was going to say that I wasn't sure whether Hugo was the marrying kind. But I hesitated, and she read my meaning differently.

"Oh, you must be absolutely sure. It would be awful to marry a man if you weren't really sure." Her eyes were soft. I guessed she was thinking of John.

"I couldn't agree more, but you see I haven't known him very long. He's great fun, though, and I like him tremendously." I wondered why I sounded defensive. Hugo's obvious attractions didn't need any boosting from me.

Chloe had been struggling with a dropped stitch and now she threw the work down with an exclamation of disgust. "I'm a hopeless knitter. I don't know why I bother."

"Let me try. The light isn't good enough over there for you to see to do it."

I carried the knitting to the window and managed to find the dropped stitch and pick it up. I smoothed the work out; it looked like the back of a vest. There was something touching about the smallness of it, the uneven stitches here and there. Chloe was right—she wasn't an expert knitter.

I took it back to her. "Here you are, I think I've got it right. It's lovely—so tiny—"

"It isn't lovely, it's awful—" came in a shaky voice from the bed. And then I saw that she was crying. Chloe crying! She looked up at me speechless, eyes brimming, then she gulped and fumbled under the pillow for a handkerchief.

At last she stopped and blew her nose. "Sorry, Kate. It just came over me." She pulled a rueful face.

"Do you good. Help you to relax. That's what they say, isn't it?"

"Do they? I've always thought it was weak and silly. I've always despised women who burst into tears when things go wrong."

"Is it about the baby? Or don't you want to talk about it?"

"I don't mind talking about it to you. I think I want to, really. I've got an awful feeling I'm going to lose this baby too. I try to think myself out of it, but I don't seem able to. I wish I could get up and keep busy. I'm sure it would be better for me than just lying here worrying."

I hardly recognized her for the bright, cheerful Chloe I was used to. Her face was drawn and anxious; even the freckles on her short nose looked paler than usual. I wished I knew more about the business of having babies. Easy optimism didn't seem to fit the occasion. "What do the doctors say?" I asked.

She shrugged. "Not much. I saw a specialist last time. He said there wasn't anything obviously wrong and that probably everything would go quite normally next time. He said I mustn't let myself get worked up, but it's terribly hard not to when you want something very badly. I suppose I'm just not the placid type." She pushed back her hair nervously. "You see, Kate, John was married before and—it wasn't a success. His wife walked out on him and took their little boy with her. They're in America now and he never sees his son. I suppose John might have got—what do they call it?—custody of the boy. But he wouldn't take him away from his mother because he felt it wouldn't be in the child's best interest. He was only two at the time. So—so you see why I want so much to give him another son?"

"Yes," I said softly, "I do indeed. And I'm sure you will."

She smiled suddenly. "Kate, you're such a tonic and it's done me a world of good just to talk about it. I've plenty of acquaintances around here, but there's nobody I could talk to like this." She scrubbed at her eyes like a schoolgirl. "Now, for Pete's sake don't let me talk about myself any more. Look, if you're determined to go back to Lambton tonight I wonder if you'd do something for me?"

"Of course."

"I picked some strawberries for Bobby yesterday evening, before the rain started. I meant to take them to hospital myself this afternoon. I wonder if you'd drop them off for me."

She explained where the strawberries were and how to find the hospital.

"I'll see he gets them," I promised. I leaned down to hug Chloe and said, "See you soon. Don't worry, pal. It's going to be all right."

I left her valiantly tackling the knitting again and went downstairs.

Ben was rather silent on the drive to Lambton and I didn't feel particularly chatty either. I was thinking about Chloe and wishing I hadn't had to leave her with Val Deering in command.

When he arrived at the White Hart he carried my case

up to my room and looked around. "Will you be comfortable here?"

The room was at the back of the hotel. Small, but light and airy, overlooked the local cricket ground, where an evening match was in progress.

"I'll be fine," I told him.

He hesitated. "I hope so. I wish— Oh well, I suppose it was the best thing. Until tomorrow morning, then, Kate. Here's a spare front door key in case you get to the practice first."

When he had gone I unpacked my case and hung up my clothes in the closet. By then it was time to start finding my way to the hospital. I went down to the reception office, found out that dinner was served from seven onward, and set out on my way.

The Cottage Hospital was about ten minutes' walk from the center of the town. A cluster of low buildings, interspersed with drives, grass lawns, and flower beds bursting with geraniums, lobelias and yellow calceolarias. Visiting time was evidently in full swing. Inside the hospital every passage was milling with people, armed with carrier bags and flowers, who all seemed to know where they were going. It took me some time to find out where I was supposed to be going, but eventually I was directed to Benson Ward.

I paused outside. Through the open doors I heard the hum of many conversations. I could see the long double line of beds, with visitors' chairs drawn up to each, and the male patients, very neat in clean pajamas. Most of them were sitting up, but here and there chairs were drawn nearer the bed and all that could be seen of the patient was a long hump under the red blankets. I wondered which of the beds held Bobby, but I couldn't remember what he looked like.

A very young nurse came out of the ward and I stopped

her and said, "I've come to leave these for Mr. Farnham. Would you mind giving them to him, please?"

"I will do that," she replied, very prim and correct in her blue and white striped dress. "Who shall I say brought them, please?"

"Miss Kate Moorcroft," I told her. "But he won't know me. I'm only—"

"Will you please wait here a moment?"

She didn't stop to hear what I had to say, but tripped away down the ward with the basket of strawberries in one hand and the parcelled book in the other.

In no time at all she was back. "Will you come this way, please?"

"But I don't know—" I began.

The little nurse was standing no nonsense from me. "Mr. Farnham's mother is here," she announced firmly. "She says she'd like to see you."

Somewhat reluctantly I followed her into the ward. There seemed nothing else I could do.

Bobby Farnham's bed was at the very end of the row. The two things I saw about him immediately were that he had red hair and the cheeriest grin in the world. The next was that his right leg was hoisted toward the ceiling by a pulley.

A large blonde woman in a beige coat stood up from her chair beside the bed. "You're Miss Moorcroft who's helping Holland," she said. "Mrs. Garrett told me about you. I'm so glad you could come. It's lovely of you to bring Bobby such a beautiful book. It'll keep him amused for hours." She pulled up another chair for me. "Sit yourself down."

She held out her hand with an affable smile that disclosed a lot of teeth. As we shook hands I felt somewhat relieved. Ben had told me that Bobby wasn't nursing any resentment against Hugo and me for being in the car that he had run into, but I hadn't quite known what to expect.

I turned to the boy in the bed. "Hullo, Bobby. How are you getting along?"

"Okay," he said. He was examining the book with obvious delight. "This is super, Miss Moorcroft. It's pretty decent of you to get it for me after all the trouble I caused you."

"Trouble?" I smiled. "It's you that has the trouble, surely?"

He squinted up at his leg. "Oh well—it's not too bad. And my Dad says it'll teach me never to be a Biker. As if I ever would!"

He grinned cheerfully at me, but his eyes returned to the book and I could see that he was just itching to taste its delights. I mentally thanked the lucky chance that had led me to find the right gift and turned back to his mother.

If Bobby was a man of few words, Mrs. Farnham made up for it. There was no problem about making conversation with her; you just sat there and listened.

The doctors, I heard, were very pleased with Bobby now and he should be home, with his leg in a cast, of course, by the middle of next week. It would have been sooner only there had been a bit of infection, it seemed. They wouldn't say, however, when he'd be able to return to work. You could never get much out of them, could you?

In the following ten minutes I discovered that Bobby's father worked for the Rural District Council, but Bobby had always been one for farming and as he had an uncle in the next county who was a farmer, they had decided to send Bobby to the Agricultural School. He'd done splendidly there, and now he was working for Mr. Garrett; he was getting on very well too.

"But he'll be joining his uncle eventually, Miss Moorcroft. He hasn't any sons of his own, so it'll all work out very well."

Mrs. Farnham beamed at me all the time she was talking. She was quite evidently one of the world's optimists. When I got up to leave she shook hands with me again.

"I've so enjoyed meeting you, Miss Moorcroft," she assured me, "and I do hope you enjoy the rest of your stay in the country. Dr. Holland seems such a nice young man. We're all very pleased to have him for a dentist in Lambton. Old Dr. White was very clever in his day, of course, but he was getting past it, poor old thing. He should have given up long before he did. Everyone was afraid he'd pull out the wrong tooth because his sight wasn't too good at the end, but he never did." She trilled with laughter. "They say that Dr. Holland is a very good dentist and I'm sure he'll be popular here. Everyone speaks most highly of him. I must really make an appointment for myself one of these days. Dr. Deering keeps telling me I should have my teeth attended to."

She paused for breath, and I began to edge politely away, but she talked on and on. There was a good deal about her operation three years ago, and how she'd never really pulled up since and it must have had an effect on her teeth.

Finally she got back to Ben. "A nice little place he's got there in High Street. Needed a lot doing to it, of course, when Dr. White went, but Mr. Pill's doing it up, I hear, and you couldn't have a better workman in." She smiled knowingly. "Dr. Holland'll want it specially nice, I'm sure, as he'll be getting married fairly soon."

The large face with the complicated mass of golden hair was very close to mine, wearing a confidential expression.

Something seemed to be expected of me, so I murmured, "Oh?"

"Oh yes, didn't you know? It's Valerie Deering, Dr. Deering's daughter. She's very pretty; they'll make a lovely young pair. And she'll be useful to him in his practice, too, as she's the doctor's daughter." She nodded and smiled with satisfaction, as if she had personally arranged the whole affair.

Suddenly I'd had more than enough of Mrs. Farnham. "I really must be going—" I began determinedly.

"Yes, of course. You mustn't let me keep you with my gossiping, but it's been so nice to have a chat. Come in and see Bobby again; he'd be so pleased. And you must come and have tea with us before you go back to London. Ask Mrs. Garrett to bring you along—"

Finally I said my goodbyes, got away and walked slowly back to the White Hart. It had been a very hot day after the thunder last night and there seemed no air anywhere. It's rare for me to feel tired: Daddy always said I was as tough as a terrier, but now my legs were beginning to ache. I felt dusty, sticky and generally out of spirits. I wished I hadn't gone into the ward to see Bobby, or at least that I hadn't had to listen to Mrs. Farnham.

There was a delicious smell of dinner in the air at the White Hart. I had a luxurious bath and decided to change for my solitary meal. Suddenly I felt a need to get away from the little white blouses and linen skirts that I'd been wearing ever since I came to Lambton. They'd seemed the most suitable things for country wear, but now I found myself yearning for something much more dashing.

My wardrobe disclosed only one dress that had any element of dash about it. I'd bought it impulsively in a boutique the day after I met Hugo. It was a fashionable one in moss-green crêpe with a wide silver kid belt clipping it in at the waist.

It was the kind of dress that demands lots of make-up, so I sat down at the dressing table and applied myself to the job. My face is small and rather pale; when I'm giving myself the full treatment I always accent my eyes because Louise says they are my best point. Louise, in fact, taught me most of what I know about make-up, so I did complicated things with liners and little brushes. Finally I stroked my lids lightly with a new shadow called, romantically, Green Glen. When I'd finished, my face looked quite different; my eyes were darker, larger and almost mysterious. It was rather fun.

I twisted and turned in front of the mirror; my dress swung out softly. I thought with a grin what a pity it was that I wasn't going to a party, instead of a solitary meal in the dining room of the White Hart.

As I ran down the stairs into the hall the first person I saw, amazingly, between the leaves of the revolving door, was Hugo.

I forgot all about my poise. "Hugo!" I squeaked gladly, and ran to meet him.

He took both my hands; the old Hugo smile spread out. The deep velvet voice said, "Katy—well met indeed! But I though you were exiled in the wilds?"

"I've just moved out," I told him, and explained briefly why.

"Fine," he said and his eyes admired me. "You look marvelous, Katy love. Like a mermaid."

My knees began to feel weak as they always did when Hugo looked at me like that, but I clutched at my poise and said, "Anyway, what brings you out here?"

"Business," he said. "I'll tell you later. First of all, I'll buy you some dinner. What's the food like here? Or would you rather move somewhere else?"

"It suits me. Though it may not meet your exalted standards."

"We'll risk it." He beckoned to a passing waiter and booked a table.

The White Hart boasted a cosy little bar so Hugo installed me at a corner table and left me with a drink while he went to tidy up. When he returned and sank into the chair close to mine I said, "I feel like Cinderella must

have felt; expecting a lonely evening and then being asked
to the Ball after all.''

His eyes smiled lazily into mine over the rim of his
glass. ''You look the part too, love, I must say. After the
fairy godmother had done her stuff, that is. Quite
ravishing, that's my Katy. Sure you haven't got your eye
on any of the local talent?''

I giggled and glanced around at the assortment of travelers, busy with their order books, and the young
propping up the bar. ''Can't say I've noticed any.''

''Lucky for me, then,'' said Hugo smugly. ''I rather see
myself as the fairy prince.''

And that, I'm afraid, set the level of our conversation
all through dinner. Not exactly highbrow, perhaps, but it
was fun. I found myself laughing as I hadn't laughed since
the last time I saw Hugo. I expect the wine had something to do with it, too. Hugo's an expert on wines.

As we sauntered into the lounge and settled down to
drink our coffee Hugo said, ''And now I've told you all
the gossip from the big city since last we met. How about
you?''

''Oh well—'' I rather halted at giving Hugo, or anybody else, an account of the difficulties I'd run up against
at the practice. It was Ben's business really, not mine.
''Nothing exciting's been happening here. We've been
pretty busy; routine stuff mostly. By the way, I've just
been to the hospital.''

''Hospital? Nobody ill, is there?''

''Hugo! The accident—the boy who was hurt!''

''Oh, that boy.'' He held up a finger to the waiter and
asked for cigars to be brought. ''How's he coming along?
Wild young idiot!''

''Improving,'' I said a little shortly, telling myself that
there was no reason why Hugo should be particularly
concerned. ''And I don't believe he is a wild young idiot.
He seems a nice, steady boy. It must have been a

moment's lack of concentration. By the way, he's a pupil at the farm where I've been staying; it's been a blow to them, having him off work."

"I bet it has," Hugo said, selecting a cigar.

"Did you hear any more about it from the police? Will there be a case?" I hoped Bobby wouldn't have to face a magistrate's court, but it seemed only too likely that he would.

Hugo shrugged. "I turned the whole thing over to my lawyer, but I haven't heard yet whether the arm of the law is going to pursue the matter. I'm in the clear, anyhow. Look, Katy, don't let's talk about accidents and hospitals. Let's talk about us. I've got to move on to Stratford tonight, worse luck. Pa's got a scheme on for a special tour for a bevy of matrons. Shakespeare country—you know, they love it. We're going to center them on Stratford and then do a round tour for them—Warwick, Kenilworth, Charlecote, the Birthplace, Anne Hatheway's Cottage—the lot. I'm supposed to be staying with the Faulkners, Mr. and Mrs. who run the big hotel by the theatre. Know it? They're taking the bookings for us and there's a fair amount to organize as it's a rush job. It's a nuisance that I'm expected there; still, I don't have to rush away just yet." He glanced at his watch. "Nine-thirty. How about a drive first? I've got the old man's car with me and she's a beauty; I'd like to show her off to you."

"Lovely," I said. "I'll fetch a coat."

I finished my coffe and ran to my room, glanced quickly in the mirror and took a light coat out of the closet. Turning to leave, I saw Hugo standing in the doorway.

"Permission to enter?" He smiled at me and came in without waiting for a reply. "I just had an idea, Katy love." He closed the door and leaned against it. "I could phone the Faulkners and say I'd been detained and would turn up early tomorrow. It wouldn't make any difference to them. The hotel here could doubtless put me up." He paused and looked around my room. "What about it?"

I wasn't going to pretend I didn't know what he meant. I'd lived in London for three years. "I think," I said, "that you'd better stick to your original arrangement."

The closet where I was standing was quite close to the door. He stretched out and touched my shoulder very lightly. "Really and truly?"

"Really and truly," I said, and smiled very matter-of-factly at him. "Lambton's a very small town, you know."

That wasn't really the point at all, but I didn't want to get involved in a fight. I hoped Hugo would be reasonable; I thought he would, but you never know.

His eyes looked me over for what seemed ages. Then he said, grinning ruefully. "Ah well, the lady always decides. Still, it would have been nice. Come on then, girl, we won't stay here. Come and sample my Pa's wonderful car."

I breathed freely again, reasonably pleased with the way I'd handled the situation and liking Hugo better for taking it so well.

The car was a dream; a great silent glossy monster that licked up the miles like a cat lapping a saucer of cream.

"I'm trying to persuade Pa that he needs a new bus, in which case he'd turn this one over to me. Look, have you seen this?"

We were a few miles outside Lambton when he pulled over and switched on the inside light to show me all the gadgets: the coffee and tea maker, the electric shaver, the built-in portable television, the tip-back seats.

Overwhelmed, I said, "It's fabulous!"

He smiled down at me. One hand went to switch off the light and the other one slid along the back of my seat. "You're pretty fabulous yourself, love," he whispered into my hair, and drew me close to him.

But we didn't linger very long. Hugo, with rare lack of foresight, had stopped on a main road, and the approaching headlights were quite an embarrassment.

"Damn," he breathed as the umpteenth ones flared up and passed us with a friendly and derisive hooting. "Blasted idiots! Oh well—" he let me go "—this is evidently no place for a dalliance. We'd better get back and wait for a more propitious moment. You are coming to London next weekend, aren't you, Katy? I've got a surprise for you."

"Another surprise? You're good at surprises, aren't you? Turning up tonight like—like—"

"A bad penny?" he suggested softly, leaning down to rub his cheek against mine.

"No, a fairy prince, had you forgotten? And now, hadn't you better drive me back—that is, if you're not going to tell me what the surprise is."

"Ah, but that would spoil it, sweetie. You must wait until Saturday."

He chuckled, reversed the car in a lane and drove back to the hotel.

"I'd love to come in for another drink," he said, "only better not, as I'm driving." He opened the door on my side. "This has been grand, Katy. A bonus for being a good boy and doing what Pa told me. Staying with the Faulkners, that is. They're somewhat of a bore. Look, I'll call you about arrangements for the weekend. I saw the garage people here a little while ago and they say the car should be ready by Friday, so I may come up to collect it Friday evening. If not, it'll be Saturday morning. Okay?"

"Fine," I said. "And thanks for the dinner, and everything, Hugo."

He smiled into my eyes. His own eyes were very dark brown, very dreamy. "It might have been better—it might have been heaven. Sure you won't change your mind? All right, I can see you won't. 'Bye then, Katy."

He put his arm around me and bent to kiss me. It wasn't exactly a lingering kiss, but it wasn't just a good-bye peck either. Something between the two.

I stood and watched the big car purr away up High Street; even when it had disappeared I still stood there. On the far side of the road, as I looked through the ranks of parked cars, I could see the blue front door of the practice. It seemed to belong to another world.

It had been too warm in the car to need my coat. Now I slung it around my shoulders and turned into the hotel. I'd have an early night, I decided, and make up for the sleep I'd lost last night.

And then as I put my foot on the bottom step, I looked up and saw Ben, outside the entrance door. He looked as if he'd been standing there for some time.

It was an odd moment. If Ben was surprised at seeing me, all dressed up in my war-paint, embracing Hugo beside a car that had no doubt cost several thousand pounds, he certainly didn't show it. His face showed absolutely nothing.

"Your watch, Kate," he said, holding it out to me. "You left it on the shelf in the bathroom."

I took it from him. "Oh, thank you so much. I hadn't missed it yet, but I expect I should have done later on. How stupid of me—I might have overslept and been late for work. Hugo turned up unexpectedly—did you see him? He's just gone off to Stratford on business. His father runs a travel agency, you know—"

The look on Ben's face effectively stemmed the flood of chatter. There was no doubt about that look; it was the expression of a man caught by a boring female and longing to get away.

"Oh well—" I trailed off idiotically. "You'll be wanting to get back, I expect. Thank you so much for this." I indicated the watch. "It was so good of you to bring it, but you really shouldn't have bothered."

"I didn't," he said. "I had to come in to the practice for some papers, so I thought I might as well drop it off for you."

He turned to his car. It must have been parked right behind Hugo's glittering monster and I hadn't noticed it.

"Well, thank you again—" I babbled.

He nodded, gave me a pleasant salute and drove away. I climbed slowly up to my room.

"Damn," I said, sinking on to the bed. "Oh, damn, damn, damn!"

I didn't really know why I said it. Even at that point, I didn't know. I just wished I hadn't dressed up. I wished Hugo hadn't come. I wished—I didn't know what I wished.

Before I finally went to sleep that night I did a lot of thinking and asked myself a lot of questions. About my job, about London, about the country, about Hugo. And about Ben Holland.

But I didn't arrive at a satisfactory answer to any of the questions, except the final one. The answer to that was very clear. To Ben, I was a London girl and as such would never touch his life anywhere at all. There was, I assured myself, no reason to wish it otherwise.

And yet—and yet—

CHAPTER TEN

It was obvious from the very start of Thursday morning that Celia Marsh was a star pupil.

I knew a little about training dental surgery attendants. In the first London practice I worked at I'd helped to train several girls straight from school. But even though they were young and keen, they couldn't compete with Celia's intelligence and unobtrusive competence. She had neat hands, a lovely soft voice; she was very quick on the uptake. I never had to tell her anything twice.

By the end of the day she was assisting Ben with the routine amalgam fillings as if she'd been at it all her working life.

I could tell that Ben himself was delighted with her. Now and again as she handed him an instrument, or took one that he had finished with, he glanced up at her with a fleeting smile of appreciation that he'd never given to me. But then, of course, I had got off on the wrong foot right from the start.

When the final patient had gone Ben heaved a sigh of contentment.

"That," he said, "was what I call a highly satisfactory day." He began to unbutton his white coat and Celia moved quickly to his side to help him off with it. "My thanks to you both for excellent team work. And now, if I'm not wanted for anything else, I'm going to cut along back to Summerfields. John wants me to do the hens for him. It's Chloe's job usually," he added with a glance in my direction. "Will you lock up, Kate, when you've finished?"

I promised to do so, and he went off. Celia and I spent another half hour going through the various forms. She asked me a few questions about general office routine.

When I'd finished explaining she nodded. "I think I've got everything fairly well now. It's just a matter of practice." Her clear gray eyes met mine with a smile. "Thanks a lot, Kate; you explain things very well."

I smiled back. "You take things in very well. Mutual admiration society!" I replaced the cards in the filing cabinet, closed the drawer, and said, "How does it appeal, all this?" I waved my hand around the surgery.

She paused before she replied. "I think I'll like it very much. It's not the same as nursing, of course, but it's the next best thing. You're helping people, making them comfortable. And you can't have everything," she added with a cheerfulness that sounded just a trifle assumed.

I said, "I heard about your mother being ill. I hope it isn't anything serious."

She was silent for a moment or two. Then she seemed to make up her mind. "I'd appreciate your advice," she said. "You've been working with Dr. Holland. You must know him fairly well?"

"I've only been here this week," I said, "and I don't think he's very easy to know. Why?"

She spread her fingers out on the desk and looked down at them. "My conscience is pricking me, that's why. You see, my mother is a patient of Dr. Deering's. She asked him if he knew of any nursing job in this part of the world. That's how I got in touch with Dr. Holland."

"Yes, I understood that. But—"

"But it wasn't because my mother is so ill that she needs me to look after her. She has a spot of arthritis, but nothing very much. I wanted to come here to live with my mother because—well, because it was the only way I could think of to keep my baby with me."

I took that in for a while, saying nothing, waiting for her to go on; after a bit she did.

She was rather pale, but she met my eyes calmly. "I

didn't think I should feel bad about this, but now I do. I should have told Dr. Holland the truth when I applied for the job. In fact, I deliberately misled him, saying I had left general nursing because I had to look after my mother. Now I've met him and seen the sort of man he is, I'm feeling guilty. He's the kind of person you feel you must be completely honest with, isn't he?"

I remembered suddenly how I'd felt the same way myself when I first met Ben. "I think you're right," I said.

Celia smiled faintly. "Now I've told you so much, may I tell you the rest? No, I'm not married, and so far as I can see, not likely to be. We were—terribly in love. It was all quite hopeless and eventually we had to make up our minds to finish it. He was going abroad. He's in the Middle East now, for his firm, and has taken his wife and family with him. He—doesn't know anything about the baby. That was my decision. I wanted his child if that was all I could ever have of him. I suppose you think I'm crazy?"

"Do you think you are?"

"No, I don't. It's what I wanted and what I still want."

"Then I don't think you're crazy," I said. "But—"

She looked up at me, smiling faintly. She must have heard that reservation in people's voices so often. "Yes?"

"Forgive me," I said, "but do you mean you haven't told him about the baby?"

She shook her head. "No. Why should I involve him? It's my show."

That rather took my breath away. At last I said helplessly, "I think you're very brave, and that's all I can say. And if you want my advice, you'll tell Ben Holland just what you've told me."

"Thanks. That's all I wanted to know. I'm sure you're right." For the first time during our strange little conversation she looked rather embarrassed as she added, "I rather wish you weren't going back to London, Kate."

First Chloe and now Celia. I was leaving some good friends behind me, I thought rather sadly.

I began to tidy up the desk. "Boy or girl?" I asked.

"Boy. Peter, and he's only four months old."

I guessed why she'd chosen that name by the way she spoke it.

"I'd love to see a picture of him," I said. "Do you have one?"

Celia's eyes lit up. "I'd like to show you in person, so to speak. Mother's meeting me and she'll bring Peter with her. Come along and see them both."

We found Mrs. Marsh in the back seat of a little red Mini, parked in the side road by the church, the baby, very much awake and alert, on her knee.

Celia bent down to the window. "Mother, this is Kate Moorcroft who's come from London for a few days to help out at the practice. She's been orientating me most wonderfully and I feel quite confident already."

Celia's mother was comfortably dressed in a blue sweater and skirt. She had soft gray hair and the same calm eyes as her daughter. I thought I could see where Celia had got her courageous acceptance of life.

"How very nice to meet you, my dear," Mrs. Marsh said warmly. "Come and sit inside for a few minutes so we can talk properly."

Celia got into the driving seat. I squeezed in beside her and twisted around so that I could see Peter. He was a gorgeous baby, with huge blue eyes that stared solemnly at me. I grinned back, waiting to see whether he approved of me or not, and was quite gratified when he gurgled and waved his arms, apparently a gesture of acceptance.

"He likes you, Kate," Celia said. "Come on, my pet, over you come." She took her son from her mother; held him for a moment, her cheek against his fine gold hair, and deposited him on my knee.

"He's simply heaven," I said to Celia, and saw her eyes glow. "I see what you mean."

It ended with my going to the Marshes' cottage for a meal. Later we talked, and I told them about my job with Dr. Hartington and how he'd sent me to help out Ben when he had lost his dental nurse.

Mrs. Marsh looked puzzled. "But I thought the letter from Dr. Deering said that Dr. Holland was without any help. Isn't that what he said, dear?"

Celia said, "I thought it was. That was how I read it, anyway. It must have been a misunderstanding. It was rather lucky for me, because it means that I'll have Kate until she leaves."

We began to talk of other things, but the thought lingered that perhaps it wasn't a misunderstanding after all. Perhaps Val was behind the letter; she might even have written it herself. I had the strange thought that she would stop at nothing to get rid of me. I supposed she just had a jealous and suspicious nature, because she certainly hadn't any reason to fear me as a rival. Quite the reverse, I thought wryly, remembering the polite coolness on his face as he drove away from the hotel that evening.

I stayed with Celia and her mother until after ten o'clock. By the time I left I felt as if I'd known them all my life. As she drove me to Lambton Celia said, "I'm so glad you could come. Mother liked you so much, I could see that straight away. It's a bit much to ask her to look after Peter all the time, but that's how she wants it. It seems the best solution. We're awfully good friends and see eye to eye on most things. I suppose we'll have to be very careful not to spoil Peter. Two women at his beck and call—you know—it might be bad for him." She sighed. "It isn't ideal. But then nothing in life is ideal, is it?"

I've never suspected myself of being psychic, but at that

moment I had the strongest possible feeling that Celia was wrong; Peter wouldn't be brought up exclusively by two women. Some day there would be marriage and happiness for Celia, I was sure of it.

But I knew she wouldn't believe me, just then, if I told her so.

That night I couldn't sleep.

Three years ago there had been a bad patch when I would lie awake for hours at night; it was so bad that the nights had become something to dread. But London had cured that. Once I started training at hospital I was so tired by bedtime that sleep came as soon as my head touched the pillow.

Now, it seemed, sleeplessness was grabbing me again. I pummelled the pillow and flopped over for the 20th time and tried to blot out the skittling thoughts.

It must have been about two o'clock that the idea came to me; it was so beautifully simple that I couldn't imagine why I'd overlooked it.

I was going back to London tomorrow and *wasn't returning to Lambton*.

Right from the beginning this project of coming to the country had gone wrong. Once you pull up your roots and plant yourself somewhere you should stay there, I argued to myself. There is, as they say, no going back. You'll only be unsettled and confused.

I wasn't needed here anymore. With one more day's help Celia was perfectly capable of managing on her own. As for Chloe, she had Val to look after things until she could take over herself again; not ideal, maybe, but the best solution in the circumstances.

No, there was nothing to keep me here. I'd speak to Ben about it as soon as possible tomorrow. After I decided that I felt as if a huge weight had lifted. I must have been asleep within minutes.

What I never expected was that Ben would get to me first.

He tackled me at the end of morning surgery. Celia had gone to the restaurant to buy our lunch, and I was on my way to the kitchen to brew coffee when he stopped me.

"Kate—just a moment."

I turned.

"I've been thinking," he said. "Now please don't get this wrong, or believe I don't appreciate what you've done here. But—well—it's fairly obvious that you're yearning to be in London. You told me so yourself at the beginning, remember? Very natural, of course."

He was smiling at me. I felt I hardly knew this courteous, smoothly polite Ben, and I didn't know whether I wanted to.

"So," he continued, "as Celia seems set to take the work in her stride there's really no need to trespass on your good nature any longer."

It was exactly the way I'd planned to put it myself (except that stuff about trespassing on my good nature). There was no reason at all why I should have felt so horribly let down.

"You mean you don't want me after the weekend?" I blurted out naïvely.

He stopped smiling; the old frown of irritation seemed to settle on his forehead. I almost laughed to think how much more familiar and—yes—more likeable he seemed that way.

"That's not what I said." He glared at me angrily. "I hoped I wouldn't be as ungracious as that, after all your help."

He turned to the cabinet, picked up a trimming knife and started to carve the edges off a plaster model.

"Oh, I didn't mean—" I began miserably, and stopped, seeing the hopelessness of explaining what, exactly, I did mean.

"Thank you for releasing me," I went on. "We'll fix it like that, then, shall we? Hugo will be picking me up either tomorrow evening or Saturday morning. Is that all right with you?"

"Perfectly. Make whatever arrangements suit you best. I've instructed the White Hart to send me the bill."

Formal. Stiff. I nearly blew up and shouted at him, *For goodness's sake, Ben Holland, be yourself!* But of course I didn't. The certain sympathy that existed between us was only in my own imagination.

"Thank you," I said again and retreated to the kitchen, feeling that I was shedding my battered poise in small fragments along the way.

Soon after Celia arrived with lunch, Ben put his head around the kitchen door and said, "I'll be out for a while. Okay?"

When he'd gone Celia said, "Does he usually go out for lunch? I bought enough sandwiches for all of us."

I put the plates on the table. "Don't worry—it's happened to me, too. He's very friendly with the Deerings and often goes there for lunch. I imagine he talks over any cases he has with the doctor. And then, of course, there's Val. Have you met Val Deering?"

Celia shook her head. "No."

She was looking inquiringly at me; there must have been something in my tone of voice, I suppose. "Don't worry, you will," I said, and changed the subject quickly by telling Celia that I'd arranged to return to London for good on the weekend.

"Oh dear, I'd been looking forward to us working together next week. Must you go back so soon?"

I'd told her the bare bones of the situation last night—about Dr. Hartington being away in Italy and so on, but nothing about Hugo.

"Well, the fact is that there's a man in London," I said, "and Dr. Holland thinks I'm yearning to leave for that reason. He thinks he's doing me a good turn by letting me go."

Celia cut a sandwich in half. "Oh," she said.

I knew she wasn't the kind of person to pry or ask questions. "The thing is," I went on, "that I'm not quite sure myself whether I'm yearning or not. I think I'd have appreciated another week here, really, but—oh well, it's all somewhat complicated and probably better this way."

Celia was regarding me thoughtfully. "I hope things work out for you, Kate," she said in her lovely, calm voice, and somehow I was comforted.

Hugo phoned me at the hotel that evening. He'd just come from Stratford, he said, and was enjoying civilization.

"What's wrong with Stratford-on-Avon?" I said quickly.

"Nothing wrong with it, sweetie," Hugo drawled. "Except that it isn't me. All so self-consciously part of England's great and glorious heritage, and horribly commercialized at that."

I could feel myself bristling, but I couldn't argue with Hugo over the phone; in a way I supposed he was right. And yet—I loved Stratford. I'd been to school there. Until I left for London it had been "my" town: the town where I went to shop, meet my friends, gossip in the Tudor tea room, and walk along by the river to watch the swans. I knew every bit of it, every narrow little side street, every funny old building, and I found now that I still nostalgically loved it. It was part of my youth that I'd left behind.

I brought my mind back to what Hugo was saying. "—so it'll be Friday evening. I just called the garage and the car will be ready to collect then so I'll drive the little jalopy up, exchange it, and then pick you up at the hotel, somewhere around seven. Okay?"

"Fine," I said. I wondered fleetingly whether to tell him that I wasn't coming back after the weekend, but decided against.

"Good. I'm busy working on that surprise I told you about. No, don't ask me about it. 'Bye for now, then, love."

"Goodbye, Hugo." I hung up, amused at the mystery. Life would never be dull with Hugo around.

Suddenly I felt eager to be away from this place and in London, where nothing had changed. My job was there, waiting for me. Louise and the apartment would be there to welcome me. Hugo hadn't, after all, lost interest; we could continue from where we left off.

Yes, all things considered, I was a lucky girl.

Friday was the busiest day we'd had since I went to Lambton. The front doorbell rang incessantly; the waiting room bulged at the seams with patients, some with appointments, some hopefully without.

"Dr. White always used to see me whenever I could manage to get here," one woman told me with a kind of weak and desperate aggressiveness. "We've only got one bus a day that goes through our village and I have to come when I can manage. I've been awake half the night with the pain and then when I did sleep, the baby woke me up again, crying. I've had to leave all the children with my husband to get here at all and he ought to be at work on the haymaking, and his boss'll be furious—"

She was a scraggy little woman, probably not much more than 30. Tired from trying to make both ends meet on a farm laborer's wages and keeping her children fed, clean and tidy, she looked years older.

I couldn't possibly turn her away. "Come and sit down," I said, "and I'll fit you in as soon as I can." I hadn't the heart to deliver the usual lecture about making an appointment.

Ben did fit her in, as well as three more emergencies that morning and two extra in the afternoon.

By the time the last patient left he was looking more tired than I'd ever seen him. His face was pale, and his dark hair clung damply to his forehead.

"I've made some tea," I said. "Come and have a rest, both of you." Celia had been coping with all the surgery work this afternoon while I did odd jobs like attending to the door, the phone and keeping the files up to date.

Celia fed the last batch of instruments into the sterilizer and levered the lid down. "Bless you," she said. "That was quite an afternoon, wasn't it?"

Ben peeled off his white jacket and threw it with a weary grunt over the back of the chair. "I should go home," he said. "I promised John I'd lend a hand. . . ."

But he came into the kitchen with us and accepted the cup of tea and biscuits I put before him on the big table.

"It looks," he said to Celia, "as if I'll have to work Saturday mornings, to cope. I've resisted it up to now. How would you feel about it?" He looked worried. "I know I specified a five-day week."

Celia smiled. "I'm a nurse, remember? I'm not conditioned to five-day weeks. Yes, I'll come in on Saturday mornings with pleasure, so long as I can take the odd hour off now and again to shop, when we're slack."

"Of course you can." Ben looked at her with amazed approval and then glanced at me. "She's wonderful, isn't she?" His mouth twisted a fraction. "I'm sure you're thinking that I don't deserve my luck, Kate?"

"Why not?" I quipped in the same tone. "Since you ask me, I'd say you do deserve your luck to have Celia. And the way you've worked today you could do with two or three more willing slaves to wait on you."

The blue eyes narrowed. "Is that how you think of me—as a slave-driver?"

I sipped my tea. Now that Ben was no longer my chief we could spar on equal terms.

I glanced at him demurely. "Would you really like to know what I think of you, Dr. Holland?"

For all our bright fooling, he was looking at me intently. Once again blue electricity seemed to sizzle in the air between us.

"I'll risk it," he said quietly.

In the outer part of my visual field I saw Celia move to the door, murmuring something about the sterilizer. Ben and I were left alone together. I knew dimly that the moment held some kind of importance; knew it with my heart, that is. My mind told me all sorts of other things, plunging about like a startled pony. Mostly it told me to stop imagining; that dreams were dangerous and that loving people was likely to hurt; that Ben Holland was a man who went after what he wanted. If I were what he wanted he would have made it plain before now. He wouldn't play about with the subject as Hugo might.

No, a girl would know when Ben was serious.

I leaned back in my chair and smiled straightforwardly and without any girl-to-man provocativeness. I said, "I know we've skirmished, but I have enjoyed working with you, and I'm sure you'll do marvelously well in the practice here."

We sat there, one on each side of the big kitchen table, the sunshine pouring through the window; shining straight onto Ben's face, making his blue eyes even more brilliant than usual. The set of his mouth was as firm as ever, so firm that it almost looked strained.

Then he relaxed and smiled. "Thank you, Kate, for those kind words. I've enjoyed our working together too. I'm sorry it's been so short."

"But Celia is splendid," I reminded him.

"Yes," he said almost absently. "Celia is splendid." He glanced at his watch and stood up. "John will be looking for me. I must leave."

Automatically I took his jacket from the hook on the door and held it out for him.

His mouth twitched. "Still playing the willing slave?"

"To the end."

Keeping up the gay badinage stuff was becoming more and more of an effort. I said seriously, "Will you please give my love to Chloe and tell her how sorry I am that I couldn't see her to say goodbye. I hope things go well for her. I expect I'll hear news from Dr. Hartington when the baby arrives."

Ben frowned. "But you could have seen her—" he began uncertainly.

I shook my head. "Transport too complicated. Besides, Hugo is calling for me about six-thirty, so there really wouldn't have been time."

"No," he said, "of course not." I thought he seemed relieved

He hesitated and then held out his hand. "Well, goodbye, Kate, and again many thanks. The best of luck to you."

"And to you."

Our hands met in a brief, firm grip. Then he was gone and for some idiotic reason I wanted to cry.

Endings of anything are always sad. There was one more thing, though, that I wanted very much to see again.

"I'll be with you in a moment," I called to Celia as I passed the surgery door on my way upstairs.

Mr. Pill and George had gone; the living room was bare and white and full of sunlight, just as it had been when I was up here with Ben choosing the wallpaper.

I went to the window and looked out. Immediately below was the neglected garden. Suddenly I saw it all as it would be when the grass was cut, the borders weeded, the ragged shrubs pruned and given room to breathe and grow. I saw it at the end of the summer; a little peaceful haven within its boundaries of beech and laurel, with a garden swing, perhaps, and tea laid out on the lawn.

Blindly I turned away from the window and almost

tripped over something I hadn't noticed before: rolls of wallpaper stacked like organ pipes against the bare pinkish plaster. One roll had fallen sideways and the end had come unstuck. I stood looking down at it, wondering if Ben would remember, as he sat here in this pleasant room, when the day's work was finished, the girl who had chosen the wallpaper. It was an odd thought; funny really, only I couldn't laugh.

I bent down and unrolled the farther.

The pattern wasn't the one I had chosen. I frowned at it, thinking for a moment that Mr. Pill or his lad George had made a mistake. Then I recognized the paper that Val Deering had enthused about—smudgy yellow roses leered up at me.

Ben must have altered the order slip after I left the two of them together, must have changed to the paper that Val approved.

Well, and why shouldn't he, for goodness's sake? Nothing could be more natural.

And nothing could have brought me more quickly to my senses. I rolled up the loose end and replaced the piece with the others.

After that it was easy to leave the practice. I was able to believe, now, that there was nothing here for me, never had been and never would be.

All that remained was to help Celia clear up the surgery, say my goodbyes to her, and walk out of the front door for the last time.

And it couldn't, I thought, be a moment too soon for me.

CHAPTER ELEVEN

"And now for my surprise." Hugo's voice was a long way away. I must have been half-asleep for the last few miles, for I opened my eyes and saw the Marble Arch slipping by on our right. The white panther, restored to glossy perfection, was turning into Park Lane.

I sat up in my softly cushioned corner, blinking. London was at its best on a summer evening, and I reminded myself how glad I was to be here, and how exciting it all was.

We followed the procession of red taillights along the smooth wide road, the park shadowy on one side, the tall, impressive buildings on the other.

I said, "If you go along past the Albert Hall and into Kensington High Street, then our apartment is near the subway station—"

Hugo grinned without turning his head. I saw the crinkles fan out beside his eyes.

"First things first, sweetie," he murmured.

The Dorchester loomed on our left and soon, unexpectedly, Hugo turned off the main road. Two minutes later he negotiated the car into a narrow passage and stopped outside a block of town houses.

I sat and stared at this typical bit of the West End, where money for the purchase "desirable residences" is no problem at all. And indeed the little houses were beautiful: low and white-painted, with geraniums sprouting from wrought iron baskets, coach lamps beside the front doors.

Hugo opened my door for me, looking very pleased with himself.

"Something nice to show you," he said as he fitted a key into the nearest front door and stood aside for me to enter.

I suppose I'd been too deep in my own blurred thoughts to think ahead. But now it dawned on me what Hugo had been so mysterious about.

I stood in a small square hall, my feet sinking into inch-deep cyclamen carpet and blinked at the elegance around.

"It's—it's yours?"

"All my very own—for the period of the lease, that is." He looked smug. "I've been waiting for just the right place to turn up. I had an apartment in Streatham before I went to Europe, but I gave it up. Too isolated. Barry Cox has been looking for a place for me ever since. This came on the market last week—furnished—everything in—and I snapped it up, needless to say. Not bad, is it?"

"Not bad" was the understatement of the century. As we approached the room on the left the sheer luxury of the place closed in behind me like a soft eiderdown. Everything was cushioned, muted; you felt that the deep white chairs and the gold velvet hangings would swallow any sound. There was a low bench of satiny wood running the whole length of the room; massed flowers in an urn in one corner. Invisible lights threw a glow over everything.

"A bit lush, perhaps," Hugo said, "but it'll appeal to the customers. I have to do a fair bit of entertaining for business."

"It's all very—elegant," I said, and for some treacherous reason another room came to my mind—bare and empty, with the sunlight flooding in. The comparison was hardly fair; as any sun which could penetrate this dark little passage had set long ago. It must be, I guessed, almost midnight, for it had been after eight before we left Lambton, and we'd stopped for a leisurely meal on the way.

"Like to tidy up, sweetie, while I fix drinks? That door in the corner."

If the sitting room had cushioned me like a quilt, the bathroom was more like diving into a tropical fish tank.

Dull green panelling, a sunken bath, mirrors everywhere.

I stared at my reflection to see a girl in a yellow dress with big, dark eyes which looked back at me questioningly.

"Well, what now?" I asked myself, but there wasn't any answer forthcoming. My mind seemed to have gone off duty.

When I returned to the sitting room Hugo said, "My turn now. Make yourself at home, Katy," and disappeared into the bathroom.

I sank into one of the buttoned white chairs and it swallowed me into its depths.

I could, I thought, just get up and walk out now. That would be the wise, the sensible thing to do, but I didn't seem capable of moving. I only knew somehow that I was facing the biggest decision of my life. Not merely the decision about whether to stay here with Hugo tonight, but about everything that would happen afterward. It was frightening.

Hugo was back too soon. "What's your drink, Katy?" He flicked open a cabinet door to disclose rows of bottles gleaming in a whitely-lit interior.

"Oh—bitter lemon, please." We'd had a bottle of wine with dinner.

"Bitter lemon and what?" He held up the half-full crystal glass.

"Just bitter lemon."

"Rubbish," said Hugo lightly. "We can't have a party on bitter lemon, can we?" He selected a bottle and tipped something from it generously into my glass.

"I don't think—" I began.

"You don't need to think, love." Hugo's voice was amused, caressing. He put the glass into my hand. "Drink up like a good girl."

When I thought about it afterward, I decided that I must have a guardian angel after all. Just at that moment he helped by stiffening my backbone. Or perhaps it was just that I suddenly saw how stupid it all was; stupid and ordinary and shoddy, in spite of the elegant surroundings.

Hugo poured a drink for himself. "Rather better than the hotel at Lambton, eh?"

Poor Hugo, I thought, how carefully he'd planned all this—his own place, the perfect setting.

I took a sip of my drink and put it down on the long bench.

"Hugo dear," I said, with more confidence than I felt, "I'm awfully tired. Won't you be an angel and take me home now, please?"

I saw his face change as he took the point. "Take you home? What are you talking about, Kate? You must have known—you came with me—"

"Not exactly," I reminded him "It was your surprise "thing," remember? I didn't expect—" My voice trailed off.

He gazed at me moodily, twiddling his glass around and around. Then as I got out of my chair he put his arm across my shoulder and pulled me close. "Let's not argue, Katy," he said softly and nuzzled his mouth into my neck.

I pulled away smartly. My heart was thudding and my conscience was delivering sharp pricks. I'd put myself into this situation and I despised myself now for doing it. Subconsciously I must have known, all the time, what was brewing. Hugo admittedly had his good points, but he wasn't the kind of man who flashes a diamond ring at you and then takes you to meet his parents.

"I'm sorry, Hugo, really I am," I said, "but I'm not a bit what you want, really I'm not."

He grinned. "I know what I want, love. I've had plenty of time to think about you, since that first evening, and now that the place is right—"

"But it isn't right," I broke in desperately. "Nothing's right. Don't you see, I'm only playing at being—at being—" I spread out my hand to the luxury and gloss "—this sort of girl, out for kicks. I'm really a country type, a cabbage. I need the—the other kind of life."

But Hugo, understandably, was in no mood for a discussion. "I know just what you need, sweet Kate, you need this drink." He held the glass to my mouth.

In another second we'd be fighting. It would be horrid and humiliating plus he was much stronger than I was. It was not good at all making some dramatic gesture like dashing the glass from my lips.

I lifted my eyes to the face that loomed above mine; with a shock I realized that Hugo was much, much older than I'd ever supposed. The lines around his eyes were deeply engraved; there was a slight looseness about his chin.

I backed away a step and put my hands behind my back. "Hugo," I said, "it's no go, I'm afraid. You see, I'm in love with somebody else. I'm—I'm sorry."

I could feel my mouth begin to tremble and then I was really crying, gulping in a most ridiculous and naïve way.

Hours seemed to pass while I sobbed and sobbed in timeless misery.

A handkerchief was thrust into my hand and Hugo's voice said, "For God's sake stop, Kate. It's okay. Here, mop up, will you?"

I mopped up. "Thanks, pal," I said at last.

"Don't blame me for being taken in," Hugo said. "Your act was pretty nearly perfect."

I sniffed. "I'm ashamed of myself."

"Put it down to a miscalculation on both our parts," said Hugo. He grinned crookedly at me and sighed. "I never knew I was such a nice, understanding chap."

He led me across the room and gave me a little push into the bathroom.

"Go and repair the damage," he said, and closed the door.

When I finished Hugo was in the hall with the front door open.

"There's a taxi waiting," he said, picking up my case. "Now go, there's a good kid, before I change my mind."

Outside he tossed my case into the waiting taxi.

"I feel a heel," I said miserably. "I am sorry, Hugo."

"You're okay," he said, and touched the top of my head with his lips. "As for Hugo—virtue must be its own reward."

The taxi door slammed, and I gave the address. As we turned the corner I looked back, but Hugo had gone.

I supposed I'd been lucky, but I felt a wretched fraud. Never in my life had I been so low in my own estimation.

I didn't see Louise until next morning. The apartment was empty when I arrived and I went straight to bed, leaving a note on the kitchen table to say I was back.

I doubted if I would sleep at all. But oddly enough I slept like a log all night and awakened to hear Louise clattering in the kitchen next to my room.

I dug myself out of bed and padded in there.

"Hullo, Kath. I got your note. Tea?"

Louise, yawning delicately, poured me a mug, and we drank in companionable silence.

"Thanks for your letter," Louise said presently. She looked lovely sitting on the high kitchen stool, her pale hair loose around her face and falling over the filmy wrapper she was wearing. I always felt closer to Louise in the mornings, before she put on her make-up and dressed her hair into a smooth high chignon. "How's it going?"

I pulled a face. "It's gone," I said. "I've finished my stint in the country. The new nurse turned up earlier than expected so that let me out."

"Good for you—that means a week to please yourself. What about Hugo?"

I put my mug down carefully. "Hugo's finished too," I said.

"Oh."

There was a short silence, but I didn't enlarge on my statement and Louise never probed.

She slid a glance in my direction and stood up. "I'm off for the day. Plenty of stuff in the fridge—have a look around."

She seemed to hesitate; then she smiled, suddenly and beautifully. "Kath," she said, "you may as well know now. I've got news for you. I'm going to be married."

When I recovered from the shock she told me about it. She was engaged to Dr. Ivor Lattimer, she said, and it had all happened very suddenly. Of course she'd known him for ages, but only as one of the consultants who had his office at Manchester Square.

I knew him too, by sight; a tall, thin distinguished-looking man with wings of gray hair at the temples, beautiful hands and an enigmatic expression.

"It's all been such a rush," Louise said helplessly. "I can't seem to take it in yet. It was last Monday afternoon—we were going though his appointments for the week and suddenly he asked me if I was free that evening; if I'd dine with him, and I did, and—well, that was it." She gave me a dazed look. "He's a widower, with two boys away at school. He's got a tiny apartment in Chelsea and a house at Redhill. We're going to be married as soon as I can buy some new clothes and find someone to take over my job."

"Lou, it's wonderful!" I hugged my cousin, and she hugged me back with unaccustomed warmth. "No need to ask if you're happy, it's all shining out of you."

She grinned shakily. "Just like the songs say. It's marvelous, Kath. You ought to try it some time, falling in love, I mean." Her face changed. "Oh lord, I'm sorry," she said. "Was it Hugo?"

I shook my head. "No, it wasn't Hugo."

"Phew, that's a relief. I thought I'd been incredibly tactless. Well, I must get myself ready. Ivor's calling for me at ten. We're driving down to the school outside St. Albans to break the news to the boys. I only hope they'll accept me."

I thought they'd probably adore her and told her so. That seemed to please her and I left her to dress. I went back to my own room and wondered what I was going to do with myself for the rest of that weekend.

I kept out of the way until I heard Louise and Dr. Lattimer leave. No doubt I'd meet him soon, but Louise and I had never overlapped much in our private lives. Anyway I needed time to get used to the idea of her as a married young woman. For so long she'd been a kind of changeless star in my sky—a bit remote sometimes, but always *there*. And now she wouldn't be there any more. Mrs. Ivor Lattimer would be there, the wife of the distinguished consultant; my cousin Louise would have disappeared.

Hugo, I thought, and now Louise. When things begin to change they change quickly, as I'd learned three years ago. But at least there was my job to anchor myself to.

I planned for the rest of the day: I'd clean up the apartment, wash my hair, visit the laundromat. I'd ring up Edna Burke and see if she was free for a film this evening. And next week I'd spend at the practice, doing all the maintenance jobs that I'd intended to do before Dr. Hartington exploded his bombshell—could it have been only a week ago?

I'd be madly, wildly, busy. For above all there must be no time to think.

Being in love did wonderful things for Louise. True, I

didn't see much of her in the days that followed, but when we were together she was quite a different personality from the cool older cousin I'd always admired and tried to copy; warmer, more approachable altogether.

On Wednesday night, when she came home, she drifted into my room, sat down on the bed and began to talk—mostly about Ivor naturally. It led to my own affairs and, rather to my surprise, she seemed glad that Hugo had faded out of my life.

"But you didn't know him," I protested.

She smiled her Mona Lisa smile. "No, but I know you, Kath, and from what I've gathered about Hugo, his scene wasn't really yours."

I sat up in bed and hugged my knees. "I tried to believe it was," I admitted, "but I don't think I was ever really right. It wasn't the real me that Hugo was a little attracted to. Only something I'd built up on top. Something without roots."

Suddenly, saying it like that, I felt a horrible sense of failure. What a mess I'd made of my life, trying to model myself on Louise, trying to be something that I really knew all the time I couldn't ever be!

Louise was looking out of the window over my head and I knew she was thinking about Ivor.

"I'll tell you something, Kath," she said at last, slowly. "Something Ivor told me. It's very obvious really, but I don't think we stop to realize it. He said that lately—since his wife died—he'd been sort of drifting. The boys are growing up and don't really need him much now. He'd thrown himself into his work, but when that was finished there was an emptiness. Then one day he went into the country and walked and walked—alone, not thinking, but just waiting and listening. And when he stopped he had the answer to which way he wanted his life to go."

"You mean," I said, "that he believes you can't plan your life?"

Louise nodded. "Something like that. You can imagine that you're thinking it all out logically and rationally, but it's really something bigger, in the end, that does the planning for you. What you have to do is to wait and listen, and then when something happens you must be ready to recognize it as "yours," and go after it. That," she added a trifle smugly, "is what happened with Ivor and me."

When Louise had left me I faced facts for perhaps the very first time in my life. I was disgusted with myself for a sham and a pretence.

I'd heard the inside voice that Ivor had spoken of. Right from the beginning I'd recognized all that was at Summerfields—the country scene that Ben loved so well—as "mine." And I'd let it slip away without even a struggle. Because of what? Pride? If I'd been honest from the beginning instead of letting them all think I was a London girl what might have happened? Would I have had a chance with Ben?

I didn't know; I couldn't be sure, anyway. But there was one thing I was sure about, even though the very thought of it made my knees wobble.

Somehow, from somewhere, I had to summon up the courage to find out.

The next day was Thursday. I stood in the middle of the Manchester Square surgery and had to admit that there was nothing more to do. Everything—the stream-lined equipment, the delicate instruments, the drug cupboard, the day-book, appointment book, record cards, correspondence—everything was in order, checked and re-checked, ready for Dr. Hartington's return.

All day I'd been more and more conscious of the outside-line telephone on the massive carved desk. Now, when I couldn't put off the moment any longer—the moment when I must call Ben—the phone seemed to have swollen to twice its normal size.

The gilt French clock on the mantelpiece told me it was

twenty-five past five. Ben would probably have finished his last appointment by now unless there had been a run of emergencies. Of course he might still be busy; on the other hand if I didn't call now I might miss him altogether.

I went across to the phone and sat down quickly because my legs felt very odd indeed. From the table a card stared up at me with the phone number of the Lambton practice. I'd had a feeling that when the moment arrived my memory would probably go blank.

Celia would be seeing the last patient out now, making the follow-on appointment, going through the end-of-the-day routine, tidying, sterilizing, switching off. She was crossing the surgery now in her quiet, efficient way, smoothly opening and closing the narrow instrument drawers in the cabinet.

Ben was signing forms at the desk. Now he was checking the aerotor, a job he always like to be responsible for himself.

The palms of my hands prickled damply. I knew it all so well; I could see him so plainly, his white coat rather limp after a day's work. I could see his hands as he held the aerotor, the way the dark hair grew at the back of his neck—

"Pull yourself together, Kate Moorcroft," I said aloud. "You may be making a fool of yourself, but isn't it worth the risk?"

My hand went out, shaking but determined, to lift the phone from its cradle and dial the number.

Too soon for me the ringing was cut off, Ben's voice said, "Hullo?"

I swallowed and tried to adjust quickly to the fact that he had answered the phone and not Celia.

"Dr. Holland?"

"Yes, speaking. Who is that?"

I recognized the faint irritation and my heart sank. It

was touch and go then whether I'd hang up without announcing myself but something insisted on my battling on. Perhaps it was my guardian angel popping up again.

"It's Kate. Kate Moorcroft," I said weakly.

"Kate!"

Surprise certainly. Pleasure, annoyance, disappointment? I couldn't tell.

"I do hope I'm not disturbing you," I gabbled. "I thought perhaps you wouldn't mind if I called up to inquire how Chloe is getting along. I didn't want to ring Summerfields in case—"

He didn't wait for me to finish my little carefully-prepared speech.

"Kate," he broke in urgently, "where are you? What are you doing?"

I could feel my eyes widening. "Doing? I'm not doing anything, really. I'm at Manchester Square, and—"

"Look, Uncle Geoff won't be back this week, will he?"

"N-no, not so far as I know. He's due to begin work again next Monday."

There was a short silence from the end of the line. I thought for a moment we'd been cut off.

Then, "Kate, I'm going to be abominably demanding, but—could you possibly come back to help us out for the rest of the week? I can't go into it all now, but things are just in one hell of a mess here. We need you, Kate. Will you come?"

It was just like music. It didn't make any sense that could be put into words, but it sounded wonderful.

"Of course I'll come," I said.

I could hear him let out his breath. "Splendid! Look, get a taxi to Euston. The trains run every hour from there. Come to Coventry, that's the nearest, and I'll be there to meet you. Don't bother to collect any gear—we can provide you with a toothbrush. Just come. Okay?"

"Okay, Ben," I said, and put the receiver back

My cheeks were burning. No doubt I was being idiotically optimistic, and I'd come down to earth with a bump very shortly, but there was only one thing that registered; I was going to see Ben again today. In a couple of hours, perhaps, if I hurried.

I flicked the switch on the intercom. "Louise, be an absolute angel and call a taxi, will you? No time to explain, but I've got to get over to Euston straight away."

Louise said calmly, "Will do, Kate. I take it you won't be home tonight."

As I dashed along to the cloakroom I thought fleetingly that Lou was going to make a wonderful wife for a top consultant.

CHAPTER TWELVE

Ben was waiting for me in the lobby of Coventry Station. I saw him before he saw me, as I was lining up to pass through the barrier; my heart began to thump wildly. I had to remind myself that this was no lovers' meeting, but simply that he needed my help, for some reason I didn't yet know.

He was frowning the small, concentrated frown that I recognized so well, as he stood there alone. But when he saw me his face cleared.

I lifted my hand in greeting, and he came over to me quickly and took my arm in a hard grip when I'd handed in my ticket. "Kate—my goodness, I'm thankful you've come! I hoped you'd manage to make this train, but I couldn't be sure."

He guided me through the big glass door to where his car was parked at the curb.

"I was able to wait here for a short time," he explained as he unlocked the door, "but if you'd missed this train I would have had to drive around Coventry for an hour until the next one was due—or else parked the car and sat in the snack bar, downing cups of station coffee."

His hand on the self-starter, he suddenly paused and turned to me uncertainly. "Would you have liked a drink, by the way?"

He was so obviously itching to be off that I was quite impressed by this unfamiliar thoughtfulness.

"No, thank you very much, I had one on the train. They seem to have a non-stop service of car attendants following each other around with trays of coffee and biscuits. I got the impression that by the time they had finished filling cups at one end of the train they started back the other way, re-filling as they went. You know—like painting the Forth Bridge."

He laughed as the car moved off. We were both being very bright and conversational; I wondered when we'd get down to the real reason for his S.O.S.

"I put my foot down hard on the way here," he told me. "I did the run in just over half an hour. But I promise to go easier this time. This bus is over four years old and makes alarming noises if I push her too hard."

We turned left at the lights and started up the hill toward Kenilworth. The traffic was fairly concentrated so I resigned myself to patience. For the moment it was enough that I was sitting here in this unspectacular little car of Ben's, rather than in Hugo's great white panther. That, at least, was one thing in my life I'd managed to put straight already.

The little car lapped up the miles. Soon we were through Kenilworth and out on the Warwick by-pass. I sat and watched the sky. The sun was going down in a fireworks display of flame and orange and green. We were only a few miles from Summerfields now. Ben would have to start soon if he was going to brief me.

It was another ten minutes before he did. Then he pulled the car into a parking space, switched off, and said, "I've given up cigarets for good but this is one of the occasions when I still long desperately for one. Look, Kate, can we skip all the explanations until another time? I'll just sketch in the position as it is and tell you why I sent out my cry for help. All right?"

"Of course."

He gave me a faintly ironic look. "That's my Kate!" I didn't quite get the point, but at least he sounded friendly.

"Now," he began, ticking the items off on his fingers, "first, Celia's mother has to go into hospital for an emergency operation. Not too serious, we hope. But it means that Celia has to make fresh arrangements for the baby while she's out at work, which she hasn't managed to do yet. So—no help for me at the practice for the last couple of days." He drew in a breath. "Second, Chloe's condition is still giving rise for concern. It's proving difficult to persuade her to stay in bed, but the doctor seems to think it's absolutely essential for the moment. So—no help in the kitchen, except for one or two of the village women who've managed to take time to drop in now and again to make the odd cup of tea and mounds of bread and butter."

"Third, John is nearing the end of his tether. Bobby's off, as you know. Chloe's laid up. I can't help much as I'm not getting back until late from the practice. He's only got the elderly cowman and Frank Bannister, who's a good fellow but not exactly a rapid worker. Poor old John's working about 25 hours out of the 24 and worrying as well. So you can see our plight?"

"I can indeed. But what about Val Deering? I thought she was helping you?"

His face seemed to close up. "Val? Oh yes, I'd forgotten you didn't know. Val went to Oxford, to relatives there. She hasn't been with us since Monday."

"Oh," I said, and waited, but nothing more seemed to be forthcoming. That meager information, however, revived me like a glass of champagne. I sat up and said briskly, "I see the position, and you certainly do need another pair of hands. I wonder what's the best way to arrange things? How about if Celia could be persuaded to entrust the baby to me? I think she might agree to do that. I could look after him, keep things ticking over in the kitchen—meals and so on—and make Chloe rest. That way, Celia would be freed for the practice work. What do you think?"

There was a short silence. "Yes," Ben said consideringly. "I hadn't thought of it that way around, but maybe it would work. Let's give it a try, anyway."

Unexpectedly he turned and smiled at me. It was a warm, friendly smile, unlike any smile I'd had from his direction before. "Thank you for coming back, Kate," he said, and my heart began to sing.

It was wonderful to arrive at Summerfields and know that Val Deering wasn't there.

Ben took me up to see Chloe the minute we arrived and left us together. She was sitting up in the big bed, just as I'd seen her last: wrapped in a skimpy pink bed-jacket, her dark hair pushed off her face, looking more like a small caged animal than ever.

Like myself, she evidently felt that we knew each other well enough to waive the formalities.

"I'm beginning to wonder," she said wryly, as I pulled up a chair, "Whether all this business of producing the next generation is as rewarding as I thought it was."

I grinned. "You'll just have to wait and see until the next generation arrives, won't you?"

"You still believe it's going to arrive, don't you, Kate?"

"Of course I do, why not? That is, if you're sensible."

She groaned. "Sensible! That's what they all say."

I leaned back in my chair and assumed a nurse-to-patient tone. "And what have you been up to while I've been away? Come on, young Chloe, let's have the truth."

She smiled feebly. "Hasn't Ben told you?"

"Ben has told me exactly nothing, except that they seem to be having a job making you obey doctor's orders. You don't mean to tell me that you've been downstairs working?"

She looked sheepish. "What else could I do after that Val Deering walked out on us? Kate, if you'd *seen* my kitchen! Great whacking piles of dirty dishes—food burned black on the pans—flies in the larder— Everything in the most awful mess."

"She walked out? But why? I thought—"

"I don't know why," Chloe said glumly. "I don't know anything, stuck up here by myself, wondering what's going on. I must admit that I thought Val's reason for volunteering to help was to demonstrate to Ben how simply marvelous she was domestically; what a wonderful wife she'd make. Of course there *may* be truth in the tale about having to go to Oxford to help out some relatives there. But I can't help thinking that when she realized what she'd taken on she decided that there must be easier ways of getting her man than slaving in the kitchen."

She wrinkled her straight, freckled little nose. "I expect I'm being horribly cynical. That's what solitary confinement does for you. Even John can't help. He's so tired out, poor darling, that when he comes up to see me after supper he just sits down in a chair and goes straight off to sleep." She smiled with tenderness.

I nodded, remembering how Daddy used to do just the same after a day in the fields. Then I explained my plans for meeting the domestic emergency.

When I'd finished Chloe said simply, "Kate, why should you go to all this trouble for us?"

I carried my chair to the window, hiding my face from her. I wondered what she would say if I told her that, when you were down to basics, perhaps my motives weren't all that different from the ones she had guessed were Val Deering's.

For a moment I stood by the window, looking out. After that gaudy sunset, great thick dark clouds were gather behind the branches of the big old pear tree which spead itself toward the house.

I went back to the bed. "Because we're friends," I said, and I knew that that was true, too. "Now, tell me what everyone's had to eat today. I'll go down and rummage in the pantry."

It took nearly an hour to restore something like order to the chaos that I found in the kitchen. By the end of that time the dishes were done, except for two burned pans put to soak under the sink; the big deal table was scrubbed, and left-overs of food dealt with.

Now for a meal. I was exploring the pantry when Ben's step sounded behind me in the kitchen.

"I've been looking for you upstairs, Kate," he said, "but Chloe told me there was no holding you from the kitchen sink."

I turned to him, smiling. "How many for supper? And when will you and John be ready?"

"Just the four of us, and John won't be long. He's just seeing the vet off. Frank's packing up for the day; he says it's his wife's birthday and 'she'll be after 'im proper if 'e don't get 'ome soon-like.' "

"Has anyone told you you'd make your fortune on the stage, Dr. Holland?"

"Constantly. It's something they're telling me all the time."

I scrounged a bowl of tomatoes, a great wedge of ham ready for slicing and a box of eggs.

"Anything I can do to help? You look overloaded," Ben said, taking the tomatoes.

"If you could put a cloth on the table and find a tray for Chloe? I haven't found out where everything is kept yet."

It was odd to be there in the big kitchen, with the smell of ham grilling and the sound of tomatoes sizzling. Ben padded about, opening and shutting drawers, muttering as he searched for the salt, getting out a clean table napkin for me. I stole a look at him now and again, wondering if I should ever know what he was thinking, seeing tension in the set of his mouth, the faint furrows between his eyes.

But at least his attitude to me was friendly. Our relationship was different now that I was here as a friend of the family, so to speak, and not as his employee. That gave me confidence.

Presently John came in, shaking the rain off his coat,

saying that it was going to be a soaker and it was a mercy they'd managed to get all the hay in.

He greeted me pleasantly and thanked me for coming. "Chloe will be so glad of your company Kate. She thinks a lot of you and she was very upset when you left us. I'll go straight up to her now."

He hung up his coat and suddenly became aware of his surroundings. "By golly, you've done a bit of tidying up here, haven't you? I'm afraid we left you an appalling mess to deal with." A twinkly smile came into the kind eyes below the thatch of gray hair. "Wonderful smell, too. Makes a man feel ravenous."

He went off upstairs. I took the tomatoes out of the frying pan, wiped it with a paper towel and slid the eggs in one by one.

"Phew!" I breathed, when this somewhat tricky maneuver was accomplished. "That's a relief. Now we're full steam ahead."

I turned to pick up a spoon and saw Ben leaning against the tall kitchen cabinet, his hands in his pockets, watching me with those very blue eyes of his. It was a typical attitude, the very same one that I'd noticed the first day, after the accident. I was conscious of the same prickling down my spine. Hastily I began to whisk the eggs.

Domestic scene, I thought, with a whiff of self-contempt. Little woman in home setting. Bah!

Somehow I transferred the eggs to the dish with the ham and tomatoes. I was self-conscious now; I'd lost my touch and made heavy weather of the operation.

But finally it was done and the dish on the table. Without looking at Ben I said, "Tell John that supper's ready, will you?"

"Yes, ma'am. Certainly." He came up behind me and said quite softly, "Did you know that you bite the tip of your tongue when you're concentrating?"

I could feel my eyes widening as I swung around, but he

hadn't waited for my reaction. He'd already gone off to find John.

Next morning, soon after eight, Celia drove up in the Mini. It must have been pouring all night, for when I opened the front door I saw that the puddles in front of the house were still dimpled with raindrops.

She waved to me from the car. When I saw her nice smile, smooth fair hair, and general serene and tranquil atmosphere, I realized just how glad I was to see her again.

She eased herself out of the car and pushed the driving seat forward and down. "Kate, how lovely! I was thrilled when Dr. Holland phoned last night and told me he'd asked you to come back. Look, if you could just hang on to the car door while I get the Karri-Kot out. Isn't it an awful morning? I've got a rubber sheet here to keep the rain off Peter. He's asleep now."

I took the cot from her and put it down in the kitchen, while Celia followed with assorted bags and hold-alls.

As we went I inquired about her mother; all was progressing satisfactorily.

"She'll be in hospital for at least another ten days, though, and she'll have to take it easy when she gets home. I've got to try and fix up something for Peter before then. I'm afraid I'm crossing over my bridges as I come to them. It's awfully good of you to offer to help, Kate."

"I'll enjoy it," I said truthfully. "I'm a bit rusty, but I've had quite a bit of experience with babies. I don't think you need worry."

"I wasn't," she said calmly. "I gave up worrying some time ago."

I stacked the bags beside Peter's cot. "Will you brief me, then? How about routine?"

"There isn't much," Celia admitted. "He's bathed whenever it happens to be convenient and when he happens to be awake. Sounds a bit casual, I know, but it seems to work all around. Don't bother to bath him today, though, unless you feel like it. I can cope when I take him home this evening. I've prepared a couple of feeds—for the rest, T.L.C. will fill the bill." There was a humorous gleam in her eye.

I said, "Tender loving care—I know." I looked down at the sleeping angel in the Karri-Kot. His dark thick lashes lay against cheeks like flower petals. "That'll be easy."

Celia laughed at what must have been my besotted expression. "Don't be taken in. He can howl with the best of 'em when he feels like it."

"I hope so indeed," I said indignantly. "Something wrong if he couldn't."

She leaned down and touched a finger lightly against her son's cheek. " 'Bye, my love," she said softly. Then she straightened up and smiled at me. "Full speed ahead then, Kate. If you can keep things going here I'll try and do the same at the practice. I've been very bothered about letting Dr. Holland down these last few days. That's something that has worried me. I even tried taking Peter along with me to the practice the day after Mother went into hospital, but it didn't work. I suppose, I was anxious myself—babies sense it, don't they?—and he simply wouldn't settle down. No, it wasn't exactly a success," she added ruefully.

Ben rushed in at that moment, filling the kitchen with cool damp air and an atmosphere of masculine energy. He'd been working with John ever since breakfast at six-thirty, and now he ran upstairs to change, flinging a greeting to Celia over his shoulder as he went.

She looked after him as he disappeared up the stairs. "That's how he's been," she said. "A mite jittery! I fancy he's got a lot on his mind."

"Yes," I said, "I expect he has."

But I didn't know what was on Ben's mind. In spite of

his present easier attitude toward me, I wondered if I ever should.

The day that followed was much too busy to indulge in such gloomy speculations, however. Busy, and rewarding too.

As soon as both Celia and Ben had left for Lambton in their respective cars I took the Karri-Kot up to Chloe and put it where she could watch the sleeping Peter.

"This is your job for today," I told her briskly. "I'm going to get on downstairs while you keep an eye on the infant. I'll leave the door open and you can give me a call when he wakes up. Then we can cope between us."

An hour passed. I'd washed up, tidied the kitchen, put a casserole in the oven, and had just finished peeling the potatoes, when I heard Chloe's voice from upstairs, "Kate! He's waking up!"

While I worked I'd been remembering what I knew about babies. In my final year at school we'd had a young married couple living with us on the farm. Gerry Hayward had finished his college training and was enlarging his practical experience of farm management. His wife, Mary, helped around the house. She and I were very friendly, although she was several years older than I was. She'd had her first baby while they were with us, and I'd had a wonderful opportunity of being in on the act.

I ran upstairs now, carrying the flowered plastic hold-all that Celia had left, and trying to look more confident than I felt.

Chloe was very quiet while I lifted Peter out of his cot and changed his diaper. I cooed at him and he didn't seem to object to me; just stared with his wide unblinking baby stare.

I held him up. "Aren't you a pet? Isn't he heaven, Chloe? Would you like to hold him while I tidy the cot?"

She took the baby rather awkwardly in her arms.

"Isn't it strange," she said in a small voice, "I've never even held a baby before."

"Good practice for you," I told her cheerfully, shaking out the blankets. "Now I'll get a bowl of water to wash him and then I'll put his bottle on to warm. You can give it to him while I get on with the chores. I expect the men will be coming in for their mid-morning snack soon?"

Chloe was gazing spellbound at the baby. "Usually about half past ten," she said absently. "Kate, look at the way his hair grows around his ears. And his little fingers—they're perfect—Oh, Kate—" Her voice disappeared in a choke.

I pretended not to notice and went off for a bowl and towels. When I returned Chloe was in control of herself again.

"Now, I'll put this low table up to the bed and spread lots of towels around; Then we can all have fun. Come on, my lovely, come to Auntie Kate."

As I took the baby from Chloe I was very conscious that she was watching, tense and wide-eyed. Deliberately I slowed down my movements, talking softly to Peter, as I'd seen Mary Howard do when she was washing her own baby. Please be good, I willed him rather desperately; please don't cry. For, in spite of my grand show of confidence, I really didn't know what I'd do if he made a fuss.

I needn't have worried. Young Peter was a true son of his mother. After a long, long stare he seemed to accept me and the situation with the utmost nonchalance, and lay happily blowing crystal bubbles while his toilet was attended to. For a while we were in the magic, enclosed world of new-washed baby, with it's talcum powder, cotton wool and clean diapers.

"Now you give him his bottle," I said to Chloe at last, "while I go down and see if the men have come in yet."

"Oh—do you think—?" Chloe drew back nervously.

I put Peter in her arms again. "Have a go," I grinned,

and took the bottle out of its pan of hot water, testing it against my cheek.

I waited long enough to see the baby begin to take his milk and to watch Chloe gradually relax, while a delighted smile came over her freckled face. Then, smiling to myself, I gathered up the odds and ends that were lying around and left them to it.

John was in the kitchen with the other two men; very wet and grumbling mightily about the weather. I was introduced to the elderly cowman, who was much more interested in getting his pipe going than in me, and to Frank, the family man, who shook my hand heartily and apologized for the mess that their boots had made on the kitchen floor.

John said, "How are things, Kate?"

"Fine," I said. "Chloe's giving the baby his bottle now."

His eyes met mine and he smiled his slow, understanding smile. "That's a brainwave," he said. "I won't disturb her, then. Tell her I'll come up and see her at dinner time."

"I'll do that," I said, and added with a grin, "I think we're winning."

He took my meaning straight away and a delighted smile crinkled his eyes into slits. To see that look of pleasure and relief would have been sufficient reward for coming back to the farm even if nothing more had been involved.

But later, when Peter had been tucked in his cot again and deposited in the front sitting room to sleep, there was a further bonus.

"Kate," Chloe told me earnestly, cradling her mug of coffee between her hands, "something's sort of happened. I can't quite explain because you see, I never really knew what it was like to have a baby until now. I think I've had it all wrong—wanting a baby so desperately to—to prove myself to John, not for its own sake at all. But now—oh, I'll do anything, *anything*, if there's this at the end of it. Do you know what I'm trying to say?"

I nodded. "I think so."

"I'm not putting it very well, I'm afraid. But I've been such a fool, getting everything all mixed up. I suppose I've been trying to show John what a marvelous wife I was—so much better than his first one—and I've wanted to do everything for him. I've just ended up by taking silly risks and worrying everyone. But I'm going to be sensible now and rest, and do everything I'm told, truly I am."

"Good," I said approvingly. "Bully for you!"

As I went downstairs again I pondered that two out of three of Ben's points seemed cleared up already. Celia was at the surgery to help him, and Chloe had seen sense at last.

There remained the third point—that John was undoubtedly working too hard. And even *that* point, chronic to farmers, showed some signs of improving. I found out when I had a word with John that same afternoon. He'd taken Chloe's tea up to her and stopped in the kitchen on his way out as I was draining my third cup.

"She's a different girl," he said. "You've worked wonders."

"Not me, Peter."

His eyes twinkled. "Maybe, but it was your idea, wasn't it?"

I laughed. "Guilty! But I just hoped it would turn out as it has done. Give the credit to Peter, he's an angel."

He poured himself another cup of tea and drank it standing up. "She worries too much, does Chloe," he said. "And she's been working far too hard lately."

He began to fill his pipe, plugging down the tobacco with steady, methodical fingers. "But I'm glad to say I'm getting the farm reorganized now; things are going to be

very different in future. You know, Kate, I'm afraid I've
let things drift these last few years. It hasn't been fair to
Chloe, and she's such a sporty kid."

His face sobered and I guessed that he was remembering his first marriage.

"But now I'm planning to amalgamate with two other
farms nearby. The one-man set-up has had its day, in my
opinion. There's still a lot to be settled, but things are
moving; it'll be easier all around when it's fixed up. For
instance, Chloe won't have have any outside work, unless
she wants to do it, and I won't get landed in the fix I'm in
now, just because one man goes off sick."

He walked to the door, but before he went out he
turned and smiled at me. His great height filled the doorway, his eyes were gentle.

"Thank you for what you're doing for us, Kate.
Without you and Ben I don't know how I'd have managed. But we mustn't impose on your good nature," he
added with old-fashioned courtesy. "You must let us
know when you have to get back to London."

"Dr. Hartington isn't due to begin work again until
Monday," I told him, "so if I'm back by Sunday evening
that will be time enough."

"That's splendid. We ought to be more or less on our
feet in a couple of days. It's a blessing we just managed to
make the hay before the weather broke."

I glanced at the steamy window. Outside, I could hear
the rain still clattering down on the roof of the out-house.

"Has it really set in, do you think?"

He opened the door, turned up his collar, and scanned
the sky. "Looks good for another few hours," he judged,
and added, "You won't take a very good opinion of the
country with you to London, will you, Kate?"

Back to the city! What an ominous ring those words
had for me now. Two more days—that was all that was
left of my two weeks in the country. Two more days be-

fore I left Summerfields for London, and this time it would be for good, wouldn't it?

I wished I could have believed that before Sunday evening arrived, something really important would happen.

Perhaps it was just as well, as things turned out, that I didn't know in advance just what would.

CHAPTER THIRTEEN

When Ben got home from the practice at five o'clock that afternoon, I was in the kitchen making a cake. Chloe had been worrying that her last batch of baking wouldn't hold out until she was on her feet again, and I'd offered to replenish the cake tin.

I recognized the sound of Ben's car. My heart bounced about in a way that was, by now, getting quite familiar. I wished it wouldn't, but I couldn't do a thing about it.

He appeared in the kitchen doorway. A day's work in the surgery had left the usual marks of tiredness and strain on his face, but there was no frown there. "Well, how are things on the home front?"

It was the new, softer Ben speaking, and my heart melted absurdly as I looked up at him. Then, I concentrated quickly on breaking eggs into a basin again.

"Everything under control," I told him crisply. "Chloe and the baby have taken a terrific fancy to each other. Having him here has really done something for her. She's quite reconciled to staying in bed for the present, so that's something. We've had a good day—only the weather's been cussed. John and the two men were soaking when they came in for tea before the milking. I had to bully them all into putting dry coats on."

I tapped the fifth egg on the side of the basin and watched it plop in to join the other four. They looked fascinating—five smooth deep-orange globes floating there like setting suns. In London I'd made fancy little iced cakes now and again, if Louise gave a party, but I hadn't made a super-big fruit cake for ages; not since I used to bake what Daddy called "Kath's Special." Every other Saturday I would make two big cakes, and they would last for a couple of weeks.

Ben fetched a pair of boots from the cupboard, sank rather wearily into a chair and started to pull off his shoes. "I'll go and lend a hand." He grinned. "I do the donkey work in the milking shed. I'm quite useful with a bucket and broom—you'd be surprised. It makes a nice change after fiddling with drills and probes and elevators all day."

I said, "Have a rest and a cup of tea before you start. I'll make one in a second." I was filling the kettle. "I expect you've had tea already, but it'll be an excuse for a few minutes' break—which you certainly need," I added firmly.

He sat back in his chair, eyebrows raised. "I didn't know you were a disciplinarian among all your other accomplishments, Kate."

"We live and learn," I said, pushing aside the flour tin and packets of currants and sultana raisins to make room for two cups and saucers. "I'll join you."

He came and sat by the table and helped himself to a handful of raisins while I made the tea. But before I could pour it there was a faint whimper from the direction of the sitting room.

"That's Peter waking up," I said. "He's been almost too good to be true all day. It's quite a relief to hear that he can cry if he feels like it. I'll go and fetch im."

I brought the Karri-Kot into the kitchen, lifted the baby out and held him on my knee against my arm. The whimper was turning into a wail.

"Oh dear, I'm afraid he's beginning to miss his mother." I rocked him and made encouraging faces, all to no effect. "There, there, my lovely, cheer up, it's not as bad as all that. Let's see if a dollop of orange juice will do the trick."

I tucked him under my arm and went to look for the bottle of ready-mixed orange juice that Celia had brought with her; Peter's lament increasing in volume all the time.

The bottle was in a blue striped insulating bag, and I grabbed it thankfully and sat down again.

"Look, lovely juice!" I waved the bottle temptingly in front of Peter's damp face and streaming eyes, but I don't think he even saw it. Then I decided to proceed by guile. I waited for one howl to stop and begun to open his mouth for the next howl. Then I popped the bottle teat inside his opening mouth. The howl stopped with a sort of squeak, as if someone had thrown a switch and turned it off. The lips closed promptly over the teat and Peter began to guzzle immoderately.

I giggled with relief. "There you are—all done by kindness!"

Ben had been watching the performance with interest.

"Fascinating," he said in a faintly awed tone. "No doubt putting in some good practice for taking his beer later on in life. You're very good with him, Kate. Just another of your many skills."

I glanced up suspiciously. "Irony again?"

"Certainly not. Wholehearted admiration. We, all of us, have a lot to thank you for."

No irony. Not even a hint of banter. He smiled at me in a warm, friendly way. In fact it was all much too friendly. Something was missing from our relationship—something that had always been there before. I couldn't have quite explained what it was, but I wished it hadn't gone.

Soon after that he went out to the milking shed. I changed Peter's diaper, sponged him and had him all clean, sweet and cooing when Celia arrived.

I saw the Mini turn off the main road and went to the front door to meet her. She pulled up the car and was out of it in a jiffy. I'd never seen the placid Celia move so quickly.

I carried Peter into the porch as she reached it. "Don't panic," I smiled. "He's still very much alive—and kicking." I held him up to show two chubby legs threshing about energetically.

Her eyes widened. "Oh, I didn't think—I wouldn't for the world—"

I put the baby into her arms. "Of course you did," I teased. "And so would I if he'd been mine. I'd have worried myself to shreds at having to leave him all day with an untrained female. You concealed it very well this morning, I must say."

She met my eyes ruefully. "You win," she admitted. "But it wasn't you, Kate. I feel just the same about going off to work and leaving him with Mother. It's just something I'll have to get used to."

She looked suddenly sad, and I said quickly, "He's missed you too. He was very good this morning, but he began to get suspicious about me this afternoon. Didn't you, sweetie?"

From the haven of his mother's arms Peter turned his head away. It was the first time I've actually felt pleased to be snubbed.

As we went into the kitchen I said, "Something good's come out of all this, though. Have you met Chloe Garrett, Ben's sister? Do you know about her?"

Celia shook her head, at the same time lifting Peter up against her shoulder and rubbing her cheek against his hair. "No, only that Dr. Holland said the doctor was keeping her in bed. I thought perhaps she'd had an accident."

I explained about Chloe, leaving out the details. "—and she was thrilled with Peter," I concluded. "Will you bring him up to say goodbye to her before you go? I said I'd ask you."

"Of course. I'd like to meet her."

The two girls took to each other straight away. I left them happily talking about babies and went down to finish making my cake.

By the time Celia came downstairs some time later I'd got it in the oven. I had finished clearing away the cooking pots and pans and was making a salad for supper.

She looked flushed and happy. "We've had a lovely chat," she said. "And I'm going to leave Peter here for an hour or so tomorrow while I go to see Mother." She tucked the baby into his cot and then straightened up and looked at me.

"You know, Kate," she said seriously, "it's wonderful to fall in love and turn your world upside down, but lately I've thought that there's something that's just as good, though not so spectacular."

"What's that?" I asked, though I thought I could guess the answer.

"Just making friends," said Celia simply.

By Saturday morning the rain had lost its frenzy and settled down into a warm, fine drizzle.

"It'll clear later on," John said to Ben after breakfast. "We might have a go at that gate in the Bottom Field if it does, what do you think?"

Ben munched a final piece of toast, standing up. "I'm game," he said. "Give me a shout when you're ready."

The two men had been busy with the milking and had come in for breakfast. They'd neither of them spoken more than half a dozen words to me, but I didn't mind that. It was enough for me that Ben would be nearby all day and that I'd catch glimpses of him as he came in and out. I was as maudlin as that! I might have been 15 and suffering the pangs of first love, the way my eyes followed him about.

The people who say it's never as good as the first time were quite wrong, I decided. I watched him clumping across the yard toward the hen-house, a bucket in each hand and John's old coat hanging loosely on his thin, taut frame. The thought that tomorrow was my last day here kept pushing its way in, but I pushed it away quickly. Today was enough.

When Ben had disappeared from sight I went upstairs to collect Chloe's breakfast tray.

I sat down on the edge of the bed. "Well, ma'am, what's the orders for today?"

"I thought a steak and kidney pie, if you feel like it. Or would you rather make it dumplings? Perhaps it had better be dumplings; John loves 'em, even in the summer."

"Dumplings it is, then. How about the meat?"

"I'm afraid I'll have to ask you to trundle into the village to collect it," Chloe said ruefully. "We don't have supermarkets here; we have a priceless little butcher's shop, sort of tacked on to a cottage—you know?"

"Yes, I know. We had one at—"

I was just going to say "at home," but that would have meant too many explanations then, so I said "—at a place in Dorset where we used to spend our summer holidays when I was little—" which was true, too.

"You could take my bike," Chloe said. "You'll find it just inside the barn—you know, where Elsie had her calf."

"I know. How's the calf getting on?"

"Coming along splendidly—not that Elsie would know, poor dear. Not much fun being a cow and losing your offspring a few days after you've taken all that trouble, is it?"

She explained to me how to find the village. Turn right and go on over the river bridge. There are four rather ugly little houses with beautiful gardens just beyond there. Frank Cartwright and his brood have one of them. If you take the right fork at the houses you'll find the village about a mile on."

I stood up. "Right. I'll just finish the dishes and get cracking."

"Mind the roads," Chloe warned in motherly fashion,

"they'll be slippery after all this rain, and my old bike is rather a museum exhibit."

"I'll be careful," I promised. "I've got to stay in one piece or Uncle Geoff will never forgive me when he's ready to begin work on Monday."

Chloe groaned. "Don't talk about Monday," she said. "It's been grand having you back, and I'm going to miss you like anything."

She looked a bit downcast again and I said hastily, "You'll have Celia now. She's leaving the baby here this afternoon, she told me."

Chloe brightened. "Yes, that's something to look forward to. She's nice, isn't she? And working for Ben makes her almost one of the family straight away, if you know what I mean."

I did know what she meant. I'd felt like that myself, but now the situation had tied itself up into knots that I couldn't unravel.

"And Dorothy will be a great help to you in the house when she gets used to things."

John had managed to arrange for the vicar's granddaughter to come in each day to help Chloe, after I'd gone. Dorothy had called yesterday evening and I'd seen her for a few minutes. She seemed a bright, pleasant girl, I'd thought. She was starting her training at a Home Economics College in September. Until then she seemed happy to get some practical experience running a kitchen and a little pocket money as well.

"You really will let her pull her weight, won't you, and not try to do everything yourself?"

"Promise!" Chloe put her hand on her heart. "I shall be calm and placid, like a vegetable marrow."

I smiled to myself as I ran downstairs. I couldn't really imagine Chloe being anything but a human dynamo, but perhaps she'd manage to quieten down, with so much at stake. I certainly hoped so.

As I pulled Chloe's old bike out of the barn, pumped up the tires and set out toward the village, the rain seemed to be easing up. I hadn't ridden a bike in years, but you never forget, and I set off down the short track to the lane in fine style.

At the gate I couldn't stop myself looking back to the two low wooden hen-houses where I'd seen Chloe that first evening. Sure enough, there was Ben now, lugging his buckets from one hut to the other. Even from this distance I could see the way his thick dark hair gleamed wetly and the easy way he strode along; truly he was in his element in the country, I thought.

Twisting my neck to keep him in sight as long as possible, my front wheel whobbled alarmingly, and I nearly fell off the bike.

Hey, steady on, I told myself, eyes on the road. But just catching that glimpse of him was enough to send me flying along the country lane with the rain in my face and a quite unjustified feeling of lightness and joy inside me.

Chloe's directions were accurate and soon I came to the bridge. I was concentrating on steering the old bike, but a glance down over the low parapet showed me the river below. This must be Uncle Geoff's fishing paradise. No fishing today, though, with the rain-swollen river rushing along urgently, nearly up to its banks. Indeed, far back I caught a gleam of silver spreading out into the fields where the river had actually broken through and was flooding the land.

Around two more corners I came to the "four ugly little houses." They were ugly too, but their flat brick faces were redeemed by the burst of color in their front yards.

Collecting the meat for dinner would have to wait for a little longer. I dismounted to stand and admire. Peonies, delphiniums, poppies, the last of the wallflowers and the first of the roses; all massed in a riot of crimson, blue, yellow, scarlet and gold. Here and there the rain had crushed the heads of the great poppies, but already they were beginning to lift again. It was a breathtaking sight, better than all the planned displays in the London parks.

"Why, if it isn't Nurse!"

I turned around, holding onto the bike, to see Mrs. Cartwright, with Rosemary and Frederick climbing about the gate beside her. She was wrapped in a large pink overall, her round face beaming with pleasure. "Well now, Frank told me you'd come back to help them at the farm. Quite a change for you, isn't it?"

I stayed for a few minutes, chatting with her and renewing my acquaintance with the twins. On his home ground Frederick was even more awful, Rosemary even more deceptively angelic.

"And this is Susan, our eldest," Mrs. Cartwright informed me with pride. "She favors her dad."

A girl of about seven or eight came outside. She had Frank's lank red hair and doleful expression, but her eyes were lovely, big and brown.

I tried to make friends with Susan, but she was as shy as the twins were forthcoming. Frederick and Rosie, indeed, were by now exploring the chain and pedals of Chloe's bicycle with alarming enthusiasm. So, after admiring the flowers and inquiring after the baby, I rode off in search of the meat for dinner, thinking once again how pleasant it was in a village, where you stopped to chat with someone over a cottage gate instead of rushing blindly and heedlessly into buses and subways with everyone pushing to get in first.

By late afternoon the rain had finally stopped and a hot sun had appeared. Everything was steaming—the earth, the grass, the puddles in the yard. I threw open the kitchen window wide.

The men had all been in for their tea and left again. The

room was hot and smoky as I finished the dishes. Celia had been to hospital to visit her mother and now was upstairs with Chloe and the baby.

Everything was going very smoothly—too smoothly, I thought, drying the last saucer and beginning to carry the crockery back to the cupboard. Too smoothly and too quickly. Tomorrow I would go back to London. The next day Dr. Hartington would begin work again and that would be that. No more reprieves!

As I reached up to put the pile of plates back on the shelf something moving on the table caught the outside edge of my vision. I spun around. There was a faint plop as soft paws landed on the floor; a dark shadow slunk swiftly across the kitchen and disappeared into the hall. The piece of cold ham for supper went with it.

I didn't stop to wonder whether the cat belonged to the farm, or whether it was a marauder from outside. I only knew it was a thief, and I was after it like a flash. I was quick enough on the trail to see it turn into the sitting room.

The window was closed in here, except for a crack at the very top.

"Got you, you brute," I muttered in triumph. "Come on, now—give!"

The cat glared at me. It was no beauty; it was large and lean and a rusty brown color; the joint of ham hung limply and rather horridly from its mouth. As I moved toward the cat, it turned and, tensing its body, was up on the top of the buffet in two leaps.

I wondered where it belonged. I hadn't seen a cat in the house or around the farm, although there were at least three dogs.

"Puss, puss," I cajoled. "Come on down, good puss!"

I hadn't much hope of its seeing things my way, and it didn't. Without loosing its hold on its prey, it backed, flattening itself against the wall. Staring down at me with great yellow eyes, a low growling noise came from deep inside it.

A cold prickle ran up and down my spine as the truth dawned. This fury was no household pet; it was a loner—probably had been living wild off the countryside for age. You treated cats like this with as much respect as you gave to tigers from the jungle.

My heart thudding, I was out of the room like a shot, with the door closed firmly behind me. This, most definitely, was when I went for help.

I reached the kitchen at the exact moment that Ben did, coming from the outside door.

He glanced at me. "Hullo. John wants a roll of wire; he says it should be in here somewhere. Have you seen—why, what's up, Kate?"

I sank into a chair, letting out a long breath. I said, "There's a wild cat in the sitting room."

He stopped his search and stared down at me, eyebrows raised.

"It stole a ham from the kitchen table," I gabbled incoherently, "and I—I went after it—but it's dangerous, so I shut it in."

Suddenly he burst into laughter. "Why, *Kate*! You look like a ghost, I though something dreadful had happened. Now, where's this awful pussy?" He turned to the door.

"Ben, stop, be careful! I tell you it's dangerous."

I moved ineffectively after him and saw him throw open the door of the sitting room. I wasn't in time to see what happened next, but I heard Ben's voice addressing the cat in the tone one would use for a domestic pet.

Silence from the cat. I could see it still, in my mind's eyes, up there on top of the sideboard, yellow eyes dilated, ears flattened back against its rusty bedraggled head.

Ben's voice became playfully impatient. "Come *on*, puss, damn you, I haven't got all day to spend here."

If I hadn't been so petrified I would have giggled. Ben's voice of authority might get results with most creatures; it would get him nowhere at all with a wild, hungry cat, pushed into a corner.

There was the sound of a chair being moved. I heard him muttering impatiently under his breath. Then everything happened at once.

There was a terrific thud, accompanied by a horrid yowling screech from the cat. At the same moment it shot out of the sitting room, slid silently across the kitchen and disappeared through the open window, the way it had come in. The piece of ham still hung from its mouth. I was glad to see it go by then.

I gave Ben a couple of seconds to pick himself up and went into the sitting room. The chair was lying on its side, and Ben was standing beside it with a dazed look on his face. I took in that much, but what I really saw, and my inside turned over as I looked, was the wide ribbon of crimson that ran down his cheek and onto his bare arms.

The next seconds are still a blur in my memory. I suppose I must have panicked at the sight of that long gash of red. Probably my imagination did the rest. I was by his side in a flash, my arms around him, and I still blush to think of what I must have gabbled.

It was like a slow-motion picture. Ben's hand went up to his cheek wonderingly, and—the anti-climax of all anti-climaxes—brushed away the ribbon of crimson. It fell onto the carpet and lay there in a twisting curl. I saw it for just what it was; a crimson ribbon. A length of half-inch wide crimson satin ribbon!

My hands dropped to my side. My voice dried up in my throat. If a deep black pit opened in front of me then I think I would gladly have thrown myself into it.

Comprehension slowly dawned on Ben's face. "Why, Kate, did you think the brute had mangled me into mincemeat?"

I nodded wretchedly. "Something like that."

He stooped, picked up the ribbon and dropped it again, glancing up at the top of the sideboard. "Left over from last Christmas decorations, no doubt. I'll have to speak to Chloe about her dusting!"

"I thought—I thought it was—"

"My life blood seeping away?" he teased. "Oh, Kate, Kate—" He was laughing in a helpless kind of way. And then I was in his arms and all my bones were melting inside me. "Thank you for minding," he said very softly into my ear, just before he started to kiss me.

I knew I must be dreaming, but it was a lovely dream and I wanted it to last forever. The barriers between us were down; I put my arms tightly around his neck and strained my body against his and kissed him back. It was as wonderful and as *right* as I'd always known it would be.

I must have been so carried away that it took me quite a time to realize that the dream was going wrong.

He stopped kissing me and put me away from him, gently but very firmly. "It won't do, Kate, it won't do at all. This doesn't solve anything, does it? Just proves that I should never have asked you to come back. You're too disturbing altogether to a weak male, and proximity's the very devil and all."

I couldn't have said a word to save my life. I just stood there and wished I could die.

He shook his head with a look at me that I couldn't even begin to interpret. "I'll just have to remove myself from temptation, won't I?" he said, and turned and left the room. I heard his heavy shoes clump across the tiled hall and into the kitchen. Then the back door slammed.

I stood where he'd left me, my hand to my lips. My mouth felt bruised, but that was nothing to the way my pride felt. If it hadn't been for Chloe I would simply have walked out of that room there and then and never come back.

The picture that he had in his mind of me was too humiliating to be funny. With horrible clarity now, I remembered the other times; the evening I'd fallen off the gate into his arms, the time in the surgery when Rosemary had planted the feather in my hair and he had taken it out; the night in the barn when I'd played the little heroine in the thunderstorm. Oh, there would doubtless be other times too, when he'd misread me and my motives. If you're on the lookout for proof of some wrong judgment you can always find it, I thought bitterly.

Then, through the turmoil of my feelings, I was suddenly aware that I wasn't alone. Someone was watching me.

My head jerked and I could feel my eyes widen into an incredulous stare. Just outside the window stood Val Deering in a blue silk shirt, her hand holding the rein of her horse loosely. She wore no riding hat so her fair hair hung straight and satiny to her shoulders. She was staring through the window and as her eyes met mine I saw that her pretty face was livid with rage.

I suppose when two people take an instant and violent dislike to each other, as Val Deering and I had done, there has to be a moment of reckoning sooner or later. It's horrible and painful, but it can't be side-stepped. What happened next had that kind of feeling about it.

She tossed the reins of her horse over the gatepost and walked straight inside to where I was standing, her eyes narrowed, her face white and drawn into ugly lines. I was quite sure she must have seen what had just happened between Ben and myself.

Even then, at that late moment, I might have been honest. I might have said, "Look, I know you think I've been out to capture Ben for myself, as you once told me. You were quite wrong then. Perhaps it's become true now, but you haven't anything to worry about. Any attraction I have for him is merely one of physical proximity, as he was kind enough to inform me a few minutes ago."

I think I might have said that—or something like it—if she'd given me the chance. I even took a step toward her.

But I got no farther. I was stopped in my tracks by the look on her face, shattered by my very first encounter with naked, uncontrolled hate.

"So you came back, did you?" There was no describing the venom in her voice. "You never meant to leave for good. You crawled back here as soon as you possibly could, you—you—"

She paused almost choking with rage and spat out a gutter-word, all the more shocking coming from the delicate mouth in the pretty, pink and white face.

Then she lifted her hand and smacked my face violently, before she spun around and furiously whirled out of the room. A moment later I saw a flash of blue as she swung herself up into the saddle and heard the hoofs of her horse slithering on the wet paving stones in front of the house.

I groped my way back into the kitchen. It seemed very quiet in there, with only the ticking of the clock on the mantelpiece and the faint crackle of fuel in the stove.

Tea, I thought stupidly. Good hot strong tea. I was trembling in a shuddering kind of way, and tea would pull me together. I'd have some myself first and then take a tray to the two upstairs. Just the thought of Chloe and Celia, their niceness and normality, restored my faith in human nature and stopped the trembling a little.

I made the tea and poured out a cup for myself, but I'd only had time to drink half of it when there was a tap on the back door.

Outside I found a little girl of seven or eight with red, lank hair.

"Hullo," I said, rather grateful for the diversion. "Haven't I seen you somewhere?"

She hardly looked at me. "I want me dad," she said shrilly. "Where's me dad?"

I remembered her then. I'd seen her on this morning's expedition to the village. "You're Susan Cartwright, aren't you?"

She nodded. Her eyes were brown and huge and fixed in a stare. "I want me dad," she repeated quaveringly.

I went down on one knee and put my arm around her thin little body. "What's the matter, Susan? Won't you tell me, then we can go and find you dad together."

Her eyes were on a level with mine now. Her hand went to her mouth. "It's—it's the lady," she faltered. "In the river. I saw her, I did that. An'—an'—the horse—"

I struggled with the idea. "In the river?"

Having got out that much, Susan became more confident. "She's lying there, she is, in the river, just by the bridge. An'—an' the horse was going off down the lane, all on its own. An' it was limping," noted the farmworker's child in her.

"The lady—did she—was she wearing a blue blouse?"

She nodded dumbly.

I was on my feet in a flash. Making my voice very deliberate I said, "Susan, your dad is in the bottom field with Mr. Garrett. I think they're mending a gate there. You know where it is, don't you?"

She nodded again.

"Well, do you think you could go there straight away, as quickly as you can run, and tell them just what you've told me, about the lady in the river. And tell them that I've gone to the river myself. Can you do that? Do you understand?"

The big brown eyes searched mine for a moment. The child was very scared, but I was thankful to see that she was intelligent too.

"Yes, miss," said Susan obediently, and she turned and scuttled away across the yard.

I stood still for a moment, debating whether I should try to explain to Chloe and Celia what had happened and tell them what I proposed to do. But that would waste precious minutes. I would have to trust Susan.

So, with cold fear inside me about what I should find when I reached the river, I flung myself on the old bike and rode off along the lane in the direction of the bridge, the water in the puddles hissing and swishing under my tires.

CHAPTER FOURTEEN

As I pedalled along the lane I found myself hoping that I would meet somebody on the way to the bridge. There was nothing—no car came along, not even a farm vehicle or another bicycle.

Soon I reached the bridge, ditched the bike, and forced myself to look down over the parapet.

It was just as Susan had told me. On the far side of the river, close to the bank, floated the shape that she had seen. I knew straight away that it was Val Deering. The bright turquoise of her shirt was darkened by the water, but the color was unmistakable. Her fair hair swirled loose in the rushing current; her body was lurching and rolling in a way that made my stomach turn over.

I threw one leg across the parapet, scrambled across and stumbled down the slope on the other side. Before I could reach the river bank I had to push my way through a thick growth of stunted willows. Their wiry branches whipped my arms and legs. When I'd finally managed to struggled through I was glad of the branches that hung low over the water. By holding onto one of them I might just be able to reach Val and pull her in.

She was lying only about three or four feet away from the bank. Some underwater root must have fastened itself around her legs and was keeping her from sinking.

"Val," I shouted. "Val!"

The sound of my voice was drowned by the noise of the rushing water. But I knew she couldn't have heard anyway. The glimpse I caught of her pallid drenched face told me that she was unconscious, even if she wasn't—

I crouched down on my heels, hanging onto the willow branch, my arms at the limit of their reach, but even so I was inches short of touching Val's body, let alone getting sufficient grip on it to pull her in to the bank.

How long before the men could get here? Would Susan find them in the Bottom Field, or would they already have finished working on the gate and moved away to another part of the farm?

My feet were being sucked into the spongy grass of the river bank; I dragged them out over and over again, never taking my eyes from that white face and floating pale hair.

Then, sick with horror, I saw that something was happening. The undergrowth that had been serving as anchor was slowly relaxing its hold. Val's face was beginning to loll sideways and down, so that with each roll of her body her mouth and nose slipped under the water.

Val Deering was actually drowning before my eyes.

Suddenly I felt very calm. I dragged off my sodden shoes. If the undergrowth could hold one body, then it would support two, I reasoned. It would have to.

I felt the shock of ice-cold water as I lowered myself into it. For a second I lost my balance and was almost swept away by the rushing force of the flooded river.

Immediately I was up to my waist in the water. But at the same time I was conscious of my legs being caught and held, as Val's must have been, by thick, twining growth under the water.

I pushed my feet down, trying to find the river bed, but there was nothing but a mass of sinuous roots and tendrils.

Swimming was impossible. All I could do was try to keep Val's face clear of the water and stop her from being swept into the middle of the river, where the current was strongest.

Grabbing again at one of the overhanging willow branches, I inched my way outward, pushing hard against the entwining roots with my feet.

Now I could touch the soggy blue shirt. I edged my fingers up to her hair; it felt slippery, like seaweed.

Winding it around my hand, I pulled hard and breathed a prayer of thankfulness as her face rolled over and up, and was clear out of the water.

Now there was nothing to do but wait and hope I could hold on. My back was to the road. I hadn't even the encouragement of looking for Ben's car coming up over the bridge.

I hung onto the branch with one hand and with the other clung desperately to the rope of hair. Every minute I could feel the pull against my arm increasing as the roots below the water gradually loosened their hold.

Minutes passed like hours. Spreadeagled, my arms felt as if they were being pulled from their sockets. The river seemed to have gone mad as it raced and surged past me.

Then I saw that the branch was slipping from the grasp of my numbed fingers. I watched it, powerless to stop it without letting go of Val's hair with my other hand. Then it snapped back and I was down in the river. The water rushed into my eyes and ears, blinding and choking me as my head went under.

I surfaced and grabbed Val's hair with both hands. She must have been entirely free of the twining roots now; the force of the water, dragging her away from me, was almost overwhelming.

My own legs were being pulled free. With a strange, sucking sensation they came up from under the water. Desperately I clung to Val's heavy body as we were both carried out into the flowing stream, carried toward the bridge, tossed like toys toward the struts that supported it.

The men's voices I heard seemed to come from a dream world.

"Let go!" someone shouted close to my ear. "Let go, Kate, you're all right!"

My hands relaxed their grip, my head went under the water again. And then there was nothing else.

Warmth was the next thing I knew. Blessed warmth engulfing me—a prickle of wool against my chin. Cautiously I lifted my head and saw that I was lying, tucked up like a mummy, on a narrow high bed in a cubicle. The blankets that enclosed me were red, the curtains around the cubicle pale green; there was an unmistakable hospital smell in the air. From outside the curtains came the clink and murmur of what I guessed was a casualty department.

I lay back again painfully, appreciating the warmth of the hot water bottles tucked inside my blankets.

Presently I began to remember, bit by bit at first; then the whole thing came back as the bits fell into a pattern. The river—and Val—

I must have called out, for a nurse appeared around the curtains. She had graying hair and a heavy silver buckle on her belt.

"There now, you've wakened up. You've had a good sleep. Feeling better? Gently now, if you want to sit up—you'll feel a wee bit groggy just for a while."

"How is she?" I demanded urgently. "Miss Deering—is she all right? Was she—?"

Sister patted me and tucked me in. "There, there, you must keep warm. You've been very chilled, you know." She wrapped a blanket around my shoulders.

"Please tell me it—"

"Now, you mustn't worry. The doctors are with Miss Deering," she said soothingly. "Her father is here."

"But she's all right," I insisted. "She wasn't—"

"She wasn't drowned," Sister said quietly. "Thanks to you, I gather. You're a very brave girl. Now, you mustn't talk any more. Have a good rest and I'll send Nurse with a nice hot cup of tea. Dr. Wade will have a look at you as soon as he's free. How do you feel? Any pain anywhere?"

"I'm fine. I'd like to get up."

She shook her head firmly. "Not until Doctor says you may."

When she'd gone I lay back and stared at the pale green curtains; questions ran like rabbits through my mind. I longed to see Ben, but of course he'd be with Val, or at least waiting near for news. Yes, Ben would be desperately worried about Val.

I closed my eyes again. Suddenly I felt very tired.

It seemed almost the very same second that a voice near my ear said, "Kate!" I opened my eyes again and there was Ben, leaning down to me. There was an odd expression in his eyes—something very strange, like tenderness.

"Kate, my dearest love, I'd thought I'd lost you."

I was dreaming, of course. Or else I really had drowned out there in the river and this was heaven. Just to make sure I wriggled a hand free from under the blankets and touched his face. His skin felt hard and rough and cold; he was wearing a funny white bathrobe thing instead of his coat.

"Of course," I murmured. "You must have got wet too, fishing us out. Did you have a job, you and John?"

He was holding my hand tightly between both of his.

"They'll send me away in a minute. The doctor's coming to see you. I just want to say—Kate, my dearest, I love you so terribly that I simply can't think of anything else, not even for a moment, except that you're safe. Tell me I've been a stupid fool—I know darned well I have—but tell me I've got a hope. Tell me you don't really want that smooth fellow with the vulgar great car."

"Hugo?"

"Yes, Hugo, if that's his idiotic name. Tell me you don't."

I smiled. This was the Ben I knew. I couldn't be dead after all.

"I love you," I said. "I always have—I thought you'd noticed. Why do you think I rushed back when you snapped your fingers?"

His eyes were as blue as the sky and intensely bright. It was almost as if there were tears in them.

He didn't move, or say anything, just leaned over the bed holding my hand and looked into my face as if he couldn't believe what he heard.

A voice said from behind, "Sorry, Dr. Holland, but I'm afraid I must shoo you out. Doctor's ready to see Miss Moorcroft now."

He gripped my hand hard and straightened up. "We'll have you home tonight, Kate love, you'll see."

Home! What a lovely word! Everything inside me was singing like a green wood in springtime. I could watch him disappear around the curtains of the cubicle now and not even mind.

The church bells were ringing for Evensong next day as Ben drove me slowly down the hill in Lambton and parked the car in the Square.

"I couldn't get you to myself at the farm," he said. "Everyone was making too much fuss about you. Besides, it'll be nice to talk here."

He opened the front door of the practice with his key and we went upstairs together to the apartment.

All day long the sun had shone. Now, in the early evening, the whole place felt warmed, flooded by the yellow light that poured out through the open doors onto the landing.

Ben paused outside the living room. "I've got a surprise for you," he said. "I—I hope you'll approve."

Ben sounding uncertain of himself! Amazing!

"I'm sure I shall," I said. I'd heard myself using that unfamiliar voice ever since yesterday when Ben told me he loved me. I don't know if every girl's voice changes when she hears those satisfying words from the man she loves—becomes soft and relaxed—but certainly mine had done.

He stood aside and I entered the room.

I just couldn't believe it. I turned back to him, eyes wide. "But, Ben, it's incredible! How—when—?"

"The stuff arrived on Wednesday," he said. "I'd clean forgotten it was coming. The men just laid the carpet down and dumped the rest, but Celia managed to get up and arrange things a bit. Do you like it—really, Kate? Because if you'd rather choose things for yourself they'll jolly well have to take it all back. Chloe did the selecting for me some time ago. I'm hopeless at that sort of thing. She chose all the wallpapers too, and the drapes."

So it was Chloe that Mr. Pill had been referring to when he said that "the young lady" had chosen the wallpapers! Chloe, not Val, as I'd assumed. How mistaken can you be, when you jump to conclusions, I thought ruefully.

"I think its absolutely wonderful," I said, moving around the room, blissfully stroking the pale smooth wood of the chair arms, gently probing the resilience of the upholstery. "This blue is just right with the carpet, and—"

I stopped, my eyes riveted to the wallpaper. The smudgy yellow roses that I'd been bracing myself to accept without comments; the paper that Val had chosen, had been stacked up in rolls on the day I left, was nowhere to be seen. Instead, the walls were covered with off-white textured paper with a fine design in black line and abstract forms of blue, scarlet and limey yellow.

"But—but it's the paper *I* chose," I said wonderingly.

Ben smiled. "Naturally."

"I don't understand," I said. "I saw the rolls of paper here, that day I left. It wasn't this paper at all, it was the one—"

"The one that Val preferred. Yes." He took his arm from my waist, where it had come to rest quite naturally, and walked over to the window, with his back to me. "I think" he said quietly, "that you'd better know what happened about that, such as it was. I don't want any more misunderstandings between us, ever."

I joined him at the window and we stood side by side.

"It seems that somehow Val must have changed the number on the order slip," he said. "She took far too much for granted, you know, all the time. You do believe that, Kate darling, don't you?"

"That you weren't in love with her? Yes, of course I believe it if you tell me, but—but you did sort of *consider* her, didn't you? Everybody seemed to think so."

"You make me sound very calculating," he said with a grin. "But—well, yes, I suppose I did, for a while, before you came to upset all my neat patterns of the way I intended my life to go."

"Chloe told me you had a great Plan for Life. She said you'd always known exactly what you wanted and gone straight after it."

"H'm. Sisters don't always know quite as much as they believe. But about the wallpaper. When I found Pill putting up the wrong one on Monday I reversed the order straight away. And when I got back to the farm that evening I tackled Val with it. One thing led to another. It all got rather out of hand. And then she said some things I just couldn't take—" His mouth was grim.

"About me?" I could imagine what they were.

"Precisely. Well, it all ended up by her flinging out in a rare old temper and going off to her uncle's in Oxford."

I nodded slowly. "Then when she'd had time to cool down she was sorry and came back yesterday."

I'd told Ben only part of what happened between Val and myself yesterday. The details were best left to fade and die in obscurity.

"She came back and found me apparently in charge of things once again. No wonder she was riding carelessly. She must have been upset."

"That's putting it charitably," Ben said. "I've witnessed an exhibition of Val's temper once. I can imagine the way she would handle her horse, if she felt angry. And over that Bridge, with the road wet and slippery—" He shrugged. "It was pretty well inevitable that he should lose his footing and throw her. It was entirely her own fault—and she involved you."

There was a pause and then he added slowly and bitterly, "When I think of what you did—when I remember how it was when John and I got there; what might have happened if we'd been another moment later—and all for the sake of that—that—"

"Don't think about it, it's all over and best forgotten," I said. "Val's going to recover, isn't she, so we can afford to let all the rest go."

"You're very generous, Kate."

I shook my head. "I don't think I am. Realistic, perhaps. Val Deering and I disliked each other on sight. It was mutual. I expect if I'd been in her place I'd have acted as she did."

He gave a sudden shout of laughter. "You! Don't give me that!"

"I've got a temper too, you know."

"I do know. I've witnessed it." He put his arm around me and pulled me down onto the new sofa. "I have a way of dealing with your temper, my lovely. Like this."

And he proceeded to demonstrate.

Much later we went out into fields behind the house. It was my idea; I wanted not only to look out of the window at my wonderful view but to get right into it.

The sun was going down and the country was very quiet. We wandered along the path bordering a field of knee-high corn, arms entwined.

Ben sighed and said, "It's pretty marvelous to know that you love all this as much as I do. And I thought you were all sold on the bright lights of London. Although—" he paused reminiscently "—there were times when I began to wonder if you were quite the city girl you seemed to be. Then you'd go all sophisticated again and I didn't think I had a hope. Do you remember that night that you went to the hotel?"

"I do," I said with feeling.

He drew me closer. "I'd sent you away because I couldn't bear to see you around any longer and know you were pining for that Hugo fellow. I went home to the farm and the whole place was like a howling wilderness because you weren't there. I plucked up my courage to come back to the hotel to look for you. And there you were—looking ready for dinner at the Savoy, and stepping out of that great splashy car—"

"It wasn't Hugo's car, it was his father's," I put in mildly.

Ben ignored that. "It seemed like the end. I hadn't a thing to offer that would match up. To expect a girl like you to exchange a gay life in London for a one-horse town like Lambton—"

"Did you really believe I was a London girl?"

"At first I did. Afterward—sometimes I wasn't sure. Why didn't you tell us, Kate? Why all the mystery?"

It all seemed so stupid now—so futile—that I couldn't imagine why I hadn't. I tried to explain, to tell Ben all about my father's death, how Denis had let me down, how I'd determined to shut out all that early part of my life and start again, with a different personality.

"It was silly of me to deceive you all, I know. I should have admitted that I was a farmer's daughter right from the start. Later on, I think I would have done, but then—well, Chloe told me how you'd got things worked out. How you wanted a country life and a girl with her roots in the country. You told me so yourself, remember? Naturally I thought that was the brush-off."

He groaned. "And I was trying to be so subtle. To give you a chance to come clean, which would have given me a bit of encouragement. Why, for goodness' sake, didn't you tell me then?"

I laughed weakly. "Oh, Ben, can't a girl have a bit of pride too? What should I have done? Put on a pantomime act by disappearing through the stage and springing back, clad in blue gingham, with a pitch fork in one hand and a pail of buttermilk in the other, crying 'Surprise, surprise, here I am, your very own rustic village maiden?'"

It really wasn't all that funny, but we laughed so much that in the end we found ourselves on the grass; and then, of course, Ben had to kiss me again.

Finally we sorted ourselves out and walked sedately, hand-in-hand, back to the house.

"I suppose you must go back to London tomorrow?" Ben said plaintively.

"Afraid I must. I can't let Uncle Geoff down. He's going to get a shock, isn't he, when he knows?"

Ben was silent for a long time. Then he said, in a funny voice, "Now I wonder!"

"Wonder what?"

"I just wonder whether he wasn't planning something all the time, the old rogue. Knowing you, knowing me, he probably figured out that we were made for each other."

Ben Holland," I said, "you've got a nasty suspicious mind, and I'll jolly well tell Uncle Geoff all the dreadful things he's supposed to have done when I see him."

His eyes were twinkling down at me, blue as blue.

"You do that," said Ben. "All the same, I rather fancy him in the role of fairy godfather." He glanced at his watch. "His plane was due in at five-forty. He might be home by now—let's call and tell him our big news."

"Yes, let's," I said joyfully.

He held out his hand to me, and, like a couple of children, we ran back across the fields toward our new home.